PERSIE MERLIN AND THE DOOR TO NOWHERE

Harley Merlin 19

BELLA FORREST

ONE

Persie

No air. *Can't breathe. Can't see.* Heavy limbs pushed through impenetrable darkness, thick as tar and clogging my mouth, my nose, my eyes. The black deadened my every sense. It wanted to choke me. It wanted to drown me, my churning body not knowing up from down, down from up. And every second that passed brought me closer to unknown oblivion.

Panic splintered my struggling chest, forcing me to take breaths that only let the dense substance deeper within. *Help! Someone, HELP!*

But I was alone, floating in this abyss of pure, blackest black. The kind that didn't exist in nature, or in any ordinary palette, the kind of nerve-shattering absence that a deep space explorer might see when staring a black hole dead in the eye. And it incited the same terror in me—of getting sucked into that hollow nothing, my atoms shattered to smithereens.

And then, it spat me out.

I hit cold, hard… something. Hunched over on all fours, I drew in breath after breath until the slimy slugs of shadow that had snuck into my lungs dissolved with sweet, sweet oxygen. Coughing, I sat up and froze. Hazy figures stood beyond a pane of blue-tinted glass, its rippled texture warping their faces and shapes until they looked like eerie wraiths, staring through the glass as if I were an animal in a zoo.

"Hello?" I called, and my voice echoed back like there were ten of me. My head whipped around in fright, forcing me to take in my surroundings for the first time. That same blue-tinted glass, embellished with faintly glowing hexwork, incarcerated me on all sides.

What's going on? My heart raced, my eyes flitting back to the figures beyond the glass. I staggered to my feet, holding my roiling stomach. Stumbling into this new place left me feeling shaky and strange, and a numbing cold made my limbs stiff and uncooperative.

"Hello? Can you hear me?" I went to the front pane and placed a palm on the frozen surface. I yanked my hand away on impact, the icy touch of the glass biting into my skin like a burn. The sting made me wonder if it was glass at all, or a thick slab of ice. A few faint wisps of black wafted up from the site of the pain—the kind of gossamer mist I'd seen before, in box after box of Purge beasts.

This isn't right... I don't puff out smoke like this... The panic from the black nothingness returned with a vengeance, piercing me like poisoned barbs. I had to believe my eyes were just playing tricks on me, or that this was some sort of sick joke. Anything to ignore the simplest explanation.

I'm not a monster. I'm not a beast. Don't lock me away!

There might have been air in this glass prison, but I couldn't get so much as a lungful. Gasping, I hammered on the pane with every ounce of strength in my shaky muscles. A dusting of frost fell away from the glass, revealing the faces of the figures who stood beyond.

"Mom, Dad, help me!" I screamed, my voice thundering in my ears. "Genie! Anyone!"

They were all there, huddled together in identical black robes as though they were standing vigil at a funeral: my mom, my dad, Genie, Victoria, Kes, Diana, Finch—literally everyone I knew and cared for. O'Halloran stood off to one side with Tobe, holding a ring of keys that jangled in a mysterious breeze. I heard the sound like a death knell, chiming out my fate. It exploded my panic into the stratosphere, and I slammed my hand into the glass until my bones shuddered.

"I'm not a monster! Help me! Get me out of here!" Hot trails of tears trickled down my cheeks as I pounded harder against the pane. "Please, let me out! I haven't done anything wrong!"

Either they couldn't hear me, or they wouldn't. I wasn't sure which was worse. My mom kept her head down, and my dad held her close as though they'd already lost me. The sight wrenched through me, tearing up my insides until the emotions had no choice but to rise up my throat as a howl of suffering. As my cries spilled over with all the anguish and terror that urged my fist to keep pummeling, my mom tipped her chin up to look at my dad. Grief and anger morphed her face into a mask of pain, but she wouldn't look at me. She refused. My desperate eyes scoured the rest of the miserable congregation, and I saw that same expression on all of their faces—a disappointed, agonized grief.

"Genie! Genie, you know this is ridiculous! Please, you've got to help me!" I stopped hammering and pushed my hands against the pane. Some foolish part of me hoped that, with enough willpower and terror, I could get it to crack. Instead, Genie turned into the arms of her father, who glowered at me over the top of her head with his alarming gray eyes. A look that said: *I always knew you were trouble.* I noticed Genie's shoulders shaking violently, and I knew she was crying. But if she was so upset, then why wouldn't she help me? Why wasn't anyone doing anything? My friends, people I'd known all my life, just… turned away, or looked at me as though I'd done something unforgivable.

"Let me out, please! I can't... I can't breathe in here! I can't be in here!" The air had gotten so thin, or my throat too narrow, and being trapped on all sides by this glass sent me into a downward spiral. The floor might've been solid, but I'd never felt less steady. Tears streamed down my cheeks and I beat the glass until my knuckles turned raw red, the first hint of mauve and vermilion bruises blooming beneath. I hadn't done anything wrong, but I was being treated as if I were a criminal who deserved to have the key thrown away.

I looked at Tobe, my last hope, through blurred eyes. "Tobe, you've got to set me free! I'm not a beast. I don't belong here. Tobe!"

Please... He bowed his head and ruffled his wings, and I swore I saw a golden tear drop from his eye and splash onto the dark, silver-veined marble below. It spattered oddly, the tiny particles glittering like specks of diamond dust.

My mom finally turned her steely gaze on me, and I saw tears swimming in her eyes, too. "Quiet now, Persie."

"You've put me in a cage!" I sobbed, my lungs swelling with heartache. "Please, Mom. I don't understand..."

She stared unflinchingly, unmoved by my pleas. "This is for the best—for your sake, and for everyone else's."

"Mom!" I yelled, thundering on the glass with everything I had left. She hadn't even given me a chance to get things under control.

"It's already decided." My mom turned her back on me, and the others followed suit. They headed toward the exit, their cloaks dragging along the ground. Glinting streaks of something dark and sticky followed them, and in the dim glow of the hall's faint lights, it shone with a hint of scarlet. It was only then that I realized *which* hall we were in.

In a final, futile attempt to get them to turn around, I screamed until my throat felt raw, streaks of blood now smearing the glass.

Once they left, I knew what would come. I could already feel his presence.

Leviathan...

No sooner had I thought his name than black smoke began to swirl in the corners of the box. A chill ran the length of my spine, as though someone had dropped a snowball down my collar. The hall grew darker as I blinked away tears, not wanting the salty sting to steal my vision. But it wasn't the tears obscuring my view... The darkness was coming from inside the box itself, the shadowy mist becoming denser. And with it came more of the bitter iciness that heralded Leviathan's arrival, prickling my skin until I was covered in goosebumps.

I have to get out! I have to get out! I tried to rake in a deep breath, but it was as if I'd forgotten the simple mechanics of inhaling and exhaling. All the while, the glass walls closed in on me and the black smoke shrank the box until claustrophobia claimed me. Frantic beyond sense and reason, I kept banging on the glass long after everyone had gone. Everyone, that is, except for a small ball of white fluff that sat watching at a distance with curious black eyes. I blinked, wondering if it was here to help, but then... it left me, too, vanishing into thin air.

"Please... don't leave me alone. Please." My knees buckled and I sank to the cold floor, my head hanging low. "I didn't do anything wrong."

"Neither did we," said that deep, musical voice, seeping through the encroaching shadows. "Would you call a satyr a criminal? Would you clap a griffin in irons for daring to live?"

"No, but—" I tried to argue, but he cut me off.

"But... you are human? Is that what you were going to say?"

I felt the caress of a misty tendril against my neck and jolted away. He didn't get to touch me like that. He didn't get to touch me at all.

I bent over until my head was practically on my knees, trying to make everything else disappear so I could breathe again. "I don't want to talk about this now." My head raised ever so slightly, and my hand touched the pane. "They... *left* me."

"You do not need them. You do not need any of them. They are a hindrance to you, nothing more." His wispy tendrils brushed my arms, but I had nowhere to run. "You will be their queen someday. There will be no glass boxes strong enough to hold you. You will smash them all."

I covered my ears with my hands. "No! Shut up!"

Leviathan's smoke grew thicker around me, the vise closing on my lungs. I needed air. I needed freedom.

"I just want to get out. I have to!"

A loud bang pierced the air, as though someone were rapping on the glass. My head snapped up as the hall, the box, and Leviathan evaporated, leaving me sitting bolt upright in my single, spartan bed at the Basani Institute. Sweat drenched my pajamas. The coarse sheets had twisted around me like a python, and, when I looked down, I noticed that my knuckles were mottled with fresh purples and crimsons. The bang echoed through the room again, more insistent this time. With a wave of relief, I realized it was coming from my door.

I untangled myself from the sheets and lumbered out of bed. As rooms went, this one was the epitome of uniform, devoid of any personality. The curved stone roof made it look like a tunnel that had been cut in half. It made me feel like I was in a cellar, but the circular window brought in the outside world and some much-needed sunlight—whenever the gray Irish weather permitted, that is. It looked onto a pretty orchard, with rich emerald grass dappled by the light that streamed through the leaves above. Plump, russet-colored apples hung from the ochre branches.

All of the rooms in the student quarters were more or less identical, from what I'd managed to glimpse. At least I didn't have to share, and the rules seemed pretty lax. No strict curfew, just a note to be considerate of others—that was the difference between life at coven school and something tantamount to college. Plus, I had my own bathroom, which was a godsend, tucked away behind a narrow door that I could barely squeeze through. These rooms resided in an annex off the East Wing, with the male quarters in a different annex nearby.

Crossing to the door, I winced at the icy nip of the stark stone floor beneath my bare feet. I had to remember to put slippers on my list of necessary items for my mom to send through.

She left me in that box... I shook away the illogical thought. It was only a nightmare—an actual one, not a Leviathan-infused hypnosis. I could feel the difference; my head didn't feel *invaded*, like it had when Leviathan had wriggled in. I took a steadying breath and opened the door to find Genie standing in the hallway.

"Finally! I was about ready to break down the door." Genie grinned at me, only for her smile to fade quickly. "What's up? You look all... sweaty and feverish. Are you sick? I heard there's this thing called Fresher's Flu that hits the new recruits in their first week. Do you need me to round up some meds for you?"

I put my hands up in mock defense. "Easy, there, I only woke up two seconds ago. I can manage a maximum of one pre-coffee question."

"Sorry. I've just been on a run around the grounds, so I'm pretty jazzed." She took a deep, meditative breath. "Are you feeling okay? It wasn't a... *you-know-what*, was it?"

I shook my head. "That was technically two questions. But no, it wasn't a Purge. It's been"—I counted out the days on my fingers —"five days since the exam, and I haven't had any symptoms. I think this place is already doing me some good."

"Either that, or this Mama of Monsters thing is like food poisoning."

"Huh?" My mind was still way too preoccupied with the dream to decipher her metaphors.

Just seeing her standing there was both relieving and triggering, since she'd abandoned me in that dream like everyone else. But I needed to push the thought away before it ruined my day entirely. After five days of settling in, we were finally having our orientation, and I wasn't going to let any stupid, separation-anxiety nightmare get in the way of my first proper day as a student. Plus, I had some catching up to do, socially speaking. While the other students had been exploring and getting to know one another at planned events, I'd spent most of my time recovering from the banshee, going back and forth between my room and the infirmary for checkups. Genie had stuck with me, not wanting me to feel alone, but I worried she might've missed out by playing nurse. Still, we'd have plenty of time to mingle now that we were getting into proper Institute business.

Genie smiled, a mischievous glint in her eyes. "The flu. It's supposed to be rough as heck for the first few days, but then it all plateaus and you don't have to keep running to the bathroom every ten minutes."

"I hope so," I admitted. This was the longest I'd gone without Purging since getting the worst birthday present in history, so either Genie was right... or I was due a doozy of a beast birth. I prayed it was the former.

"So, why all sweaty? I know you haven't been running." She squinted curiously, as if she could read the problem on my face.

"That's because, as you know, running is for psychopaths. You'll never convince me otherwise." I bit the bullet and told her: "I had a dream. A bad one."

She gasped and lunged forward, pressing her palm to my forehead to check for a fever. "Like, a Leviathan dream?"

"He was in it, but it wasn't one of his, if that makes sense. At least, I don't think so. It didn't have the same vibe as before, and he wasn't doing any romancing, unless you count a few unsavory brushes." I removed her hands and held them for a minute as I explained the dream. When I finished, she looked at me with genuine horror.

"You know I'd never do that, right? They'd have to go through me if they ever even *thought* about putting you in a box."

"I know. It was just a dream." If I kept saying it, I was certain I'd eventually convince myself. "Everything's new here. I'm in a strange bed in a strange room that doesn't feel like home yet, and we've got orientation today, so I think it was probably an anxiety dream."

Genie nodded in understanding. "I'm with you on that. I had a horde of seahorse-mounted Atlanteans chasing after me with tridents last night. Stereotypical, totally implausible, but *very* unnerving."

I laughed, the residual jitters dissipating. "Did they catch up to you?"

"I don't know. I woke up when I got pronged in the butt cheek." She ushered me gently back into my room. "Now, get your peachy butt into some clothes so we can get coffees before orientation starts. And trust me when I say I wouldn't let anyone put you in a box. You could Purge elephant-sized chickens for two weeks straight, and I'd still bite anyone who came near you."

"I thought Victoria warned you about the biting?" I asked, smiling.

"She said I couldn't bite any of *her* people," Genie reminded me.

After the banshee debacle, she'd apparently bared her teeth—figuratively and literally. It certainly explained why a few of the other students had been wary around her when we'd done some exploring of the Institute.

Genie waited as I took a clean T-shirt and my mom's fancy leggings from the old-timey wardrobe crammed in beside my bed.

As I changed, the scent of the clothes briefly whisked me away to the SDC, the home I couldn't go back to. *Crap, I'm going to have to learn how to do my own laundry...* It was just the dose of independent reality that I needed to stop dwelling on the bad. O'Halloran had made his position clear—I still wasn't welcome back home, as long as I was a perceived risk—but so had my parents and Victoria Jules.

And so had I. I was here to learn and get this curse under my control, and once I'd succeeded in doing that, I could go back to O'Halloran with a diploma in my hand that said to the world, *I'm in control. I belong, no matter what I am.* Frankly, I couldn't wait to get started, and figuring out a washing machine couldn't be any harder than Purging a beast... right?

After throwing on my clothes, I walked a few steps toward the mirror that hung on the opposite wall. I scooped my dark hair into a messy bun, which looked more sleepless-chic than casual-chic. But I wasn't there to be part of a fashion parade, as my mom would've said. I was there to become the best damn hunter I could be.

"What if all these nerves make me Purge?" I checked my reflection. The gray complexion and the dark circles under my eyes definitely told of uneasy dreams. Purging was never far from my mind, and the anticipation grew with every Purgeless day that passed.

"You're in an Institute full of hunters whose primary purpose is to capture Purge beasts. That's why we chose it," she said matter-of-factly. "There's no safer place for you. Even your mom agreed on that, in the end."

I faltered, having a momentary crisis of confidence. "What if they never truly accept me, though? If I end up being a liability, they'll have a hard time viewing me as anything but a... problem." The word *monster* had almost come out, but I'd stopped myself. Even if I Purged them, I wasn't one myself, and a curse couldn't change that.

"Victoria is gaga over you!" Genie swooped in with a bit of bolstering. "You think she hands out invites like a broken candy machine? She chose you *because* of your Purge ability. She's not scared of it, and neither am I. I doubt anyone will be. They might be curious about you, but then the novelty will wear off and you'll fit right in with everyone else. I feel it in my Atlantean waters, and they're rarely wrong."

I chuckled. "You and your waters."

"Besides, Victoria will have put hunters on standby in case of emergency, and you've got your beeper thing." Genie leaned out the door and pointed down the stone hallway. "There's a dude at the end of the corridor who's been loitering there since last night, and there's only one reason he'd be hanging out in the ladies' dorms. Actually, there's two, but I'm going to give him the benefit of the doubt. Victoria has all bases covered, so all you need to worry about is—"

"Learning how to hunt and capture properly, so I can turn this curse into a gift." I finished the sentence for her as I gave myself a stern look in the mirror.

"Exactly." Genie smiled at me like a proud mother hen.

It was going to be a long, hard process, but I hadn't come all this way for nothing. This was what I'd wanted—a new start to my independence, where I could make a change. Sure, I hadn't expected to have to give up the SDC for this, but it had played out that way, so I had to make it worth it. And Genie was right—until I had more knowledge and practical training under my belt, I had the Institute watching my back.

And I had my best friend at my side, going through all of this with me.

It's definitely a start. I looked back at my reflection and smiled. I had to remember; I'd asked for this. I'd wanted to do more for myself so I wouldn't have to rely on friends and family—or other hunters, for that matter—to save my ass when I puked up a Purge beast. And I was only going to learn this stuff here.

Victoria knew what she'd gotten herself into when she'd seen me unleash a banshee, and she'd still accepted me. I had to trust her judgment.

And if it's not enough and I fail, they can always put me in a box... I hadn't meant to think it, but the dream clung to the back of my mind. It had scared the bejeezus out of me because it had felt so painfully, desperately real, devoid of the usual fluff and trickery. Maybe, all things considered, my mind actually was my own worst enemy; I didn't need Leviathan to show me my gravest fears because I already had them lined up and ready to go. Despite my determination to ignore it, I had a feeling I wouldn't be able to shake the dream entirely. Not with my knuckles still sore and bruised, each dull ache a reminder of what I'd experienced.

"We need to get a move on," Genie said. "Charlotte Basani is leading our tour, and I don't want to be late!"

I grabbed a notebook and shoved it into a backpack. "Is she one of the instructors?"

"Charlotte?" Genie giggled like a schoolgirl. "No, she's Shailene Basani's daughter."

"Right, got it." I remembered now—Fay and Shailene were the twin founders of this place, and it stood to reason that one of them would've had kids. I slung the backpack over my shoulder and headed for the door. "Kes had us cram so much into our skulls that I think a lot got pushed out right after."

Genie made an airy, whistling noise. "It was literally in one ear and out the other with me, but I know all about Charlotte from the ever-helpful grapevine." She turned and we walked down the corridor together, past the hunter who had apparently been keeping watch all night. He gave a discreet nod and immediately walked off in the opposite direction. "Everyone talks about her. She's apparently one of the best monster hunters to have ever come out of this

Institute. Top-ranking, future head-huntswoman material, with a Bestia ability that I'd kill for! And she's got the name to go with it."

"Bestia? I don't know that one." We fell in step, and the chatter helped ease my increasing nerves.

"It means she can turn into all sorts of creatures and get into their mindset, which gives her a massive edge when hunting."

"Isn't that just Shapeshifting?"

"Kind of, but it's exclusive to animals. I hear she can even change into a few Purge beasts, but you know what the rumor mill is like." She sighed, as if she were already besotted with this Basani woman. "Still, it'd be amazing if she *could*, and it would definitely explain the glowing resume."

Turning the corner of the cavernous hallway that led into the main body of the Institute, where the old collided with the modern, I spotted two more hunters who were doing a terrible job of acting nonchalant. They'd obviously been stationed there to keep an eye on me. I didn't mind, given my history, but their presence made me feel like a pariah before I'd even gotten started. A watched enemy in the ranks, one who could go rogue at any moment. I was really trying to be optimistic, but every time I glanced at my knuckles and thought of the curse that had brought me there, my lungs seemed to shrivel like prunes and my throat got tight.

You will smash them all. Leviathan's words hadn't sounded at all comforting while I was deep in the tangle of the dream. But now... I remembered the panic I'd felt pummeling that glass, willing it to break beneath my futile fists. Faced with the prospect of life in a box if I couldn't make this work, those words now acted as a weird salve to my fears. And that worried me most of all.

TWO

Persie

"Would a signpost be too much to ask for?" Genie came to a stop beside a display case containing two wrist cuffs that had belonged to Artemis herself. They gave off distinct Wonder-Woman vibes, but they wouldn't give us the superpowers required to find the main assembly hall. We'd spent the better part of twenty minutes trying to find the banquet hall so I could pick up breakfast and a coffee, and had spent another twenty minutes running around, looking for the assembly hall. Shaky splashes of coffee had spilled out of the paper cup in my hand, leaving a wet trail behind us like I was some kind of caffeine-deprived Theseus.

"I was sure it was this way." I was wheezing, thanks to my general aversion to cardio. "But then, I thought the banquet hall was in the opposite direction to where it was, so I'm not much of a tour guide."

Genie huffed, putting her hands on her hips as she scoured the Institute's baffling layout. Every hallway looked the same, with endless corridors leading to endless destinations.

"I could've sworn I put the orientation map in my bag," I lamented. I had a sparkly new pencil case, a bevy of empty notebooks, a half-filled sketchbook, and a pastry wrapped in a napkin from the banquet hall, but no map to speak of. I must have left it on my desk this morning in my nightmare-addled state.

"Well, we need to keep going and hope the assembly hall throws us a bone and appears out of nowhere." She checked her phone. "It's ten to nine, so we've got nine minutes and fifty-nine seconds to get there. I can almost hear the whispers already—can't you?"

No whispers, please... I knew the curiosity would come, but if they kept it for another day—tomorrow, even—I would be forever grateful.

Genie took off again, and I followed on weary legs. I'd recovered from the banshee-Purge, but last night's dream had taken more out of me than I'd first realized. My hands and wrists and arms throbbed as though I'd been... well, slamming them helplessly against a sheet of glass. And my chest still felt heavy and clenched, like some of that unnerving dark sludge lingered in each lung.

"There! Cadets!" Genie punched the air and picked up speed, chasing after a gaggle of cargo-panted students who appeared to know precisely where they were going. It made me feel a tad uncomfortable, seeing how professional and clean-cut they looked, while Genie and I ambled along in our civilian get-up of T-shirts and athleisure pants. They'd probably spent the last five days studying the orientation map religiously instead of recuperating and strolling around like this was a holiday camp.

We hurtled after the militant contingent, our shoes screeching on the polished concrete as if we were doing laps of a basketball court. In focusing on the other students, we might have neglected our spatial awareness. Skidding around a corner into a narrower corridor so as not to lose sight of our unwitting guides, we crashed straight into a figure hurrying out of a doorway on the right.

The three of us went flying. Papers and folders erupted in a snowfall, the sheets fluttering down in a chaotic whirlwind as I bounced backward and hit the floor with a thud that knocked the wind out of me. My coffee arced into the air and landed in places unknown. Staring up at the paper blizzard, I cocked my head, distracted from the pain shooting across my shoulders. Every sheet was etched with intricate illustrations of monsters, labeled and detailed with technical jargon in elegant handwriting. They were on par with my own drawings, though I noticed some discrepancies from my useful angle: too-small wings on a gargoyle, scales on a serpent that should've been feathers, a wrongly proportioned loup-garou, that sort of thing. Minute details that only someone who'd been up close and personal with these creatures could have noticed.

"They're beautiful," I blurted out as I maneuvered into a crouch and started picking up the pages. I was so engrossed in the images that I barely even saw the person we'd careened into.

"Yeah... beautiful." Genie tapped me on the shoulder. I peered up at her and saw her wide eyes and open mouth directed at the mystery artist. Following her gaze, I glanced over my shoulder to see who she was gaping at.

A young man, somewhere in his early twenties, dusted down a gray tweed suit jacket, shot through with delicate threads of vivid purple that formed checkered squares. A stylish kind of tweed, like something from those old *Kingsman* films my uncle adored, but mismatched with a white polo shirt that had a fresh coffee stain down the front and faded black jeans that I would've described as "dad fit." He had a nice face, though: unusual green-blue eyes that reminded me of Amazonite, with a dark ring around the iris. His sweeping mane of unruly golden-brown hair had been hastily gelled into submission, and defined, manly features and blonde stubble added to his Tobe-like leonine look. His fair eyebrows knitted together in consternation as he looked down at the stain on his shirt.

He bent down for a pair of rectangular glasses that had survived the fall and cleaned them on the edge of his polo shirt. "I prefer to *drink* coffee, but maybe the caffeine will sink in via osmosis." He put the glasses back onto the bridge of his nose, and then it was his turn to start gaping like a beached fish as his gaze fell on Genie. "I mean, not that I... uh... mind. No, osmosis is good. Um... accidents happen. It's nothing. I can just... uh... fasten the button and hide it."

Realization dawned as I connected that the coffee all over him was *my* coffee. "Oh, my goodness, I'm so sorry! That was me." I scooped more papers into my arms, checking them for liquid damage. "I hope it didn't get on any of these. It'd be a shame. They're... nice."

I was thoroughly mortified that I'd doused him in coffee, but he didn't seem to be paying attention to his shirt or sketches. Nope, my friend had all of his interest. There were very few who could look Genie straight in the eyes and *not* get stung by the smitten arrow, but it was far rarer for Genie to look into a man's eyes and get hit too. And, unless I was mistaken, it looked like she'd been hit.

Genie looked toward me, severing their connection. "Sorry about that, and all of this." She gestured to the sheets in my hand. "We were trying to find the assembly hall, and we weren't watching where we were going."

Flustered, he took the papers from me and jammed them into one of the folders. "It's fine, really. Happens all the time. More than I'd like to admit." He cast her a shy look, but she was deliberately avoiding his gaze. I knew my friend, and she was definitely in shock. "And they'll dry out, if any of them are wet. It might make them look a bit older, give them gravitas. You know, like those history projects when you were a kid, where you'd tea-stain a piece of paper and singe the edges to make it look old-timey?" A faint flush of pink tinged his complexion as he sought Genie's eyes again, but she carried on pretending to be absorbed in the sketches he'd already tucked away. "I'm talking too much, aren't I? Sorry. I can take you to the assembly hall—I'm actually headed there myself."

"That'd be great, Mr.—?" Genie waited.

"Nathaniel O'Hara. No 'mister' necessary, Nathan's fine." He appeared to rally, making a show of pushing the stray pages into the folder. "And who might you be?"

I knew he didn't mean me, but it didn't bother me in the slightest. Actually, it did a bit, but only because I wanted to know more about his illustrations. Who was this guy, and why did he have folders of beautiful drawings that matched my own endless sketchbooks? True, we were in a monster-hunting Institute, so it wasn't exactly odd, but there was something undeniably intimate about his artistry. Each touch of shade and light was painstakingly crafted, the creatures made three-dimensional with skill and thought until they almost leapt off the page.

"I'm Iphigenia Vertis, but Genie's fine," she copied him. "And this is my best friend, Persie Merlin-Crowley."

He adjusted his specs. "Merlin-Crowley? As in—"

"Yep, my famous parents." I rubbed the back of my neck, bracing for the usual torrent of compliments for my mom and dad. Even here, I couldn't escape their legacy. I wished I could've been more mature about it, but it did tend to grate after a while. Instead, he just furrowed his brow, as if he were more irritated than impressed.

"I corresponded with her a few times when I was younger," Nathan said, "trying to gain access to the Bestiary for research purposes. All my requests were denied."

Huh, how about that... Of all the institutions in all the world, I happened to come here and meet the one person who didn't immediately turn gooey-eyed at the sound of my family name. It was kind of refreshing.

Genie chuckled, though I spotted a subtle blush in her cheeks. "Maybe they know you're clumsy. Being around all of those glass boxes and narrow walkways would probably push them up to DEFCON 1."

"*I'm* the clumsy one? You're the ones who barged into me!"

"Only because you were backing out of a doorway," Genie retorted. I wasn't entirely sure she wasn't teasing him. That tended to be a defense mechanism for her, but it was never easy to tell. Either way, I doubted it would diminish her charms in his clearly curious eyes.

He straightened slightly. "Don't forget, you're the new students here. I know my way around, and I'd urge you to be more careful in the future."

"We really are sorry," I cut in, before Genie could make another ill-considered joke. "You're right, we should've been more aware, but we were frazzled about missing our orientation assembly. It's not good to be late on the first day, you know? And I'm so sorry we made you drop all of your incredible sketches. Are they yours?"

He focused his attention on me, but I saw him steal another look at Genie as he spoke. "They are. I'm a scholar's aide here at the Institute, in the field of Monster Research." His body language relaxed as he struck more comfortable territory, his fingertips adjusting the arm of his glasses. "I delve deep into Purge beasts and their individual natures, though my main interest is in all things ancient and obsolete. Of course, that's not as useful to the Institute, as such creatures are unlikely to pop up during a hunt." He gave an awkward laugh, as if we were supposed to understand an inside joke, before hurriedly continuing. "But I still think there's value in the history of beasts, because that can give us insight into current and, potentially, future creatures."

Well, he'd certainly had the right person bump into him, if he was into all creatures ancient and terrifying. I'd seen one just over an hour ago. I could still feel the cold touch of his wispy tendrils against my neck if I allowed myself to think about him for too long.

The truth was, I wanted to know more about Leviathan—what made him tick and what his history was—for a reason similar to why Nathan researched that kind of creature: to gain insight. Plus, as the old Irish proverb went, better the devil you know. Being in Ireland and all, now seemed like the perfect chance to put that into practice.

"Ancient? You mean, like Echidna and Leviathan?" I laid the big names out on the table, and uttering Leviathan's gave me a momentary shudder. Chaos, I hated him, and I hated that his words were the ones that brought me comfort.

Nathan smiled. "Precisely. True monoliths of Purge beast history. That's actually why I messaged your mother initially, as she's one of the only living people with any first-hand knowledge of the fabled Mother of Monsters." I could practically feel his excitement bubbling up to the surface. "Say, she didn't tell you anything about Echidna, did she?"

I shrugged. "Probably nothing you haven't already heard." That wasn't exactly true, but I didn't want to get into the naming curse thing with the clock running down to the wire on our getting to the assembly. Still, it served to know that there was someone in this Institute with an interest in Echidna who might be able to shed some light on her in return for some anecdotal tidbits. I could call in that exchange later, perhaps.

"I hate to interrupt this monster fan club meeting, but we really need to get going unless we want to be unfashionably late," Genie interjected, tapping an imaginary watch. "Which way?"

Nathan gestured to a cluster of black-suits striding along up ahead. "Follow them. I need to drop these papers off before I go to the assembly, but I'll see you again soon." He looked at Genie, but his words were directed at me. "I really would like to bend your ear about Echidna, if you can find time over the next week or so? You might have some information that you don't think is important but could radically help my research."

"Sure," Genie replied for me. "She'd love to, and you can compare monster sketches until the cows come home. But, right now, you need to do your thing and we need to do ours. So, thanks for the directions, and sorry for knocking you on your ass." She grabbed my hand and hauled me away, and the two of us sprinted down the corridor to catch up to the dwindling group turning left at the top of the hallway. I glanced back to find Nathan watching us go. He jolted a second later and gathered his folders to his chest, as though remembering what he was meant to be doing. I saw him muttering to himself as he cut down a different corridor in the opposite direction.

Poor guy... I doubted he'd forget Genie in a hurry. Then again, I'd never seen Genie so astonished by a guy before, unless you counted Marius. But that was mostly for show on Genie's part—Marius wasn't truly Genie's type. In fact, I had no idea what Genie's type was, in the real world. She did always have eclectic celebrity crushes. And maybe Nathan fit that eclectic bill, too.

We pursued the black-suits down another hallway as they breezed through a set of double doors at the far end, and we, less than gracefully, stumbled in after them. The moment we entered, we were dragged into a current of people, all jostling for space in what looked like an annex room. Another set of towering double doors loomed up ahead, but they weren't open yet—which meant we weren't late, after all.

"Why are there so many people? I thought orientation was just for new hunters," I whispered to Genie, grasping her hand tightly to keep from getting separated. I knew the Institute was home to more than just students—new and seasoned alike. Like a coven, the fully-fledged hunters also lived and worked here, using this facility as their base of operations. But that didn't explain why they were all here to witness this assembly. Did they just want to get a peek at the newbies, or was this some kind of tradition we didn't know about?

"I have no idea," Genie replied, swiping an orientation leaflet from a nearby cadet. Her eyes devoured it rapidly. "Ah, that makes sense."

I became aware of strangers' eyes fixing on us, and a prickly heat rose up the back of my neck. "What?"

"It's a *general* assembly." She pushed the leaflet under my nose. "This is where we meet everybody, trainers and scholars included. And it looks like everyone who lives here gets an invite. They're probably just here out of curiosity, I guess. Anyway, after the assembly, we get shown around the building, probably so we know where to go when classes start tomorrow. I'm guessing the scholars are the equivalent of preceptors."

"Yeah, Nathan mentioned those." I cast her some serious side-eye. "Speaking of which, he seemed more interested in you than his monsters. And I can't remember the last time I saw you blush like that. Do I sense a little crush?"

She crinkled her nose, like she smelled something sour. "Not a chance. He's got no sense of humor, and I can't deal with that. He has the looks, sure, but what's the point if he's lacking the *je ne sais quoi* that actually makes me blush? I was just warm from running."

"If you say so." I grinned at her.

She rolled her eyes. "I *do* say so. I even threw in some French so you know I'm serious. A guy has to have a... spark of something, you know? He can't just be nice to look at, or you might as well get a hologram of a movie star."

The double doors opened with a ground-shaking *boom*, and the crowd began to move like water draining down a plug, pouring into the room beyond. As Genie pulled me forward, she flashed me a mischievous smirk. "I liked his tweed, though."

Men had always fallen over themselves at the merest sight of

Genie, to the point where she could have had her pick, but her heart had some major walls around it—a by-product of her upbringing, where the words "arranged marriage" had been bandied about frequently over the years. She hated the subject, so we didn't talk about it often, though it always saddened me when we did. It was a tradition I'd never be able to wrap my head around. Anyway, I sensed the prospect of romance was the furthest thing from her mind. We were there to work and study and learn, even if men were literally tripping over their own feet in her presence.

Careful not to get wrenched apart in the rush of people, we squeezed through the crammed doorway into the assembly hall. Genie tugged my hand, leading me to a cloistered walkway off to the side, where there were fewer people. Everyone else seemed eager to get a front-row seat, fighting over chairs to get as close to the stage as possible.

"Forget that." Genie hopped up onto a stone ledge between the cloisters, and I jumped up beside her. "I'm not about to get claustrophobia for the sake of an assembly."

I laughed nervously. "No, me neither."

"I'd say we got the best seats in the house." Genie leaned out, her arm wrapped around the cloister pillar. Keeping up my I'm-totally-fine façade, I peered out with her.

"Wow…" The scale of the hall took my breath away, though that might have been the memory of not being able to get any air. Regardless, it made the SDC's assembly hall look like a pipsqueak of a gathering spot. A cavernous dome arched overhead, forged of stained glass that depicted great monster battles of bygone days: vast giants waged war against tiny mortals; jeweled thunderbirds struck at their human captors; silvered selkies swam in seal form through cobalt water, while in the next frame they stood in their beautiful human forms on pebbled beaches—shedding their sealskins while oblivious to the hunters lurking behind glass trees, waiting to strike.

The colors of the conflicts spilled down onto the congregation in rainbow shards, as though there'd been a happy ending to the tales.

It wasn't happy for the Purge beasts, though. I drew my eyes away, realizing that I'd fixated on the stained-glass monsters instead of their human counterparts. A part of me had wanted to cry out to the selkies and warn them off the beaches. But that story had already been told, and the real selkies were likely in the Bestiary somewhere, or in a coven Aquarium, being used as back-up generators.

Genie plucked me out of my thoughts by pointing out the towering septet of white marble dragons. There was one at the head of the room, standing sentinel over the stage, and three down each side of the hall. I didn't know if they were loadbearing or just decorative, but they packed a heck of a punch. They glowered down at me with golden eyes, which sparkled in the rainbow light cast by the overhead dome.

"Do you think they've got dragons in all these places?" Genie asked, giggling. "How did we end up with bronze ones at the SDC? I wonder if it's a hierarchy thing—a sign that a coven or an institute is compensating."

I clung tighter to the cloister pillar. "I don't know, I kind of like our bronze ones. They're homey, and this is all very... regal."

"Maybe that's why I feel like I should be whispering." Genie beamed, drinking in the atmosphere.

Everything had a clean, luxurious air, down to the rows and rows of plush white and gold chairs that everyone shuffled to. And beneath all of that were white marble floors streaked with veins of pink and gold. The stage rose up in a balustrade of that same veined marble before giving way to a semi-circle of polished white stone that was neither marble nor the Institute's favorite concrete. There, figures began to emerge from the wings, but I only recognized one: Victoria.

Two of the women were sharply dressed in identical tailored

suits of ruby red. Very fitting, considering they looked identical, too. I assumed they were the famed Basani twins. Beside them stood a younger woman who bore a startling resemblance to the twins. She was a bit older than Genie and me, dressed more casually in dark gray pants and a crisp white blouse.

"That's Charlotte, right?" I nodded toward the younger woman.

Genie gave an approving nod. "Bingo!"

A few marble statues caught my eye as my gaze drifted away from the stage and back across the hall. I'd missed them the first time. They were embedded everywhere, gracing the front of the stage, the recesses in the walls, and all the cloisters opposite. Smaller than the dragons, they were no less striking. I spied a chimera, a griffin, a unicorn, a quartet of kelpies pulling a chariot, a pair of loup-garous, and a cluster of feathered snakes, amongst more obscure monsters that I'd seen in my dreams. Wherever I looked, I found more, as if I were playing an elaborate game of hide and seek with these statues, and I was "it."

Gradually, the hubbub of the crowd died, and Victoria Jules took center stage. Her voice boomed around the hall, making me think there was some magical amplification on display there. I couldn't see a mic, but it sounded like she had twenty.

"Welcome, everyone, to a new season at the Basani Institute," she began, drawing everyone into her formidable gravitational pull. "As we draw away from the hardships of winter, we must look to the buds of oncoming spring—the nascent sprouts who will bask in the Institute's knowledge and bloom into fearsome hunters under the tutelage of our expert educators. Please, put your hands together for the new arrivals, for it may be the encouragement they need to endure the trials to come."

She paused for applause, and the crowd gave it to her. Reverence hung thick in the air.

"For our new students, I would advise patience and modesty as you learn what it is to be a hunter. There will not be a single day that passes that you will think of as easy. If you do, you are not doing it correctly. As those who have graduated will tell you, the real world of hunting is far more challenging than anything you will face here. We will prepare you, but your education will never stop." Victoria surveyed the hall with her intense black eyes and swept a hand through her oh-so-cool hair. "You will hurt, and you will curse the day you came here, but you will build bonds that last a lifetime. And you will understand that your limits are merely guidelines.

"To our existing classes, I would advise continued patience and modesty for you, also. You walk in the shadows of giants: the great hunters who have gone before you. There are still mountains to climb, and you would do well to remember that."

A rumble of laughter made its way around the hall, with those in black suits giving each other knowing nudges. They were the graduates—the ones who'd made it. It wouldn't be an easy ride to get there, and I didn't want it to be. I would work my ass off to get one of those black suits and prove that I could make something of myself, curse or no curse.

"To the graduates, I also advise patience and modesty, for you are not kings amongst peasants. Your purpose is to keep the magical and the human worlds safe from the dangers of monsters. You will never have laurels or glory, nor should you expect them. That is not why we do this. If you still think you will gain glory out of this, I have to assume you've got wax in your ears or you think I'm joking."

A richer chuckle rippled around the hall. There was a reason she'd ended up as the head huntswoman, and this speech went some way toward proving why. The crowd hung on her every word, even though they weren't all rainbows and butterflies. She told it how it was, and I appreciated her for that.

Victoria raised her hands and settled the hall again. "You might have noticed that I mentioned patience and modesty a few times there. That wasn't an accident." She cast a fleeting look at me. "No one is born with all the knowledge, or all the skills, or all the talent. This is a perilous profession with a low survival rate. There are no assurances. One mistake can cost even the finest hunter dearly, but that is part and parcel of the life you have all chosen. It is the tough grunt work that keeps the world safe, with our only reward being the continued security of the global covens, fueled by the energy that the beasts we capture give to the Bestiary. We are hunters and captors, not killers."

We are not fuel... Leviathan's voice crept into my skull, a memory of a past encounter, and his words raced to attack Victoria's. My heart began to race, my throat filling with cotton wool as I tried to drag in a breath or two. All my life, that had been the status quo—beasts were fuel, and magicals needed that fuel. But to think of those creatures in their boxes, maybe feeling the same way that I'd felt in my dream... It swung my moral compass a little, letting in a trickle of doubt that I hoped wouldn't shatter the dam and unleash hell inside my head.

"Are you okay?" Genie put a hand on my shoulder, interrupting my small panic attack.

I closed my eyes for a second to let the world calm around me. "It's warm, that's all."

I leaned against the pillar for support as Victoria carried on. "There is nothing glamorous about this profession. If you are looking for celebrity, you are in the wrong place."

I wouldn't say that around your founders. I glanced at the Basani twins and saw a flicker of annoyance cross their identical faces. Once upon a time, my uncle Finch had told me tales about those two, and he hadn't exactly been generous with the flattery. He'd met them in some strange monastery back in the day, and he'd said the twins had been charlatans with an impeccable PR team who'd made sure the duo was splashed on the front page of every magical magazine in circulation. After that encounter, however, Finch guessed the Basani twins had gotten a kick up the caboose and had actually put in the legwork for their legacy. In the aftermath, they'd traveled far and wide to catch beasts, dedicating years to it, until the truth finally matched the lies they'd formerly told—namely, that they were responsible for 15% of the beasts in the Bestiary. And now, this was their empire.

"It is messy, it is bloody, and it is dangerous." Victoria put her arms behind her back, standing proud. "But I have faith in your courage and determination, which you have already shown or I would not be speaking to you now."

Bloody. I still had my qualms about beast-kind, but I also understood the merits of monster hunting. Without it, monsters would swarm the world, free to hurt and kill innocents who couldn't fight back. Without it, Leviathan's vision of Hell on Earth would be reality. It might've looked unkind out of context, but it was necessary... right? I had to remember that, no matter how much Leviathan tried to nudge the needle on that compass of mine.

"Now, it is my pleasure to introduce you to our honored guests, and the people who will become a large part of your lives." Victoria gestured toward the Basani twins. "Please greet our founders, Shailene and Fay Basani: two of the best monster hunters who have ever lived. And Shailene's daughter, Charlotte, who is well on her way to becoming a legend in her own right."

Rapturous applause erupted from the congregation as the ruby-suited twins gave a bow. Charlotte, on the other hand, only dipped her head. Either she hated crowds, or she wasn't as well-versed in public adoration as her mom and aunt.

"Continue your applause for Ingram MacLoughlin, head of Monster Research." Victoria introduced a frankly massive man with a shock of bright copper hair and a beard that birds might easily confuse for a nest. He strode out and gave a bow as another figure stumbled along behind him.

"And, apparently, Mr. Nathaniel O'Hara wishes to make himself known to you all. Please, be particularly generous in your applause for Ingram's assistant, everyone." Victoria smiled as Nathan turned beet red in the center of the stage. He fumbled awkwardly, not knowing what to do with himself, and everyone duly gave him a bout of explosive applause.

This really isn't his day. I clapped for him, feeling sorry for the man as he scarpered off the stage like a startled mouse. Casting a subtle glance at Genie, I saw her head turn to watch him hurry away. Not quite as disinterested as she'd claimed, but I wasn't going to rib her for it.

After Nathan's fumble, the rest of the faculty paraded across the stage to the tune of Victoria's introductions. "Tarif Hosseini, master of the hunt. A living legend, who will never allow you to forget it." She smiled wider as she introduced him—a giant of a man, with a noble look about him, snappily dressed in a red silk suit with a high collar—though I could hear her speeding up to get through everyone.

"Naomi Hiraku, chief engineer, responsible for all of the devices that keep us alive and have provided us with greater safety over the past few years. Argo Ridgeway, head of logistics—or the gatekeeper of fate, as some of you like to call him. Johannes Noah, head of the arena—or Captain Pain, as he has been so graciously nicknamed. Lisbeth Oriel, head of Monster Sciences..." She rattled off a few more names that passed me by, as I was too engrossed in Naomi Hiraku to take them in.

If I was going to succeed here, this smiling, cheery-faced scholar held the keys. Without magic, I'd have to rely on all of the devices and technical wizardry I could get my mitts on to capture even the simplest of monsters.

Victoria settled the crowd again and resumed her power stance, though her black eyes paused on me as she shared her parting words. "All I have to say now is… good luck, everyone. Regardless of what stage you're at, there is always more to learn. Push past your limits, welcome challenge, and pursue every step with patience and modesty. Don't be disheartened. Use setbacks as a springboard to keep you moving forward. If you remember that, you cannot fail."

I won't let you down, Victoria. I didn't think I was the sole target of her advice, but it struck me as though she were speaking directly to me. She'd taken a chance on me. A big one, one that could very well change my entire life for the better. And I didn't plan to forget—or fail, if I could help it.

THREE

Genie

Holy *Ganymede, this is insane!* I had chills by the crapload. The good kind, fizzing up like a shaken soda bottle and ready to pop. We walked through a main hallway in the South Wing, not as spectators but as legit students. Even the layout began to make more sense after looking at the stained glass—different colors for different wings. Sweet, sweet freedom jiggled deliciously in my fair hands, delivered by the most awesome place imaginable. I felt like all my dreams were coming true at once. Even dreams I didn't know I'd had.

"I wonder what we'll see first," Persie whispered. My compadre in life. My sister from another mister. The yin to my yang. Call me a cheeseball, but I'd have gone to the ends of the Earth for her, and then some. And it felt so freaking good to be there with her, stepping out into our brave new world together, knowing we'd earned the right to stand in these hallways.

"These are the training halls." Charlotte Basani, the badass of her mom's Institute, opened the doors to let us take a look. I wasn't one for hero worship, but heroine worship—yeah, I could do that. And I had some major heart eyes for this woman. She had the kind of hunting rap sheet that turned me green with envy, but I wasn't jealous—global, cross-continental missions to wrangle the rarest and most dangerous beasts of all: bahamuts, wendigos, and basilisks. But, at the end of the day, everyone was in a one-horse race against themselves, so jealousy was a waste of time. I preferred to champion folks instead of creating an enemy that didn't exist.

I craned my neck to get a look at the training facilities. No surprise that the cadet corps was up front, hogging the doorway. "Can you see?" I asked, looking down at Persie.

"Just about," she replied from her tiptoes.

A row of glass rooms lay beyond the main door, sort of like squash courts but way bigger. The panel sets were frosted, but I could make out hazy shadows moving behind, and I could hear Grand Slam grunts from within. Hey, even hunters needed their privacy while training. It wouldn't have been too impressive to watch the blooper reel on our first day. We needed to see the slick end-product, the thing that would trick us into thinking everything would be smooth sailing—even though we all knew this was going to be the hardest thing any of us had ever done. And I included the GIs in that.

"You'll train here with Hosseini. He'll teach you to hunt. It goes up in stages, so you'll start with the basics—types of attack, defensive strategies, the use of devices—then work toward intermediate level, which is more to do with your personal hunting style, and so on." Charlotte kept things straight and to the point, and I liked that. No messing about, just "here's this, and here's how it'll serve you." I imagined she had the same approach to her hunting. "If you ever get lost, ask for directions. It takes a few weeks to get the hang of the layout, so don't be too proud to get help. That goes for most things in this place."

If only the rest of us had an advantage like yours. I didn't mean that in a bitter way. Having an edge was useful, and she had the Basani well of monster knowledge at her fingertips. Honestly, it was kind of freaky how much she looked like her mom and, obviously, her aunt as well. Charlotte had the same hazel eyes and olive skin, though her golden blonde hair verged on the strawberry persuasion. A hint of her dad, probably.

"If you've seen enough, we'll move on." Charlotte walked off without waiting. She knew we'd follow.

She pointed out various studies and suites as we headed back along endless corridors, containing know-how that we didn't need in our first year. Persie wasn't in a very chatty mood, and I couldn't blame her. She was clearly dog-tired from playing defense against her nightmares. My best pal had been through some gnarly crap lately, troubles that didn't show any sign of letting up. We both hoped her Purges had waned, but we also knew wishful thinking when we saw it. Even though I knew it was stupid, I hated dream-me for not stepping up. I didn't always get it right, like with the scorpion fiasco, but I wouldn't ever stop trying to help my best friend. If anyone ever tried to lock her up, I'd throw everything I had at them.

"Here, we have the Theorem Complex." Charlotte paused in front of two enormous double doors. They really had a thing for those, here. Turning the huge, clover-shaped handles, she pushed both doors open like a dramatic movie heroine.

A cathedral-like beauty of a room invited our necks to strain upward. "Room" didn't even begin to cover it. You could've fit an aircraft hangar in there and still had wiggle room. Curving stair-cases snaked up to elaborate balconies, where trainees and gradu-ates sat at mahogany desks, flipping through the million dusty books that lined never-ending shelves. On the ground floor, modern glass boxes masqueraded as study cells. In one, I spotted that bear of a scholar, Ingram something or other, teaching a small class.

"Hey, isn't that—?" Persie gave me a nudge in the ribs.

"Who?" Of course, I knew who she meant. I wasn't blind. He stood at the back of Ingram's glass box, taking notes.

Persie smiled. "Mr. O'Hara."

"Oh... yeah, maybe. I can't tell from here." I could smell the BS, and there was no way my pal hadn't caught the reek. Fortunately, Charlotte saved me.

"This is where you will learn Monster Theory, if you hadn't guessed from the name. MacLoughlin and his assistants will be teaching you." She gestured up to the yawning rafters. "It also serves as a library, if you want to study privately. Although we do have five libraries, so you can take your pick depending on your needs."

She didn't even announce that we were moving on this time. She just turned and headed off, leaving us to trail after her like eager ducklings. There was something about her cool, matter-of-fact attitude that intrigued me. I'd yet to see her break a smile. Not that it was necessary, it just made me wonder if she'd been roped into this against her will, as a favor to Mama Basani. As with all legacies, I guessed she felt the Basani name weighing on her shoulders. I guessed she had other, more complicated dimensions to her, ones she didn't want to show to the newbs.

I could understand the crushing heft of legacy, and not just from being friends with Persie. Being the only Atlantean at the Institute came with novelty value, sure, but it also singled me out. I didn't look like everyone else. I had tattoos on my face, for one. And I had more power than everyone else, for another. I wasn't tooting my own horn or anything, it was plain fact. A gift and a curse. Normally, I didn't let that faze me, but I remembered the words my dad had whispered in my ear when we parted ways: "You will be our nation's representative. Make Atlantis proud."

Ah, the motherland... The double-edged sword that loomed over my life. But I wasn't doing this to make Atlantis proud. Long before

Persie had even suggested this place, I'd daydreamed about becoming a monster hunter for one woman and one woman alone: my mom. She'd been one of the finest hunters in Atlantis. Yes, it had taken her away from me in the end, but she'd loved her job with everything she had. I'd sat on my dad's knee and listened to his stories about her death-defying captures and the weird and wonderful monsters of the deep, and I'd been so awestruck that I'd forgotten to breathe. I had known even then that I wanted to be like her, without ever having known her.

"Take a breath, baby shrimp," my dad would whisper to me. Apparently, it had been her pet name for me because I'd slept curled up like one. And he'd continued it, in her memory. Though it had been a long time since he'd called me that.

I want to make you proud, Mom. I want to be as great as you were. Maybe, it'll make me feel like you're... still here. I had to blink away unexpected tears and pretend to stare at a few display cases filled with hunter paraphernalia. If Persie saw, she'd worry, and she didn't need my problems on top of hers. There was so much I hated about Atlantis: the traditions, the arranged marriages, the paternal expectation. But it was where I was born. It was where I was loved by her. It was where I'd said goodbye to her, even though I'd been too young to remember. And that bound me to that backward little world, no matter how far away I roamed.

"Don't get too close, she might hex you. They're sentients, you know—sneaky buggers." My head whipped around. The two closest cadets, with ponytails so tight they had permanently startled expressions, shot me daggers and descended into furtive giggles. I didn't know which one had said it, and I didn't want to cause a scene. But this wasn't the first instance of this. There had been sly looks and whispers for the last five days. I'd ignored them, for the most part, hoping they'd wear out their petty bigotry, but it got harder each time.

"I wouldn't waste the energy," I hissed back.

They exchanged a worried look and scuttled to the front of the crowd.

Persie looped her arm through mine. "You okay?"

"All good here." I forced a smile and kept my chin up. But a nagging doubt crept into the back of my head. *Is this what Dad was talking about?* He hadn't always been a stuffy traditionalist. He'd gotten us out of Atlantis precisely because he didn't agree with a lot of what they did. But that had changed over the years, after he'd started working as an Atlantean envoy for the integration program. There had been a slow shift in his mindset. He'd sat me down a thousand times and warned me that the wider magical world didn't think kindly of us. It was his main reason for wanting to cart me off back to Atlantis. I'd called nonsense on it, but... what if he'd been telling the truth?

"Seriously, did someone say something? You look... sad." I couldn't pull the wool over her eyes. She knew me too well. Although there was one thing she hadn't caught onto just yet. A secret, of sorts: that I needed her as much as she needed me. A fearless façade did not a fearless woman make.

"I was thinking about someone, that's all."

She nodded in understanding. "She's rooting for you, Genie."

"Yeah, I think she is." I dipped my head and battled more tears until they gave up. Jeez, this independence thing came with a lot more weepy moments than I'd expected. But there was an old Atlantean sentiment that I kept close: "Loved ones never leave us, for they are within us. You cannot lose what is intrinsic to your heart. It is but a brief parting, not a forever farewell."

Charlotte stopped in front of more familiar doors. "This is the banquet hall. First-year students take their breakfast in the old chapel at the back, if you didn't already know from your orientation packages."

"What packages?" I shot a confused look at Persie.

She shrugged. "Maybe ours got lost in the post?"

I took a quick look at the banquet hall, though I'd already seen it once today.

"This way." Charlotte walked on, pointing out the way to the infirmary, four of the smaller libraries, and the laundry room. Apparently, they weren't interesting enough to take a peek at. But we could always investigate more later, schedule permitting. We were supposed to receive our schedules at the end of the tour, and I guessed they'd be jam-packed.

Trekking on through the labyrinth, she halted halfway down a vast hallway and swung open a set of medieval doors. I expected a classroom or another library. Instead... well, what a view. To the right, there was a beautiful courtyard with pear trees growing along the perimeter, and benches beneath the rustling leaves. To the left were manicured gardens with vivid flowerbeds in full bloom, despite the chill in the breeze. Beyond the sandstone walls, from Charlotte's curt description, were more gardens, where hunters and students liked to stroll. And, down a central path, rolling green hills stretched as far as the eye could see, even beyond the confines of the Institute. From inside, it was easy to forget that the outside world existed. But here it was, in all its lush green glory.

"This place is so beautiful, isn't it? Everywhere you look, there's something new and exciting to see!" Persie gushed breathlessly. "I wonder if those pears are ripe enough to eat?"

I shook my head. "They'd give you the collywobbles, make no mistake."

"What?"

"A tummy-ache." I grinned, feeling better with some fresh air in my lungs. Ironic, considering I'd spent most of my earliest child-hood in a manufactured bubble, but hey—I didn't make the rules.

"Even without the pears, I'd love to sketch out here," she said wistfully.

I leaned my head on top of hers. "Then sketch you shall."

In the distance, I noticed the ghost of a gray, church-looking building—a smidge of non-magical civilization. Churches had always unnerved me. And this one had a flavor of the eerie about it, intensified by the bruised swell of rainclouds rising up on the horizon.

"You can walk out here whenever you like, but don't go outside Institute limits without express permission," Charlotte warned. "It's nicer in the summer."

I'll bet it still rains. I smirked. In the five days we'd been there, it had rained on four of them. Ah, Ireland. No wonder everything was so green.

Moving on, she showed us the common areas: big lounge rooms with roaring fireplaces, comfy sofas, and cozy vibes—the perfect defense against grim weather. Though maybe we'd just been spoiled by the San Diego sunshine. At least here, I wouldn't have to lather on about forty layers of sunscreen to avoid getting crisped. Ghostly Atlantean skin and that burning orb in the sky did not a happy pair make, though I did miss the heat of the SDC.

"And this is the Monster Repository." Charlotte led us through black doors with gargoyle-head door handles. I skidded to a startled halt as major flashbacks bombarded my brain. My mom's colleagues, who had been like aunts and uncles to me, had taken me to visit the Atlantis Bestiary a few times, with the permission of King Ovid. And this place looked… identical, just in miniature. A sea of various-sized blue glass orbs attached to silver poles were arranged in neat lines from wall to wall, resembling a forest of bubbles. Black mist swirled inside each one, and nobody won a prize for guessing why.

Before I'd fully recovered from the shock, a patter of footsteps made the group turn. A stressed-looking Nathan sprinted to Charlotte, then stooped to catch his breath. His eyes caught mine for a split second before I hurriedly looked elsewhere. No point in making doe eyes at anyone. I wasn't here for that. And there wasn't much point, anyway. My dad had made it clear that I could either accept an arranged Atlantean marriage for bloodline reasons or never marry at all. Not that I was thinking about marriage; Ganymede, no—that was the furthest thing from my mind.

"Sorry I'm late. Time got away from me," Nathan apologized.

Charlotte took her phone out of her pocket. "Actually, this is perfect timing. I need to make a call. I trust you can take it from here?" She didn't give him a chance to answer. Already dialing, she walked into the hall and left him to it.

He stood there for a moment, like a deer in headlights. Finally, he straightened his jacket cuffs and smoothed a hand through his lion's mane, all the while ignoring the flirty giggles from a gaggle of girls close to the front.

Did they teach you that *at cadet school?* I watched a black vortex of smoke in a nearby orb, though I felt a prickle of heat on the back of my neck—a telltale sign that he had his eyes on me. Well, I wouldn't be looking back. Nope, nope, nope. Good-looking guys spelled trouble. And I couldn't afford any distractions.

"Uh... Well, this is the Monster Repository. I am responsible for the upkeep and intake here." He gestured to the bubble forest. "In case you were confused, this is where the monsters are brought after being captured in the field. I identify them, classify them, record their information into the logbook, and generally care for them until they're shipped off to the Bestiary. Sometimes, I even give them names." He laughed awkwardly, but nobody else did.

Feeling sorry for him, I mustered a chuckle. "Like what?"

"Oh... um... It depends. There was a goblin I was particularly fond of, and I called him... Goodness, this is embarrassing." Nathan swept his hand through his hair again. A nervous tic. "I called him Ptolemy."

"Was he particularly good at math? Or astrology, perhaps?" I teased, while Persie smothered a laugh.

Nathan squirmed, pushing a flustered hand into his back pocket. "Truthfully, I just like naming them after famous theorists." He turned his back and started pointing aimlessly. "As you may have noticed, we don't use the same boxes as the Bestiary. We used to, but they were upgraded to emulate the... uh... Atlantean design."

Persie stiffened at my side, no doubt freaked out by the mention of glass boxes. I tugged her closer to me to let her know I was there.

"Pfft, as if we need their technology," said a classmate with hedgehog hair and muscles that looked like they'd been inflated by a bike pump. Bike-Pump Biceps was what I'd call him for now. I shot him a dark look. He hadn't even dared to actually direct his comment at me. Coward.

Nathan turned back around. "Actually, their technology is proven to provide the creatures with a more comfortable experience."

"Who cares about their comfort? They're mindless," another classmate chimed in, a smug grin on her face. One of the ponytails who'd snarked at me before.

"If you think that, you shouldn't be here." It was the first time I'd seen a bit of fire in Nathan. His eyes narrowed, and the girl's grin vanished. "They aren't mindless. They are sentient beings with very real personalities, and every creature is unique. I'm not even sure that keeping them caged is the best way of harnessing their energy, but they are necessary to magical society, so it's my job to make sure that they are, at the very least, comfortable while they are in my care. And I have no doubt that the Beast Master of the Bestiary behaves the same way, because *he* understands these creatures and their merits in a way that you clearly don't. I hope that changes, or you'll find life as a hunter a thankless task."

"Why don't you ask the SDC's finest?" the musclebound jackass grumbled.

Nathan smiled at Persie and me. "That's an excellent idea. You must know the Beast Master quite well, I'd imagine. What does he believe?"

Persie nodded. "Tobe knows every creature, and he cares for each of them with the biggest heart. Even the ones who might not deserve it."

You say that, but he'd rip Leviathan a new one if that slimy son of a biatch ever actually tried to hurt you.

I didn't say it aloud. There was no use in bringing him up when he was clearly already on Persie's mind all the time. She always shuddered when she heard his name, and I hated the hold he had over her. She should've been enjoying her life, not worrying about what Leviathan would do next. I'd never forgive him for that, or for ruining my best friend's eighteenth birthday. Who did that? The slippery snake clearly had zero manners.

"If you love him so much, why didn't you stay there? You could've added to the Bestiary," the other ponytail muttered under her breath, growing some serious sour grapes.

Fortunately, I liked the taste of sour. And I wasn't about to let anyone talk to my friend like that. I knew she could defend herself, but she wouldn't.

"Why, you worried it might give us an advantage because we've seen more real-life monsters than you've had hot dinners?" I retorted.

Ponytail #2 sneered. "I'm not afraid of you, Genie."

"You're the one who said it, not me." I smiled, sweet as anything. "Now, I'd like to hear more from Nathan and less from you."

Nathan nodded enthusiastically. "Yes, thank you, Genie. I'm

pleased to hear that the Beast Master is everything I thought he would be, and I'd like to speak with you about him in more detail, but… that can obviously wait." He walked up to one of the bubbles and coaxed the creature inside to appear. It flitted around like a dragonfly, with wings that looked like browned leaves. It resembled a stick insect with its crooked arms and thin body, with the exception of an eerily human face that observed us with milky white eyes. "This is a sprite called Archimedes. He's very shy, and he likes—"

"Long walks on the beach?" I joked. This time, I got a proper laugh, free of nerves.

"I imagine he would, though he'd probably prefer a long flight in the park," Nathan replied, smiling. "Many people used to believe that sprites were the spirits of the dead, who could be benevolent or malevolent, depending on how they were treated. They are ancient and were feared, but not so much anymore. This one is an Earth sprite, with weak spellcasting abilities that it uses to grow flowers and fruits, and to help crops. But the point is, there are sprites who would batter against this glass, or shrink away, or not emerge at all. I've gotten to know this one, and it's proof of my theory that they have awareness and are far more complex than people make them out to be."

A long-haired dude folded his arms across his chest. "You'll be saying they have souls, next."

Nathan put his palm to the glass, and the sprite raised a crooked, twiggy hand to his. "Actually, there is a great deal of evidence to suggest that they do, but proving the presence of a soul in a Purge beast would be like proving the existence of a soul in a human being."

Nice comeback, O'Hara! The long-haired guy huffed grumpily. Nathan had silenced him without so much as raising his voice. He'd slapped him with a wet fish of intellect, and I had to admit… it was kind of sexy. Not the wet fish part, but the smarts part. And he'd shown me a flash of a sense of humor, when I was fairly sure he'd had a humorectomy. Still, I wasn't sure he would be much use in an actual hunting scenario. Not to sound shallow, but I'd always gravitated toward brawnier types. The kind of guy who could hold their own. Borderline alphas, that sort of jam. Nathan had some tasty looks, absolutely, but he was so... awkward. Cute, in its own right, but I didn't usually go for that.

"Are we done in here?" Charlotte reappeared, as blunt as ever. Maybe even a little thorny, but who wouldn't be if they'd been saddled with a tour group by their mom? I'd shown a similarly blasé attitude when my dad made me take new Atlanteans around the SDC, though I'd managed a few smiles and a joke here and there. Just like Nathan's theory about monsters, humans had their own individual styles and responses to situations. Charlotte was just riding with hers.

"I believe so," Nathan replied. He cast a look at me, and his face brightened in a disarming smile. It would've been rude not to smile back.

"Right, then, let's get moving. Our last stop is the future new wing of the Institute." Charlotte disappeared and the group exited, in a rush to catch up to her. This time, Nathan joined us. I pushed away the hopeful thought that maybe he'd joined because of me.

We got halfway up the corridor when something caught my attention: a faint light bobbing in the rafters overhead. I paused and stared at it, convinced my eyes were playing tricks on me. I blinked, but the light didn't go anywhere. It looked like a hazy purple orb, with flaming blue wisps coming off it.

I nudged Persie. "Do you see that?"

"What?" Her voice sounded weird. Strained. Glancing down at her, I gasped. The color had vanished from her face, and a sheen of sweat glistened on her forehead. Her lips were blue and trembling. Either we had a panic attack on our hands, or a Purge. Since it had been five days since her last spew of scary mist, my money was on the Purge.

"Okay, Mama, we need to get you sitting and breathing." I tugged her gently toward a bench against the wall and sat her down. The others hadn't noticed and gone on ahead, including Nathan, which was fine by me. Persie didn't need an audience of gawping vultures. Kneeling in front of her, I took her hands in mine. "Breathe with me, Persie. Can you do that?" I drew in a slow inhale, counted to five, and exhaled again. She stared at me, terror in her eyes. I gripped her hands tighter and breathed again, with the same slow deliberation. "Come on, baby shrimp. In for five, hold for five, out for five."

Baby shrimp? My heart jolted. I hadn't meant to say it, it just spilled out. As I kept up the rhythm for Persie to copy, my mind turned to my mom again. Maybe she really was here, watching over me. Tragically, my mom would never get to meet Persie. I somehow knew they would've adored each other. But, right now, I had to take care of my best friend.

Persie nodded. With a rattling rasp, she took a breath.

"That's it, you've got this. I'm here," I urged. "Just keep breathing. I've got you."

As she drew another breath, slow and steady and clear, I dared to steal a look back up at the rafters. But the glowing orb, or whatever it was, had gone. And I had to wonder... had it caused this?

FOUR

Persie

I knew it couldn't last. Five days without a Purge had been blissful, but that run of luck had come to an end. I tried to clench Genie's hands, but it was as though I'd fallen asleep on my arms and now numbness spread from shoulder to fingertips. A new symptom, perhaps? I wouldn't put anything past this curse. I was just a vessel for unleashing beasts into the world... a means to an end.

"My... chest. I can't... breathe." I hunched over, my surroundings swimming in a kaleidoscope of color. The straight walls and curved ceiling melted into one, and the seat beneath me felt spongy and strange, like it could twist away at any moment. Panic scampered into the spotlight, sending dark sparks of adrenaline through my veins. Even though I'd known my Purges were inevitable, I hadn't wanted this one to come. Not here, not on my first real day.

"You can, Persie." Genie ducked underneath my bent shoulders, so I had no choice but to look into her slate gray eyes.

"Are... they... watching?" I couldn't stand the idea of having a crowd observe me in my lowest moments. We weren't children anymore, but that didn't mean they wouldn't use anything they considered ammunition against me. I didn't want to be an outcast forever, especially not here, where I'd hoped I'd belong.

Genie shook her head at an awkward angle. "No, it's just me. Don't worry, you have nothing to be ashamed of."

So why do I feel like it's my dirty little open secret? This was part of me now, and I knew there'd come a time when I had to own it, but I doubted I'd make peace with it anytime soon. With an ability so chaotic and haphazard, how could I? It flat-out refused to let me enjoy one good thing in my life. First my birthday, and now my orientation day.

"I... hate it," I rasped, as tears sprang to my blurry eyes. "I... hate... it!" I held onto Genie with every ounce of strength I could muster, focusing on the faint lines that crisscrossed her fingers and the chipped varnish on her nails. Anything to keep me anchored in this storm.

"I know you do. I'm sorry I can't take it away from you or find someone else who can." Genie's breath hitched and I saw tears shining in her eyes, too. "But you're tough as heck, Persie. You can shove this sucker down and show it who's boss. This is your power, and that means you run the show."

My tears splashed onto the polished concrete floor.

"I can't... even breathe," I muttered, trying to follow Genie's rhythm. Five seconds in, hold for five, then five seconds out.

She peered up at me. "Can I use some Chaos on you?"

"It can't... make it worse." Famous last words, but I was desperate.

A shivering white tendril, hair-thin and barely perceptible, slithered out of her without the need for any hand commands. The glowing thread slipped between my lips and traveled down into my chest. The Air expanded my lungs, and a loud gasp erupted from my throat as I took a genuine breath. After calming down, I realized I'd caused this attack myself. I'd been holding my breath the entire time, panicking like a drowning person, intent on reserving whatever oxygen I had left—a survival tactic that could've gone seriously awry if I'd held on a few more minutes.

"That's it, you gulp down that tasty, tasty air." Genie smiled widely as my body remembered what it was supposed to be doing. I unlocked the vise that had clamped around my ribcage and drew in breath after breath, letting the adrenaline and anxiety drain from me. The melting world returned to solidity, and my swimming vision cleared.

I laughed like a loon. "It wasn't a Purge!"

"No?" Genie didn't sound convinced, but I knew the difference. If this had been an oncoming Purge, the lingering need to expel would still be inside me—a perennial nausea in the pit of my stomach, like those tarry slugs that I'd coughed out in my dream.

"I think I was just overwhelmed. A panic attack, or something," I replied, my manic laughter subsiding.

"You've been through a lot." Genie rose to her feet and sat next to me on the bench. "It's only natural that your body wants to go into protective mode. After all this, it probably thinks you're under constant attack."

"I couldn't have put it better," I agreed. "I've been waiting and waiting for my next Purge, and I've been waiting for Leviathan to make a move, and I keep thinking someone's going to comment on me being dangerous. I guess all the stress was bound to take its toll at some point."

I had Genie, but I didn't have the rest of my support system within easy reach. I'd come to a brand-new place to follow my own path, with the shadow of my "gift" looming over me. And the transition had been anything but smooth. The joy of finding out I would be studying here had been marred by the news that I was no longer welcome in my own home and couldn't even go back to fetch my things. Sure, I had big hopes for the future, fueled by a furnace of determination, but I couldn't quash the idea that all of this would somehow blow up in my face. This morning's dream hadn't helped matters, amplifying my worst fears. Since arriving at the Institute, I'd tried to seem okay on the outside so I didn't stand out as the perpetually nervous weirdo who might blast out a monster at any moment. But, on the inside, mayhem reigned supreme. To say that I was a mess would've been putting it lightly. I wanted to find my way through this new world without stirring up any trouble, but Leviathan's gift had made trouble my middle name.

Genie bumped her arm gently against mine. "Silver lining. No Purge beast."

"Right." I tilted my head back against the wall and tried to stick with the positives.

"I just... don't want to end up in a glass box," I said, more to myself than Genie.

"You're not going to." She turned to me, and I met her earnest gaze. "I realize everything is a bit topsy-turvy at the moment, but you've got so many people on your side, Persie. People who won't let that happen to you: me, Victoria, your parents, Tobe. And maybe I sound like a broken record, but you've already taken the first step toward controlling your ability. *You* made that happen, and if that doesn't show grit, then I'm a circus clown."

I smiled at her. "Your cheeks do look a little red, but that might just be the lingering effects of Nathan's presence."

She squeezed her eyes shut and clasped her hand to her heart dramatically, making me chuckle. "Oof, you wound me, Persie. I've told you, this Atlantean has her romance blinders firmly in place." One eye peeked open. "But I'm glad you're cracking jokes. The funnies are the first sign of recovery."

I really did feel calmer. The tension I'd been holding in my muscles had released, and I'd gone back to not noticing how air came in and out of my chest.

"Thank you for being here, Genie." I weaved my arm through hers.

She waved a hand through the air. "*Ach*, where else would I be? Taking elocution lessons in Atlantis, gearing up to take a husband?" Her expression turned more serious. "We've been a pair since you were born. A team. And I know you'd have gotten yourself out of that"—she twirled her hand through the air, indicating the panic attack—"even if I hadn't been here. I saw you during your exam, Pers. You didn't let anything stop you... Well, until *I* stopped you." Sadness flickered across her face, mingling with a smidge of guilt.

"You *helped* me," I corrected. I knew she still had some mixed emotions about that day, and how she might've messed up my admission into this Institute. But I didn't blame her at all for stepping in. She'd seen me go all Purgey and had done what any good friend would.

She gave me a grateful smile.

"So, do you think we should catch up with the group?" I said.

With a concerned eyebrow arched, she asked, "Are you sure you feel better?"

"Steady as a rock." I held out a hand to show the shakes had gone.

"Then let's go and see what we're missing." With my arm still looped through hers, Genie led the way up the hall. I had to lean against her a little bit as we walked, but she didn't make a point of it, just tightened her muscles so she could bear as much of my weight as I needed. We were our own two-person unit, and we left no woman behind.

Fortunately, the labyrinth of the Institute had decided to be kind. At the end of the long hallway, there was only one route: to the left. We followed it until we spotted the rest of the group in the distance, standing in front of a wall of stained-glass panels that appeared to be in the middle of construction. Half-formed friezes of monster battles, in fiery shades of scarlet, gold, and burnished orange, were arranged around a partially-built archway that gaped darkly.

We were halfway up the corridor when Genie yanked me back. "There they are again!"

"What?" I squinted up at her.

"Those... glowy things." Her forehead furrowed. "Do you feel sick again? Any chills?"

"No, I feel fine." I followed her line of sight and froze in wonder. Gaseous spheres of light, about the size of baseballs, bounced around in the rafters overhead, trailing wisps of duck-egg blue, jade green, and lavender. The colors intensified in the center of each dancing light, like a candle flame, though the centers didn't necessarily match the trails they dispersed; one of the blue lights had a vibrant violet core, while one of the green ones had a center of sunshine yellow.

They mesmerized me as I watched them whirl and somersault above. "What are they?"

"I don't know, but I saw one before you got sick back there. I thought they might've had something to do with it, but since you haven't gone all pale again, I guess I was wrong." Genie tilted her head, her mouth set in a curious line.

A few seconds later, they melted into the ceiling, only the mystery remaining.

"Maybe they were dust motes," I suggested. "Really big ones."

It wasn't much of a theory. I'd never seen any sort of mote act the way those glowing orbs had, but light had a way of fooling the eye. And the Institute's stained glass, inserted into almost every roof, certainly could've explained the pretty colors.

"I don't know. They looked magical to me." Genie stared at the spot where they'd been.

"Ireland is meant to be teeming with Chaos, right? Maybe it has something to do with that? Residual energy?"

Genie pursed her lips. "Could be. Or they're a part of the Institute we haven't learned about yet. Security hexes that patrol the whole place on a loop, that kind of thing."

I nodded uncertainly. "I think I've heard of that before." Her theory definitely worked better than mine, but those orbs had given me a peculiar feeling of... I didn't know, it was hard to describe. A magnetic pull, similar to Leviathan's hypnotic angler-fish appendage. Anyway, they'd disappeared, and it didn't look like we'd be getting any answers.

We seized our moment and hurried the rest of the way to the group. They had their backs to us, listening to Charlotte as she swept a hand across the gaping archway. It gave us a chance to slot into the back of the cluster without anyone noticing we'd been gone, though it seemed Nathan had noticed Genie's absence, judging by the relief that washed over his features when we returned. He really seemed taken with her, but I wasn't sure how that worked in a place like this—was it okay for assistants to have the hots for a student? I guessed so, or he wouldn't be so open about it.

"This is the future site of the new Monster Repository. Please be mindful that it's still under construction and try not to touch anything." Charlotte didn't even turn around before pressing on through the archway.

Entering behind the rest of the class, I realized why it had looked so dark from outside. Several hunters stood at intervals around the space, working their magic to build this addition to the Institute's interdimensional bubble. Sacks of raw building materials sat on the ground beside them, and above it all stretched a gargantuan black tarp that blanketed the space below in semi-darkness. In fact, the only light these workers had to see by were a few wall-mounted lamps and the glow of their own Chaos. With their palms up, they drew out the materials and crafted girders from metal and stone bricks, replicating the architecture of the rest of the Institute. They pulled up shards of glass, which formed more of those stained-glass masterpieces. The end products floated up and slotted into place in the grand puzzle of this new wing.

"I've never seen an interdimensional bubble being built before," one of our classmates whispered, though it was too gloomy to see who'd spoken.

Charlotte glanced back. "It's impressive. Our Magnetons, Masons, and Igneons work in shifts during the day to ensure it'll be completed by the deadline." She pointed into the darkness ahead. "Once the main parts are finished, they'll start on additional rooms for research and testing, and quarters for visiting hunters."

"Igneons?" I looked at Genie.

"It's an ability that blends Earth and Fire, to turn things molten," she explained. "I guess it's good for glassmaking."

Nathan and Charlotte led the group through the tarp-covered entry hall, only to stop again where the construction gave way to an enormous open section. Nathan formed a fireball and tossed it into the yawning beyond. It hovered like a flare in the center of the cavernous addition, though the dense darkness seemed to suck away the majority of the light, leaving behind only an anemic glow. Even so, I could see enough. It didn't look like much had been done here yet. It only bore the metal and glass skeleton of a massive sphere, the bottom half falling away below the precipice where our guides stood. The bones of metal walkways were partially erected, but it was hard to see how far they stretched, considering this sphere provided almost no light to see by.

"Is this where the monsters are going to be put?" a classmate asked.

Charlotte stared out into the sphere. "Eventually, yes. The bubble poles you saw in the old Repository will go floor to ceiling, with circular platforms that run up and down each pole, accessed by these walkways."

Suddenly, the glowing lights reappeared on my right and fluttered across the tarp overhead. I pulled on Genie's arm and jabbed a finger upward. Her gaze flitted toward them, her face scrunching in confusion. Charlotte and Nathan appeared to notice them at the same moment, the latter's eyes widening in surprise as the lights whooshed about the black sphere.

"What are they?" I piped up. "We saw them a few minutes ago, in the hallway."

Nathan squinted at the pastel trails, watching the orbs twist around each other before they plummeted down into the lower hemisphere and their glow sputtered out into gaping nothingness.

"I have no idea," he said, after a moment or two. "I've never seen them before."

"So, they're not security hexes?" Genie called out.

"Not that I know of." He rubbed his chin thoughtfully. "They could be remnants of a hunter's magic, maybe. Sometimes, when a magical is powerful enough, they leave shards of their Chaos behind when they die."

Charlotte cut in, clearly unimpressed by the light show. "If that were the case, I'd have seen them before. I've been here all my life. They're probably just aids for the workers, to help them see."

"Then why did they just take a nosedive into this... sphere thing?" I pointed out. Hexes could sometimes have a mind of their own, but these orbs didn't feel like manufactured puffs of light to help with construction.

Charlotte shrugged. "They could be additions to the décor—magical fairy lights. It wouldn't be the first time some continental hunter decided to spruce the Institute up a bit. We once had a visiting hunter from Paris who decided to try something out for size and wound up turning the whole East Wing pink. And when I say pink, I mean *pink*. So bright, I don't think my eyes ever fully recovered." A hint of a smile turned up the corner of her lips. It was the first sign of personality I'd seen since I first heard her name. "Or it could be students messing about. A prank that'll burn itself out."

"Yes, perhaps a joke of some kind." Nathan took off his glasses and cleaned the lenses with the edge of his polo shirt before putting them back on. "Let's just hope they don't let off an eggy stench or start exploding. We had to close the East Wing once, after a student decided to unleash a cloud of gas that made people talk in high-pitched squeaks for an hour. Seeing Ingram try to keep his class together during that debacle... I'll never forget it." He chuckled to himself, and Genie joined in. Man, did he seem pleased about that.

"It's always the East Wing," Charlotte muttered before weaving through the group to lead the way back. "Anyway, we need to get moving."

Genie grinned at her. "Where to next?"

Next to her, Charlotte paused. "Wherever you like. Once I take you back to the entrance hall, the orientation is over." Her ghost of a smile had gone. "But you should keep up this time. Don't want to be getting lost."

It was hard to tell if she was concerned or sarcastic. I just hoped she thought we'd been sidetracked back there, by looking at the glowing lights and not by something else—AKA, my mental state. I hadn't Purged, after all, so it really didn't need to be talked about. Just some first-day jitters, leading to an all-out panic attack. Nothing too serious... Well, not as serious as a hydra or something worse, like a bahamut or a dragon, loose in the corridors. Who knew what I was capable of Purging?

"No problem." Genie sounded a touch hurt by the cool response. As the old adage went, never meet your heroes. I guessed Charlotte wasn't quite what Genie had hoped for. For my part, I wasn't overly impressed by her general attitude. She might've been a talented hunter, but she behaved so coldly to people. I thought it was odd, too, that she hadn't seemed particularly warm toward her mom and aunt when they were on stage together.

Charlotte turned her attention to me. "I hope there wasn't an issue?"

"Not at all," I replied, a beat too quickly.

"Good. I don't like cleaning up messes." Charlotte strode on, her frostiness leaving me a little stunned. If she had any idea how painful and taxing multiple Purges could be—on top of not knowing when they'd strike—I'll bet she would've shown more understanding.

Genie gave me a reassuring jiggle. "Ignore her."

"I plan to," I mumbled. The rosy sheen had well and truly worn off of Charlotte, judging by Genie's clipped tone.

No one has any idea what this is like. Becoming a hunter would be the challenge of a lifetime, made all the more difficult by my unique, one-of-a-kind power. I had a lot to learn, and, honestly, I felt like those builders, speeding toward a deadline—if I didn't figure out how to capture my Purges fast, then there *would* be messes that I couldn't clean up. But I'd come to the Institute to prove to myself, and to everyone else, that I was capable. I wouldn't let Charlotte knock down my confidence before I'd even started.

"I don't care how many monsters she's caught, I bet you've seen things she's only heard of in books." Genie lowered her voice to a conspiratorial whisper. "Soon enough, you'll have a grip on this catching thing, and you'll probably end up with a list of captures longer than anyone in the history of the Institute. Rarer and cooler, too."

"Maybe. Right now, I'd be happy to just catch one." We walked along with the rest of the group, though we hung back to bring up the rear. "But thanks for the ego boost."

As much as I liked to think I could've done this alone, I was grateful to have my stubborn friend there with me. After all, I'd almost blacked out from the mere threat of an oncoming Purge. Without her, I'd be on the ground somewhere, willing the overwhelming anxiety away. But, like I'd sworn to my mom, I wouldn't get in the habit of relying on someone else. I needed to learn to control my emotions and my creations. They were the lynchpin to this whole Purge thing, and it was better to take the bullets out of the gun than to fire at a bulletproof vest.

FIVE

Persie

Evening snuck up on Galway like a child playing a trick, chasing the sun down to the horizon. I sat by the window and let the vivid colors wash over my face, my fingertips eager for paint and canvas, both of which were still waiting to be sent over from the SDC. So, I let my eyes be the artist, picking out the tones and marveling at each: the bursts of oxblood fading into tawny orange, deep notes of plum foreshadowing the oncoming night, and the residue of daylight hiding in notes of citrine and yellow ochre. San Diego had some stunning sunsets, but this was otherworldly, as though Galway itself were ablaze.

The nights in Ireland were proving to be the hardest. I'd never realized how loud my family home was until I wasn't there anymore. The familiar tread of my mom's footsteps in the hall, the sound of doors opening and closing, the rush of the faucet in the bathroom, the murmur of my parents talking before bed.

Louisa May Alcott's words came to mind as I watched the sunset an ocean away from my mom. *Mothers can forgive anything!* she wrote. *Tell me all, and be sure that I will never let you go, though the whole world should turn from you.* Mom was the one I usually spoke to about my dreams, and I worried about what dreams awaited me once I slipped into my narrow bed and closed my eyes.

"Maybe speaking to her would make me feel calmer," I said aloud to the stark room. Anything to dispel the stony silence. My nerves had eased up throughout the day, but I still didn't feel peaceful. Frankly, I wondered if I ever would again. And, you know what? No matter how old a person gets, sometimes, you just need to talk to your mom.

I set my phone on the windowsill and dialed. It would only be about eleven in the morning where she was, so maybe she wouldn't be too busy with work yet. Five rings later, the call connected.

"Persie!" My mom's face appeared in slightly fuzzy hologram form, but her smile came through crystal clear. "I was just about to have lunch and give you a call."

My hands fidgeted out of sight of the camera. "Oh. Did I interrupt you?"

"Not at all. I was just plowing through paperwork. Super boring." She lifted up a folder, as though I needed evidence. "What time is it there?"

"Nearly seven." There was something about technology that stilted conversation. If I were home, there'd be minimal small talk. We'd just jump into a rundown of our days over dinner or coffee, but it was different over the phone when we'd hadn't spoken in a few days.

She chuckled. "Don't you have more exciting things to do than call your mom? Socials, mixers—whatever they're called now."

I shrugged. "There's nothing going on tonight except a movie in one of the common rooms. I didn't feel like going, so I came to my room to do some... reading and stuff, but then I saw the sunset and thought of you."

"You did?" Her smile turned bittersweet. She didn't need to say it

—I could tell, from the pitch of her voice, that she missed me. But my mom was a tough cookie. She wouldn't say she missed me unless I said it first.

"Yeah." I had no idea why I felt so shy. This was my *mom*, for Pete's sake.

"It was your orientation today, right?" she prompted. "How did it go? Are you making friends? Do you know your way around yet? Have you started classes, or was it just an introduction to the Institute? Is there anything you need? I'm working on your art supplies, so don't worry about that."

I laughed, my discomfort ebbing. "I didn't realize I'd called the Spanish Inquisition."

"There's just so much ground for us to cover, and I want to know everything!" She propped her chin on her hand and waited expectantly.

I didn't know where to begin. Did I start with the good stuff and go into the dream and the panic attack afterward, or did I spill the bad news first?

"Well, we had a welcome assembly, then Charlotte Basani showed us around. I saw the training halls and library, and they've got really pretty grounds. We didn't get to meet the scholars yet— that's their version of preceptors—but I'm sure that'll happen soon."

I'd decided to keep it short and sweet. Weirdly, I found it a bit disappointing that I couldn't produce more high-octane excitement. My first foray into the world of independence was, at present, a bit banal. But that would change when the hard work started, so I would try to enjoy the calm before the storm.

My mom's eyes lit with intrigue at the mention of Charlotte, so maybe I hadn't painted as boring a picture as I thought. "Charlotte Basani, eh? What's she like? I've heard great things about her. They say she might actually deserve the title of legendary monster hunter, unlike her mom and her aunt. Are the twins at the Institute a lot? Maybe I should bring Finch one day, just to see their faces."

I glanced at the sunset. The colors had turned darker and muted, like someone had accidentally streaked navy blue onto the palette. "She's... kind of hard to gauge. You'd call her a cold fish, but I only met her while she was giving us a tour. Maybe she's one of those people who grows on you when you get to know them better." I paused, realizing what she'd said. "Chaos, no, please don't bring Uncle Finch while the twins are here! I don't want them kicking me out because he makes some joke about them being con artists."

My mom grinned. "Good point. He'd definitely have a few choice words for them, after the stunts they pulled at the Mapmakers' Monastery." Her image sharpened as she leaned closer to the phone camera. "But you're having a good time, right? Do you feel like you made the right choice?"

"I do." I swung my legs, trying to unkink the knots that had taken root in my thighs. I ignored the other question because I didn't have an answer to it.

Was I having a good time? I hadn't really been here long enough to know yet.

Genie had partaken in more socializing than I had. She'd gone to a couple of the "organized fun" events during the settling-in time: lectures, a few dinners, a baking competition, and a "disco," which showed the age of the organizers a bit. She hadn't said much about them when she'd returned to check on me. I guessed she hadn't wanted to hype them up since I hadn't been able to go.

My banshee recovery had put a major dent in my mingling time, and so had the restless nights, but then I'd never been one for parties or gatherings. Besides, I would get to know my classmates better once classes started. It would beat standing off to one side with a soda in hand, painfully bobbing along to music I hated and wondering how much longer I had to stay, out of politeness, before I could vamoose.

"And Genie's getting along all right?" If my mom noticed I'd skimmed over her question, she didn't give anything away. "Her dad's worrying about her."

I toyed with a pencil, tracing random lines and shapes across the bottom of my sketchbook. "She's fine. I think she might actually be at that movie, but I'm not sure. She still hadn't made up her mind at dinner."

"That's a relief." My mom pushed a strand of hair out of her eyes. "It's not always... easy for Atlanteans to integrate, especially when they're the only ones. Hector will be pleased. He's so happy you're there with her, and so am I. As long as you've got each other, I know you're not alone, and sometimes that's all a mom needs to know."

I chuckled stiffly. "You know me. I can only put one toe out of my comfort zone at a time."

"You'll get there. It's always difficult when you strike out on your own." She lifted her hand, as though she was about to touch it to the camera. Evidently thinking better of it, she put her hand back down. "I had Ryann and the Smiths to lean on when I got my first apartment, but when the front door closes, it's just you, you know? That takes some getting used to, but one day, you'll wonder how you ever coped any other way. Change is good, in the end."

I realized if I dithered any longer, we'd have a whole conversation without me mentioning the dream and the panic at all. "I'm not sleeping very well," I blurted out. The instantly concerned expression on her face made me wish I'd worked up to it a bit more. My mom was still getting used to this new situation, too. In a way, I thought it might be harder for the one who let go, as opposed to the one who went away.

"Why not? Is it—" Before my mom could finish, I heard a door opening and my dad's voice cut through the feed.

"Hey, I just got back from Astrid's," he said, sounding out of breath. He clearly hadn't realized my mom was on a video call. "Marius and Azar found a handful of witnesses who've been able to piece together the last 24 hours of the missing magicals' where-abouts. This is big—"

"Wade!" my mom interrupted him, panic on her face. "Persie's on the phone."

He appeared a second later, looking sheepish. "Persie?"

You were *busy*. They clearly had major fish to fry with the missing magicals, but my mom hadn't mentioned it at all.

"Hi, Dad." I waved awkwardly.

His face broke into a broad smile. "About time, stranger. We thought you'd dropped off the Giant's Causeway."

I played up to his cheer. "How long have you been waiting to say that? You sound like Uncle Finch."

"Hey, your dad can be funny, too. Finch doesn't have a monopoly on jokes." He gave a full-belly laugh. "But, truth be told, I've been holding onto that one since you last called."

"I got kind of caught up with recovering and stuff. Sorry about that." I drew some swirls with the tip of my pencil, soothed by the quiet scratching sounds.

My dad frowned. "And how are the... Purges?"

"I haven't had one since I came here. Five days and counting." I forced a hopeful smile and hoped it didn't look as fake as it felt.

Now that my dad had pulled back the curtain on the strain my parents were under, it no longer seemed right to bother them with my dream and anxiety attack. Would I go running to them every time I had a nightmare or crumbled under pressure? No, not if I wanted to stand on my own two feet like I'd promised myself I would. Besides, I had Genie as my sounding board.

My mom made a bizarre half-squeal, half-gasp. "That's really promising, Persie. Maybe the Purges are slowing down? And it's becoming more manageable? Not that I'm minimizing what you're going through," she added quickly. I had an inkling she'd been hitting the "How to Speak to Your Offspring" section of the library. A week ago, she would never have said anything like that. "In fact, your dad had to hide my phone last night to stop me from checking in on you and your Purges."

My dad squished his head against my mom's, even though they had plenty of room on the screen. "I did. I said, 'She'll call us when she wants to, and if she has a Purge, she'll let us know in her own time.' I thought she'd smother me in my sleep after that." He kissed Mom's cheek and she smiled up at him.

"When you said you were having trouble sleeping, I thought it might be Purge-related." My mom segued back into our previous conversation, and I braced to gloss over it. They needed to hear the Hollywood version of how I was doing, not the grainy, indie version. Sitting there in my room, a continent and an ocean away, the distance between us had never felt bigger.

I widened my smile until my cheeks hurt. "No, no, nothing like that. I'm just getting used to all the noise. There are women down the hall who have their music blasting all hours, so I'm not sleeping until late, and then I have to get up early. Sure, that makes me sound like a granny, but a girl's got to have her eight hours, right?"

My mom's expression relaxed immediately. "Oh, thank Chaos." She turned slightly to face my dad. "She was just telling me she'd been having some sleeping issues when you came in. My heart's been pounding for the last five minutes, thinking it was something awful. I'll send you some earbuds to help. If that doesn't work, you should bang on their door and, when they answer, act all shocked and say you thought someone was strangling cats."

I smirked. "I'll think about it." Now, it was my turn to do a bit of segueing. "What about the two of you? It sounds like there's been a breakthrough with the missing magicals cases?"

My parents exchanged a solemn look before my dad answered. "You know that's sensitive information, Persie. We can't disclose details of the investigation yet, since it's in such fragile stages. You shouldn't have even heard what I said when I came in. There are protocols we have to follow."

"How come Marius and Azar know all about it, then?" I might've been coming across a little petty, but the point stood. Last I'd checked, Marius and Azar weren't part of my parents' Secret Agent Squad. Actually, last I'd checked, they were in freaking Mexico. They were the same age as me, and they weren't carrying around a big "Merlin" target on their backs. Surely I deserved to be in the loop— or was that forbidden, now that O'Halloran had decided I was a menace to polite society?

My mom sighed, and I saw the depth of the fatigue she'd been hiding. "They've been assigned to the SDC's agent training program. They both showed an interest in wanting to make careers out of it, so they signed the NDAs and all the forms and they were brought on board."

"In a week?" I might've snorted.

"It was already in the works before you went away, Persie," my mom explained. "They were given their first tasks when they got back from Mexico two days ago."

My dad offered me an apologetic look. "However, if our investigation goes anywhere near Galway or the Institute, we'll let you know what's going on."

Yeah, because that'll happen. My dad was just paying lip service to stop me from trying to pry more information out of them. Still, I knew a hopeless cause when I saw one. Without an NDA, or my dad bursting into the room again without spotting me on video call, I wouldn't find out anything else. And the sudden spike of annoyance and jealousy made my stomach churn in a deeply unsettling, painfully familiar way—a Purge was coming. The shivers would be next, then the chest pains, and then the need to expel.

"I get it." I drew shaky fingertips across my lips. "Ask you no questions, you'll tell me no lies, right?"

My dad gave a reluctant nod. "It's just red tape, Persie. You know we'd tell you if we could."

Best not to open that can of worms... A comeback tingled on the tip of my tongue, but I let it stay there. Leviathan's gift had already been given, so there seemed little point in dragging up old quarrels and old lies for the sake of landing a jab. Especially with the nausea rising and the shakes settling in.

"Kes has been asking about you." Mom switched back to fluffy small talk. "He's insanely jealous of you and Genie. Tobe had to carry him out of the Bestiary at least six times this week. He's been trying to spring some beasties loose so he could start up his own monster hunting program. Last I heard, Tobe went to ask O'Halloran if he could put a magical bell around Kes's neck, so he'll know where Kes is at all times. Finch keeps joking that it's Victoria Jules's fault for mesmerizing him, but I think he's keen on the bell idea."

"Really? That's... uh... very Kes." I wrapped my arms around my stomach, the nausea still bubbling up. Sweat began to bead on my forehead, while the telltale prickles began to scuttle up the back of my neck like ants. "Maybe Tobe could... teach him?"

My dad chuckled. "He's too young. In three years, maybe, but not yet. The potential backlash, if anything went wrong, would be enough to put anyone off."

"Oh, yeah, I guess... I hadn't thought of... um... that." I jiggled my legs, fighting back the swell of the sickness. "Look, this is awkward, but I'm going to have to say goodbye and nip off to the bathroom. We had tacos for dinner, and I think I ate a bad one."

"Bad tacos? Are you sure it's—"

I cut my mom off. "Okay, I'm going to sign off before I need to... uh... trash these pants. Bye! Love you, bye!"

The last thing I needed them to see was me Purging up whatever happened to be coming. If they saw, they'd come crashing through the mirrors before it was even over. I ended the call before they could respond and flopped off the chair onto all fours.

Oh no, oh no, oh no... Pain splintered from my stomach up into my chest, forming a heavy ball of agonizing weight that threatened to crush any organs in the way. Blinding bolts of white-hot lightning ricocheted away from the lump in my chest and sizzled down my arms and legs until my fingers went into frantic spasms. Hugging my knees, I rocked back and forth while sharp stabs pinballed between my temples. Black spots danced in my field of vision—the evil twins of the floaty orbs from the hallway.

"I can do this. I can do this. I can do this." I repeated the mantra in a panicked whisper as more symptoms crept over me. I hated Leviathan so much, I wanted to snap off his stupid glowing hypno-thing and shove it down his throat.

My heart hammered hummingbird fast. Sweat drenched my white T-shirt and my sweatpants, darkening the gray fabric until it was closer to black. And then the punches came, socking my stomach, my chest, my legs, my back, my arms, my throat, until everything hurt. It didn't take a genius to figure out that this particular Purge would be a sizeable beast. And I wished I had the strength to push it back down into the ether, but that wasn't part of the game Leviathan had forced me to play.

Wrenching pulses launched my body into convulsions. I raked my fingernails across the stone floor in an attempt to stay connected with something solid, until the floor scraped my skin rusty-red. This didn't feel like any Purge I'd had before. In my chest, I felt that heavy ball moving upward. When it reached my throat, my eyes bulged. I wasn't aware of much beyond my own pain, but I could've sworn I heard the bones in my throat creak and strain to make way for the foreign object.

Finally, with one exhausted retch, a smooth orb, trailing black smoke, erupted from my mouth and hit the floor in an explosion of black fire. A second later, dozens of tiny creatures burst out of the flames and took flight. They zipped around the room in darts of vivid color, fluttering gossamer wings so fast it looked like they weren't moving at all.

One landed on the ground by my trembling hand and looked me dead in the eyes. Similar to the sprite that Nathan had showed us, its wings looked like paper-thin sycamore leaves, tinged with an alarming shade of red. It wore what looked like a tiny bird skull as a helmet, with two beady black eyes glinting behind the eye sockets. Tufts of mossy hair extended from the bottom of the skull. As for its body, it had frog-like legs and arms, minus the webbed feet, which were banded with streaks of pearly white and indigo. Its thin torso didn't look like it could hold the creature up, but somehow, it did.

It grinned at me, flashing a miniature set of razor-sharp teeth. Then it gave a sarcastic bow, like it knew it was about to make my life hell, before taking flight again.

I managed to drag myself into a sitting position to assess the mayhem. A few of the creatures wore the bird skull helmets, while others sported upturned walnut shells and some had no headpiece at all. But I had little time to wonder if it was a hierarchy thing, since at that moment two of the fluttering beasties were pulling a lamp off my shelf. It plummeted to the ground and smashed, sparks flying. The creatures giggled raucously, pointing at the debris and grinning those sharp-toothed smiles.

On my bed, four of them were gleefully in the process of putting my Thread Bear through torture. They had a limb each, pulling with all of their tiny might, trying to rip him in four directions.

"Hey! Stop that!" I jumped up on shaky legs and ran to the bed, and not a moment too soon. I lunged for Thread Bear just as the critters dispersed in a cacophony of jangling laughter. They chattered to one another like monkeys, but I had no idea what they were saying. I probably didn't want to know, either, as one pointed at my soaked sweatpants and started giggling. Its buddies joined in. Clutching Thread Bear to my chest so they couldn't hurt him, I stared in abject disbelief. They whooshed in every direction, taking no prisoners: a cluster swung from the light fixture overhead, shrieking with naughty delight; two ran at each other across my desk, jousting with pencils; another dipped his butt in the cold coffee I'd left atop my wardrobe, then dragged his cheeks across my sketchbook. Still another group was causing all kinds of bedlam in the bathroom, whooping and trilling, with a few very worrying splashes thrown in. I knew I should've been trying to stop them, but their sheer volume overwhelmed me. I couldn't have moved if I'd wanted to, not even knowing there was a whole team of butt-painters going to town on my sketchpad.

Another crash jolted me out of my deep freeze. One of the idiots had toppled my scented candle from the side table against the wall. It cackled and danced a jig on the edge of the table, giving it the full hoedown as the candle flame licked the border of the thin rug in the center of the room. The fabric caught abruptly, and the creatures all paused and "oohed" at the same time, unconcerned that fire threatened to consume the entire thing.

"What the heck did you do?" I yelled, finally shaken out of my daze. With no useful magic, I'd have to put the fire out the old-fashioned way. I raced into the bathroom, only barely registering the destruction I saw. Toothpaste had been squirted all over the walls, creatures dripping in goopy shampoo were flinging handfuls of it at each other, and two of them were having a whale of a time in the toilet bowl, using it as a personal jacuzzi.

I drenched my towels under the faucet while batting away the buzzing creatures. With the towels fully doused, I sprinted back out and threw them over the flames. Smoke and steam billowed from beneath, filling the room until I had to cover my face with the collar of my T-shirt. From somewhere within the smoky haze, I heard a ripple of mad laughter and the echo of tiny applause.

They're freaking mocking me! The absolute audacity of these things. When this smoke cleared, they'd learn a valuable lesson. All I had to do was lock them in my room, find some puzzle boxes, and catch the little pests. I had a few pre-hexed Mason jars in my luggage, but not enough for all of them. Then again, with them being so small, maybe several could fit into one. I steeled myself to return to the mayhem.

But when I poked my head out of my T-shirt to check on the state of the smoke, the joke was definitely on me. Heavy, significant silence hung in the foggy air. No laughter, no whoops, no shrieks. Deadly silence. *Holy crap, no!* With my arms outstretched, I ran in the direction of the front door—and where the door should've been, my hands felt empty space.

Terrifying realization struck like a thunderbolt. I'd just Purged a horde of tiny, chaotic monsters, and now... they'd all escaped.

SIX

Genie

I lurked by the hot chocolate urns, assessing the situation like an army general plotting out the best course for socializing. It paid to know your enemy, though thinking of them as the enemy probably wasn't the best mentality for striking up friendly chat. The banquet hall filled with a steady stream of students and graduates, all branching off into their own ranks and gunning for the best seats: first years, second years, yada yada. The long wooden tables had bowls of snacks in the center, ready for mid-movie munching. A few folks were wrangling with a projector to get the movie going, arguing over the mechanics.

Man, I should've dragged Persie along. She called me the social butterfly of our outfit, but it was looking more like I was the mangy moth that nobody wanted fluttering around them. My classmates had rebuffed all my previous charm offensives over the last five days, but I hoped tonight would mark a shift in dynamics. I'd never really felt out of place before. I knew everyone at the SDC, and they knew me. More to the point, they liked me. Still, I wouldn't be beaten. No siree. This moth was determined to get some flames to at least give me a friendly smile.

Sipping my hot chocolate as if it were high-dollar champagne, I unfurled my social butterfly wings and drifted over to a table with a few familiar faces, about ten classmates in all. They didn't even look up at me. And, judging by the oh-so-stony silence, I'd just interrupted a volley of banter.

"Anyone know what the movie is tonight?" I hid my nerves, smooth as anything.

Mr. Bike-Pump Biceps shrugged. "No."

I really need to learn their real names. I tried to sift through my brain for them: Brian? No, that wasn't it. Xerxes? Definitely not. I knew I should've pleaded for name tags at orientation, not that I had that kind of say. The best way to get someone on your side was to call them by their name; every psychologist worth their salt knew that. First rule of negotiations—keep saying someone's name to get a rapport going.

"Can I get anyone a refill on the hot chocolate?" I powered on. "It's good, right? Usually, you get that powdered stuff that tastes like diluted mud, but this might actually have some real chocolate in it."

Ponytail #1 took a pointed sip from her mug. "We're fine."

"Sorry, I'm not very good with names. I'm Genie." I sat on an empty part of the bench. They looked at me as if I'd just suggested we go and drown some kittens.

"We know," Ponytail #2 snarked.

"Right, but I'm saying I don't know your names." I resisted the urge to give her the evil eye. "They go in one ear and out the other, so why don't you tell me, and I'll remember for next time?" I glanced at a round-faced girl with equally round glasses. Her name came back to me like a boomerang. "You're Colette, right? Any French ancestry, or did your parents just like it?"

She puckered her lips until they looked like... well, it wouldn't be polite to say. "French-Canadian."

"Ah, *les Quebecois*. Do you follow ice hockey, or is that a stereotype?" I smiled to show I meant no harm. Only chimps grinned when they meant to do some damage. A warning first, a bite later. And I'd promised Victoria I'd sheathe these gnashers, not that I'd ever actually bitten anyone. Not since I was a kid, anyway.

"What do you think?" she replied coolly.

A long-haired guy, who might've been called Adrian, snorted. "Yeah, it'd be like her asking if you ride seahorses."

"Have you seen a seahorse? They're tiny. What, you think Atlanteans have massive seahorses hidden away? Unless you're talking about Kelpies, but they're not the same thing. Sea *horses*, with a space, not seahorses." I kept my tone breezy, despite the cold front blasting off these guys. Discomfort wriggled into my stomach, destroying all the cozy work the hot chocolate had done.

A girl with a severe blonde bob blew hair out of her eyes. "Who knows what goes on in Atlantis."

"It's not like they let people in to see," said the guy beside her, a stunningly good-looking dude with ebony skin who was putting on the most aggressive chip-chewing display I'd ever seen. He was probably picturing those fried slices of potato as Atlantean necks. Charming. "Right, Ayperi?" He looked at another classmate, an overeager, shaky kind of girl who needed to ease off on the energy drinks. She had buzzed hair, a Middle Eastern complexion, and big dark eyes highlighted by winged eyeliner—super beautiful and edgy.

She managed a jittery nod. "I hear they're building weapons."

I laughed it off. "You shouldn't believe everything you read online. Propaganda is alive and well, unfortunately. King Apollo is a decent guy, and he doesn't go in for the whole weaponry thing. He's more likely to bore people into submission by holding endless summits about trade deals."

"Says you." Ponytail #1 smoothed a palm over her plasticky hair. So lacquered, you could probably bounce a penny off it.

I'd have felt more welcome at an anti-Atlantean rally— I'd never seen one, but I'd heard they happened now and again. At least those protestors didn't use sarcasm and sourness to sugarcoat the way they felt about my people. They just spewed outright hatred. Worse, sure, but more honest. This awkward jelly-feeling in my chest—no, that didn't suit me at all. I wasn't one for bottling things up in the face of underhanded nastiness.

I set down my mug, cool as a cucumber. "So, is someone going to come out and tell me what the smacked-ass faces are about, or are you just hoping I'll give up and run away with my tail between my legs? If it's the latter, you'll be waiting until after graduation." Possibly not the best approach to making pals, but I wouldn't grovel or kiss ass or whimper like a puppy for the sake of integrating. If I stayed silent, they got to chalk up another win against "people like me." Not just Atlanteans, but people like Kes, whose differences rubbed folks the wrong way. Society's targets, magical and otherwise. No way was I about to let them do that.

Colette stared down into her hot chocolate, all talk until it came to confrontation. "We didn't invite you to our table."

"Oh, excuse me, I didn't see names carved into the wood. Now, why don't you give me the real reason? You've clearly got beef with me, and I'd like to know what it is. So far as I know, I personally haven't done anything to piss you off."

Bike-Pump Biceps piped up, their fearless, meathead leader. "We don't *want* you at our table. We're not interested in having an Atlantean hanging around us at all, right now or any other day."

"Nice to see that you've all picked up some deep-rooted discrimination along the way." I held my ground, wrapping my hands around my mug on the table until my knuckles whitened. "Let me guess, your parents told you that we're all sly devils who should be avoided at all costs? Or did you learn it at your covens, maybe? Oh, I'd love to have a word with your Magical History teachers—everyone loves a clear-cut, black and white enemy, don't they? But, tell me, have any of you or your parents or your history teachers actually *met* an Atlantean?"

I should've lowered my voice. A crowd had started to gather, beady eyes watching and waiting for the Atlantean girl to lose her cool and explode in a shower of Chaos sparks. They were forgetting how long I'd been alive. They couldn't rile me up or get me to throw a punch just by being nasty to me. Their words hurt, and it sucked, but I wasn't about to give them the satisfaction of seeing me throw a fit.

This was the catalyst, I realized, as I waited for the clammed-up crew to respond. My dad had been so happy about our transition into the wider magical world. That happiness had cracked and faded over the years because of people like this. People who sneered and jeered at him. People who made him feel less than he was. People who battered his pride and his heritage, until the world we'd left no longer seemed like the worst place we could be. He'd dealt with this for nearly twenty years. I was just getting my first proper mouthful of it, out in the open, instead of snide, under-the-breath comments.

"Atlanteans are backward and dangerous." Ponytail #1 glowered over a half-eaten candy. "They nearly destroyed the magical world, thanks to Princess Kaya and that maniac Davin Doncaster! We wouldn't be sitting here if *our* people hadn't stopped yours."

I glowered right back, taking a shaky breath to steady my voice. "That ended twenty years ago, and it wasn't just 'your' people who helped prevent outright war. My father nearly got killed fighting back. King Apollo helped stop Kaya, and his best friend, Thebian, gave his life to get the jump on Davin Doncaster. You wouldn't be sitting here if they hadn't gone against their own queen. I'm not saying we don't have our bad eggs, but so do you. Davin wasn't

Atlantean, was he? Neither was Katherine Shipton—a way worse scenario, which you're conveniently ignoring. Or am I getting my histories crossed?"

"Katherine Shipton and Davin Doncaster were two individuals. Your whole race is messed up," the ebony-skinned guy shot back.

"How did you work that one out?" I tightened my grip on the mug. "I came from the SDC, where the heroes who saved your mostly unborn asses from Kaya and Davin all live. They don't have a problem with me, so what makes you think you have the right to? Did you fight Kaya and Davin? No, you didn't. You don't know anything except what you've been spoon-fed by your bigoted parents who, by the way, didn't fight either!"

Our argument was attracting attention, and classmates had begun to crowd around us like bloodthirsty spectators at a boxing ring—the kind who wanted to smell the sweat of the boxers and feel the splash of blood on their faces.

"Typical of an Atlantean to start with low blows. Who says this has anything to do with our parents, and who do you think you are, branding us as bigots?" This attack came from a young woman with a sleek dark braid and smug blue eyes, someone I knew to be a part of Charlotte's hunter clique, although Charlotte herself was nowhere to be seen. Apparently, this had turned into a free-for-all. Hurl an insult at the outsider for two dollars a pop. Unleash your anger at an Atlantean, five for the price of three. Win a stuffed seahorse every time.

"Uh, are you listening to yourselves? Would you like me to whip out a dictionary and show you the definition of 'bigotry?'" I retorted. "You don't know anything about me. You see these tattoos on my face and you judge me without having ever interacted with anyone of my race! I've tried talking to so many of you in the hallways, and you've run away or turned up your noses like I'm covered in frigging scales. Which I'm not, by the way, contrary to popular belief."

Okay, maybe I'd been wrong. It really hurt now. *They* were hitting with the low blows, not me. I liked to think I could keep my cool in almost any situation, but I was getting a serious lesson in self-control today. I hadn't realized just how much venom the wider world had stored up for my kind. And the acid of it burned me, deep in my heart. I might not have considered myself a "proud" Atlantean, but they were prodding at a defensive streak of patriotism I hadn't known existed. *How dare they?* How could they spew such hatred as though it were nothing?

Bike-Pump Biceps snorted. "And who cares if you came from the SDC? They're a bunch of saps for letting you people in in the first place. They might be happy to integrate with your kind, but that doesn't mean everyone else is. As for your 'hero' friends, they cause more trouble than they prevent. Funny you mentioned Katherine Shipton—she's got family at that beloved commune of yours, so who's to say they can be trusted? Maybe they saved us from Atlantis because they saw an opportunity. I hear the SDC has secret technology they got from your people, so it's not hard to believe."

"Are you out of your tiny mind?" I hissed back, my anger rising uncontrollably. "Their lives were ruined by Katherine, just as much as everyone else's. They *killed* her, you freaking idiot. And they stopped Davin. And they've saved the magical world more times than you'll ever know, and they don't ask for anything in return. As for the SDC having secret technology—how about you take a long walk off a short pier? You're clearly a few sandwiches short of a picnic."

"What did you say to me?" He leaned across the table and slammed his palms down, hunching over so he could get right in my face.

I didn't even flinch. "You heard me."

For a moment, everything was dead silent, punctuated only by the sound of the door swinging open as Charlotte Basani walked in, joining the dark-haired friend who'd attacked me. She looked around, sizing up the situation. "What's going on? she asked.

"Oh, just some run-of-the-mill discrimination. Specifically, your friends attacking me for being Atlantean." At this I made eye contact, briefly, with Charlotte, and I knew we were wondering the same thing: would she side with her friends or speak up? Would she, with her family name over the entrance of the school, come to my defense in the face of discrimination?

No. She dropped her eyes to the ground, looking guilty and conflicted. I was on my own.

But then she seemed to find her courage and turned to Bike-Pump Biceps. "Is that true, Teddy?"

"It's not discrimination," Bike-Pump Teddy said. "It's fact."

Charlotte's friend chimed in again, saying, "The truth is, you don't belong here. Frankly, I don't give a crap what you say your people did or didn't do, or who your friends are. I just know you shouldn't be here. You've got, what, six abilities, judging by those grubby marks on your face? That's like using a talisman to cheat the exam system, while the rest of us have actually worked to get here. We studied, we slogged, and we earned our places. You make a mockery of that just by sitting in this room."

"Hey, that's stepping well over the line," Charlotte said, looking around the room like a disappointed mother who'd discovered crayon all over the walls. I saw, for a moment, the kind of hunter she was—she radiated something electric and potent. Even if she had a terrible choice in who she considered friends. "I think I speak for my mother and my aunt when I say that Genie—or any other Atlantean—is welcome here."

Her best pal didn't look convinced. "I'm just voicing an opinion, Char."

"Would you tell Harley or Finch Merlin that *they* don't belong here?" I spat at the friend. "They're as powerful as I am, but I bet you wouldn't say a damn word because they look like you." I willed myself not to cry. I wouldn't show weakness, no matter how hard they beat me down, but my heart ached. It didn't just hurt—it stung in the very essence of my being.

The friend shrugged, casting a cautious glance at Charlotte. "If the Merlins came here—you know, aside from that dud you strolled in with—I *would* say the same thing to them. You shouldn't be tested the same way we are. There could be someone sitting here, right now, who deserved a place more than you, but because they weren't pumped full of serums and spells since birth, they missed out."

"Hear, hear," said Bike-Pump Teddy.

"That's *enough!*" Charlotte shouted. But she hadn't interjected in time. A few minutes earlier, I could've kept my cool. Not now. Now, that friend of hers had crossed *my* line.

"Don't you dare bring Persie into this," I said. My breath hitched, and I saw red.

Charlotte's friend opened her mouth like she wanted to chip in again, but Charlotte's nostrils flared in anger, a clear warning signal, and the girl fell silent.

"Why not?" Bike-Pump Teddy asked, oblivious to Charlotte's demeanor. "She definitely doesn't deserve a place here. She's the exact thing that we put in glass boxes."

I lost it. They could call me what they liked and I'd take it, but not Persie. They feared what they didn't understand. Fine. But they needed to educate themselves. And they'd pushed a big red button that they really shouldn't have pushed.

Blue waves of pure Chaos surged out of me, scattering the crowd. Yelps and cries went up, but they hadn't seen anything yet. My Water ability spread over the entire banquet hall. Hot chocolate rose up from mugs. Water erupted from bottles and urns and faucets. I even dragged in some water from the decorative fountain in the garden outside. It crashed against the windows, making them swing open. More screams and shouts echoed through the room, a few people diving for cover. Of course, they thought I was going to attack. That was all they thought an Atlantean was good for.

Instead, I drew all the liquid together into a swirling vortex in the center of the room. I only had to feel the atoms of it to get it to do what I wanted: the beauty of being a sentient. If they envied my skills, they could stuff it where the sun didn't shine. I would never be ashamed of my abilities. I transformed the vortex into a huge sea serpent, which chased several students around the room. Next, I made it morph into a moving mass of watery women riding gigantic seahorses—a joke, to cool things off a bit. The riders dispersed to pursue my insulters, wielding frothing spears and slicing with wet swords. Nothing that could hurt anyone, just frighten them.

For my last trick, I brought the water back into the center of the room and transformed it into a giant middle finger. Everyone froze in fear, bracing for another chasing serpent, or something worse.

"Genie." Charlotte stepped closer, her voice measured like she was trying to talk me back from a ledge. I ignored her, Basani or not. I was going to say my piece while I had their attention.

"Yes, I'm an Atlantean." My voice echoed through the hall. "I believe in unity and kindness and peace. I hoped the wider magical world felt the same, because I want to be part of it. If I wanted to follow the Atlantean way, that's where I'd be. But I'm here, getting abuse thrown at me for something I had no part in." I unraveled the flowing middle finger and stretched the water out over the heads of my peers until the liquid formed a second ceiling of sorts. "Maybe if you got your judgmental heads out of your asses for a second, you'd see that getting to know me and Persie is a way better prospect than being the bad guys, hurling hatred for no reason. Make an opinion based on fact, not fiction."

I let the water drop. Gallons of it collapsed, drenching everyone.

I put up an umbrella of Air to stop me from getting wet. But the others... they deserved it. Not just for me, but for Persie.

Every expletive known to man exploded from the soggy, peeved gathering. Those who'd stayed sitting jumped up, and they didn't look happy. Charlotte and her clique had taken a hefty bucketload of water. The one who'd insulted me squawked, whining about her hair. But Charlotte just stood there, dripping and quiet, as inscrutable as ever.

"What the hell?" Bike-Pump Teddy shouted, waving a water-logged vintage watch in my face. "You wrecked my dad's watch! You're going to pay for this."

"Nope, that'd be you." A few sparks of red flared out of my body, a warning of Fire, which I whipped around me in a spiral.

He reeled back, spitting out a petulant, "You'll see."

A snarl of agreement ran through the crowd. Apparently, they hadn't listened to a word I'd said. Now, they wanted to take out the irritation of their unexpected shower on me. Well, they could bring it. Either they heeded me or they didn't. Whatever. I didn't want to fight, but I'd defend myself if I had to.

"What is the meaning of this?!" A stern bark made everyone jump.

I turned to find a livid Tarif Hosseini at the door. Standing at an imposing height and built like an Ifrit, he had Arabian features and curly dark hair flecked with gray at the sides. He'd looked like a gentle giant at our general assembly, but now his strong features were hardened into a stern expression.

Everyone fell silent.

"Well? An explanation, NOW!" I knew the others would start pointing fingers soon, so I jumped in first.

"I soaked them, Mr. Hosseini. Apparently, I don't deserve to be here because of what I am." Some might've called it snitching, but I wouldn't let these people put the blame entirely on me. "They've been saying all the things they've been wanting to say to an Atlantean, and they threw in a few comments about Persie while they were at it."

Hosseini's eyes narrowed. "Is this true, Charlotte?"

What, you don't believe me? I sat back and wondered whether Charlotte would back up her friends or tell the truth.

Charlotte sighed. "Yes, Hosseini." I looked at her in surprise, thinking that when push came to shove, she would have sided with her friends, not me. But she looked... disappointed. Her mouth was serious, her eyebrows pinched. Perhaps she didn't want to carry her mantle any more than I wanted to carry mine. "There are some"— her eyes fell on Bike-Pump Teddy—"who've gone out of their way to make Genie feel unwelcome here."

"This is disgusting behavior!" Hosseini cast a piercing stare at everyone in the hall. "Discrimination is not tolerated under any circumstances. You all should know that. You're not children, or perhaps you all need re-educating on how we treat people?"

A grumble of apologies echoed around the room.

"Atlanteans are amongst the most powerful beings on Earth, and we've come to rely on much of their technology. Our puzzle boxes, our glass orbs, our training methods, and our healing methods. Their blood is the blood of our ancestors, and they existed in a world without war for centuries. Can you say the same about ours? No." A lilt of the Middle East came through in his commanding voice, though it was less of an accent and more of a musical note. "You should be honored to have an Atlantean here. She is descended from lauded hunters, who saw and caught creatures that even our most decorated hunters have never seen. You could learn a great deal from Genie."

A wave of surprised whispers rolled through the crowd. I guessed that showed just how little they knew about my homeland. Did they think we didn't have hunters?

That's right. You didn't know that, did you? My mom's career made me prouder than anything. If they'd wanted to hear stories, I'd have happily regaled them. But they'd only just described me as a powerful upstart who hadn't earned her spot. And now, Hosseini had delivered a few home truths. That made him my new favorite, usurping Nathan from the top spot.

"Get out, all of you, and take this evening to reconsider your actions here. If I so much as hear a hint of this sort of thing happening again, there will be far greater consequences. Consider this a first, and last, warning." Hosseini dismissed everyone, and they all went running. He turned back to Charlotte. "Charlotte, you'll help clean this up?"

Resentment passed over her face, but it was quickly replaced by her usual armor. "Yes, Hosseini."

He noticed and visibly returned to that gentle giant I'd seen on stage, touching Charlotte's shoulder in a friendly fashion. "People look to you as a leader." He gestured to the room-turned-aquarium. "We want to set a good example for those who are... ignorant. When people in authority stand back in the face of discrimination, it gives validation to the act itself. We must always fight that battle."

Charlotte bowed her head. "I know, I could have—no, I should have intervened more firmly..."

I wondered if she was sincere, or if she was thinking about her mom. Shailene wouldn't be happy to hear about this. Places like the Institute received integration grants from the UCA. She'd be irked if she found out the bigotry of some of her hunters, and I was sure neither she nor Charlotte wanted their surname tied up in it in any way.

Hosseini looked at me. "Genie, I'm sorry you had to go through that. I hope you can forgive the idiocy of mob mentality."

"I'll give Charlotte a hand," I replied. "In the spirit of peace. It was my mess, after all."

"Very honorable of you." He dipped his head. "For my part, I'm looking forward to training you and turning your talents toward less chaotic ends. If you have Water abilities that can cause this, then your future as a hunter is very promising, indeed."

I grinned, though my insides felt hollow. A futile victory. "The feeling's mutual."

"I'll leave you to it." Hosseini walked out, leaving me with a sullen Charlotte. She hadn't argued against the punishment, but I could see she wasn't jazzed about cleaning up. I couldn't blame her. If anyone should have been mopping up, it was Bike-Pump Teddy and his fan club.

I stalked over to the counter, where one of the banquet hall workers was gathering mops. He handed two to me, complete with rusty buckets. I carried them back over and set one down beside Charlotte.

"Thanks," I said, "for speaking up."

She merely nodded, remaining cool to me as we cleaned, extinguishing any notions I had of a budding friendship between the two of us. Maybe the others would have a change of heart, maybe they wouldn't. I couldn't control anyone but myself. What hurt most was knowing my dad had faced this for years and had shielded me from it. But he'd hung on, thanks to the few who'd made him feel he belonged. That was enough to help me cling to my faith in the magical world. There was room for me in it. And I'd find my nook, sooner or later.

I was stubborn as a mule. It would take more than this for me to give up.

SEVEN

Persie

With everything rapidly slipping out of my control, I flung open the window, snatched up my backpack of pre-hexed Mason jars, and raced out the door, slamming it behind me to try to keep the smoke from setting off any alarms. How would I even begin to explain the mess in my bedroom to anyone who caught a glimpse? It looked like a bomb had gone off. Eyes watering and still shaky from the Purge, I took off down the hall to find the little monsters.

You're not screwing this up for me! I ducked into doorways and hid behind walls to avoid being seen, keeping my eyes well and truly peeled. They couldn't have gotten far, right? Oh, who was I kidding… of course, they could get far. They had freaking wings and a frightening determination to cause as much mayhem as possible. And I had absolutely no clue what they were. I'd never met them in a dream before, and though they resembled the sprite that Nathan had shown us, they definitely weren't the same thing. Different bodies, different colors, different wings, and a penchant for bizarre accessories.

"Where the heck are you?" I hissed to the empty hallways as I entered another part of the Institute. Still living quarters, but not a section I'd visited before. Amber light flickered from the sconces on the wall, creating shadows that flitted and darted like the very creatures I was after. It left my head spinning and my stomach churning, until I had whiplash from turning left, right, back, and forward in an endless rhythm. But the tiny critters were nowhere to be seen. It was only the shadows messing with my already screwy head.

Okay, let's think about this logically. How much harm can they actually do? I pressed on down the hallways, a million worst-case scenarios thudding in my brain. What if they got into Victoria's room and scrambled her wardrobe, or got into her bathroom and did what they'd done in mine? What if they reached the main assembly hall and started smearing muck, or worse, on all that clean, white marble? What if they snuck into the Repository and let the monsters loose? They might not have looked violent, but they were really freaking mischievous. And there were so many things in this place for them to smash! They seemed to love smashing. And throwing things. And, holy crap, they'd really loved the fire.

"Why did it have to be these beasts?" I muttered, peering around a corner to make sure the coast was clear of people. Meanwhile, my eyes squinted through the gloom for the glint of a monster. "At least one big one would've been easier to spot."

This would all come back to bite me if I couldn't capture them. Speaking of which, where the heck were all the hunters who'd been stationed to watch over me? The one at the bottom of my corridor hadn't been loitering there, and I couldn't see any suspiciously placed personnel on my sprint through the hallways, either. I really hoped Victoria hadn't called them off because I'd gone five days without a Purge. What if I'd lulled her into a false sense of security at the very moment when I could've used some help? Not because I couldn't handle capturing what I'd created, but because there were so *many* of them. I'd estimated thirty, maybe more, had exploded from that weird black ball of mist.

Should I go to Victoria? I weighed the options as I pressed on. She'd given me a direct line to her office phone and an emergency beeper for occasions like this. But if I went to her with this incident or sounded the alarm, perhaps she'd worry that this might be a common occurrence in the future—Purging multiple beasts at once. What if that swayed her to reconsider my position? My insides wobbled at the thought of being forced to leave. I mean, I hadn't even started training yet.

No, I had to fix this myself. There were no two ways about it—I had to catch them, or all those thoughts of independence and self-reliance could take a flying leap out of the window. At the very least, I had to give it my best try, or I'd be back where I was before I came to this place. Always running for help at the first sign of trouble, with everyone looking at me as a dud or a hopeless case, not worthy of the Merlin name. Maybe if I'd Purged a stampede of griffins or Cerberuses, I'd have no choice but to phone her and call in the cavalry, but these weren't huge, devouring beasts. They were small and hadn't seemed bloodthirsty. They were a good jumping-off point to start testing my skills as a hunter who deserved her place here—a follow-up to what I'd started, and never got to finish, during my exam.

So far, I hadn't seen any smashed glass or signs of miscreant behavior, which meant I still had time to remedy the situation. Hadn't I asked for an opportunity to prove myself? Sure, I hadn't expected there to be so many critters to catch at once, but this would give me a chance to put my money where my mouth was when it came to cleaning up my own problems. My mom would've tried to clean things up herself before reaching out for assistance, and it was about time I started acting more like my mother's daughter. Then, if things *did* go awry and I couldn't wrangle all of them, I had Victoria and an Institute full of hunters to fall back on. But, if it came to that, I'd be able to say that I'd tried to fix things myself first. Proof of my perseverance.

"I don't suppose you could make this easier for me and friggin' show yourselves?" I grumbled, scouring every possible nook and cranny for the buzzy bastards. I searched cupboards, storage rooms, behind statues, under side tables, inside vases, in bathroom cubicles, behind every curtain—just about every dark hiding place they might've snuck into.

Peering through open doors, I checked over common rooms, bathrooms, and kitchenettes, listening for any startled screams. The halls lay uncomfortably silent, like the little creatures were deliberately toying with me. With every corner I turned, I half expected one to leap out and shriek in my face, just to get a good laugh. And, perhaps, to get a giggle out of seeing my sweatpants turn soggy again. I would've preferred it if they *had* tried to frighten the living daylights out of me. At least then I would know where they were.

This is hopeless... The Institute was enormous, and these creatures were teensy by comparison. Even if I searched every corner, it wouldn't stop them from hiding somewhere else. I leaned against a wall to catch my breath. Part of me felt like crying, and part of me felt like descending into a heap of hysterical laughter. Of all the stupid things I could Purge, it had to be a hive of giddy critters with the collective maturity of a five-year-old.

My head whipped around as I saw a flash of color down the corridor—one of the creatures, hovering in front of a doorway, twisting the door handle in its pesky hands. It swung the door open and disappeared inside. *Oh no, you don't!* I bolted down the hallway, only to skid to a halt in front of a low-swinging sign that read "Scholar's Quarters."

Whatever blood I had left in my face must've drained away at that moment. No wonder the corridors hadn't seemed familiar—we weren't allowed in this part of the Institute, and now a little monster had just gone inside one of the scholar's rooms. Which one, I had no idea. It wasn't very late, so I hoped the scholars wouldn't be in their rooms yet.

Steeling myself to enter, I just hoped I could get in, get the monster, and get out before anyone found out I'd been snooping around these parts.

Please don't wreck anything before I can get my mitts on you. Sending up my plea, I tiptoed inside the room the creature had fluttered into. Darkness shrouded what looked like an apartment, lit by a solitary lamp which had probably been left on so the owner wouldn't return to pitch blackness. I froze, listening for any sounds that suggested someone was home. Silence echoed back, and I edged further into the apartment, only for my eyes to snap toward the kitchen. The sound of clinking bottles came from behind a jutting island. My heart pounded as I crept around the back edge of the island and peered behind it. Silhouetted in the glow of the fridge, one of the naughty critters—female, I guessed—struggled with a bottle of milk. And she was about two seconds from upending the whole thing.

Lunging forward, I dove for the flitting beastie. With more light to see by, I might've noticed the rug in the middle of the kitchen floor. Unfortunately, tonight wasn't going my way. My foot caught on the edge of it and I tumbled downward, faceplanting on the cold stone floor with a thud. A groaning wheeze puffed out of my lips like a sad balloon, and the creature, who'd no doubt witnessed my fall, began to laugh. To add insult to injury, she mimicked the sound, doing it over and over again until I managed to jump back up. Seeing me on my feet, she gave a shriek that sounded a lot like a curse word.

"Come here!" I muttered, swiping at the fridge. The creature darted upward, and a pack of cheese and a trio of yogurts took the hit intended for it. The yogurts toppled onto the floor, a spurt of strawberry goo splashing out from under the lid.

So much for not creating more of a mess. I'd deal with that later. But if I lost sight of the tiny creature, then I'd be back on my wild goose chase with nothing to show for it. Stepping over the rug this time, I raced after the monster as she made a beeline for one of the doors on the far side of the living room and vanished inside.

Cautiously pushing the door wider, I took out my phone and shone the flashlight across the room, something I probably should've done earlier. A fastidiously neat bedroom was illuminated by the cold blue glow, with every corner of the bedsheets perfectly tucked. Seeing the room empty, I went ahead and flipped on the light switch. Bright orange light flooded the space, revealing a room that barely looked lived in: a desk with nothing but a lamp on it, bedside tables with short stacks of precisely aligned books, and no pictures or personal touches to speak of.

Whoever lives here must be a bit of a square. A clatter distracted me from the rest of the room, coming from a partially opened door on the other side of the bed. I bounded over the mattress, action-movie style, and wrenched it open. The creature had opened every drawer of a large mahogany chest, and was flicking out underpants, socks, and ties as if she were in charge of a confetti cannon. I didn't have time for embarrassment. The monster was so engrossed in her mischief that she didn't notice me approaching, and if I lost this shot, who knew when I'd get another?

I snatched up a pair of gaudy, pixie-discarded, Hawaiian-style boxers. Before she could fly away, I wrapped the beastie in them like it was Christmas Eve and the family was coming over. Realizing she'd been caught, she twisted her head back to glare at me. I half-expected her to turn into black mist and disappear, but she didn't...

or couldn't. I wasn't sure which. Either way, her tiny arms thrashed underneath the Hawaiian fabric and she began to chatter furiously.

"Would you stop? I'm not going to hurt you." As I spoke the words, I meant them. Holding this creature in my hands felt stratospherically different from squaring up against a griffin or a hydra. If I wanted to, I could've crushed her between my hands. I had no desire to do so, but it felt odd to have that kind of power over a living creature. A sudden protective instinct flickered inside me, something I hadn't experienced before with any beast I'd expelled.

She paused for a moment, as if she understood. Beneath my clenched hands, her little chest rose and fell frantically. In the bedroom light, I got a better look at her face. Iridescent scales formed a halo around her sharply pointed features, the colors shifting from blue to green to pink to purple, depending on how the light hit them. Mossy curls of pale green hair sprung up in tufts from her head, and I noticed detailed striations of yellow and blue banding that ran from the tops of her shoulders up to her neck. The banding contained minuscule swirls in a darker shade, and multicolored spots across the pale portions of her skin pulsated in time to her rapid breaths.

"What are you?" I whispered.

She chirped back, but I didn't speak… whatever language she was speaking. Her big, round black eyes peered up at me, filled with emotion. The sadness and panic in them struck me like an arrow through the heart, making me loosen my grip slightly. Like Tobe and Nathan, I wanted her to be comfortable. I didn't want her to feel trapped. I couldn't explain why… I guessed I just didn't want to see that sadness in her eyes and think I'd caused it. Sprouting out from between her unwrapped shoulder blades, her gossamer wings fluttered anxiously. I'd scared her, and she didn't know what I was going to do with her. Right now, I wasn't sure either.

"Persie?" said a voice from behind me. I whirled around as

Nathan walked in, his expression stern and confused. "What are you doing in my room?" A horrified gasp escaped his throat, his gaze darting to the creature ensconced in his undergarments. "Are… are those my boxers?"

Oh, boy, this was going to be a toughie to explain.

EIGHT

Persie

"It's not what it looks like!" I squeaked, nearly dropping the monster parcel. I wasn't even sure what it *did* look like, but my mind had gone completely blank.

Nathan took a step forward, his palms raised as if he were approaching a wild animal. "Okay, then, why don't you put my... um... boxers back where you found them, and we can talk about this outside."

"I'd love to, I really would, but—ow!" The tiny monster whipped her head around and sank her sharp teeth into my thumb. Nathan had made the mistake of edging closer, his presence well and truly freaking out the parcel in my hands. Either that, or she'd been biding her time. Startled, I dropped the creature. Boxers and critter plunged to the floor, and my heart might as well have left my body. "Crap, *no*! Don't let her get away!"

Quick as a flash, Nathan swooped the jacket off his shoulders and hurled it with impressive accuracy toward the spot where his boxers had fallen, right when the critter attempted an upward escape. The heavy tweed swamped her, knocking the monster back down, and my heart re-entered my chest. With the door wide open, that thing would've beelined for freedom faster than I could have said "Don't you freaking dare!" Her tiny form writhed underneath the stuffy fabric, unable to find an exit. I heard her shrieking and chattering savagely, and it was clear she wasn't singing my praises.

I dove onto the jacket and gathered the sides into a sort of old-timey sack—the kind put on the end of sticks in cartoons. "Thank Chaos for that." I heaved a sigh of relief as I lifted the pouch. Meanwhile, the little monster dropkicked the heck out of her tweed enclosure. The whole thing swung like a pendulum, tiny dents appearing with each defiant punch and roundhouse.

She might not have been inside a Mason jar, but I was halfway there. Part of me wanted to unleash an almighty scream of relief, but that would only alarm Nathan more. So, for now, I'd keep it to a quiet half-victory. Maybe not even half, considering I still had dozens more to capture.

"Okay, I'm really going to need an explanation." Nathan came nearer, eyeing his jacket with a mixture of curiosity and confusion. "What's in there?"

I gripped the top of the sack tighter, feeling the tiny monster trying to force her way out. "Honestly? I don't know. A monster of some kind. She looks a bit like Archimedes, but not quite the same."

His eyes widened. "She?"

"I mean, I'm no expert, but I think she's a she," I replied.

"May I?"

I hesitated. "Close the door first. If she gets out, you're going to have to help me catch her again. I've been chasing her for ages." I paused, my cheeks heating up. "And there's some yogurt on your kitchen floor. Sorry about that."

Nathan closed the bedroom door. "No problem. I can catch monsters when I have to, you know…" He arched an eyebrow. "But I don't much care for it. I suppose that's why I ended up a researcher instead of a bona fide hunter. You see, there comes a moment, for some people, during training where—I'm digressing, apologies. Please, let me see the creature, and I'll try not to let it loose."

I wonder what he was going to say... It sounded like the beginning of something profound, but it would have to wait—the ferocity inside the makeshift sack had amped up a level. My fluttery friend strained against the opening, and I realized I'd probably frightened her by trapping her in a dark mass of tweed. Maybe if I gave her some air and made her feel more comfortable, she would calm down.

Feeling for her thin body through the fabric, I wrapped a hand around what I hoped was her waist and peeled back a few pieces of the gathered jacket. Her head poked out, her needle-sharp teeth gnashing at me as more rude shrieks pierced my ears. Those big black eyes narrowed as she sucked in deep breaths and tried to shimmy her shoulders out. I let her wriggle her arms loose, but made sure to keep the wings locked down.

Nathan yelped so loud I almost dropped the monster again. "No way! This isn't possible!" He took off his glasses and wiped them on his polo shirt before putting them back on, like he couldn't quite believe his eyes. "For the love of Chaos, this is... this is incredible! Never in my life did I think I'd see one in the flesh!"

"Would you mind sharing?" I asked.

The tiny monster looked pretty cool, for sure, but she didn't look special enough to get a grown man jigging around like a little kid. He'd leave boot marks on his super-clean floor if he wasn't careful.

"Sorry, yes, of course." He clasped his hands together, grinning so wide the corners of his glasses dug into his cheeks. "Persie, you have no idea how amazing this is. The creature you're holding in your hands is... goodness, I can't believe I'm saying this. It's a pixie!"

I nodded dumbly. "And that's... good?"

"Good?" He gave the first real guffaw I'd ever heard in my life.

"It's more than good, Persie! This might be the rarest monster I've ever laid eyes on. In fact, they're archived under 'obsolete' in just about every monster research library you're likely to come across. Pixies are... Oh goodness, oh goodness, this is so exciting!"

"They're what?" My Purge not only made him dance like a marionette with the shakes, it had also made him *very* distractible.

He clamped a stunned hand across his mouth, then removed it, saying, "They're supposed to be extinct, Persie! Extinct! Defunct! Nonexistent! Pick your synonym! And you're holding one in *my* jacket!" He laughed so hard I worried for his blood pressure. Even the pixie stopped squawking for a second and stared at him with scathing judgment. She turned her face toward me, and I swore she rolled her twinkly black eyes. It took everything I had not to snort and ruin Nathan's moment of euphoria.

"Well, then, they can't be extinct," I said sagely, but Nathan shook his head.

"That's just it! Even the rarest of creatures will pop up on our radar from time to time, but the last sighting was over a hundred years ago. This... this is an impossible monster." He held out his hand to touch her, and she snapped her teeth at him. His fingertips recoiled out of harm's way. "She's certainly spirited. Now, you have to tell me, did you create her or did you find her? They're of Celtic origin, though they used to be found primarily in Devon and Cornwall in England. Perhaps they've reappeared here of their own accord, or perhaps the land itself has manifested them back into existence? Ireland is famously rich in magic, so it would not be entirely out of the question. Chaos, that would be thrilling! It would change everything we know about monster creation! Oh, think of all the theses I could write." He went off into a daze, evidently dreaming of sleepless nights at his computer and mountains of research. In fact, I wasn't even sure he still knew I was there. I felt almost reluctant to burst his academic bubble.

Wait... what do *I tell him?* My mind forked into two roads. Nathan knew more about monsters than I did, which meant he could be useful in figuring out what these things liked and how to wrangle a whole bunch of them. Although I supposed he could do that without knowing I'd created them. On the flipside, I thought about the implications of what I'd done. I'd expelled a horde of formerly extinct pixies, which was an oxymoron in and of itself; something was either extinct or it wasn't. What if people worried about the other extinct things I might Purge—creatures with far more dangerous motives than these mischievous things?

The glass box loomed large in my fears.

"Persie?" Nathan prompted, waiting impatiently.

I glanced down at the pixie and she gave me a shrug. "I took an evening stroll, and I happened to see her moving down the hallway. I chased her because I figured she probably shouldn't be running wild, and I found her rifling through your underwear drawer." I settled on a compromise—not the whole truth, but not a lie, either. It seemed like the best course of action, though the little she-pixie didn't appear to agree. She snickered into the tweed, muttering something that sounded a lot like "big fat fibber."

Nathan laughed, then asked nervously, "But where did she come from in the first place?"

"Right... that." I couldn't conjure up a believable excuse out of thin air, and I didn't know that I wanted to. But the truth... that would mean admitting that things had gone horribly awry.

He offered me a reassuring smile. "Persie, it's okay. You can be honest with me. The scholars and their assistants were all briefed about your unique ability, and if this pixie came from that, then I won't judge you for it or get you into any sort of trouble. Truthfully, I will be in utter awe of you."

"You will?" An unexpected lump formed in my throat.

"Did you not see me before? I think I squealed like a piglet when you showed this creature to me, Persie. I would be over the moon if you *created* it!" He grinned from ear to ear. "There are some fairly gaping holes in a land-emission theory, so you would be saving me a great deal of wasted time and effort delving into how that could be possible."

The pixie chirped and gave my hand a nudge that said, "Go on, stop being a coward."

"Shush, you," I muttered.

"You understand her?!"

I mustered a nervous laugh. "No, but I get the gist. You know, when someone shakes a fist at you, or glares at you, or rolls their eyes, you generally know how they're feeling." I sighed, my stomach doing somersaults. "Okay, so I Purged her. That's where she came from. Me. I'm so sorry that I invaded your space. I wouldn't have done it if I wasn't—"

He cut me off with a sudden round of applause. "What are you apologizing for? This is momentous, Persie!" He waggled his hands in another bizarre dance, shuffling his feet a bit. For just that moment, I was glad Genie wasn't here, more for his sake than hers. She always said that the moment a guy made you cringe, especially in the fledgling stages of flirtation, it was game over.

I looked back down at the pixie—who had started smoothing a dramatic hand across her mossy hair, relishing the praise—and I found a smile tugging at the corners of my lips. She certainly had personality, even if she had given me the run-around. I mean, if someone had been trying to catch me, I imagined I'd do just about anything to give them the slip, too.

"You've got no idea how envious I am," Nathan said, continuing to gush. "Don't misunderstand me, I'm sure it has its drawbacks, and I don't want you to think I'm making light of it, but to create something so wonderful—that is everyone's dream, isn't it? To make a masterpiece. Some see it in their children, some see it in their first novel, or in a piece of artwork, or a play, or a dance. Some see it in successful business endeavors, or landing a dream job, or making a difference in someone else's life. Some see it in research, or teaching, or—I'm rambling again, aren't I?"

I smiled. "A little."

"What I'm trying to say is, some people spend their entire lives pursuing this, and you have already achieved it. You, and what you are able to do... It's nothing short of astonishing." He reached toward the pixie again. Now that she'd received his endless flow of compliments, she allowed him to get a smidge closer before she gave a warning snap of her teeth.

"I've never thought of it as anything but a curse," I admitted. If he fully understood what my body and mind went through in order to expel these creatures, I sensed he wouldn't be nearly so envious. And yet, glancing at the pixie, I couldn't deny her beauty. Just looking at her made me want to grab a pencil and start sketching, so I could put every feature to paper-memory. She had life because of me. Sure, her and her wrecking-ball crew weren't using that life so wisely, but they would've gone on being extinct if not for my Purge. There had to be some magic in that—if not the Chaos kind, then the emotional kind.

I held her in my hands and felt her chest rising and falling, felt the toughness of her muscle and bone, as real as Nathan or me. Maybe that made me more than a conduit. Or, maybe, Leviathan's gift had a way of tricking me into thinking that, the way a mother forgets the specifics of the intolerable pain of childbirth. If they remembered, no one would be crazy enough to have more kids, right?

Nathan nodded. "It's your cross to bear, and I'm not going to tell you what to think about it. But I will marvel at the outcome." He put a fingertip on a pleat of the tweed jacket, and the pixie slapped it away with a shrill chatter. "You might not like me much, pixie, but you're remarkable."

"I don't think it's personal." I eyed the pixie and she blew a raspberry at me. Not exactly polite, as far as creations were concerned. The griffin had been much more reverent toward me, though it was hard to imagine a griffin sticking out its tongue.

"We should get her to the Monster Repository," Nathan suggested. "I would offer her some closet space, but I have a feeling she would take the first opportunity to escape."

Before the pixie could argue, I juggled the makeshift sack and my backpack and took out a Mason jar. Removing the lid, I loosened the neck of the sack and clamped it over the jar's entrance, watching as black mist poured inside. I had the pixie trapped.

"Sounds good to me. I don't have the energy to chase her any more tonight. Tomorrow, my bruises will have bruises."

He paused awkwardly. "And if we could forget the underwear part, I would be eternally grateful, as I'm sure you would be?"

"No problem. Your secret is safe with me." My cheeks seared with embarrassment. "But... there's one other thing you should know."

"What's that?" He raised an eyebrow.

I had to tell him. "There are a lot of these loose. Thirty or more."

He mustered a deep, calming sigh. "Well, let's deal with this one first, and then we can think about the rest. This will require some reading."

With the pixie's black mist kicking up a royal fuss inside the Mason jar, we set off for the Repository.

Entering the realm of the silver-poled, blue-tinged glass orbs, I stopped dead on the threshold. For a good few seconds, I wasn't sure I'd stepped into the same place as before. The light of the Repository had shifted as night had crept in sometime between my Purge and my wild pixie chase. The blue glass now looked navy, bordering on true black, dulling the silvered moonlight that touched the surface. Shadows moved across the white floor, which appeared unnaturally pale against the contrasting dark.

I put a foot forward, and the darkness appeared to follow, the shadows closing in somehow. The glass orbs hadn't frightened me before, but now that the night had transformed them, I felt as if the monsters inside could burst out at any moment, becoming one with the glass in order to overwhelm their enclosures. I couldn't even see the black mist swirling inside anymore. It set my nerves on a knife-edge, the hairs on the back of my neck tingling as if I were being watched.

I'm being stupid. I'm just tired.

"Over here." Nathan beckoned me to a nearby orb. "We've got smaller ones, but I don't like using them unless we're reaching capacity. She deserves some space to stretch, you know?"

I eyed the Mason jar; the pixie, in mist form, hadn't stopped swirling violently the whole walk over. "I guess so."

But when someone or something was in a cage, did it really matter how big the cage was? It didn't change the fact that they were trapped. I shook off the thought, knowing it had to happen. The thought of a free-range pixie was nice in theory, but I'd seen what they were capable of. If this one didn't go inside an orb, what else would I do with her? Let her go so she could wreak more havoc? No matter how I considered it, I arrived at the same conclusion: She had to go in the cage.

"Can you hand her to me?" Nathan asked, still visibly buzzing from the night's events. I had to say, it felt nice to have someone treat my Purge as a cool ability instead of something to panic about. I hadn't known I'd needed a fresh perspective, but it had helped.

Genie and my parents claimed they weren't afraid of what I could do, but when a Purge threatened, I saw it on their faces. Nathan was different.

I gave him the jar, and he proceeded to work his magic on the orb. His mouth moved silently as he conjured the spell that would crack it open. Soon enough, a twisting iris opened in the glass surface, expelling a rush of cold air. Nathan took off the jar's lid, shoved the top into the opening, and gave it a gentle shake, prompting the mist to cascade into the orb. As quickly as he could, he snatched the jar away and the iris twisted shut again before the pixie had time to react. Still, she more than made up for it once the iris had closed. Erupting back into her physical form, she pounded her miniature hands against the glass, the faint spots across her body throbbing violently. Her black eyes turned in my direction, filled with rage and sadness, and I knew she blamed me for this. Who else was there?

"I'm going to grab a few books that might be useful, as there's not much lore on these creatures. Are you okay to stay here, or do you want to come with me to my study? It's just over there." He gestured toward a door, tucked away on the far side of the Repository behind the bubble forest.

I shook my head. "I'll be fine here."

"Okay, I'll only be a minute." He darted away, practically skipping to his study.

I couldn't muster the same enthusiasm, even though, technically, I'd done what I'd set out to do. I'd caught and caged my first real-world Purge beast. Regardless, my fingers itched, albeit illogically, to let the pixie back out of her prison. It might not have been shaped like a box, but it served the same purpose as the box from my nightmare—the same ones that housed countless monsters year after year. I hated to see her thudding her tiny fists against the glass, the same way I'd done in that petrifying dream.

"I'm sorry," I whispered.

The pixie glared back, hammering harder for the freedom she couldn't have. In the end, I had to turn away from her, even though I felt like a chicken for not facing her. Why had I bothered giving her life at all, if this was where she'd spend it?

Nathan came back a few minutes later, his nose already buried in a book. He had an entire stack in his arms, his eyes flitting left to right as he plowed through the information within. "Ah, here it is! I knew I'd seen it somewhere."

He stopped abruptly, one step from bumping into a low-hanging orb. With a grin, he turned the pages toward me before flipping them back.

"So, it says here that pixies are curious and playful creatures, with a distinct mischievous streak. They are known to play tricks and jests and cause trouble, but they are not evil or malicious by nature. They love to dance and gather in large numbers. They will defend themselves when they feel threatened, but they won't attack unprovoked." He licked his finger and flicked through a few more pages. "Oh… and they love milk and sweet fruits. In the old days, it was believed that if you left a saucer of milk outside your house each night, then the pixies wouldn't play tricks on you. They were even thought to bring good fortune on homes that left milk out for them."

"That's why she went into your fridge." With new understanding, I pictured her struggling with the large bottle of milk.

He peered over the book. "Huh?"

"Never mind."

"Books aren't always correct, but this is a good starting point." He snapped the volume shut, looking pleased with himself. "We'll have to do some more research, considering what you told me about there being a lot of these creatures on the loose."

I gulped. "Yeah, sorry about that…"

"Why should you be sorry? You don't have any say over it." He didn't look scared, per se, but he certainly looked a bit warier. However, I found myself distracted by the prickle up the back of my neck. It got worse, all of a sudden, turning into a searing burn that made my ears tingle. A quick look around at the Repository revealed the reason. The monsters inside had all transformed out of their mist states and fixed their eyes firmly on me. They watched me with a mixture of expressions: intrigue, caution, disappointment, excitement, to name a few.

Why are you staring like that? I didn't want to draw Nathan's attention to it. Had he been less invested in pixie lore, he'd have noticed on his own. The creatures had gone very still, but their eyes spoke volumes, like a thousand cries calling to me in a language I didn't understand. Oddly, I felt entirely at home among these beings, as though I were somehow attached to each and every one, yet there was this huge divide between us. A fear, a me-vs-them kind of feeling. Plus, on a more literal level, I stood on the outside of the glass and they were trapped behind it. And that wrenched at my gut. I sensed the thrum of their energy resonating inside my chest, and the sadness swelled like a balloon, making my breath hitch.

"Persie?" Nathan cut through my strange reverie. "Are you ready to look deeper into these pixies, so I can help you?"

"No." The refusal blurted out of my mouth as though someone else had said it. "I caused this; I'll fix it. I caught one, I can catch the rest. You've given me enough to go on." I bolted away from him, driven by an uncontrollable sense of urgency that spiked in every vein. I owed it to these creatures to be the one to gather them up. Maybe that didn't make sense, and this wasn't the time to be a maverick, but my mind was made up.

Nathan ran after me, cutting me off before I crossed the Repository threshold. "Persie, hold on a second. I'll let you do this, as I can see what it means to you, but I can only give you a brief window before I *have* to say something."

"Just… give me until tomorrow." My eyes widened, imploring him. He was right—it did mean a lot to me, because if I didn't at least attempt it solo, then I wasn't sure I deserved my place here. Otherwise, everyone would always be on their guard, rolling their eyes, wondering when my next screw-up would happen.

"On one condition. You come back with every pixie you manage to capture, so I can safely deposit them in the orbs. You'll quickly run out of space if you don't," he said firmly. "And then, come tomorrow; if it hasn't worked, we'll discuss our next course of action."

It was an offer I couldn't refuse. I *would* need somewhere to put the pixies, given that I only had a few of the pre-hexed Mason jars. With a subtle nod, I agreed. "That's fair."

"And come back here if you decide you want further help. I'll stay in my study all night so you can easily find me." He offered a reassuring smile, and he didn't chase me this time as I took off out the door.

I didn't want to depend on the Institute's aid, but there was one person I could call without feeling like I'd handed off my responsibility. Taking out my phone as I ran, I dialed Genie, only to get her voicemail. I remembered the movie, and realized she'd probably turned it off. Still, I'd keep trying while I went after these annoying pixies.

I've got a good feeling about you, Nathan O'Hara. You're one of the nice ones, I can tell. I smiled as I slowed my pace. Genie might not have thought much of him, but I knew she'd feel the same as I did once she got to know him better. And I guessed we'd be seeing a lot more of him now that he'd seen what my Purge ability could do.

Settling into a brisk walk, I roamed the hallways, watching every corner and crevice for the slightest sign of a pixie. I kept my ears peeled, too, if that was a thing, listening for the sound of their fast-fluttering wings. Even if it took all night, I would find those mischievous critters.

An hour later, after circling back to the main common areas empty-handed, I froze at the sight of a figure storming toward me. It was Charlotte, her face like thunder, striding along and taking out her foul mood on the floor. Her hazel eyes narrowed as she saw me, her footsteps quickening.

"What is it with the two of you?" she barked. I wouldn't get a trophy for guessing who the other half of that duo was.

But I didn't have to pretend innocence. "Is something wrong?"

"Like she hasn't already told you." Charlotte folded her arms across her chest. "I just spent the last two hours mopping up the banquet hall. It wasn't exactly how I wanted to spend my evening."

I shrugged. "I don't know anything about it. I haven't seen Genie since dinner."

Charlotte eyed me, clearly debating whether or not to believe me. "You shouldn't be out at this hour."

"It's not even ten yet," I replied, keeping my calm. "I didn't realize we had early curfews here."

Her small frown told me I'd called her bluff.

"I was trying to be nice," she said, though her expression remained indecipherable. "Hosseini goes hard on his students, and you'll be a wreck tomorrow if you don't get a decent night's sleep. When you do badly in a class, it reflects badly on the whole Institute. So, like I said, best not to be out at this hour."

"No problem. I just wanted to make a snack first, but I guess I can go without." I smiled sweetly, though I had no intention of following her orders. She might have been a big shot in this Institute, and I respected the work she did and the success she'd achieved, but nothing was going to keep me from catching those pixies. Her warning just meant I'd have to be particularly vigilant to avoid another unwanted run-in tonight.

As Charlotte walked away, I hurried toward the dorms, wondering what had happened between Charlotte and Genie. I remembered what Charlotte had said to me at the orientation tour: *I don't like cleaning up messes.* The irony was... entertaining, to say the least. Still, I wondered what lurked beneath her cold exterior.

I turned down my corridor, still hunter-less, when a light caught my attention. Not the glint of pixie scales or the flutter of wings, but a fuzzy glow that I knew all too well: the orbs from earlier.

You don't look like decorations to me. I squinted at the lights as they danced along the wall ahead, tempting me to follow their pastel trails. Figuring I was headed in that direction anyway, I set off after the glowing orbs.

They bobbed and floated through the air, seemingly pausing at every corner so I wouldn't lose them. A shiver of unease bristled in my chest, but I didn't know if it stemmed from the missing pixies, the reappearance of the orbs, or the residual fatigue of my Purge. It was probably a mix of all three.

Where are we going, huh? I took a left when the orb went left, and almost cried out. A pixie darted up ahead, transfixed by the fiery purple center of the glowing Pied Piper. It was the first one I'd seen since leaving the Repository, and just when my hopes had begun to wane. With renewed determination, I raced down the hallway toward the pixie, ready to leap onto the pest if I had to. Veering down the right-hand corridor at the end of the hallway and sprinting full-on, I could almost feel the pixie in my grasp. Then something, or someone, crashed into my chest, and I sailed backward, the air rushing out of my lungs as I slammed into the ground.

No, no, no, no, no! Wheezing slightly, I struggled to my feet as quickly as I could, but it was no good. The glowing lights and the pixie had gone. Dusting off the back of my pants, I sought out the culprit.

It was Genie, who, like me, had been knocked down by our collision.

"Genie! Chaos, I'm so sorry, I didn't even see you." I hurried to help her up.

"Yeah, I figured that after I went flying." She offered a crooked smile and rubbed her chest. "But I think I'll live. Just a few cracked ribs, a deflated lung, and a severely wounded ego. How about you? You okay?"

I took a deep breath. "Not exactly." Talking a mile a minute, I explained everything that had happened since we'd parted ways at dinner. She listened intently, her eyes widening with every twist and turn of the tale. "So, as you can probably tell, I've got to catch the suckers before they wreck anyone else's rooms... or worse. I've done it once, I can do it again, but I could use an extra set of eyes and ears."

Genie gave a low whistle. "And I thought I had a bad evening."

"I just saw Charlotte," I said leadingly. I knew that Genie, not unlike the pixies, only attacked if provoked. And I had to wonder what Charlotte had done to piss off my friend. The pixies could wait a few more minutes—Genie was always there for me, and I wanted to repay the favor.

She chuckled grimly. "You heard about it, then?"

"Only that Charlotte got punished. What happened?"

"She wasn't *exactly* punished. She actually stuck up for me. A little." Her eyes glinted with pain as she began the rest of the story. Genie was tough, and there weren't many things that could make her hurt like that. "It was a bunch of bigots and assholes," she continued, "and their archaic beliefs about Atlanteans. Which my dad warned me about, and which ended with me dousing everyone in water... and a bit of hot chocolate. Anyway, it's over now, and

Hosseini sent everyone away to 'think about what they did,' so things should be quiet for a while. Anyway, he asked Charlotte to mop up, and I helped. I think she thought it was unfair because she was the only one who stuck up for me." She gave a tired shrug, but I sensed she was holding something back from me. But she was weary, and I decided to let her evade. "It's nowhere near as exciting as your evening. A horde of pixies... I don't know whether to applaud you or grab a butterfly net."

I smiled. "That wouldn't be a bad idea, actually."

"Well, we can work out a proper plan of action tomorrow." She gave a pointed yawn. "We've both had a tough night, and you've had a doozy of a Purge, so you need to sleep before you keel over. No offense, but you look shattered. And if you want to catch these things, you need to have your mind clear and not all loopy from exhaustion."

I shook my head. "I can't risk the pixies doing something terrible while I'm asleep. Everyone will know it was me, and... I don't want to be the liability they already think I am."

Genie took my hand. "I know your dream has you freaked, and it's totally understandable, but the Institute won't do that to you. If you'd Purged an army of freaking Godzillas, maybe they'd think about it, but even then, they wouldn't just march you off to a glass box and throw away the key." She led me gently back down the corridor, toward our rooms. "If the pixies are evading you and haven't wreaked havoc anywhere else, chances are they're trying to hide. If this place seems huge to us, then it probably feels cosmically massive to them. Besides, they're not going anywhere—the Institute is warded against escaping monsters. They'll still be here in the morning, awaiting your expert capturing techniques. I told you I liked the tweed, didn't I?"

I sighed reluctantly. "And I guess they'll sound the alarm if something does happen."

"Exactly!" She flashed me a tired grin. "But I have a feeling they'll keep a low profile. Harsh as it sounds, even the pixies must have a sense by now of what happens to monsters in a place like this. Plus, if things *do* take a nosedive, we can go to Victoria or you can go back to Nathan to get help."

"He'd be our best bet." My cheeks warmed up a smidge. "About that... There was one part I left out. I chased that other pixie into his room—I didn't know it was his room, just so you know—and she may or may not have gone into his bedroom and rummaged around in his underwear drawer. And I may or may not have had to wrap the damn thing up in a pair of bright orange, Hawaiian-print boxers."

Genie grabbed me. "Hawaiian print?!"

"Believe it or not." I nodded, giggling with humiliation.

"Well, well, well, the fashion disaster reveals new and horrifying layers." She grinned. "I'll be sure to mention them the next time we see him."

I grabbed her arm. "No! You can't! I swore I wouldn't say anything!"

"Then I'll just have to picture them." She cackled, and my spirits lifted.

After walking back the way I'd come, she dropped me at my door. I resisted opening it, so she wouldn't have to see the decimation inside. The thing was, I had no intention of going in there and catching some zzzs, but I needed her to believe it. Not in order to lie, but because she looked absolutely exhausted. She'd taken such good care of me during my banshee recovery, and I wanted to return the favor, even if it meant carrying on this pixie-catching fiasco on my own. I'd seen one, and that had to be a good sign. They couldn't hide from me forever, and if I left it until tomorrow, there would be no telling what they might do in the daylight. It would certainly be harder to cover up their existence from Victoria and the rest of the Institute if they decided to go on a chaotic rampage during waking hours.

Genie eyed me. "You're going to go to sleep, right?"

"It'll take a while with so much going on, but I should eventually drop off." I could rest once I had the pixies captured. If I managed it in the next few hours, I might actually get some sleep before morning came around.

"Okay." Genie stretched out her arms. "Well, I'm pooped. Try not to think about it too much, and we can keep looking between classes."

I nodded slowly. "Sleep well, Genie."

"And you." Yawning loudly, she sauntered back down the hall to her bedroom and disappeared inside. I waited a few minutes, to make sure she didn't come back out, before backtracking to where we'd collided. The orbs and the pixie had gone, but I knew they had to be around here somewhere.

If I'm not resting tonight, pixies, then neither are you. The search had well and truly resumed. I just had to hope I had no more run-ins with anyone before dawn rose, unless those run-ins happened to be with my pesky Purges.

NINE

Persie

I awoke with a jolt, to find foggy, gray-tinged sunlight trying to sneak through the gap in the curtains. My bedroom still smelled like the aftermath of a bonfire, but most of the smoke had escaped before I'd returned from last night's adventures. Well, it was more like last night and this morning's adventures. I hadn't made it back to my room until after five, when the sun had started to come up over the horizon and the cleaning staff had thwarted my continued search attempt.

Today is going to hurt. I'd be working on three hours of sleep, and the idea of getting stuck in training knocked me sick. I'd probably need to duct tape my eyes open by lunchtime. Lucky for me, I had the adrenaline of pure panic pulsing through my veins. I'd scoured as much of the Institute as possible since leaving Genie, and though I'd seen traces of pixies in knocked-over plant pots, smudges on the walls, and a few glimpses of wings, they'd managed to stay one step ahead of me. I'd even outright spotted a few after leaving out some milk and slices of apple I'd found in one of the kitchenettes, but they'd puffed into black mist before I could get my hands on them. A reminder that something peculiar had definitely happened with that first pixie, to stop it from disappearing when I had it in my grasp. Still, the Institute's defenses wouldn't let them out of the building, even in mist form.

Now, however, there was a greater chance of their discovery. The sun had come up, and people would be going about their daily lives again.

As for the bombsite formerly known as my bedroom, I'd done my best to clear things up before hitting the hay. The rug had gone in the trash, and I'd probably be billed for it after I graduated... Oh, and for the lamps, the light fixture, and the crack in the bathroom mirror where a wedge of soap had been launched like a missile by a pixie.

Coffee. Must have coffee. With my hair transformed into a bird's nest, I swung my legs over the edge of the bed and took a moment to properly wake up. Even with so little sleep, I'd slipped into the nightmare again. Same room, same crowd, same glass box, same claustrophobic terror, same screwed-up pep talk from my friendly neighborhood Leviathan. But the fear hadn't followed me into the real world the way it had yesterday. My chest had a slight vise-like clench, but I wasn't gasping and spluttering.

I don't paint dreams or nightmares; I paint my own reality. I'd always loved Frida Kahlo's artwork, but her words were just as remarkable. And I had the opportunity to paint *my* reality instead of letting my glass box nightmare dictate my days. At the moment, I felt... buoyed up, on a fresh swell of determination. I could view the glass box as an omen or a cautionary tale, and I chose the latter. I wouldn't be ending up in one, thank you very much.

"Play nice, pixies." I lumbered out of bed and padded to my messy vanity. My brush had tangles of mossy pixie hair in it, which I quickly plucked out, and the mirror was covered in smudged lipstick scrawls. I could deal with that later. I had a bigger mess to wipe clean, and today would be the day I proved myself a capable hunter. Last night had only been a warm-up. And Nathan had promised me he'd give me until today, but we hadn't set an exact time. So, it wasn't game over just yet.

I'm coming for you all. Hide if you like, I'll still find you. I smiled at my reflection. Sure, I still looked like I hadn't slept in a month, but I had a glitter of vitality in my eyes that came from deep within. I needed all the vigor I could muster—I had a naughty gang of pixies to wrangle.

A knock at the door disturbed my inner monologue. "It's open!" The pixies had broken the lock when they'd escaped last night, so that would probably get added to my ever-growing repair bill.

Genie appeared, wielding a brown paper bag and two expertly balanced coffees. "Delivery for the Queen of the Pixies." She flashed a grin. "I got you a plain bagel with cream cheese. Figured I'd go easy on your stomach after your Purge." Her nose wrinkled as she sniffed the air. "Oof, I bet that smokey smell clings to this room until you graduate."

"Thank you!" I reached for the bag, but she swiped it back. "I opened a window, but I think I might need to get some air freshener or something, to take the edge off."

"We can get you all the smoke cover-up you need later. No time to laze around, my friend. We've got half an hour before training with Hosseini kicks off, and we need every spare second to find your wily offspring." She nodded to my fluffy PJs. "Get into your training gear, and you can wolf this down on the way."

I grimaced. "Don't call them my offspring."

"Noted. I'll go with ankle-biters." She tapped an invisible watch on her wrist.

I gave up on the brush and pulled my dark hair into a bun. "Right, yes, got it. More haste, less chat. Give me a second."

As she headed back into the hall and closed the door, I pulled on bottle-green workout leggings and a soft gray T-shirt, then yanked my black SDC sweatshirt over my head. It would probably draw some choice looks, but I didn't care. If the GIs could be proud of where they came from, so could I.

Ready, in more ways than one, I grabbed my backpack and ran out to meet Genie. I felt like a new woman—if slightly bruised and battered and thoroughly exhausted. The huge welt on my elbow that had appeared after Fridgegate was the worst of my injuries—my first at the Institute, and I hadn't even started training yet. I supposed it was best to get accustomed to pain, considering what everyone, including Victoria, had warned us about the challenges ahead. *Bath salts. Remember to ask Mom for bath salts.*

"Where to?" Genie handed me the brown sack, and I duly stuffed the bagel in my mouth.

"Repository." Crumbs flew everywhere as I devoured a massive chunk. What could I say, Purges made a girl ravenous. "I think the pixies might gravitate toward the one that got put there last night."

Genie raised her coffee cup. "Ingenious!"

"No, that'd be you." I chuckled, tearing off another huge bite. With hunger like this, there was no room for table manners. "So, are you going to tell me what really happened with Charlotte yesterday?"

Genie pulled a sour face. "Like I said, bigots and assholes."

"Come on, you've got to give me the details. I told you every-thing about the pixies. I know it's not the same, but I want to know," I insisted. "I realize I've been a tornado of mayhem lately, and you've been here the whole time, helping me through it all. But I'm here for you as much as you're here for me, and I can't hold a grudge on your behalf if I don't know who's in my bad books."

She sipped her coffee with a faint smirk. "I'll give you the abridged version. Basically, I was trying to make friends and our classmates decided to really dig in with some deep-rooted hate for me. Well, Atlanteans, but since I'm the only one here, I got the whole barrage. Nasty words were hurled, and some stuck-up snoot from Charlotte's clique hogged the mic a lot." She paused.

My intuition told me we'd arrived at the part of the story Genie didn't want to share. "And?" I pressed.

She looked at me apologetically. "Then, they took a stab at you. And I lost it. I dragged up all the water in the banquet hall, had a bit of fun, then dumped the whole wave on their heads." She shrugged. "What can I say? They were getting a bit heated, so I figured I'd cool them off. Hosseini walked in, demanded to know what just happened. He basically guilted Charlotte into cleaning up because she's a Basani. Face of the Institute and all that. She wasn't happy about it. I helped mop up, because I'm just that nice."

"You should've told me that last night!" I swallowed a lump of bagel. "I wouldn't have gone on about pixies if I'd known what you went through." Anger crawled into my chest, making my hand clench around what was left of my bagel. I'd seen a glimpse of Atlantean prejudice during the exam, but when Victoria had snapped at the culprit, I'd figured it was a one-off. Or, at least, that no one would dare be outwardly hostile after that. It burned me up inside, to think that my best friend had faced that alone.

Genie drained her cup. "Pixies are a way bigger deal, Pers. Although, I wouldn't mind if they left some well-deserved 'gifts' in Charlotte's pal's room. Maybe a few in our classmates' rooms, too. You know, as long as they couldn't be traced back to a bunch of tiny monsters on the loose."

She always makes jokes, even when she's hurting. She could hide it pretty freaking well, but there was a subduedness in her face that revealed her pain. No one could come out of an encounter like that and feel okay. Not even the toughest woman I knew. A twinge of remorse lay on top of my anger; if I hadn't bailed on the movie, I could've been the one to stand up for her.

"Do you want to speak to Victoria about it?" I asked as she passed me my coffee.

She looked off toward the wall to hide her expression. "Nah, there's no point. I'm not going to change anyone's mind overnight." She gave me a forced smile. "I'll win them over with exposure therapy—be so in their faces that they won't be able to see a big, bad wolf when they look at me anymore."

"This is what your dad was worried about, huh?" She was trying to comedienne her way out of this, but I didn't want to watch her sweep it all under the rug.

"Yeah..." Her eyes scrunched up, as though she was fighting tears. "I thought he was being a drama queen or using it to prod me back toward Atlantis. I guess he's seen more of this than I have. And you know what the funniest thing is?"

I frowned. "What?"

"I never thought I was sheltered before I came here. But my dad shielded me from so much." She coughed suddenly, and it sounded like a covered sob. "The SDC made me think Atlanteans were already part of the gang, you know? Fully integrated, accepted members of magical society. Now, I see more clearly."

"I'm so sorry, Genie." I threaded my arm through hers and gave it a squeeze.

She sighed. "It's fine. Either they'll get used to me, or they won't. It doesn't matter. I'm going to graduate and be a hunter, regardless." Her expression hardened. "But if they say anything about me or you again, they'll get another impromptu shower. I might not be able to change their perspectives, but that doesn't mean I'll put up with their hate-spewing."

"Neither will I." I didn't ask what had been said about me, because I already knew. It was about my Purge ability, my lack of useful magic, or both. Plus, even if they had their issues with me, they'd likely only dragged my name into the fray to get a rise out of

Genie. Clearly none of those idiots realized they were playing with fire. They had no idea what Genie was truly capable of. Drenching them was a walk in the park for her, as easy as snapping her fingers, and I knew she'd shown restraint when she could've gone all-out on them. But she hadn't, because she wasn't like that, and because she valued her place here. Still, I was glad she'd fought back. They'd clearly deserved it.

We dropped our breakfast trash in a bin as we entered the hallway that led to the Repository. We scanned the ceilings, investigated statues, flung back curtains, peeked into classrooms, and cracked open study doors, looking for any sign of the pixies. We were on high alert; even the whistle of the wind through the rafters turned us into nervous wrecks. We even ducked into a couple of recesses to lie in wait for the pixies, but the creatures were nowhere to be found. It looked as though they'd gone into ultra-covert mode, steering clear of the hunters who'd waste no time dropping them into a Repository orb.

"Just how small are these things?" Genie whispered as the pair of us ducked behind a chimera statue to search for the creatures.

I showed her with my fingers—about six inches, head to toe. "I think you were right about them being scared. I mean, I saw two yesterday, after the great escape. But today, it's like they've... gone." I avoided highlighting which part of the day, since she didn't know about my early-morning exploits. "Which is obviously impossible, since the Institute is protected against potential runaways. They're definitely here, but they aren't taking any chances with their freedom."

Genie peered out from behind the chimera's rump. "Does that mean we should be relieved? Maybe they're planning to go about their lives without causing any fuss at all. You know, like roosting bats or pigeons."

I shot her a dubious look. "I think it's more likely to blow up in our faces at some point. They're quiet now, sure, but these aren't wilting wallflowers we're talking about. They thrive on mischief."

"Damn it. That's what I was thinking, but with cruder words." Genie puffed a sigh. "Well, we'll have to carry on the search later. Don't want to be late for our first training session with Hosseini. He might look like a gentle giant, but I saw his stern streak last night. I don't want to be on the receiving end of it."

Please, don't step out of line, pixies... My time this morning had run out, and it would be hours before I had another opportunity to look for them. Hours filled with crippling anxiety that someone would see them and report the news to Victoria. I wondered if anyone had been expelled on their first day? Maybe, I'd be the first.

Unless... A sudden resignation dawned. I'd made a promise to Nathan last night. I had to come clean to Victoria. I'd tried to fix it alone and I'd failed. Maybe she'd give me some credit for attempting to stand on my own two feet and solve my own problems. Maybe not. Either way, this morning's search had been the final nail in the coffin—I couldn't do this alone. I owed Nathan for giving me the chance, but I couldn't even do it with Genie at my side. I'd wanted to, but it wasn't possible. As soon as my first classes were over and our lunch break came around, I'd go to the head huntswoman and tell her everything. And pray she understood my reasoning.

I nodded. "They'll have to show themselves some time, even if it's not me who coaxes them out." I sounded calm, but my insides jittered like crazy. One mishap from these pixies, and it'd be front page news before I had a chance to get to Victoria myself. And that prospect came with additional fears. I wished I could believe the comforting things Nathan and Genie had said about Victoria not losing her mind over this, but O'Halloran's reaction was stuck in my head like a barb. I hadn't expected him to react the way he did, and I didn't want to get into the habit of believing I'd get a free pass every time I messed up.

"And hope they don't get any stupid ideas before then." Genie stepped out from behind the chimera and, together, we headed for the training courts.

At Genie's suggestion, we jogged the whole way to get ourselves warmed up—though, I mostly just wanted to wake myself up—and arrived five minutes early to a room full of awkward looks and shamefaced silence. After Hosseini's talking-to last night, everyone had their tails tucked firmly between their legs. Hosseini himself crouched in the corner of the huge glass-and-stone space, sifting through a trunk full of unusual sea-green cubes. I couldn't see them very well from my spot, but silver embellishments glinted as he turned the boxes over in his hands, assessing them. Hexwork of some kind, I supposed, as these were likely the famous puzzle boxes that Kes had told me about—Institute patented.

I could use about thirty to forty of those. I tried to keep up a calm façade, my eyes flitting toward every corner in the training studio for a glimmer of pixie. Stupid as it sounded, above all else, I didn't want my classmates to see what I'd done. They were already wary of me.

Choosing a box, Hosseini straightened to his full height. He'd looked a lot smaller on the stage in the main assembly hall, but that was perspective for you. His dark curls were held back by an embroidered band of coral-red silk, which covered most of his forehead and tied in the back. The matching buttoned-up tunic was decorated with delicate gold patterns sewn into the cuffs and high collar. His pants were white and flowing and his feet were bare, maybe to give him some freedom, or to keep him in touch with the ground. I'd never seen a person with more natural nobility—aside from Victoria.

Please don't expel me, Ms. Jules. Please... I just needed a few more hours, and I'd reveal everything to her. The pixies just had to hold off until then.

"Good morning. I trust everyone rested well and took pause for self-reflection?" His voice was lilting and musical, but the inference in his words was anything but soft. A grumble of assent made its way through the class of twelve. His obsidian eyes glanced at Genie for a moment, as if offering her the opportunity to speak. When she didn't, he continued.

"I am partial to the saying: 'This is the first day of the rest of your lives.' However, that would be untrue, in this instance. Instead, I will say that this is the first day toward saving your lives. Monster hunting is complex and uniquely personal, as you will discover throughout your education here. There are the basics, but there is no one-size-fits-all approach." He gestured to the group. "You each have your own set of skills and talents, of varying levels of intensity and utility, and you must decipher which are of the most value to you when facing a monster in the field. Monster hunting is as much about the mind as it is about the physicality, for one lapse in judgment can cost you everything. Now, you will find that I have a very practical approach to teaching. It's easier to learn by showing than telling, though textbooks do have their uses."

And what if you only have your bare hands? A different current of nausea churned in my belly. The normal, anxiety-driven kind—not the imminent-Purge kind—blending with the missing-pixie kind. I'd made it through several stages in the exam before the banshee happened, but what if I didn't have a satchel to swing or a convenient lightning bolt at my disposal? We hadn't even begun, and I already felt like I was at the bottom of the class. Not in a self-pitying way, just in a practical, logical sense; I'd come to a firefight with a blunt spear.

Hosseini raised the sea-green box in his hand. With a better view, I could see that each face of the box was covered in intricate silver designs etched directly into the matte metal. A sheen rippled across the surface like a mirage, the etchings glowing faintly.

"What's in there?" said a meathead with enormous biceps, jabbing a sausage-like finger at the box. He was actually called Theodore Isherwood, I learned—or Teddy, to his friends.

Hosseini smiled. "Let us find out, shall we? Genie, if you would be so kind as to demonstrate for us?"

"Demonstrate?" Genie looked startled. I gave her a gentle push forward, setting aside my pixie thoughts for a second. Evidently, Hosseini had high hopes for my friend, and wanted to show the rest of our class what a remarkable magical they had in their ranks. He was giving her the platform she needed for the exposure therapy she'd been scheming.

"Yes," Hosseini said simply. "If you come up, I will unleash the creature."

"Go," I urged in a whisper.

Genie stepped out of the crowd and took up her position in the open space at the far side of the room. Lines were drawn at intervals across the rough stone floor to mark out a pitch of some sort— much better for running and fighting than the smooth concrete. To test our capturing skills from different distances, perhaps? Without prompting, she moved behind the farthest line, while Hosseini went to the opposite side. He set the box on the floor and pushed down on a harp-shaped symbol. Then, he backed away, retrieving a baton from the trunk where he'd gotten the box. No, it wasn't a baton… It looked, unless I was mistaken, like a shock stick.

That can't be right. They wouldn't use something like that here, would they? Maybe it was solely for the new recruits, in case anything went wrong. When it came to the safety of students or monsters, the students would always come first. Still, it left an unpleasant taste in my mouth. Anger, maybe. Using a device like that was cruel, plain and simple.

Before I could think about it for long, black mist erupted from the box and started to take shape on the stone floor: stringy legs covered in dark, maroon scales, which gave way to a plump, slimy body and a set of leathery black wings that flapped furiously. Bulging, thread-veined eyes glowered at Genie, while glinting fangs the size of my index finger dribbled with an oily ooze. Its midnight-blue tongue slobbered around thin lips, like it had just eaten a blue-raspberry sucker.

A gargoyle... Immediately, I thought of my mom and my uncle. They probably wouldn't have liked to hear that, but they had an affinity for these creatures. So many of their best stories included gargoyle sidekicks. Murray had been my favorite as a kid, though I realized later on that they'd PG-ed the tales about Murray and Davin for child-friendly consumption. Still, he was a hero to me, and I used to beg to visit his box in the Bestiary. He adored my mom and uncle but hated my dad, always lunging at the glass to try and scare him. I'd been so envious of my mom and uncle for their gargoyle exploits, so seeing this one in the proximity of a shock stick was a bit jarring. True, I'd Purged one of my own, but I hadn't been given time to think about it the way I was thinking about Genie's target practice.

Genie smiled at the gargoyle, already familiar with this type of monster. She launched into an attack without hesitation, green ripples pulsing down her body into the stone floor, where a crack formed and snaky vines slithered out. They twisted around the creature's legs before it could even move.

Something's not right about this. The gargoyle had my full attention, its expression contorted with a tangible fury that shouldn't have been there. Gargoyles had a nasty streak, for sure, and they had no trouble getting aggressive, but this felt different. I could almost sense its frustration and wondered how often this poor thing got dragged out of its prison for the sole purpose of being battered into submission, only to end up back in that puzzle box at the end of it. I mean, no wonder it looked pissed.

"Look how ropey that thing is," someone whispered.

Someone else chuckled. "You ever seen a punchbag after a few years? Same difference."

Don't any of you care? My heart broke for the gargoyle. It wasn't much of a positive, but at least other creatures were taken care of and given some comfort in the Repository or the Bestiary. But this one was here, stuck in a box, waiting to be used over and over again. No wonder I could feel its frustration so potently. And a shock stick on top of that... It was inhumane.

The gargoyle hunched over and tried to rip the vines away with its sharp fangs, growling in exasperation. While it was distracted, Genie launched another burst of Earth at the beast. More vines wrapped around its body, constricting it. I wanted to shout for her to stop, but quickly realized that wouldn't go over well. The trouble was, I could feel its pain. It couldn't breathe and was starting to panic.

It thrashed wildly, trying to get free, but Genie was in the flow of the fight now, however one-sided it was. She drew water from the flasks of the students, whose eyes widened in fright. No doubt they were having flashbacks to last night. She shaped the water into a large rectangle of liquid before maneuvering it around the gargoyle. Its fear amped up, and so did mine, in parallel. I felt what it felt, empathizing with its awful situation. Without breaking a sweat, Genie used her Glacial abilities to transform the liquid into a block of solid ice. In the space of a few minutes, she'd immobilized the creature.

"If you would like to do the honors, Genie?" Hosseini held out the puzzle box. "Press the harp to open it."

Stepping over the line, Genie walked to the other side of the room and took the box. She set it down in front of the gargoyle and did as Hosseini had instructed. Red flashes shot out of her, mingling together in a sheet of Fire that made its way down the ice block, melting it away. As the gargoyle's form emerged from its frosty prison, it disintegrated inch by inch into black mist that spiraled down into the waiting puzzle box, until there was nothing left and the lid snapped shut.

"Excellent work, Genie." Hosseini picked up the box and twisted it. Thin, rotating panels appeared in the metal. He spun them into a particular pattern, and the silver designs flared with white light before fading to a barely perceptible glow.

Applause exploded from the class. Even Teddy put his hands together for Genie's flawless display. In fact, I was the only one not clapping. I wanted to be thrilled for my friend's accomplishment, especially since this was our first class and she'd already aced it, but the gargoyle's pain and anguish still throbbed in my chest. How could I applaud, knowing that gargoyle would spend its life as a punching bag?

In the end, I put on a smile and hoped Genie didn't notice that my hands were behind my back.

TEN

Persie

An entire morning passed before I knew it, and barely a minute had gone by that I didn't spend thinking about the escapees and my impending discussion with Victoria. Seeing that poor gargoyle had amped up my anxiety. If someone caught the pixies before I could explain to the head huntswoman, maybe they'd end up as training material. And though they might've pissed me off, I didn't want that for them. Plus, the longer I spent in classes, the more time they had to cause some damage or get found.

The rest of Hosseini's class had involved basic drills with artificial monsters: how to deal with preemptive attacks, surprise attacks, aerial attacks, every kind of attack. For the first, he'd made us sit and meditate, listening for the sound of a monster approaching to sense their incoming direction. I'd been pretty good at that, able to feel the artificial emotion coming off the hologram beasts. As for the surprise attacks, those had mainly involved retaliating with magic, so I'd been forced to improvise, which had mostly involved ducking and rolling, and aerial attacks weren't much different in terms of how I could defend myself. Hosseini had unveiled different augmented reality scenarios at the touch of a snazzy button—woodland, desert, mountains, and water—and taught us how to use the surroundings to our advantage.

When he'd asked me to try and capture an artificial monster, I'd muddled through. He'd put me up against a loup-garou in a barren wasteland scenario that weirdly emulated an old dream of mine, minus the red sky and hot wind. The rest of the class, aside from Genie, had watched with smirks, waiting for me to fail. But I'd done my best, following Hosseini's instruction to try and stun it with rocks. I'd missed, deliberately, but distracted the loup-garou for long enough to skim a puzzle box under it. Regardless, I'd definitely heaved a sigh of relief when it was over.

"You just need to find your own way, that is all," Hosseini had told me. "Hunting is not about magical prowess. That merely simplifies the act because these beings stem from magic. Though your road may be more interesting in its challenges, a method will come to you, I am certain."

Those had been Hosseini's parting words to me. I let them bolster my resolve that I belonged there, even if the gargoyle display had left me unsettled.

After, sitting in Naomi Hiraku's engineering lab with a view of the steely sea and its frothing whitecaps, the sour taste of the training session faded. The chic, silver, beech-paneled walls and clunky worn workbenches had a homier flavor than the glass training courts, and I knew no monsters would pop out unawares. *Unless the pixies show up.* I gulped with every reminder, unable to get comfortable. This should've been my zone, but I was too distracted to enjoy it. Still, this was where a non-magical hunter could find their "way." And if I wanted to get an advantage over the pixies so I could plead with Victoria to let me help later, maybe I'd find it in this class. After all, when magic failed, everyone relied on technology. And the weird and wonderful stuff in here was enough to blow anyone's mind.

"Here we have four options for capture. Can you guess which is my favorite?" Naomi laid out four objects on her personal workbench. She had an effervescence about her that proved infectious. When someone called her for help, she hurried to them as if the world might end if she didn't move fast enough. She never walked anywhere, and I'd seen her sit for all of two seconds before she'd jumped back up to make herbal tea, which she'd then offered to the class. It would've looked exhausting if she hadn't done it all with a bright smile on her berry-stained lips. Her face had an impish quality, framed by a sleek, blunt bob. The drab light, when it hit right, revealed shades of darkest cherry in her black hair.

I raised my hand. "The puzzle box?"

"Ah, excellent! But no." She giggled, and I couldn't help smiling, despite my nerves. "The puzzle box is a great all-arounder, and I know you'll all come to wonder how you ever lived without them, but *this* is my favorite."

She picked up a perfectly round, sleek sphere, about the size of a baseball and the color of a black pearl. Which is to say purplish, with tones of pink and gold and gray—not black at all.

"This is an Omnisphere. Now, call me biased, but this happens to be my baby—designed, patented, and realized by my own two hands. It can catch anything, regardless of strength. There are still a few kinks to iron out and it requires a complex spell to use, so not yet practical. But it will be! Once I've had my eureka moment and everything works properly, it'll be the best new toy in town!"

Not for me. I admired her enthusiasm, and it looked beautiful, but I needed simpler options. The rest of the class was staring at the Omnisphere agog. She'd made some bold claims, but I doubted an experimental capture object would be of much use to anyone. Still, I hoped she'd iron out those kinks. If she did, she'd go down in magical history.

"How about this one? Not my favorite, but can anyone tell me what it is? This is easy!" Naomi picked up a Mason jar.

The class rolled their eyes, a warm collective chuckle spreading through the lab.

"Mason jar," everyone chorused.

"Yes! Very good!" Naomi set the jar down and clapped her hands together. "It's the most prevalent method of monster capture, used in covens worldwide, but it uses extremely basic hexwork and can be easily broken if you've got a case of butterfingers. Most are pre-treated with hexwork these days, to avoid hexing on the go. Useful in a tight spot, but there are better choices. Namely, this one—the puzzle box that Persie mentioned." She showed off one of the boxes and nodded toward our workbenches. "You've all got one at your stations, and I'd like you to write down as many observations about it as you can. Then we'll reconvene and go through what you've found and what it means."

One of the Ponytails, Suranne Redmond, raised her hand. "What's the fourth one?"

"Goodness, good thing you asked! I'd have forgotten all about it." Naomi smacked her forehead dramatically, and possibly a bit too hard, and picked up the fourth object. It was an old, neatly painted ceramic bottle, similar to one I'd seen in a display case.

"This is an Artemis vase. We don't use them anymore, but these were the forefathers of the Mason jars and the puzzle boxes. The oldest monsters in the Bestiary were caught with these. Powerful, reliable when you've got the knack, but notoriously tricky to get the hang of, as they require a complex spell and the right sequence of buttons. Now, back to the puzzle boxes. Make your notes and be ready to share in ten minutes."

Genie cast a glance at me. "Atlantis still uses them."

"Huh?" I leaned closer to her.

"Those vases. Atlantean hunters use them, even now, and they don't have any trouble getting them to work. They caught Jörmungandr—a freaking World Serpent—with one, for Chaos's sake." She shrugged, as if she'd surprised herself by jumping to Atlantis's defense. "I bet I could catch a pixie in one, given the chance."

I propped my chin on my hand. "To do that, they'd have to come out of hiding. I thought we'd at least catch another one during our search." Especially after a whole night of being duped by them.

"Maybe they're living it up in the orchard. Didn't you say they liked apples?"

I tried to remember what Nathan had said. "I don't know if it's apples, specifically. I think it's just sweet fruits, so probably not. Blackberries, maybe? They do like the outdoors, though. And Nathan said they love a party." A horrifying thought crept into my head. "Oh no, what if they throw a huge gathering outside? That'll definitely attract attention."

I just needed to get through this class. Then, I could go to Victoria, and my anxieties would hopefully be lifted a bit. The pixies just needed to stay hidden until then.

"We'll just have to keep a watch out for any tiny keg deliveries." Genie offered me a reassuring smile. "For now, they're behaving. Let's take that as a good sign, until it's not."

"Was that supposed to be comforting?" I lamented.

She laughed. "Did it work?"

"Yes and no." I focused on the puzzle box to distract myself. "Anyway, we'll have an hour at lunch to… try something else. If they stay hidden, then there's nothing we can do about it until classes are over. And I refuse to start slipping in my lessons on the first day, pixies or no pixies."

I wasn't furtively keeping my plan to go to Victoria from Genie. I just didn't want her to sit through these lessons, worrying that her best friend might be in huge trouble. She'd been in her element this morning, with Hosseini, and she deserved to ride that buzz for a while after the night she'd had.

"I think the staff must've put some extra fire in your bagel this morning." Genie winked, and I smiled back. But the ironic thing was, it wasn't the bagel or the dream that had kicked my behind into gear; the pixies were responsible for this newfound surge of determination. One pixie, to be precise. She'd shown me that I was capable of hunting, even if putting them in cages afterward didn't sit too well with me. I just had to remind myself that they had to go in those orbs, and eventually into glass boxes, for a valid reason—the protection of the magical world, and the energy it relied on. Only, that didn't feel like an entirely valid reason anymore. There had to be a better way.

Picking up my pen, I started to make notes on the puzzle box. The contraption had clearly been designed by someone with an artistic eye. Each panel displayed a specific image: a sea serpent on one side, a phoenix on another, a Caladrius on the third side, and a rock golem on the fourth. The bottom and top panels had identical pictures of a unicorn dipping its head into a pool.

"Water, Fire, Air, and Earth," I realized with a bristle of excitement. "And these panels must be the fifth element: Magic itself."

Genie's eyebrows shot up. "Oh, this is *so* going to be your forte."

"It's a universal language, so anyone can use it." I jotted my theories down and picked up the box. I felt for those hair-thin indents in the metal that Hosseini had used. Curious, I copied what he'd done, and the images instantly twisted into warped versions of each panel: a sliver of a serpent in the middle of a phoenix, and the back end of a rock golem taking the place of a Caladrius's head. "That must be how you get the box to lock. The lid opens when you line up the patterns, and you stop the monster escaping by twisting the box out of sync."

Genie peered over my shoulder for a better look. "What about that harp thing Hosseini showed me?"

"It must let the monster in and out again, manually," I replied.

Naomi scurried over and paused at our bench. "You certainly have a talent for this, Persie. You're absolutely right!" She grinned so wide that it felt like a pat on the back. "Once a monster has been captured, the interior hexwork memorizes the unique signature of the beast inside. That means it can be released at the touch of that harp and drawn back in again with a second touch. Twisting the box is the only way to ensure everything is fully locked in. Then, once a new monster is caught, it forgets the old signature and remembers the new one. Nifty stuff! I wish I'd invented it."

"I'm sure your Omnisphere will replace these, one day," I replied. I felt compelled to give her a compliment since she'd given me my first compliment at the Institute.

She waved a hand at me. "Ah, who knows. One can hope! If I made the sort of money that the inventor of these boxes makes, I'd buy an island somewhere and—"

I never found out what she'd have done on that island. The lab door burst open and Victoria Jules stormed in with a tempestuous look on her face. A four-strong squadron of hunters flanked her, as well as Hosseini and Nathan.

"First years, apologies for the intrusion." She swept a hand through her stylishly short crop. "This is highly unorthodox, and I resent disruption to the Institute's routine, but classes are suspended until further notice."

Colette Requin, a stern-faced French-Canadian, raised her hand. "Why, Ms. Jules?"

No... Don't do this now. I was coming to you, I swear! My heart turned somersaults, and Genie grabbed my hand under the workbench. She clearly thought the same thing—we'd left it too long, and now the secret was out. Victoria had discovered the pixie situation before I could tell her, and she was putting the whole Institute on lockdown until they could all be found. Judging by the grim expression on her face, I was about to be in major-league-trouble.

"I was getting to that," Victoria replied with uncharacteristic snappishness. "It has come to our attention that a member of the senior class, Xanthippe Evershot, has been missing since last night. She attended the film screening in the banquet hall, left when it dispersed, and has not been seen since."

"Isn't that Charlotte Basani's friend?" The other Ponytail, Gem Phillips, nudged her hair twin.

Suranne nodded, lowering her voice, but not so low that I couldn't hear the gist. "She's the one who said all those things to little Miss Atlantis."

Genie paled as she heard that last part. "Crap..." She turned to me with worried eyes. "They're going to think it was me, aren't they? They're going to start pointing fingers. I swear, I didn't have anything to do with it. I was mopping up. I—"

"I know," I interjected, understanding her anxiety. Genie would never put anyone in harm's way, no matter how much they antagonized her. It wasn't in her nature. But she was right—people *would* want someone to blame, and she'd be their first port of call. If they tried it, though, I'd be right there at her side, backing her up. She had alibis, including Charlotte, and those were watertight. Still, there was a tiny silver lining in this awful news—at least this wasn't about pixies. Which meant I might still get my opportunity to come clean.

Victoria gestured toward Nathan. "Show them what has been recovered."

Huh? Had they found evidence already? Victoria wouldn't have canceled class if it wasn't serious, which meant they suspected

Xanthippe wasn't coming back, or that some foul play had gone on. Horror washed over me as I envisioned crime scenes, blood, victim's clothing, and then fresh horror washed over me as Nathan produced a Mason jar with three pixies inside.

Chaos no... Please, no. My mind and heart were strapped into a rollercoaster of emotions. I'd gone from worrying about my secret being uncovered to worrying about Xanthippe, and now I was back to the pixies again. Victoria would immediately guess I was responsible. But, aside from my fairly glaring part in it, she surely didn't think the two factors were related—the pixies and the disappearance?

"These unknown creatures were captured early this morning, prowling around the Repository," Victoria explained, her tone ice cold. "Any information regarding them would be greatly appreciated at this concerning time."

Was she talking to me? Victoria didn't look at me when she said it, but Nathan had his eyes firmly fixed in my direction. His expression didn't give much away, but I caught a hint of furtiveness. Had he told Victoria about my Purge, because he presumed our agreed deadline had passed? Was she asking me to come forward, in front of everyone? No... if she knew everything, then she would have called me out in private. Maybe he suspected my pixies of causing the girl's disappearance. My heart lurched into my throat, my head throbbing with too many thoughts. Did anyone else suspect me of creating the pixies? I tried to steal a discreet glance around the room, and everyone seemed to be looking at me. Undoubtedly, they were all thinking the same thing—the pixies were mine.

Just then, Charlotte appeared in the doorway, her face twisted with anger and her eyes red with tears. "I'd say it's pretty suspicious that we've just found these things loose in the Institute less than a week after Persie Merlin-Crowley's arrival." She glared at me, saying what everyone else was already thinking. "Isn't that what you do, Persie? Purge monsters?"

Sitting beneath the fierce heat of so many eyes, I had no answer to give that they would accept. Everyone knew what I could do. It wasn't a secret, though I wished it could've been. Genie squeezed my hand tighter to let me know she was there. But I doubted she, or anyone else, could get me out of this scrape. I'd made the pixies, and a girl had gone missing. Deep in my heart, I felt certain that the two couldn't possibly be related, but there was no way anyone else would believe it.

"Persie. Come to my office." Victoria's voice cut through my pounding heart. "Immediately."

With those words, she all but painted "guilty" on my forehead.

ELEVEN

Genie

B*alls, balls, balls, and more balls!* I perched on a bench outside
Victoria's office, clicking my heels like I wanted a one-way
ticket back to Kansas. The head huntswoman had tried to get me to
stay behind. Yeah, as if that was going to happen. Who knew what
was going down in the dragon's den right now? Where Persie went,
I went. Hell, I probably wouldn't be in this Institute if she wasn't
here. My best pal would know I was nearby, and I hoped that would
give her some comfort.

There's no shouting. Should there be shouting? Is this a good sign?
Chaos, the looks our classmates had given Persie when she'd
followed Victoria out. They might as well have been ringing bells
and shouting, "Dead woman walking!" They didn't have a friggin'
clue. Sure, they'd put two and two together with the pixies and
Persie. But who the heck looked at a six-inch fairy and went, "Oh,
yeah, you know what, they definitely did it." Did those idiots think
the pixies were like ants, lugging around 5000 times their own
bodyweight?

Fate works in mysterious ways though, eh? Xanthippe had gotten some serious just desserts. Not that I thought she should have been abducted or anything. But after the mud she'd slung at me last night, it was hard not to feel a teensy-weensy bit like she'd deserved it. Did that make me a terrible person? Probably. Which was why I'd decided to help find her, if I could.

My heels stopped clicking as a figure skidded around the corner. Carrying a pile of books so high they covered his face, he nearly tripped and dumped the whole library into my lap. He froze, the tower wobbling, and leaned this way and that, balancing his books like an expert accountant. I could've sworn I'd seen the same move in some grainy old movie that Finch insisted on showing us. Slapstick gold.

"Were you born with two left feet or something?" I teased.

Nathan peered around the side of the stack. "Oh, Genie. I... uh, didn't see you there."

"I doubt you can see anything but book spine." I gave him a feeble smile. I didn't feel much like grinning right now; not until I knew my pal wasn't about to get booted out of the Institute.

"Has anyone ever told you, you're very..." He trailed off, grabbing the top book as it tried to slide off.

"Charming? Debonair? Hilarious?" I offered.

He swayed over to the bench and struggled to sit. "No, abrupt."

"I prefer mysterious, but I'm not going to put words in your mouth." Feeling sorry for him, I reached for the stack and took half. "There, now you might be able to see where you're going."

"Why would I need to do that when I'm sitting down?" He frowned at me, apparently serious.

I set the tomes down beside me. "You might want to check out a book on humor and read the chapter labeled 'sarcasm.' It'll change your life."

He'd picked the wrong time if he wanted my sugar-and-rainbows side. After all, he'd shown the pixies off like a cheesy presenter on QVC. It sort of felt like he'd set Persie up for a fall. He knew the whole story. He must've known how it would look. So why hadn't he done anything to avoid this? My friend was inside, getting a grilling. And he'd more or less put her there.

"Are you... annoyed with me?" He put down the rest of his stack. A pro in fidgeting.

I stared dead ahead. "Moi? Why would I be? It's not like you got my best friend in a crap-ton of trouble or anything."

"I... I didn't!" he protested. He clasped his hands together as if he were about to pray. Well, I wasn't a deity, and I wasn't listening. "Have you heard anything? Is Persie okay?"

"What do you think?" I snapped back. "Of course not! You saw the way everyone stared at her, like she was some kind of messed-up science experiment. Plus, let's not forget that I know what she told you. If she let you in on her Purge, then she trusted you. You broke that, and that means you and I have a major issue."

I was scared for Persie, and it was at least partly this guy's fault.

His face fell. "I'm sorry. I didn't mean for this to happen. I tried to catch those pixies without anyone finding out, but... Victoria has a sixth sense for these things. She walked into the Repository while I was trying to chase down the second one." His cheeks reddened. "And let's just say I wasn't being as quiet as I should've been. I crashed into a pillar of orbs and she heard me. But I never meant to put Persie in the spotlight. If I did, I'd have gone to Victoria as soon as Persie told me everything last night. Instead, I stuck to my promise of giving her until later today to try to fix this first, because I could see that was what she wanted... Needed, actually."

I turned to face him, confused. "You didn't tell Victoria? Forgive me for pointing out the obvious, but it sure looks like you did. Who's to say you didn't already decide the deadline had passed? Why else would she have shown the pixies to our class?"

"She showed the pixies to every class!" Nathan went into uber-fidget mode, jiggling his knees anxiously. "But Victoria isn't stupid. She picked up on the same coincidence Charlotte did. She just wanted to make it fair before she came to your class. I think, truly, she wanted to give Persie the benefit of the doubt. Students play pranks here all the time, so there was a chance someone would break and confess to some joke gone wrong, but no one did. Victoria had no choice but to look to the obvious: Persie. And that wasn't because of me. Like I said, I tried to hide what I was doing. I wouldn't have caught the third one without Victoria's help, anyway."

I refused to back down. "Did Victoria ask if you knew anything about them?"

"No," he replied simply.

Too simply. I smelled a rat.

"You'd be terrible at poker."

He twisted a leather bracelet on his wrist. "I told her what they were, that's all, and that there are probably more. But I used my own knowledge, just showing her pages in a book. I didn't mention Persie at all. She didn't ask anything else after that. Maybe she didn't need to. So, perhaps you shouldn't be so quick to blame me." He fiddled so hard with the bracelet that it snapped.

"I'm just trying to piece everything together, since my friend is now swimming in major doo-doo." I couldn't believe I'd just used that word. That spoke volumes about my mental state.

He sighed. "Then here are my two cents, if you're willing to listen."

I shrugged, verging on petulant. "Sure, why not. I've got nothing better to do."

"Charlotte shouldn't have called Persie out so publicly. She should've left that to Victoria to deal with privately. However, Charlotte said something Victoria couldn't ignore. If she had, everyone else would have turned vigilante. Extinct creatures turning up in the same week as a person who can Purge beasts—it's not a big leap, Genie."

You think I don't know that? I reined in my exasperation. He was right. If Victoria had swanned out of the lab without saying a word to Persie, the class would've gone all interrogator on her. Shining lights in her face, the whole shebang. And he sounded genuinely sorry that Persie had been incriminated. Still, that didn't mean we were cool.

"Fine. Say I believe you—here's the million-dollar question. Do you think these pixies had something to do with Xanthippe's disappearance?" I left it lingering in the air like a terrible fart. He looked sweet and unassuming, but maybe that was all some kind of elaborate ploy. I wasn't sure how far he could be trusted.

He hesitated. "Do you?"

"No, of course not!" I barked. How could he even ask that? Even the village clown could see that six-inch critters had nothing to do with the disappearance of a grown woman—and one who had no qualms about hitting back, if the incident in the banquet hall was anything to go by. I didn't care about his credentials. I didn't care that he'd seen that first pixie with his own eyes. It didn't take Einstein to figure out the two events couldn't be related. Unless... maybe they really were like ants, able to carry many times their own body weight? They *were* known to be mischievous. What if they'd taken it too far?

No, I wasn't going down that path. Persie needed me to believe in her. If I had any doubts, I needed to bury them immediately.

He jittered awkwardly on the bench. "I know what you're thinking."

"Do you? Are you a secret Telepath?" I retorted, worried for my friend. And still busy digging a grave for my doubts.

"No, I didn't mean that." He dropped his chin to his chest and sighed heavily. "I just mean, you probably think I'm a fool. How could I look at those creatures and think they had anything to do with Xanthippe's disappearance, right?"

I narrowed my eyes. "Hmm. Maybe you're a bit Telepathic, then. You got the fool part right." Perhaps I was being too hard on him. But his show-and-tell, in addition to Charlotte's snotty words, had resulted in Persie having a one-on-one with the head huntswoman. If that wasn't cause for being stern, then I didn't know what was.

"Allow me to explain." Nathan tugged on the collar of his polo shirt. Seriously, how many of those did he have? "One may look innocuous enough, but when you take into account a horde of these pixies—them being... dangerous isn't that outlandish. Persie didn't have an exact number of how many she'd Purged, but she estimated thirty or more. That's clearly a lot. Pixies are little rascals. They probably don't realize that taking a student is far more than mischief."

"They didn't do this," I replied stubbornly, but my resolve had waned a little.

He paused and hit me with an intense stare. "Why are you so sure?"

Honestly? I don't know. But I couldn't say that, so I let my quick mind do the talking. If only to talk myself around, too.

"Put yourself in their tiny shoes, Nathan. If they've got any sense, they'll have tried to escape the Institute. Once they realized they couldn't get out, they'll have known they were in trouble. And if they saw the pixie Persie caught, they probably understand that they're stuck in a place that traps monsters *professionally*. You were the one who said these things had more pizzazz than people give them credit for. Why would they even risk showing themselves, much less incurring punishment for kidnapping a student?"

Unless they want leverage to bargain for their freedom... The thought came out of nowhere. I guessed I hadn't buried my doubts deep enough. Everyone seemed to think they were responsible, and the timing *was* pretty suspicious... What if... *dammit, no! No what-ifs!* I had to keep these doubts at bay. Didn't I?

Nathan tapped the stack of books. "That's precisely what I intend to find out, if only to take them off the list of potential culprits. You have to understand, pixies haven't been seen for hundreds of years, and we don't know why they stopped being Purged." He took off his glasses to wipe them clean. A nervous tic, I'd noticed.

Or maybe a thoughtful one.

"Sometimes—and this is only a theory of mine—Chaos appears to remove certain beasts from the Purging roster, if you will, because they're considered very dangerous. In the old days, magicals would even pray to Chaos to eradicate certain Purge beasts due to crop failures, attacks, deaths in the family, that sort of thing."

I nodded, partially understanding. "So, you're saying we don't know enough about their behavior or their past rap sheets to exonerate them?"

"Yes, exactly." A curious smile appeared on his lips. Like I'd impressed him. "I haven't found much in the lore to suggest they're particularly dangerous, but I need to do more intensive research before I can say that with certainty. I've already requested access to old archives from the Cornish coven, which might help us understand why they went extinct. Until now, I mean."

His broken bracelet fell to the floor. I automatically picked it back up and handed it to him. "You don't waste time, do you?"

"With a girl missing, we can't hesitate." He took the bracelet from me. Our fingertips brushed, and he looked like he'd been jolted with 1000 volts. Fumbling, he tried to tie the bracelet back on. I thought about helping him, but he'd only have wigged out again. Poor guy had clearly spent so much time with his books that he'd forgotten what human contact felt like. And, dammit, it was kind of endearing. But he'd caught me at a sensitive moment. My friend's fate hung in the balance. Of course, I was going to be affected by his kindness.

I turned to the office door, mostly because I wanted Persie to come striding out, everything a-okay. But partially so Nathan wouldn't feel self-conscious about botching his bracelet repair.

"What's the bracelet for? Hippie mumbo-jumbo?" He didn't strike me as the holistic sort, but if I asked too nicely, he'd have been on his guard.

He braced one of the leather ends against his chest, threading the other end through the loop. "I've had it forever. Someone... uh... sent it to me in the mail for my sixteenth birthday, and I've worn it ever since. I realize it may look like this is the first time I've fixed it, but it's not."

"I bet you had a puka necklace too, huh?" I gave him an olive-branch smile.

He chuckled. "Only until an ex-girlfriend told me it looked ridiculous."

A flicker of irrational jealousy reared its head. "Would you just let me tie it for you? It's killing me, watching you fumble with it."

"Oh... uh... that would be very kind," he said tentatively.

Eager to pivot away from the subject of his ex-girlfriend, I leaned forward and grasped the two ends. He smelled *really* good. Expensive cologne, masculine and clean. "What's going to happen to her?" I needed someone to lie to me and tell me it would be fine.

"Persie?"

I rolled my eyes. "Who else? The Queen of Babylon?"

"Ah... yes, sorry." He adjusted his jacket. No tweed today. Instead, he wore an academic corduroy number over a white polo shirt. Why did he like that look so much? Judging by the anecdote about the puka necklace, his fashion sense must always have been a bit... quirky. "Honestly, I think her ability is too unique and rare for her to be dismissed."

I squinted at him and released his now-tied bracelet. "You have 'but' face."

"Pardon?" He frantically wiped his face with the sleeve of his jacket. I would've laughed if things hadn't felt so serious.

"I mean, you look like you're about to say 'but.' Ergo, 'but' face."

He lowered his arm and turned beet-red. "Oh... very good. Very funny. Perhaps you're right about me checking out that book on humor. You say everything so deadpan. You could tell me there was a nine-foot flamingo behind me, and I'd believe you." He chuckled, embarrassed. "As for my 'but' face... We can't deny the dangers of her ability, much as I'd like to. Personally, I think it's astonishing. However, if, one day, her Purge ends up killing someone, or if the pixies *did* abduct a student, then there may be only one option for her."

Don't you dare say it. My heels started clicking again.

"She may have to be locked away," he said.

"What, like Echidna?" My anger peaked again. "Persie's not a monster, Nathan. She's not the same. And you can't just chuck someone in a box because their ability goes haywire. *Anyone* with magic is capable of messing up. I could, I don't know, freeze someone for a minute too long and accidentally kill them. Would I deserve to be put in a box?"

Nathan's eyebrows knitted together. "That's apples and oranges, Genie. But, yes, you would be culpable if you did something like that, though the accident part would be taken into account. Avarice and Purgatory don't fill up for no reason."

I shuddered at those names. The magical prisons—one for little crimes, one for the nastiest. Persie had freaked out over the average Bestiary box; I hadn't even thought about the biggest glass boxes of them all. Did he mean they might put her in prison? Somehow, that felt way worse than a Bestiary box. She wasn't a monster, but she definitely wasn't a criminal. She didn't deserve to be locked away, end of story. For the first time, I fully realized the validity of her panic. If level-headed Nathan could jump to that idea, then everyone else was probably thinking the same thing.

"She didn't ask for this," I murmured, my heart heavy. Leviathan had wedged her between a rock and a hard place. And she only had me to protect her from the cage-happy ideas of everyone around her. But, if that sentence ever came down on her head, what would I actually be able to do about it? I had Atlantean mettle, sure, but against an army of Victorias, O'Hallorans, Charlottes, and the UCA... I'd be as helpless as my pal. And that scared the heck out of me.

Nathan put a tentative hand on my shoulder. "I know, and that's the worst part about it. This is all new to her. She's had no time to train or prepare. I'm not sure if there's anyone alive who would've been able to make this transition smoother for her." He took his hand away again and looked at it for a second. "But not everyone knows how to sympathize with that."

"Like Charlotte, you mean?" The woman had gone from being my heroine to my nemesis in the space of twenty-four hours. For her to just corner Persie like that... It boiled my blood. I understood that she was worried about her friend, but Persie was *my* friend. And nobody did that to her. Nobody.

"She's not thinking straight. Her best friend has vanished. I'm not siding with her, but be kind to her, if you can. She acted poorly, but can you say you wouldn't have done the same?"

I shrugged. "I like to think I'd have been less of a cow."

He laughed. "Then just do what you do so well and be there for Persie when she gets out. She'll be shaken up, but it won't end here. Charlotte has lit a powder keg of suspicion, and she'll likely have a bone to pick with Persie about these pixies."

One that would undoubtedly turn into a whole skeleton of trouble if a connection really existed between those creatures and Xanthippe's disappearance.

TWELVE

Persie

Silence stretched like taffy being pulled, sticky and terrifyingly mesmerizing. A power play of sorts, each of us trying not to break first. Victoria and I had been sitting quietly for five minutes, and she showed no signs of relenting. She just sat there, in her cream-leather, wingback armchair... watching me. It felt like a test, and my every move could give away valuable information.

I turned my nervous attention to the view. Gray rain pattered against the tall window, and I chased the droplets down the pane with my eyes. Beyond lay an expanse of emerald hills and drystone walls packed with pervasive olive-green moss, stark in contrast to the gloomy sky overhead—though the weather suited my mood perfectly.

There is a luxury in self-reproach. When we blame ourselves, we feel no one else has a right to blame us. It is the confession, not the priest, that gives us absolution. Oscar Wilde might have been onto something there, even if Dorian Gray wasn't exactly the best role model. Part of me felt like I might feel better if I spilled all the beans and got this exhausting mess off my chest once and for all. If it was just about the pixies, I probably would have. But I didn't want to admit my guilt over the pixie debacle if it would instantly tie me, and them, to this missing girl. Not without solid evidence that they were involved, which I refused to believe.

"You may begin whenever you feel ready," Victoria prompted. She'd broken the silence first, but it didn't feel like a victory. It felt like a warning: speak, or I'll have no choice but to take your silence as culpability. That sort of thing.

I looked away from the window. "I don't know what you want me to say."

"There are a few less-intellectually-gifted students in this Institute, Persie, but you're not one of them." She leaned forward and steepled her fingers, the default setting for an adult with an axe to grind. "Xanthippe is missing, and there are extinct monsters loose in the Institute. They didn't just wander in, Persie, and Xanthippe didn't just wander out."

I shrugged, picking at the hem of my sweatshirt. "She might have."

"Then let's set Xanthippe aside for a moment." Victoria forced me to hold her intense gaze. I'd never seen eyes so dark, not up close. Dark eyes were usually brown, but her irises appeared to bleed directly out of her pupils. "The pixies, Persie. What do you know about them?"

"Uh… they're rare." I gulped loudly.

Victoria lifted a finger. "Not rare. Extinct. A subtle but important difference. One that you're hopefully going to shed some light on. Any information, at this point, is vital."

But they didn't take her! I wanted to shout it until I turned blue in the face, but a nagging doubt held my tongue. I sat with the idea that they might've been capable for a second, trying to make sense of it. Perhaps it was a mischief that had gone too far, and they didn't intend to hurt her. Maybe they'd give her back when they got bored of the trick. My mind took a dive into darker territory. What if it was a hostage situation? We took one of theirs, so they took one of ours. My stomach jittered with nervous butterflies. I'd seen the she-pixie's reaction when she'd been put in the Repository orb, and if that anger happened to spread across the whole horde... Perhaps it would be enough to warrant an abduction.

"I don't know much about them, Ms. Jules." It wasn't a lie. I knew about as much as Nathan.

She cut to the chase. "Did you create them, Persie?"

I swore not to disappoint you, didn't I? I thought about lying to save my own butt. But she clearly already knew. I exhaled and said, "I Purged last night, after five days without one. I've never Purged more than one creature at a time before, but it happened, and the pixies came out of it. They wrecked my bedroom and set fire to the rug. I tried to get a handle on it, but by the time I put the fire out, the pixies had opened the door. I went out looking for them and caught one in Nathan O'Hara's room. He found me in there, and I didn't want to lie, so I showed him the creature and we put it in the Repository together. He wanted to help with the rest, but I ran off because I wanted to clean up my own mess. I wanted to prove I could control this, and I was... embarrassed that I'd screwed up again." I took a deep breath, and realization dawned. I'd just accidentally thrown Nathan under the bus.

I'd completely forgotten to keep him out of it. I opened my mouth to blurt an excuse for him, but Victoria interrupted before I could.

"It's okay, Persie. I already guessed Nathan was helping you when I found him ricocheting around in the Repository, trying to catch two more." She gave the ghost of a smile, her eyes twinkling with surprising warmth. "He's a good lad. But I wanted to hear it from you, anyway."

I lurched forward in my chair. "It wasn't like I swore him to secrecy or anything, Ms. Jules. I know he would've told you if you'd asked, and I was going to come back to him for help if I needed it, but I was so desperate to get these pixies back on my own. I've been looking for them relentlessly—the whole night, actually. And I came close to catching a few. I only stopped because of the cleaners, and then my classes. But I *was* going to get you involved if they did anything bad. In fact, I made the decision this morning, after I realized the job was too big, that I was going to come to you and tell you everything at lunchtime. But, obviously, things didn't work out that way." I paused for another breath. "Please, Ms. Jules, you have to know that I was trying to do everything possible not to get expelled... or worse. I *did* intend to tell you. I just wanted to prove, to some degree, that I don't need to rely on anyone else to scoop up my Purge debris." I sank back in the chair, breathing like I'd run a marathon.

Victoria observed me quietly, her expression unreadable. Did she believe me? Did she think I was an idiot for trying to go it alone? Did she respect me for deciding to tell her, even though I hadn't gotten to her in time? Did she have an expulsion form at the ready, to kick me out for making all the wrong decisions? Even the warmth had gone from her eyes, replaced with a cool, blank nothing.

All the while, I shifted uncomfortably on the chair, willing her to release the hounds or tell me everything would be okay. One or the other, but quickly, before I exploded with nerves.

"And when did this Purge occur?" she said, eventually. A weirdly innocuous question, considering everything I'd just thrown at her.

"Uh... around seven-thirty. I'd just gotten off the phone with my parents."

She nodded slowly. "You didn't say anything to them about an imminent Purge?"

"No." My head sagged forward, to hide the heat in my cheeks.

She continued with an unsettling composure. "And did you happen to see Xanthippe Evershot at any time during your scouring of the Institute?"

"I wouldn't know if I had, Ms. Jules. I've never met her, but I can say that I didn't really see anyone while I was out searching for the pixies. I bumped into Nathan, Charlotte, and Genie, but that's about it." I scooted forward on the chair cushion. "I'd still like to help catch the pixies, Ms. Jules. That's what I was going to ask when I told you everything. I don't understand their language, but they seem to understand me. Maybe they'd be able to give us some idea of where she is, if they saw her, or if they know what happened to her."

Even if it's just to get people off my back. I felt awful about Xanthippe, but I also wanted to give the pixies a chance to prove themselves innocent. It was funny to me—and not funny ha-ha—that people immediately laid blame on monsters. In my experience, humans were usually the culprits, especially if they had Purge-beast scapegoats to pin their misdeeds on. Aside from Leviathan, and the will of his dead mother, I'd never heard of a single beast who wanted to wreak havoc on the world, but I'd heard of plenty of humans.

Then, a curious notion came to me. "The first priority is, obviously, making sure Xanthippe is safely returned." I paused, gathering courage. "But what if this has nothing to do with the pixies at all? Don't get me wrong, the timing is very suspicious, but that doesn't mean they're to blame. What if this has something to do with magicals instead?"

"Go on..." Victoria urged.

I knew I might get into trouble with my parents for revealing this, but it made a lot of sense. More sense than a bunch of pixies spiriting away a student.

"Well, my mom and dad are in the middle of an investigation. They're looking for magicals who've been abducted across the US. It's happening more and more frequently, and they don't know who's doing it. What if it's more global than they realize? What if it's linked to Xanthippe's disappearance, too?"

Her sleek eyebrow raised a quarter of an inch. A hint of surprise. "I admire your flexible thinking, but I find that highly unlikely. We currently have no clear evidence that Xanthippe has been hurt, nor any sign of a struggle or external abduction." She flattened her palms onto the black marble desk, where veins of gold slithered through the darkness. "It's my hope that the lass will show up on her own, but we do have to consider other possibilities."

I nodded eagerly. "That's what I'm trying to say. Talk to my mom at the SDC about this. You might find out you're investigating the same thing, and a problem shared is a problem halved, right?"

Victoria physically sat back, as though she couldn't even be near the idea. "This is an internal matter, Persie. Liaising with outside territories is out of the question, but we will conduct interviews with those who were close to Xanthippe within the Institute. That said, until we are able to exclude the pixies as suspects, they will be considered an immediate threat and hunted accordingly."

"What?! No! Sure, capture them, but don't kill them!" I blurted out, my protective instinct flaring. The same one I'd felt when I'd held the she-pixie in my hands and knew I could've crushed her or spared her.

Victoria mustered a bemused snort. "I didn't say I'd have them killed, Persie. That's not what hunting is about. You know that." Her eyes narrowed slightly, as though she was wary of my impulsive outburst. Nathan sympathized with the monsters, in his own way, but I wondered if anyone had outright suggested an alternative to catching and trapping them. Maybe there wasn't one.

"Sorry…" I forced a smile. "It's been a long day. My head's not on straight."

She visibly relaxed. "They'll be captured in the usual fashion and sent to the Bestiary, though I don't imagine they'll be much use to the Bestiary's energy supplies." Her fingertips toyed with a small, silver clover on her lapel, with the tiniest emerald in the center. "Although we'll have to keep some specimens for training and research purposes, given their... recent resurgence into the world."

Specimens? The word riled me up, and I struggled to conceal my distaste. They weren't lab rats. They had thoughts and personalities, and sass by the bucketload. I didn't like the idea of them being prodded and poked by the Institute's researchers. I knew that not all of them would be like Nathan.

"How many pixies are we dealing with? An estimate will suffice," Victoria said.

I tried to picture the mayhem in my bedroom, my mouth moving in a silent tally. "Um... a couple dozen, I think."

Truthfully, I had no clue—except that there were definitely *more* than two dozen. By giving her a loose number, I'd leave some wiggle room to find some on my own and find out if they knew anything about Xanthippe's disappearance. Getting them to trust me enough to tell me, however, would be the tricky part, and time was of the essence. Everyone knew that the first 72 hours in a missing persons case were the most crucial.

"That shouldn't be too challenging." Victoria seemed pleased. If I'd said there were a thousand, even as a joke, I wondered if her calm façade would've cracked at all. What did it take to rattle the fabled Ms. Jules? I wasn't sure, but I liked that she seemed completely fearless. It made the rest of us feel more at ease.

Once I've caught some... then what? If I put them in a Repository orb, I'd hate myself for it. I hadn't been able to stop thinking about the she-pixie and her abject misery. Perhaps if I talked to Nathan about options, I might be able to come up with a better solution for the pixies. I could hide them somewhere safe, or set them free elsewhere, far from the Institute. Anyway, I'd have to cross that bridge when I came to it. What mattered now was capturing as many pixies as possible before the hunters got to them. Some would end up in boxes, but not all, and that was the most I could ask for at the moment.

"That'll be all, Persie." Victoria stood and nodded to the door.

My heart swelled. "Does that mean I'm not expelled?"

"Why would I expel you?" Her expression softened a touch. "You showed perseverance and fortitude by trying to remedy the situation yourself. You were honest when it mattered. You sought help when it mattered. The Institute is here to teach you control, not to punish your mistakes. Do I wish you'd come to me sooner? Yes. That is why I gave you a direct line to my phone, and an emergency beeper. Do I understand why you didn't? Also, yes. Though I believe you when you say you made the decision to come clean with me, even though the pixies were discovered prior to that. That shows an understanding of your limitations. So, no, you're not expelled, though you *will* leave the pixie capture to the experts now."

"Thank you, Ms. Jules." I scraped back the chair and hurried away before she could change her mind. Plus, I didn't want my face to give me away.

I had no intention of leaving it to the experts. Not entirely, at least. If I could use the pixies to find Xanthippe and exonerate them in the same breath, then I would. That way, everyone here would understand that it wasn't always the monster's fault. I had nothing but respect for Victoria, but her "they're fuel and nothing more" attitude left a bitter taste in my mouth.

If it's not the pixies, then who is responsible? That was a perplexing thought for another day. And not one I could consider just yet, not with the pixies at the top of the culprit list.

THIRTEEN

Persie

I walked out to find Genie waiting, midway through a tense conversation with Nathan. He shot up like I'd caught him doing something wrong. Genie jumped up with him and threw her arms around me.

"Persie! Thank Chaos, are you okay?" She clung to me and I held her back.

Meanwhile, Nathan scrambled to get a pile of books together. He made an awkward bow in our direction before disappearing into Victoria's office. The door closed behind him with an ominous thud. I wanted to warn him that I'd unintentionally thrown him to the lions, but Victoria hadn't seemed remotely surprised by Nathan's involvement. I hoped she'd go easy on him. She'd said he was a nice "lad," after all.

"Well, I'm not expelled." I mustered a stilted laugh. "But we've got work to do."

She pulled away. "We do?"

"Oh, yes, and we're starting with the engineering lab." I led her away by the arm, filling her in on the way. "So, you see the predicament here. We've got to beat the hunters, and that calls for puzzle boxes."

"If you downplayed it to Victoria, how many pixies are we *actually* talking about?" She eyed me with a glimmer of approval, and a hint of "I'm not going to like this, am I?"

I pretended to count on my fingers. "Maybe thirty to forty."

"Holy crap, Persie!" She clamped her hand over her mouth, eyes bugging. "That means… we need to catch, like, three dozen?!"

"Something like that." I dragged her faster through the halls. By now, everyone would have dispersed from engineering. They were probably in the common areas or their bedrooms, having a long old gossip about how unsuitable I was to be a student here. They'd have to vent their energy somewhere now that Victoria had put the Institute into a loose version of lockdown, with no classes for the foreseeable future. At least it would make my classmates easier to avoid. I just hoped Naomi had hung around so we could ask her for some puzzle boxes. After dodging an expulsion, I didn't feel like sliding back into the firing line for stealing.

"Let me get this straight." Genie strode along beside me, our arms still linked. "While the Institute is investigating Xanthippe's disappearance and the potential connection to your ankle-biters, we're going on a mission of our own to try and catch as many pixies as possible? Aren't we just doing the same thing as the hunters?"

I shook my head. "Nope. We're going to get the pixies to help us."

She spun me around and put her palm to my forehead. "Are you feeling okay? Do you need to sit down and take a few minutes? I think you've lost the plot."

"This is the only way," I insisted, removing her hand and continuing down the corridor. "They can sneak into places that we can't. They might've seen something nobody else did. And, on the off chance that they did this, I can hopefully persuade them to come clean and show us where Xanthippe is."

"Is this about the dream? Don't get me wrong, I see why it'd frighten the crap out of you. But if Victoria didn't expel you or anything, then maybe everything's peachy. She'll just give her hunters a piece of her mind for not watching you when they were supposed to, and that'll be that."

It's not enough. I pressed on, as determined in my stride as I was in my mind. Clearing the pixies of Xanthippe's disappearance might have been the one thing that could stop the whole Institute from looking at me like a ticking timebomb. Victoria had not been unsympathetic, but if enough people pressured her to get rid of me, maybe there would come a time when she had to buckle to keep the peace. If I could nip that in the bud, then I could get on with the training I came here for.

I glanced at my friend. "I just want the blame to fall on the right culprit, that's all. And I want to try and get Xanthippe back with the pixies' help, to show that they're not a threat... and neither am I."

"Aye, aye, captain." She pretended to salute, seemingly satisfied. Weirdly, it used to be me who went along with *her* madcap schemes. Now the tables had turned, and she was once again demonstrating why she was my best friend.

Ringleader or accomplice, here she stood, at my side, ready for anything.

The halls lay eerily empty on our speed-walk to the engineering lab, our footsteps echoing loudly, as if a gang of people were following us. I had to look back a few times, just to make sure we were alone. I listened to the percussion of our footsteps until we reached Naomi's gadget sanctuary.

"Ms. Hiraku, are you in here?" The lab appeared to be as unoccupied as the rest of the Institute, the room miraculously cleared of any evidence that there had ever been a class.

Without the clutter, I saw more of the lab as a whole. Shelves filled with gleaming metal devices, and jars with vividly colored powders and liquids inside. At the back of the room was a diorama of sorts, showing the evolution of the Repository orbs. I imagined, since they used a lot of Atlantean technology, that the Institute's engineers had melded the old glass-box tech with new knowledge to make the orbs they had today. Away to one side, I spotted one of Naomi's Omnispheres in a state of mechanical undress, connected to a beeping machine with red and green wires.

An abrupt bump, followed by a sharp "ow," cut through the silence. Naomi popped up from beneath her workbench like a cartoon gopher, rubbing her head. "Girls. Didn't you hear Ms. Jules? Classes are canceled until further notice." She winced, trying to squint up at her head injury. "Honestly, I'm not sure what I'm supposed to do with myself. I know, I know, teachers are meant to daydream about snow days and vacation days, but I like to be busy! I don't like things quiet."

I leaned against one of the workbenches. "We know, we just came by to talk about something."

"You did?!" She looked incredibly relieved.

Genie chuckled as she came to stand beside me. "What were you doing down there?"

"Cleaning. I thought I'd make a start. It's spring, after all." She scurried off to an old tin kettle, which she, rather alarmingly, put on top of a tripod and lit a Bunsen burner underneath. Even in tea-making, she was a scientist to the core. Then she set about preparing three mugs and three elegant, painted ceramic strainers for the tea leaves. I wasn't much of a tea drinker myself, but I wasn't about to turn it down, under the circumstances. "Now, what can I do for you lovely ladies?"

Genie and I exchanged a conspiratorial glance before I answered. "Could you show us how the puzzle boxes work, again?"

"Absolutely!" She checked her vintage wristwatch—a rose gold face with a blush leather strap. "In exactly... thirty-eight seconds.

Oh, and make sure you let the leaves steep, or it'll taste like trash."
She stood, timing it to the last moment.

What I guessed to be thirty-eight seconds later, the kettle started
squealing. Watching Naomi had the same effect as watching an elaborate ballet. In one fluid motion, she plucked up the kettle, poured
the water into each teacup, set the kettle down, and lifted the cups
on a tray. Balancing them perfectly on one hand, she scooped up a
puzzle box with the other and made her way to our workbench.

"I don't suppose this technically counts as a class, with just the
two of you." Naomi spread the cups equidistant from each other.
She was probably one of those gifted people who could draw a
perfect circle freehand. "It's more like a tutorial, in a way. Ah... I
remember those from my days at Cambridge. Best years of my life."
She stared wistfully into the distance.

Genie propped her chin on her hands, gazing at Naomi with
newfound admiration. "You went to Cambridge?"

"Both of them, yes." Naomi scooted around to the other side of
the workbench while Genie and I sat down.

I tilted my head. "Huh?"

"The magical one and the non-magical one, but I loved them
equally. Punting down the River Cam, cycling through the town on
a summer's day. Wonderful times." Naomi shook her head like a wet
dog. "But you haven't come here to hear me reminisce. Though you
can, if you like? I'll have a lot of time on my hands—too much time,
until Victoria asks me to join the search. Where was I? I guess you
could say my train of thought left the station."

"Puzzle boxes," I prompted.

"Yes, these magnificent beauties!" Naomi picked up a sea-green
box, with the silvered patterns. "Simple enough once you know how,
as with most things. First, make sure all the designs are aligned.
Then, when you've managed to immobilize a monster, you press the
harp button and throw this luscious bit of ingenuity at it. It'll get

sucked right in, and the lid snaps shut. After that, it's a case of twisting the box so the designs get all muddled, and you have it locked in and ready for transport."

Genie nodded along. "And how do you get the creature into a Bestiary box or a Repository bubble?"

"That's the easiest part. Twist everything back so the designs align again, press the harp button and, presto, you've made a deposit at the Bank of the Bestiary."

Naomi showed us, turning the narrow slats of the box backward and forward. She pressed the harp button and the lid slid back, revealing a blood-red interior. Fragments of gemstone and glowing hexes shone, neatly arranged on the inner walls like a circuitry board. For such a small box, it was overflowing with magical technology. It certainly put the plain Mason jars to shame, though I liked the familiarity of those.

"Can I try?" Genie asked eagerly.

"Of course you can." Naomi pushed the box toward her and turned her attention to her cup of tea. I watched her take out the strainer and set it delicately on the workbench. She lifted the cup to her nose ceremoniously and inhaled, her eyes closing contentedly. Only then did she take a sip. I wondered if a whiff of the stuff would relax me for what I had to do next.

Instead, I took a deep breath. "Could we get a crate of those boxes, to help with the pixie hunt?"

Naomi stilled mid-sip. "Has this request been sanctioned by Victoria?"

I stared down into the lurid green liquid of my cup, thinking for a moment. I considered lying, but I didn't want to get Naomi in trouble.

"No." I sighed, choosing the righteous path.

"Persie, I'm sorry, but I can't hand over any puzzle boxes without Victoria's permission." Naomi sounded apologetic. I'd already known the answer when the truth had tripped off my tongue. Nobody defied Victoria lightly, if at all.

Genie set down the puzzle box. "Shouldn't, not can't. What if we were to tell you that we had a really good reason for wanting them?"

"I would listen, but that doesn't mean my answer would change." Naomi smiled, her eyes glittering with curiosity.

"How about this: These are Persie's creations that are on the loose, and she wants to tidy up the mess she made." Genie cast me an apologetic glance. "You're all about showing and not telling at this Institute, so how is Persie supposed to learn if she's not allowed to fix the situation herself? It'd be like one of your Omnispheres glitching during an experiment, and someone telling you that you can't make tweaks so it doesn't glitch next time."

Naomi swirled her tea. "Interesting."

"Plus, she knows these creatures better than anyone." Genie dove back in. "Victoria's worried about them snatching other students, but that won't happen to Persie. She made them, so they respect her. If anyone can catch them, it's her. But she needs puzzle boxes to do it."

Naomi looked back at her private project, the exposed inner workings of her Omnisphere on display. I saw the cogs whirring behind her eyes, as intricate and sensitive as her self-made device.

"I created them, Ms. Hiraku," I said softly. "All I'm asking for is an opportunity. They're my Omnispheres, and I want to make sure they don't hurt anyone. Please think about it before you decide. Who are they more likely to listen to—hunters they're afraid of, or the woman who brought them back from extinction?"

Naomi took a lengthy sip of her tea, leaving Genie and me on tenterhooks. "You make an excellent argument, but..."

My heart sank. It was going to be another no, and I really didn't want to have to steal the boxes. Nor did I want to rely on the handful of Mason jars I had in my backpack. They wouldn't be close to enough, but with a decent number of puzzle boxes *and* the jars—then we'd be in business.

"But?" Genie urged.

Naomi sighed. "I can offer you five boxes. That's all I can spare."

"Seriously?!" I yelped with excitement.

"Yes, but I have provisos." She waggled a stern finger at us. "They are to be brought back as soon as you're done with them, and all captured pixies are to go to the Repository every single time. No keeping them as pet projects, tempting as that might sound. The Institute is already on edge about this fiasco, and they will be until Xanthippe is returned. Don't make me regret this, do you understand?"

I grinned at Genie. "We won't let you down, Ms. Hiraku. Thank you, thank you, thank you!"

"Why do I already feel like I'm making a huge mistake?" Naomi griped, but she didn't rescind her offer, and that was all that mattered. After a relentless day and night, things were finally starting to go my way.

FOURTEEN

Persie

Puzzle boxes and Mason jars safely stowed in my backpack, Genie and I set off on our two-woman mission through the Institute. Keeping things nonchalant, of course, so as not to attract any unwanted attention. We paused beside display cases and pretended to read the notes, all the while eyeing our surroundings for any whisper of a pixie. Black-suited hunters swarmed the main corridors and common areas, encouraging us to stick to the paths less traveled. The pixies wouldn't be foolish enough to come out where their would-be captors were congregating, which made me wonder why they were being so obvious. Perhaps the hunters had some sort of flushing operation to siphon the creatures into one spot.

Anyway, their plan of action didn't concern me too much. We just had to stay out of their way and keep our heads down. Not literally, though, or we wouldn't be able to scan for the mischief-makers.

"Anything?" Genie whispered, as we walked down a narrow corridor that housed a bunch of study doors. They had bronze plaques outside, bearing names I didn't recognize: *Scheherazade*

Rouhani, Advanced Tactical Practice; Damian Greatorex, Covert Operations; Kofi Smithson, External Affairs. I guessed they weren't people we needed to know in our first year. There were so many people in this place, from students to teachers to graduated hunters to visiting hunters to general administration, that I doubted anyone knew everyone's name.

I shook my head. "Not even a wing flutter."

"They can't, like, go invisible, can they?" Genie stopped for a swig of water.

I shrugged reluctantly. "I don't think so."

"I love you dearly, Pers, but why did you have to Purge something that's been extinct for ages? Couldn't you have gone for a critter that at least has a crystal-clear entry in monster history?" She pretended to flip open a book and run a finger down the imaginary page. "Bullet-point one: this creature *can't* disappear at will. Bullet-point two: leave out a cookie and it'll come running. That'd be sweet right now."

"I don't get a lot of choice in what I Purge." I took the water flask she offered and gulped down a mouthful. This secret-agent stuff made a girl sweat. No wonder my mom always came back from her missions looking disheveled. "Hey, maybe when I get better at this Purging stuff, I'll be able to decide what I create."

Genie laughed. "Promise you'll make them small and singular?"

I crossed my heart.

"Come on." Genie made to continue up the corridor. "Let's check the orchard, see if we can notice any signs of a pixie shindig."

Twenty minutes later, we had fresh air on our faces. It made for a nice change from being stuck indoors. There didn't appear to be any black-suits out here, either. It gave me hope that we were on the right track.

"I should've worn an extra sweater," Genie grumbled as we ambled through the trees. The spitting rain pattered at the leaves, and misty rays of dulled sunlight sliced through the canopy, dappling the ground below. The weather might've been grim, but the rain and soft light soothed my raw nerves. The earth was covered in a mass of foliage in various stages of decay: fresh green leaves on top of their dry, russet-toned forefathers, with the browned mulch of older dead carpeting the ground beneath. Tufts of grass pushed through, creating a pretty patchwork of color.

Admiring the scenery, I almost forgot why we were really there. In fact, I was so engrossed in the shade and light that I didn't see the figure stalking toward us until she was beside us.

"Shouldn't you be in your rooms, staying out of the way?" Charlotte shoved her hands aggressively into the pockets of her jacket. Her hazel eyes fixed me with a stony glare. "Hunters are sweeping the place, and I don't want anyone holding them up."

I rubbed my arms to chase out the cold. "There weren't any hunters out here, so we figured it'd be okay." I understood her frostiness more than she knew. If Genie were missing, I'd be hostile to anyone who I thought was remotely responsible.

"Well, it's not okay." Her voice hitched for a split second, exposing some serious subtext. She was torn up about this, and who wouldn't be? She wanted her friend back, even if her friend did happen to be a bigoted snob. After all, friends were the family we chose for ourselves. Maybe Charlotte saw something in Xanthippe that we didn't.

Genie looped her arm through mine. "Do you want us to go back inside?"

"I can't make you." Charlotte scuffed her boot through the dead leaves. "I'm just saying, don't get underfoot. There's important work going on."

"We know," I said softly.

Charlotte's head snapped up. "The Institute has never had anything like this happen before. My mom is so proud of that, and so was I. But the two of you are here for a week and all hell breaks loose." She hissed a breath through her teeth, visibly trying to calm down. "Do you have any idea what kind of damage this could do to my family name, if it ever got out? We're just lucky it's Victoria in charge, and not some sap who cracks under pressure. Meanwhile, my friend is…" She trailed off, dragging in unstable breaths.

"I'm sorry. I understand that you're hurting." I tried to offer an olive branch, but I'd never been one for good timing. She didn't want sympathetic words from me right now. She wanted someone to blame.

Her eyes narrowed. "I just want to ask one thing, and I want an honest answer because I'm on the verge of a nervous breakdown. Did your monsters do this? And don't pretend they're not yours; the math isn't hard." Bitterness dripped from her words.

"Why don't we take the animosity down a notch, huh?" Genie cut in, pulling on my arm so I ended up a half step behind her.

I smiled at my friend. "It's fine, Genie. It's a valid question." I held my ground and answered Charlotte. "Not that I know of. They're not cruel or malevolent by nature, so it doesn't seem like something they'd do."

"What, are you also best buddies with the things you Purge?" Charlotte chewed her bottom lip.

"No, but I read up on them."

She snorted. "Is that what you're carrying around in that massive backpack? Books on all the creatures you've spat into this world?" Her eyes flitted upward, like she was trying to blink away tears. She was the model hunter with a perfect record and a famous mom—she carried a lot on her shoulders. And, hey, at least she could actually match up to her mom's legacy. That couldn't be said for everyone. But it was sort of humanizing to see that exterior slough away, leaving behind a sad girl who just wanted her friend back. It certainly made it easier to ignore the insults.

"What did you say to her?" Genie straightened, shoulders squared. I nudged her gently to get her to back down, but it was like trying to wrangle a bull who'd seen red.

"Oh, come on, you can't say you admire that messed-up ability?" Charlotte refused to look at me. "It's unnatural."

You're not wrong there... I doubted she'd believe my sincerity if I agreed, though.

Genie laughed coldly. "Isn't that what your friend thinks of me?"

"I didn't tell them to gang up on you!" Charlotte's eyes widened, a flicker of guilt crossing her face. "I had nothing to do with the other night. I stood up for you!"

"Yeah, to save face," Genie shot back. "But that doesn't mean I think your friend should've been taken. We're not out here to cause problems. I hope your friend gets found, because I'd be out of my mind, too, if anything like that happened to Persie."

Charlotte gaped like a beached fish, and I breathed a subtle sigh of relief. I didn't want a repeat of last night. Impulsively, I made a bold move. "Believe it or not, we're trying to help. That's why we're out here." I pulled one of the puzzle boxes out of my bag and showed it to her. "We're looking for the pixies so we can catch them. Same as everyone in there."

Charlotte eyed the box. "Where did you get that from? Did you steal it from Naomi's storage?"

"No, of course we didn't." Genie rolled her eyes. "You're not listening, are you? We. Are. Trying. To. Help!"

"You expect me to believe—"

Just then, the intercom system screeched to life, cutting her off. A deafening siren blared three times before a familiar voice crackled through the speakers: Victoria's voice.

"This is your head huntswoman speaking. Another magical has been reported missing. As of this moment, the Institute is now on high alert," she boomed. "Everyone, return to your rooms immediately and remain there until further notice. The Institute is now officially in lockdown." Three more piercing sirens sounded, ending the transmission.

Charlotte rounded on us. "No way. You two are going straight to Victoria's office for stealing Institute property."

"We didn't steal anything! Do you think I'd have shown it to you if we had?" I held the puzzle box to my chest, in case she tried to take it. We didn't have enough to lose one. "Look, we really are trying to help. Naomi gave us these—after a *lot* of persuading, I might add—because I have to learn to get my ability under control. That means being able to capture what I Purge. I know these pixies better than anyone, and doing my part is the best thing I can do for myself, your friend, and the Institute right now."

Charlotte hesitated and I watched a flurry of emotions skitter across her face, morphing between fury, confusion, sadness, pain, and something else. Understanding, maybe? It could've been wishful thinking, but I wanted to believe that Charlotte had some faith in me. In a lot of ways, we weren't so different.

"Charlotte, you and I are in the same boat." I paused, hoping I was hitting the right nerve. If she didn't buy this, I'd be back in Victoria's office sooner than I wanted. "We both have a lot to live up to. Expectations that we didn't ask for. And we both care deeply for our best friends. I'm trying to meet those expectations, but I can't do that if you don't help us to help you."

Charlotte frowned, her hard eyes scrutinizing me.

Should I have kept quiet? Only she had the answer.

She unleashed a frustrated sigh. "Do you really think you can make a difference in finding Xanthippe?"

"Yes." For the first time in a while, I spoke with genuine confidence. One way or another, I felt certain my pixies were the key to solving this.

Her teary eyes held my firm gaze. "Fine, but if you screw up the hunt, I'll turn you in. Just stay out of everyone's way and focus on catching the pixies." She looked over at the door leading to the building. "I need to get to Victoria's office. There'll be another briefing now that she's put us on high alert."

"But you won't say anything?" Genie interjected.

"No, I won't." She shook her head, like she couldn't believe what she was doing. "I get why you want to do this, and we need as many hands on deck as possible. People who know the enemy. You Purged them. They might listen to you, or at least come out of hiding for you."

They're not the enemy. I held my tongue to avoid shattering this fragile treaty.

Charlotte walked away, her shoulders slumped. The walk of a weary woman. I watched her go, my chest uneasy. "Do you think she'll tell Victoria?"

"I hope not, for both our sakes."

I put the puzzle box back in my bag. "Well, one thing I know for certain is that Victoria just threw a massive wrench in the works. How're we supposed to sneak around, hunting pixies, if everyone who isn't a hunter is on lockdown?"

"Carefully." Genie flashed me a reassuring grin. One of her best ones.

"And what about this other magical?" I readjusted the strap of my bag. "I might've believed the pixies were responsible for one disappearance. But two? I don't buy it at all. These monsters are new to the Institute. They wouldn't have a clue where to hide two people."

Genie looked away. "How can you be sure?"

"I've got a… weird sense about it. Like, I can feel they're confused, and they're frightened, but I don't feel any malice." I didn't know how else to put it. Like the gargoyle in the training room, it was like our emotions were running parallel, giving me a vague sense of how they were feeling—though it was, admittedly, a distant sense.

"You're certain?" Genie still didn't look at me.

I nodded. "I don't think I've ever been more certain."

"Then… things don't add up," she agreed, with a note of reluctance that threw me slightly. Had they gotten to her, too? I guessed the fact that she was still standing at my side meant she had some faith in what I said. I hoped it prevailed, because I didn't know what I would do if I lost my last source of support.

I drew a lungful of fresh air. "Why is no one suspecting someone closer to home— someone who'd know where to hide abductees? In true crime shows, nine times out of ten the murderer is someone who knew the victim."

"Don't go throwing the 'M' word around, Pers. We don't know that they're dead, yet." Genie urged me toward the door. "But I think you're onto something. All we've got to do is clear the pixies' name before anyone will listen to alternatives."

If only it were that easy.

The stakes had risen with the addition of a new missing person, but that was all the more reason to keep going. I wouldn't sit in my room and leave it to hunters who had no emotional link with the pixies and obeyed the party line of "capture at all costs." The connection between my creations and the disappearances seemed murky at best, but we wouldn't change anyone's mind by arguing. We needed hard evidence, which would prove tricky to find if my wayward beasties kept up the Houdini act. Or worse, if the Institute caught them all and sent them away before I could gain their trust and get answers.

"Help me out, wherever you are," I whispered to the orchard. "Help me to help you, or we might all end up in a box."

FIFTEEN

Persie

I took refuge in Samuel Beckett after a fruitless day of pixie-searching and hunter-avoidance. *Ever tried. Ever failed. No matter. Try again. Fail again. Fail better.* Considering we were supposed to be on lockdown, there had been a few close calls with the black-suits, but Genie's bag of tricks had gotten us out undetected. I owed her expert thief of a grandfather a huge debt. If I ever went to Atlantis, I'd pay homage.

"Why won't you come out?" I asked my bedroom, though I'd already checked the place twice for any lingering critters. Now, I sat at my desk in the glow of my last lamp, the sun having gone down hours ago. If I'd known yesterday how much things would change in the space of twenty-four hours... Well, what would I have done? Maybe I'd have tried to block the door or opened the window to let the pixies out. Maybe I'd have done the exact same thing. Maybe I'd have just called Victoria from the outset, though her talk of turning the pixies into 'specimens' had confirmed that we viewed things differently. It had confirmed why I'd tried to catch them alone in the first place, too. For their sake. If only life were like a painting or a sketch, where I could swipe white paint over the bits I didn't like or erase the wonky parts and start fresh. But reality didn't allow for do-overs.

At a loss, I took out my phone and called home. It rang twice, and my mom's face appeared in fuzzy hologram. Truthfully, I had an ulterior motive for calling her. If she could just give me an iota of intel that I could link to the disappearance of the magicals here, that would be a heck of a start to my alternative abduction theories.

"It must be Christmas, getting two calls in two days!" She grinned, and my heart felt a tiny bit lighter. "How are you feeling, sweetheart? You hung up rather abruptly last night. Everything okay with the... taco incident?"

I nodded. "I managed to sleep it off, though you should see the bathroom. It looks like a colony of bats had a fiesta in there." I couldn't bring myself to tell her about the Purge or the missing people, so I bent the story slightly. If you squinted really hard, a pixie could pass for a brightly-colored, really skinny, humanoid bat.

"Lovely." My mom pulled a funny, disgusted face. "I hope you're drinking plenty of fluids and sugary things to get your electrolytes back up?"

I chuckled. "Lots of tea. The Irish love their tea."

"Tell me about it. Your dad used to go crazy whenever he came back from a trip to the motherland—he'd have crates of Barry's Tea and bottles of red lemonade in his luggage. Weird stuff, but apparently it's a huge deal over there. Maybe you could get a bottle to help your tummy?" She leaned closer to the camera, as though she could reach me through it.

"I'm already much better," I promised, which wasn't a complete lie. The effects of the Purge had worn off after I'd gotten my three hours of sleep this morning, and I only had a few aches here and there to suggest I'd Purged at all. Aside from what came out of me, the recovery time on Purging appeared to be the second biggest surprise of this ability. With the banshee, it took days; with the griffin, the hydra, and the gargoyle, it had been hours; and with the others, I was more or less fine immediately afterward. I guessed it depended on the power of the monster. Sure, I'd Purged lots of pixies, but maybe their cumulative power wasn't as big as other things I'd created.

I wanted to tell my mom everything, but she'd only have worried. And not the usual motherly worry, either. She'd have been battering down the mirrors and trying to take over Victoria's investigation before I could even end the call. I did *not* want to see a stand-off between the head huntswoman and my mom, but I *did* need to pry some information out of her regarding the missing magical cases. A delicate venture, which would call for stealth and dexterity.

"You still haven't Purged?" A note of expectation hung in my mom's voice, like she suspected I had and was giving me the chance to come clean.

I picked up a pencil and doodled nervously on the cover of my sketchbook. "No, still nothing."

"You can tell me, you know. I won't go all tiger-mom." She looked through the camera so earnestly that I hated not telling her everything. But with the pixies at the forefront of this investigation, I couldn't tell her one thing without revealing the other. And I didn't want to betray Victoria's trust, after she'd just let me off the hook… not any more than I already had by hunting the pixies when she'd told me not to. More than that, I didn't want to dump a new layer of stress onto my mom's already packed plate.

I made sure to look into her hologram eyes. "Honestly, aside from the bats in the bathroom, I'm fine. But what about you? How are things at the SDC?"

"Busy," my mom admitted. "I've got paperwork coming out of my eyeballs."

"Did anything come of what Marius and Azar found?" I pressed a little more.

She smiled sadly. "You know I can't talk about that, sweetheart. It's all still under investigation, so it's secret information."

"No emerging patterns or anything? You can tell me that much, can't you? I promise I won't say anything." I refused to stand down. This was part of my "failing better" mantra, and I'd keep at it until failure turned into success.

She tilted her head, thinking for a moment. "I suppose so." She lowered her voice to a whisper, as if the forces that be were listening in. "As of yet, we haven't been able to find any patterns. Magicals are vanishing from all over the US, so there's no geographic pattern there. The returnees show up hundreds of miles, even states away from where they were taken, which muddies the waters a lot."

I gave a *humph* of exasperation on her behalf. "And what about global disappearances? Do you think this might be a wider problem?" This was the question I'd been leading up to.

"We're trying to dig into that, but there are always issues with international collaborations. A lot of jumping through hoops on both ends, so it's a slow process." Mom sighed. "Until the UCA agrees to hash out a deal, we can only track US disappearances."

Crap! I probably shouldn't have hoped for a simple solution. Even so, I had one more angle up my sleeve. "What if you reached out to a local coven? Would they be able to tell you about any disappearances?"

"I could, but they wouldn't be under any obligation to share information." My mom frowned. "Why do you ask? Is something going on? Are people going missing in Ireland?"

I kept up a calm façade. "I just thought it was strange that these disappearances cross so much distance, but are only happening in the US. What if it's happening all over, and you just don't know about it? Is there no way to kick the UCA in the butt?"

"I could take a hot poker with me next time I go to the head office." My mom laughed, not understanding how infuriating this was for me. It wasn't her fault; I hadn't told her about the dire straits the Institute was in. Still, I could only muster half a snort at her joke. There needed to be another culprit so the pixies weren't the ones in the firing line. And I just *knew* someone else was responsible for this.

"Or maybe a clown shoe?" I offered, trying to keep things light.

My mom smiled. "I forgot to ask, how did your first day of classes go? I'm sorry, Persie, my head is overflowing right now—I can barely remember what I had for breakfast." She looked down sadly. "I guess I won't be winning any Mom of the Year awards this year, huh?"

"I think you're still in the running." I didn't want to see her downhearted. "And classes were fine—not much to tell. I'm still wrapping my head around physical training, but I really like the engineering. There's so much to learn, and there are some super cool devices. I think that's the class that's going to help me the most."

Mom's face brightened. "That's great! I'm so glad you've found a class you like already." Her smile stretched wider, looking genuinely thrilled. "Engineering, eh? Is that where they make the puzzle boxes?"

"Yeah. They're genius, and the craftsmanship is amazing." I allowed myself a little geekery before signing off for the night. "I still like the Mason jars, but puzzle boxes are going to revolutionize monster capture once they're available to covens."

My phone pinged, a message from Genie flashing up on the screen. *We still on for tonight? You said 11:30, right? X*

I checked the clock on my home screen: 11:26pm. The clock had a habit of dragging along or speeding up when I was alone, and I still had a lot of work to do before I could sleep.

"I'm happy you're settling in. Is there anything going on tonight?

A movie, or a get-together?" Mom looked anxious. She'd always fussed over my lack of social interaction, thinking it would stunt my development or turn me into a bona fide hermit. But, to me, friendship was about quality, not quantity, and I had every friend I'd ever need in Genie. Still, the irony wasn't lost on me. There was a whole heap of mayhem going on in the Institute tonight, and I couldn't tell her a thing about it.

I shook my head. "Not tonight, no, but there's a social in the gardens next week that I'm thinking about going to," I said, throwing her a bone so she wouldn't fret too much about me fitting in.

"You are?!" Her eyes nearly bulged out of her head. "Persie, that's wonderful news! You absolutely have to go, and if you need a dress, or jewelry, or anything from my wardrobe that isn't exercise pants or my favorite jeans, I'll send them over ASAP!"

I chuckled. Little did she know I already had her favorite jeans in *my* wardrobe. Dad had slipped them into my luggage for me, under the sanctity of the father/daughter secrecy pact. "I'll let you know." I pretended to yawn, covering my mouth with my hand. "I should really take a shower and get to bed—I didn't realize how late it was. Will you give my love to Dad?"

Mom nodded sadly. "Of course, sweetheart. This time difference thing takes some getting used to, doesn't it?"

"I promise I'll call again tomorrow when I get chance." My fingertip hovered over the end-call button. "Night, Mom. I love you."

"I love you, too. Speak to you soon." Her eyebrows suddenly shot up. "And I want pictures of next week!"

I smiled and hung up so I wouldn't have to make a promise I couldn't keep. I hated having my picture taken. The thought of dressing fancy and having Genie take photos to keep up the ruse made my insides wriggle with discomfort. But that was a smaller problem for another day.

Hurriedly, I texted Genie back. *Still on. Heading out now.*

The reply pinged a second later. *Be safe. Keep those peepers peeled. Good luck!*

You too, I typed back before slipping my phone back into my pocket. I paused to grab my backpack, with half our puzzle boxes and Mason jars inside. Genie had the others. After our fruitless day of hunting, we'd come up with a plan to split up for pixie duty tonight so we could cover more ground. There would be fewer people to avoid now that everyone had been consigned to their rooms, and I figured the hunters would be working in shifts, which would thin their numbers out, too.

This would be my second night chasing down pixies, but this time, I knew I wasn't alone. Shouldering the bag, I snuck out of my bedroom door and checked that the coast was clear. The corridor beyond lay blissfully empty of guards, all the hunters evidently otherwise engaged with tracking my monsters. I supposed, a little guiltily, that Victoria had figured I wouldn't disobey her hunting ban. "Come on, pixies. Let's finish what I started."

SIXTEEN

Genie

This *ain't gonna be pretty*. Gritting my teeth, I flooded my body with Grandpa's invisibility trick. I'd already used it a few times that day to get Persie and me out of some hunter confrontations. Using it again felt like rubbing lemon juice in a papercut, but a body-wide papercut and a shower of lemon juice. My skin burned; my insides caught fire. Just trying to open my eyes felt like having a stare-down with the sun.

I waited a few minutes for the burning to settle into a bearable agony. Doing this was a royal pain, but it gave me a twenty-minute search window. If a hunter came my way, I could get close enough to see behind their pointless sunglasses or sniff cheap cologne without them knowing I was there. Painful, but crafty.

I hoped Persie had gotten good news from her mom. She'd planned to do some subtle questioning, trying to find a possible connection to the other abductions so we could absolve the pixies. We'd agreed to divide and conquer.

Skin crackling, I scoured the area through the greenish haze of the spell. Everything swam weirdly, like I was seeing things through a pair of comedy lenses. My very own Hall of Mirrors at a carnival sideshow. The monster statues morphed into horrifying caricatures of themselves, all bulbous noses and saucer eyes. And the handful of hunters down the way looked like swollen ogres. Heads too big, bodies too round, limbs too long. I shuddered. But at least I couldn't be seen.

Taking out my phone, I set a twenty-minute timer. If I held this spell much longer than that, I'd risk second-degree magical burns. My grandpa's right calf had never been the same after a thievery gone wrong—he'd had to stay inside the spell for an hour. Badass that he was, he'd gotten his whole calf tattooed with cool monsters and an Atlantean curse word. I was young at the time—Grandpa died when I was six—but my dad used to shut him up when he tried to show me the full tattoo and point out the word in question, and Grandpa would cackle like no one's business. Apparently, I'd had a habit of repeating words I shouldn't... even then.

I set off through the Institute, making a beeline for the Repository. The spell's side effect of burning-skin torture faded to a dull throb, so I could walk at normal speed. On my way, I breezed past hapless hunters. One of them turned and sniffed the air, her nose wrinkling. I braced for an insult, ready to add her to my list of Institute enemies. That was another unfortunate side effect—the invisibility spell could get a bit whiffy after a few consecutive uses.

"Do you smell... popcorn?" she asked her colleague.

A guy in ridiculous shades frowned. "It's more like ozone."

"No, it's definitely caramel or toffee or something," a third hunter chimed in.

A fourth took a huge sniff. "You need your nostrils checked. That's roast potatoes. I wonder who's cooking at this hour?"

I grinned and snuck past them, leaving them to play "what's that smell?" without me. At least there hadn't been any bad scents. If they'd mentioned fish, I might have had to give them an invisible smack. Atlanteans didn't, and never had, smelled of fish. Another false stereotype spread by the magical media, like the seahorse-riding and secret-weapon-hiding.

A few minutes later, I reached the wide hallway that led to the Repository. I paused for a breather, only for a clumsy clown—Nathan, of course—to skid out of said Repository and almost tumble to the ground. Miraculously, he managed to do some flailing wizardry and stay on his feet. With a mortified look, he glanced up and down the hallway to check if anyone had seen. But I was the only one there, and he couldn't see me. Relief washed over his features, and I giggled under my breath. He might have been a walking disaster, but it really was kind of cute. And he'd gone all casual in jeans and a gray T-shirt, showing off broad shoulders and an eye-popping physique usually hidden under tweed and corduroy.

Mr. O'Hara, you're really spoiling us... I crept closer until I stood next to him. Standing dead center in the hallway, he lifted what appeared to be a magnifying glass with a red-tinted lens. Scrunching up one eye, he peered through it.

"No way!" I blurted out, and immediately clamped a hand over my mouth. Specterglass was the stuff of myth and legend. There'd been a fragment of it in one of Atlantis's thousand museums, guarded by round-the-clock security. But Nathan had a whole lens of it, stuffed inside a fancy bronze frame with a handle. If legend was believed, it revealed spirits, showing them in misty forms of red and white particles. A huge benefit if you wanted to locate the dead and didn't have a Necromancer or someone with Medium abilities handy.

He whirled around, almost dropping the magnifying glass. I might've screamed into my palm. "Who's there?" he demanded.

Dammit! Maybe if I stayed perfectly still, he'd think it was all in his head. The ruby-red glass glinted like wet blood in the hall's lamplight. Specterglass was a magical phenomenon, supposedly occurring naturally in the core of the Kolumbo submarine volcano off the coast of Santorini, where it could only be found on the seafloor after an eruption. In fact, the origin wasn't known for sure. What we knew about specterglass was myth, spread by the ancient Greeks.

"Who's there?!" Nathan put up his fists and spun 360 degrees. Coming back to face me, his nose crinkled up. "What is that smell? Is that... vanilla?"

I decided to give up the ghost. "No, it's burning flesh."

He shrieked so loud my eardrums rattled. "What the—!" Hands shaking, he raised the specterglass and peered through it. But I knew he wouldn't see anything. "Are you... a s-spirit?"

"Maybe," I said playfully.

Are you a good spirit or a bad spirit?"

"That depends on who you ask." I grinned inside the spell shield. He hadn't recognized my voice. The fierce energy from the spell must have distorted the sound, which meant more opportunities for pranks.

His brow furrowed. "Why can't I see you through the glass? If you're a ghost, I should be able to see you."

"Maybe I'm not a ghost." I tiptoed around to the other side of him. I couldn't resist. "Boo!"

He shrieked again. "No actual ghost would ever say 'boo'! Who are you? Why are you invisible?"

"I thought I'd come and haunt you for a bit." I chuckled, having way too much fun. "You're not scared, are you?"

He narrowed his eyes grumpily. "No, I'm not scared. And you can't haunt me if you're not a ghost." He lifted the spyglass in my general direction. "I don't imagine you know what this is, whoever you are? You can't trick me."

I laughed. "It's specterglass."

His eyes widened. "How did you know that? Hardly anyone

knows it exists."

"I come from an ancient line of magicals. I know a lot of things." I knew I'd have to drop the spell shield soon, but I liked having him on his toes. Not in a crazy way, but it was nice to see him less uptight.

"G-Genie? Is that you?" His expression morphed into a different kind of panic. An embarrassed kind.

Reluctantly, I undid my grandpa's spell. Starting at my toes, I released the tension of the spell from my body, like slowly shedding a super heavy coat. Bit by bit, the green haze lifted, revealing me in all my glory. "Ah, you got me."

"What are you doing out of your room?" He grabbed my hand and pulled me through the Repository doorway, no blushing or messing about. He didn't even seem to realize he'd touched me. His palms were rougher than I'd imagined. In a nice way.

"All students are supposed to be in lockdown. There are two people missing, Genie! What if you'd been snatched? And... what sort of spell was that? I've never seen such a seamless invisibility spell before. Usually, they cast a mirage. Yours didn't." He shook his head. "But first, answer the why-you're-out-of-your-room part!"

"Why do you think?" I smiled at him. "Pixies."

He groaned. "You and Persie are supposed to be leaving it to the professionals."

"Like you, you mean?" I cast him a knowing look. "Specterglass isn't just for spooks, Nathan. It also traces the magical signature of ancient creatures. My dad told me about it, saying that my mom always wanted some to help with the tougher hunts. I'd say pixies fall under that category, wouldn't you?"

"That's what I hoped," he admitted. "But I haven't found anything other than one milky streak of mist that led nowhere."

I tutted playfully at him. "Are you sanctioned for pixie hunting?"

"Uh... not exactly." A warm laugh bubbled up between us. He

pulled a puzzle box out of his back pocket. "I might've lifted this from Naomi earlier."

"I didn't take you for a thief, Nathan. If I didn't know any better, I'd say you had some hidden depths." I took out one of my own puzzle boxes, and he gaped. "But I asked for mine."

I just couldn't wipe the pleased grin off my face or take the flirty note out of my voice. He needed to shine that spyglass over me again, because I could've sworn I'd been possessed.

Nathan chuckled, his pretty eyes lighting up. "Says you. Where did you learn an invisibility spell like that?" His mouth turned up in a resigned smile. "You saw me almost trip, didn't you?"

"Not at all." I gestured to the specterglass. "Just don't drop that during one of your clumsier moments, okay? All of Atlantis would give up their Elemental abilities for a chunk that big. Oh, and I'd appreciate if you didn't rat me and Persie out. It's only fair, since you're not exactly playing by the rules, either."

"I won't," he promised. "But I have to ask, why are you two so insistent on catching them yourselves?"

I turned the puzzle box over in my hands. "Persie thinks the pixies are the key to solving the disappearances. She's confident she can ask them where Xanthippe and Randolph are, even if they've got nothing to do with it. They've been watching the Institute; they might've seen something no one else did."

Randolph Klopp was the second victim. At first, they hadn't announced the name, but there'd been a second loudspeaker declaration about an hour after the one in the orchard. He was a hunter, four years past his graduation. It had taken a lot of people by surprise; he was apparently known for being tough as nails and a bit of a hard-ass. The fact that he'd been swiped made people ten times more nervous—and bolstered our theory that the pixies weren't responsible. It would've taken a huge amount of strength to abduct someone like him, which had put folks firmly into panic mode.

As far as magical involvement went, if it was someone in the Institute, they'd have to have seriously powerful Telekinesis to drag a dude like that away without making a scene. The antsier people got, the more that panic would rise. And folks were already freaked. Not that anyone would be able to leave out of fear. Lockdown meant lockdown. Doors closed, exits forbidden, until this got solved. Some students had already improvised, barricading themselves into their rooms while everyone else was on hunting duty.

"That's actually a very intriguing idea." Nathan rubbed his faintly stubbled chin. "Persie did appear to have a limited rapport with the one she caught."

I eyed him curiously. "How about you? Why are you tracking them alone?"

"Ah, well... I know the hunting protocols in cases like this. Chances are, I won't get to see a single pixie before they're shipped off to the Bestiary. Any that are kept for research will be wired up to machines, and I'm not fond of that approach." A muscle twitched in his jaw. "I'd prefer to study them in a more natural setting, and... well, I'd like to protect them as much as I can, which I won't be able to do if I leave it to the hunters."

I smiled at him. "You don't think they did this, do you?"

"I... well, it's not as simple as... It's rather more... The thing is..." He struggled for the right words. "Essentially, there's not enough evidence of their behavior to know for sure, but I haven't read anything to suggest they're cruel or dangerous. I said as much to Victoria, but she's convinced it's too timely not to be the right answer. And I could be wrong, so I didn't try to force it."

I nodded my understanding. "Doesn't she think monsters have the ability to be good? Most of the ones I've met get a bit fierce, but I think that's how any animal would respond if they felt threatened." My mind fixed on Tobe and Iso. "And then there's the Beast Master and Beast Mistress, who've got hearts of gold. They've got souls, for sure."

"Beast Mistress?" Nathan looked stumped.

"Her name's Iso. She runs the Atlantis Bestiary. She showed me around when I was little, cuddled me right up into her furry arms and let me ride on her back." I grinned at the memory. "If magicals can create Purge beasts like them, then it stands to reason that the other varieties are cut from similar cloth, right? They might not be able to speak and drink tea, but they can't be totally different inside, you know?"

His expression softened, and his eyes grew warm and inviting. "I do know. That's precisely how I feel about them." He dropped his gaze, and I felt weirdly disappointed. I wanted more of his twinkly eyes. "However, we are a rare breed. To Victoria, and most other hunters, monsters are monsters. They either belong in glass boxes or in Chaos. That's why they won't listen—unless I present water-tight evidence that it's not the pixies."

"So, you could say we're on the same team?" I willed him to meet my gaze. When he did, the air rushed out of my lungs. With all this determination, and all these defiant sides to him, I was starting to see him in three dimensions. And that was dangerous.

He pushed his glasses up the bridge of his nose. "Yes, I suppose you could. Though, I'd really like to learn more about that invisibility spell. It might be useful for covert searching."

I tapped the side of my temple. "Family secret, I'm afraid."

"You Atlanteans truly are remarkable. You have all this power and all these spells, and, in comparison, we've barely scratched the surface of magical possibility." He sighed wistfully. "I envy you."

"You shouldn't. It comes with countless insults, and traditions that would make your retinas detach." I laughed, but it sounded hollow. What was the use of admiring his pretty eyes when, in a few years, my dad would try and foist me off on an Atlantean with a good bloodline? All for the sake of some dumb "purity" business that made zero sense to me. We'd spent centuries hoarding our power—why not spread the love?

His eyes hardened. "Someone insulted you?"

"It's not important." I waved away his concern. "I'm a big bad Atlantean—I can fight my own battles. And we've got pixies to find, remember? How about we split up to cover more ground? Persie's taking the South Wing, so I'll take the North. You could take the East or the West, or both, if you're feeling fiery?"

"I wouldn't say I'm feeling fiery, but I'll sweep as many areas as I can. Hopefully, the specterglass will come up with something this time." He smiled, but some of that defensive glint still lingered in his eyes. It would give me a few warm-and-fuzzies to think about when I didn't have pixies on the brain.

I had to have a final bit of fun before seriousness set in. "And sorry for spooking you before. I couldn't resist."

"You realize I'll be watching my back from now on?" He chuckled. Humor suited him.

"Don't worry, I won't go digging in your underwear drawer." I turned and walked away, stifling a giggle. Halfway down the hall, I glanced back. He was staring at me, open-mouthed and utterly horrified. And then, to my surprise, he snapped out of it and moved his hands in a hula dance. Our laughter collided, echoing off the walls. And I could've sworn I heard a quieter, shriller laugh joining ours. The cackle of a pixie.

Oh, you are so getting caught tonight! I pressed on toward the North Wing, feeling fired up. I'd just reached the archway that led into it when I took out my phone to check for messages from Persie. The screen sat black and dead, the battery drained. It wasn't ideal, but I'd make do without it. If I turned back now and waited to juice this puppy up, I'd lose precious time. And we couldn't afford to waste a single second.

SEVENTEEN

Persie

A lone in the South Wing, ducking out of the way of hunters on duty, I stole a glance at my phone from behind a dragon statue. Just one of its enormous, white marble legs was enough to shield me from any prying eyes.

Come on, Genie! My inbox had no new messages, though I'd texted and called my friend a handful of times since leaving my bedroom. Location updates, check-ins, that sort of thing. All I'd gotten in return was a Genie-less home screen and a voicemail recording. Now wasn't the time for her to go radio silent on me. For all I knew, we could be covering the same ground without realizing, and it irked me that I couldn't get through to her.

Taking my bag off my shoulders, I double-checked my inventory: three puzzle boxes, two Mason jars, and three little cartons of milk that I'd nabbed from the banquet hall. Something Genie said earlier had struck a curious nerve—I think it had been on bullet-point number two: leave out a cookie, and the creature will come running. But pixies didn't like cookies, they liked milk. Maybe, just maybe, they'd take the bait. Meanwhile, Genie had two puzzle boxes and three Mason jars. As the magical one in our team, we'd figured she'd have better luck with the Mason jars than I would. And, Genie or no Genie, I planned to do better at catching *something* tonight.

Putting the bag back on, I waited until the nearest hunters passed by before darting out and sprinting down the hallway full pelt, on high alert for any sign of pixies. I raced past the bedrooms of visiting hunters, more studies, and private libraries for the invited guests to use at their leisure. I poked my head into the libraries, but they sat dark and empty, with no hint of a monster disturbance.

Eventually, having found an emergency stairwell between two studies and running all the way down into what appeared to be a basement, I breathed a much-needed sigh. There didn't seem to be anyone down here. A long, stark corridor lay ahead, lit with unflattering strip lights that shone a cold blue hue on everything. A musty scent filled my nostrils, suggesting this part of the Institute didn't get used often. That had to be a promising sign.

Listening for footsteps or wing flutters, I walked along the corridor, leaving footprints in the fine layer of grime that covered the plasticky floor. Black signs were pinned to the doorways that branched off the main hall: "boiler room," "janitorial staff room," "storage unit 1," "storage unit 2," and so on and so forth. I seemed to have found the utility underbelly of the Institute, which undoubtedly had a multitude of secluded spots for pixies to hide.

I tried some of the door handles, only to find them locked up tight—until I came to a door marked "Refuse." It swung open with ease, the aroma of stagnant trash overwhelming my senses, sickly and rotten and foul. Pinching my nose to keep out the worst of it, I peered into the gloom... and my heart almost leapt out of my body. There in the corner, fighting over banana skins, a half-empty bag of candy, and what looked like the remains of someone's fruit salad, was a small group of pixies. Five, to be exact.

Terrified they would bolt if they saw me, I used their intense argument to my advantage and I tiptoed off to the side, ducking behind a dumpster. I could hear their high-pitched chatter from where I was, and it didn't sound friendly. Who knew banana skins could be such a hot commodity?

Okay, quietly does it. Painfully slowly, I unzipped my bag and took out a puzzle box and the little carton of milk. I placed the puzzle box on the ground and kept the lid firmly on, twisting it until the designs aligned. Still moving at a snail's pace so I wouldn't startle the pixies, I peered around the corner of the dumpster and set the puzzle box just in front of it. My fingertip hovered over the harp button for a second before I pressed down. However, another button, which looked like a bushel of leaves, caught my eye. I realized this wasn't the time to get experimental, but something drew me toward it. An instinct, perhaps. Figuring I could use another box if I messed this one up, I pressed down on the symbol. Immediately, the puzzle box flattened out like a bear trap and the sea-green sides blended into the sticky vinyl floor, leaving it totally camouflaged.

I almost hissed in frustration. *You could've told me about that, Naomi!* Still, I had to admit, this was insanely smart and cool. All I had left to do was lay the bait.

Popping the carton open, I placed the milk in the center of the hidden box—at least, what I hoped was the center. That was the trouble with a successful camouflage. Part of me feared the milk carton would set off the trap, and all I'd get for my efforts was captured dairy. But the box stayed open, still invisible to the naked eye.

Now what? Do I just wait? I sat back against the dumpster and took out a mirror, angling it so I could see approaching pixies. Nerves pummeled through my chest, my heart racing a mile a minute. If they didn't take the bait, they might escape, and I'd be back at square one. Basically, this had to work, or I'd start flipping dumpsters.

Sing, my Persephone... A voice slithered into my head, one I knew so very well.

What are you doing here?" I asked, my chest hot and horrified. He was an ocean away—he wasn't supposed to be able to come near my mind.

Sing... he said again. But it didn't feel the same as when Leviathan had spoken to me on my birthday. It sounded far away, like I'd dredged it up from the darkest corner of my mind. Even so, the violation wasn't dissimilar. The idea that he'd embedded these words in me, somehow, made me want to pour mosquitoes into his glass box.

And what did he mean, *sing?* If he'd ever heard me at karaoke, he'd wish he'd never mentioned it. For me, singing was relegated to the shower, where I could have a private concert without anyone thinking someone was dying. And yet, the moment the thought involuntarily crept into my head, a tune began to form on my tongue. A song I didn't recognize, in a language I didn't understand, but my mind seemed to know every word.

"Thig a-mach às an dorchadas. Mo chlann, mo chlann. Èist ri mo ghuth mar a bhios mi a 'seinn do chridhe. Bu chòir dhut a bhith còmhla rium. Dannsa còmhla rium ann an solas na gealaich agus a 'faireachdainn gàirdeachas. Is e mo chridhe do chridhe. Tha sinn mar an ceudna. Tha ar spioradan ceangailte. Mo chlann, mo chlann. Èist ri mo ghuth mar a bhios mi a 'seinn do chridhe. Bheir mi dhut mo ghràdh. Lorg comhfhurtachd. Tha thu sàbhailte a-nis."

My voice rose, clear and sweet, as though my lungs and voice box had been taken over by a cosmic force. It sounded ancient and sad, as though it wasn't supposed to be heard by human ears. Strange tears welled in my eyes as I repeated the phrase, and a memory came back to me. The song, I realized, was similar to a lullaby I'd heard Tobe sing to a box of faeries when I was a child (and shouldn't have been eavesdropping).

The pixies stopped chattering. Lifting the mirror up, I saw them creeping toward my dumpster in the reflection. They gave me such a fright that I almost stopped singing, but my voice held on, ringing out with that mesmerizing sadness.

Edging closer, they spotted the milk and unleashed a collective "Oooooh." I wasn't even sure I needed the song anymore, but I carried on regardless. As I started the third repetition, all five pixies eagerly pounced onto the carton, apparently entranced. One had just stuck its hand down the opening to scoop up a handful of the white stuff when the box snapped shut around the quintet and the lid sprung closed, locking them inside.

"Chaos, YES!" I lunged for the box and twisted the designs out of sync. Muffled yelps and squeals babbled inside the box for a second, and then... silence. I held it up to the light to observe my victory. Wispy threads of black smoke puffed out of the lid and the designs glowed brightly—a subtle confirmation that I'd freaking done it!

"I'm sorry, but I promise it won't be for long," I whispered to the inmates. "I just need to figure out what to do with you. We might have to hide you in an orb for a bit, but only until we can come up with something better. Okay?"

The pixies didn't reply. After all, the box had turned them back into black mist. But I was definitely going to chalk this up as a victory. I'd gotten ahead of the hunters and caught five pixies of my own accord—six, if you counted my first. It comforted me to think I might be able to save some of my creations. I didn't know how, just yet, but I'd find a way. But, first, I had to get them to a safe place so I could ask them what they knew about Xanthippe and Randolph. I hoped they'd tell me in exchange for their freedom.

Feeling on top of the world, I slipped the box into the front pocket of my bag and took off down the hall. I hadn't gone more than a few yards when my bubble of elation was popped by a hunter-shaped needle. A trio of them, not far ahead. I froze, they froze. The only way out was up the stairwell they were blocking. I could lock myself in the refuse room, but they'd either batter it down or wait until I came out.

"What are you doing down here?" barked a tall guy in the customary black suit. "No one is allowed to be out without permission."

I gulped. "I just wanted to drop off some cardboard boxes."

"Nice try." A glowering woman with white-blonde hair folded her arms across her chest. "Why don't you tell us what's in the bag?"

"It's nothing," I replied, a beat too fast. "Books and stuff."

Their third colleague—a huge woman, built like a bull—stepped forward. "Hand over the bag. If it's nothing, we'll find nothing."

My legs urged me to run. Perhaps I'd find another stairwell at the opposite end of the hallway. Before I could move a muscle, the guy called out, "And don't even think about scampering off. Only the guilty run."

I'm guilty in your eyes. For the first time ever, I wished a Purge would pour out of my mouth then and there—a big one. Something that would keep them occupied while I made a hasty exit. But I had no sweats, no nausea, no nothing.

"I'm not guilty, but I don't see why I should give you my personal things." I swallowed the tremble in my voice.

"Because we asked," the bull-woman grumbled, striding toward me. As hunters went, these ones were really freaking threatening. Her colleagues followed her, and they were on me before I could even contemplate hurtling through the refuse-room door.

The smaller woman yanked the bag off my shoulders while the bull-woman wrenched my arms behind my back. Pain splintered through my bones, my face contorting. I wondered if Victoria was okay with this sort of violence. Whatever happened to innocent until proven guilty? Though that wouldn't have helped me much. In two seconds, they'd see all the evidence they wanted.

"Are these... puzzle boxes?" The guy plucked out the one with the pixies inside. "How come it's glowing? Did you catch something?"

The other woman sifted through my bag. "She's got three of them, Gerry. And two Mason jars."

"Dearie me, looks like you weren't just getting rid of cardboard boxes." The man glared at me. "And you're not authorized to use this stuff. Did you steal it?"

I said nothing, not wanting to implicate Naomi.

He surveyed me for a moment, then said, "You look like a troublemaker."

The platinum-blonde whispered in his ear. "That's Persie Merlin-Crowley."

"Is that so?" The guy's expression changed in a split second. "You're the one who caused all this in the first place, aren't you? From what I hear, you might just be the mastermind, making these things do your bidding." He smirked at his colleagues. "Apparently, some student saw her chatting to a pixie. Stinks of deceit to me."

"What?! Who said that? That isn't true! I was just trying to help!" I gasped. "I wanted to clear up my mess, I'm not masterminding anything."

He sneered. "Or you wanted to save your little aberrations, so they can keep doing your dirty work." He glanced at the box, seeing something in the faintly glowing lights that Naomi clearly hadn't taught us about yet. "Being able to control them would certainly explain how a beginner like you managed to catch five of these."

"They're not aberrations!" I blurted out, instantly regretting it. Evidently, the glow from the box told him how many monsters were inside.

"Aww, how cute." The man laughed coldly.

Flustered, I tried to form the right words. "And I'm not making them do anything. I don't control them, which should be freaking obvious since they're evading me as much as they're evading you! I used knowledge to catch these, not some ability. Oh, and for the last freaking time, they're not responsible for the disappearances!"

I'd say it until I was blue in the face, or someone listened—whichever came first. And this group definitely wasn't listening.

"Agnes, get her in Cuffs," the blonde instructed. "We're taking you back to your room, and we're going to make sure you stay there this time, until Victoria decides what to do with you."

Panic fluttered in my chest as cold metal closed around my wrists. A weird prickly sensation followed, like static electricity—not painful or sapping, just odd, similar to the way it felt when I got too close to Genie in full Verso mode. Magic of some kind, though I could only feel the slightest hint of it. I guessed these weren't ordinary Cuffs, though slapping a pair of Atomic Cuffs on me seemed like overkill. I wondered if Atomic Cuffs would be able to stop a Purge, if I could make one come? Having felt the force of my previous Purges, I highly doubted it.

Ignoring my pleas, the huge woman and her fellow hunters marched me down the utility corridor and back up the stairs, all the way to my bedroom. I wondered if these were the same hunters who'd been stationed in my hallway to keep an eye on my Purges.

I was shoved inside and pushed onto a chair while they set about laying charms and hexes to prevent me from leaving. It took all of ten minutes, but it felt like forever. Finally, with scowls that could've curdled the pixies' milk, they unlocked the Cuffs and stormed out. These hunters weren't playing around. They had orders to follow, and I'd made the mistake of crossing their path.

Now I had no way to search for the pixies, and they'd taken the five that I'd already captured. I wasn't just back at square one, I wasn't even at the starting line anymore.

EIGHTEEN

Persie

_____

Pixieless and fuming, I paced my bedroom floor and tried to think of a hundred ways I might get back at those hunters.

"Aberrations? Who does he think he's calling an aberration?" I snarked, unable to sit for more than a few seconds without jumping back up again.

In that one sentence, he'd cemented something in my head. These creatures deserved more than the lot they had in life. They hadn't asked to exist any more than humans had, but we had to share this world, and they'd wound up with the short end of the stick. They gave their energy for our magical empire, for Pete's sake, and still that hunter had dared to speak about them like they were crud on his shoes.

When injustice becomes law, resistance becomes duty. Thomas Jefferson's words inspired fresh anger and determination inside me. I just *knew* these pixies could help us, if only they were given the chance. Infuriating didn't even begin to cover this situation. And now, I had to wait for Victoria to come along and bite my head off for breaking her lockdown rules. *Two* meetings with the head huntswoman, a

Purge of pixies, two missing magicals, and I hadn't even reached a full week at the Institute yet.

Why couldn't they see that the pixies weren't the enemy? The only monster I'd ever met who reeked of evil was Leviathan, but the rest... They had their quirks, sure, but they weren't the under-your-bed, hiding-in-your-closet, bloodthirsty villains they were made out to be. Those who knew them best and longest all understood that: Tobe, Nathan, and me. Genie had even told me once that her mom and fellow hunters used to have ceremonies to thank the creatures for their service. They were grateful, respectful.

"Did you do this, Leviathan? Did you scramble my brain when you gave me this curse?" I all but shouted. "Is this what you wanted me to see? Is this how you wanted me to feel?" I had no other explanation for my no-matter-what instinct to protect the pixies. Was this his attempt at strengthening our bond? Had he left secret messages in my head for me to find along the way so he could prod me around to his way of thinking? Before I could Purge, I'd loved visiting the beasts in the Bestiary, but I hadn't given much thought to what they did or what they gave. I'd seen them the way everyone else did—as fuel for a greater cause. All that had been turned on its head when I'd held that she-pixie in my hands. No... before that. When the griffin bowed, and then when it squawked sadly, like it didn't understand why I was trying to capture it.

There's so much you don't know. So much you don't understand. I aimed my furious thoughts at the hunters, and everyone whose minds were so narrow that they couldn't even contemplate a different perspective. Heck, there was so much I didn't know and didn't understand, but I was, at least, open to learning. Truthfully, my brain didn't feel scrambled at all. It felt clearer than it ever had; I just feared where that clarity had hailed from.

I sat at my desk and held my head in my hands. Just when I thought

I was swinging one way, something else pushed me back in the other direction. And I was tired of being jostled from pillar to post, not knowing if my thoughts were my own or if they'd been jammed in there by Leviathan. What else had this curse done to my body without my knowledge? Only he had the answers, and he was a world away.

My head lifted at the sound of the door opening, and Victoria strode through a moment later.

"Persie." That one word struck terror into my heart. "I didn't think we'd be having a chat like this again quite so soon."

I sat up straighter, to be polite. "Neither did I."

"You flouted my rules. What else did you think would happen?" Her voice sounded strained, her black eyes hard as onyx pebbles.

"I… just wanted to help. I caught five pixies, didn't I? That's not flouting, that's assisting."

Victoria ran a stressed hand through her hair. "Be that as it may, the situation calls for obedience. I *told* you to leave it to the experts. I'm not keeping everyone in their rooms for my pleasure, Persie. I don't give instructions like that without thought." She walked to the desk and leaned against it. "While you were out hunting, against procedure, five more people went missing. That brings the total to seven. One of those people could've been you, Persie. If someone had checked your room and found you weren't there, that could have caused problems. We might have wasted valuable resources and effort trying to find you when you were fine all along. This isn't a game, Persie. This is serious, and you *have* to let the experts handle it."

Five? My stomach lurched, but my resolve didn't waver. There was absolutely no way the pixies could have taken seven people. I'd found the creatures squabbling over rotten fruit, for crying out loud. They weren't bothered about snatching personnel—they just wanted to go about their business. I mean, they were probably oblivious to the fact that the Institute was in a state of mass upheaval.

"Wait... That means those five people got taken during the lockdown." I squinted, trying to work out the logic. There hadn't been an announcement about it, which meant Victoria was keeping secrets. I guessed the Institute would be under intense scrutiny if the outside world found out about this, and she'd likely have done anything to avoid its reputation being tarnished. "Why hasn't anything been said about them?"

Victoria straightened up, if that were even possible given her exemplary posture. "That is the best course of action for now, to avoid mass panic. If people attempt to flee, it will be impossible to know who has been taken and who has simply run away. Should this continue, however, I will be making other arrangements for the safety of the Institute and its residents."

"So, not to be rude, but it wouldn't have mattered if I was walking around the Institute or stuck in my room. Whoever is taking people is doing it regardless," I said coolly. Her excuse balanced, just about. Even if it smarted of dishonesty. People deserved to know if the numbers were increasing, but she was the head of this place. To her mind, its longevity and position of respect was likely as important as people's lives.

Victoria sighed. "We don't know if the other abductees were also walking around against protocol, so that's no certainty." She pushed off the desk and walked a few paces. "Nevertheless, the Institute will be going into its code red scenario as of now. You will hear the announcement shortly."

"What's that?" I wasn't sure I wanted to know. What security measures could possibly be higher than the lockdown already in place?

She turned slowly. "It's regrettable, but pixies will now be considered lethal, and therefore we will use all force necessary to make sure they are stopped. I don't like to give this kind of order, because I don't believe in the killing of Purge beasts, but it's the only choice I have left."

I leapt from my chair. "You can't do that! They haven't done anything wrong. I don't understand why you're not looking into human culprits. How many in this place would know *exactly* where to hide seven people? You've seen the pixies with your own eyes, Victoria. They can't have done this. You're sentencing innocent creatures to death!"

My protective streak kicked in with a vengeance, and so did my certainty that my creations hadn't hurt anyone. Seven people was unfathomable. Pixies liked milk and fruit, and a bit of destructive mischief. They weren't coldhearted kidnappers. But I could see in Victoria's stony eyes that I wasn't going to get through to her. She'd already given the order; this was nothing more than a courtesy call to let me know that my Purge beasts had been sentenced.

"You are biased, Persie. You might not be able to see it, but magicals can often forge a connection to their Purge beasts. You aren't immune to that, and ordinarily there's no harm in it, but this is different." Victoria kept her voice steady. "Xanthippe disappeared after you Purged. We know that because she was accounted for during the time you said your Purge occurred, and for a couple of hours after. Come morning, she was gone. That's the sort of coincidence I can't ignore. Had there been a longer gap, I might've had a different theory. Maybe I'd have agreed that it was a human act, and said human had used your Purge as a diversion. But nobody knew about it until *after* Xanthippe went missing. So, if it looks like a dog, and barks like a dog, it has to be a dog... Do you understand?"

I scrunched my hands into fists. "Not when the dog is six inches tall and hasn't got any history to suggest it's malicious!" I jabbed a raging finger at the door. "You posted hunters in the hallway, but somehow, they weren't there after I Purged. What if they heard me?

What if they saw the pixies and took their shot to kidnap Xanthippe? *That's* more logical than blaming a bunch of tiny beasts for seven people vanishing into thin air!"

Victoria's expression tightened. "The hunters were dismissed because you seemed to be faring better, and I thought you'd prefer not being under constant watch. I hoped the direct line to me would be enough. No one was in your hallway from five o'clock on that evening. They couldn't have seen you Purge, or what you Purged."

I fell silent, tears threatening. I had nothing left to convince her. It had been a hopeless endeavor from the get-go. She was hell-bent on making these pixies pay, and, maybe, if I were in her position, I'd think the same thing. And without a better explanation, I didn't have a leg to stand on. She thought I'd gone soft on my Purges, and she was right. I did have an affection for them, but so what? Santana carried her Purge beast around on her shoulders most of the time, and nobody batted an eyelid. It wasn't a weakness.

"I think it best that you stay here for the duration." Victoria broke the tense silence. "I want to trust you, Persie, but your ability is still beyond your control. And you have clearly been compromised, which is nothing to be ashamed of—I've been fond of a few of my Purges. However, it does mean your involvement in the pixie hunt ends here. And I mean it this time."

"Please, Victoria…" I had nothing left to say.

She smiled sadly. "Once this is over, we can continue our work in helping you control your ability. You've shown great promise by catching those five pixies tonight, and I do thank you for that, but it isn't the right time." She moved away from me. "For now, I need to get seven people back from wherever they were taken. So, please, don't make me come back here. Follow the rules, for everyone's sake."

As she went to the door and opened it, one last idea exploded in my head. "At least talk to my mom about this. Please. She's dealing with missing magicals, too. It could be related!"

"We are concerned with pixies, not what your mother is investigating." Victoria looked back. "Indeed, if I know the US and its magical secrecy, you shouldn't even have told me that."

She walked out without another word. The door closed behind her with a damning *click* followed by the subtle thrum of hexes kicking back into action, and tears began to trickle down my cheeks.

O'Halloran had cast me out of my own home, I had dreams of the people I loved putting me in a box, my parents were on the other side of an ocean, I'd been marched out of the engineering lab like a traitor while everyone gossiped and whispered about me, and yet this was the moment where I felt more helpless and alone than I ever had before.

To add insult to injury, the loudspeaker kicked in fifteen minutes later, and Victoria's warning went out to the Institute, loud and bitterly clear: "We are now on code red lockdown. Hunters, this is now a matter of life and death. Lethal force may be used on the enemy. Everyone else, remain in your rooms until you are otherwise instructed. Do not be alarmed that comms have been blocked in and out of the Institute. It is necessary to avoid interference with hunting devices and will resume function when it is safe to do so. Internal calls can still be made, if you feel isolated and need to speak someone. Any disobedience will result in hexed imprisonment for the duration. We are in this together. Have courage. We will not fail, as long as everyone does their part."

I'm sorry, pixies. I tried...

NINETEEN

Genie

No need for burning invisibility spells when I had razor-sharp reflexes. I'd slunk through the North Wing like a cat burglar. Now, I liked to think I had a decent grasp of surface-world lingo, but I'd never fully understood that term. Did they steal cats? Were they catfooted? That was another weird one. Humans didn't have foot pads to soften every step. I supposed it didn't matter. Basically, I was being super stealthy, avoiding hunters like a boss.

But still no friggin' pixies. It was getting stupid now. I hadn't even caught a glimpse of one, and I'd been searching for a good hour. At least I had some nice things to think about, to pass the time between non-sightings.

I wondered if Nathan was having better luck. I pictured him James Bonding around the East and West Wings with his specter-glass. He still didn't strike me as the hunting type, but he had to have some skills or he wouldn't be here. Unless he'd gotten in purely on intellectual merit. I supposed that wasn't impossible.

It still felt pointless to dwell on him in a romantic sense, but I couldn't resist. He'd seemed so different. More relaxed, despite my haunting attempt. And he hadn't been as nervous or shy around me this time. It felt like we were slowly getting to know each other's idiosyncrasies. You know, like when you introduced a new pet to the old one, and they needed a bit of time to settle into the idea. Plus, I'd been told I made an intimidating first impression. My sense of humor wasn't to everyone's taste, but maybe he was learning to like it.

Such nice eyes. I grinned, envisioning the way they crinkled up when he smiled. The smile suited him better than bumbling confusion, although the bumbling confusion wasn't without its charms. Man, I sounded like such a cheesy romantic. Was that even how I thought of him? I'd enjoyed our talk. I liked his company. Did that spell romance? Not necessarily. It could just as easily be the start of a friendship. Then I remembered the gray T-shirt and the sound of his laughter, and my heart did a weird clench. If I wasn't careful, butterflies would be freed from their cage. And that signaled the rise of awkward, tongue-tied Genie—a rare creature who hadn't been seen for many, many years.

"He's not even my type," I told the statue of a unicorn. But did types really matter? All my crushes on men who were "my type" hadn't ended well, so maybe not. And change was a good thing, right?

I leaned on the unicorn and wrapped an arm around its neck. "Who am I kidding? It's not like it could go anywhere, so what's the use?"

It didn't matter who the guy was, my dad would never agree to it. He'd laid down the law on that front. I could have my pick of stuffy Atlanteans, but no regular magicals. And while a secret romance sounded exciting in theory, in reality it required a lot of exhausting logistics. I wasn't denying there were some absolute peaches in Atlantis, but an arranged anything didn't float my proverbial boat. Romance and love shouldn't be forced. It needed to be organic, or it would always feel like it was lacking. I believed this as someone who had no idea about love or marriage or any of it, of course, but my heart told me that was how it was meant to be.

"He did a hula dance. Can you believe it?" I asked the unicorn. A guy who could be silly was attractive as heck. Perhaps it was because he was slightly older and didn't take himself as seriously as younger guys. Whatever it was, it had reeled me in—hook, line... but not quite sinker. Not yet.

Strolling away from the unicorn, I realized I'd somehow circled back to the Repository. It was technically part of the center, not belonging to a particular wing. And it felt rude not to investigate further up the hallway. I'd always stopped beside the Repository instead of pressing on to the new wing. I guessed none of us had mentioned searching there.

"Might as well cover all our bases, eh?" I winked at a dragon statue and continued down the hall. I followed the route Charlotte had taken us on during orientation, and it wasn't long before I reached the building site.

Approaching with caution, I flattened myself against the stained-glass entrance and peered around the corner to check the situation ahead. The workers who'd been putting together the bones of this place had probably clocked off ages ago, and they'd taken their lights with them. I doubted they'd be back anytime soon, with the Institute on lockdown. Impenetrable shadow shrouded the foyer of the new wing, eerie and unsettling, like someone was watching me from the darkness. The flap of a tarp did nothing to ease my discomfort. It sounded like enormous wings, snapping violently.

I pulled out my dead phone and cursed under my breath. "I'm going to have to go in there alone, aren't I?" With no one around and plenty of shadows to melt into, it was the perfect hideout for errant pixies. Usually, I wasn't bothered by the dark, but there was some-thing about this place that freaked me out. Namely, the huge black dome at the far end that I knew lay unseen. The current Repository had a welcoming feel to it, but this new one… not so much. A definite case of style over substance. Seriously, it looked like something out of a horror sci-fi.

Putting the useless phone back in my pocket, I conjured a big ball of Fire to light my way. A woman-made torch, to chase off any nasties that might be lurking.

Tentatively, I stepped into the foyer of the new wing. It might've been the light flickering off me, or just my imagination, but the shadows seemed to swarm closer. They danced across the glowing pool of light my Fire cast around me, moving like sentient creatures with thin tendrils that reminded me of clawed fingers and globs of black that looked like skulls. I shuddered, the hairs standing up on the back of my neck.

"You'd better be here, pixies," I muttered. Glancing over my shoulder, I couldn't see the hallway anymore. The shadows had swept in and drowned out the light. An optical illusion, probably. My eyes just hadn't adjusted to the Fire, that was all.

Get a grip, Genie! I'd told Nathan I was a big bad Atlantean, and I needed to start acting like one. I had six abilities at my beck and call, for Ganymede's sake; there weren't many things in this world that could take me down. Not without a decent fight, anyhow.

Feeling less jittery, I swished my ball of Fire to the left and right, shining it on all the construction. Sacks of raw materials, half-built walls, nearly finished stained-glass masterpieces. But no pixies.

I shone my light over a doorway. It didn't have an actual door installed yet, but I saw a hallway beyond it. I tried to remember what Charlotte had said about this place. Something about how they were building rooms for visiting guests and more research facilities. This would probably lead to those, once it was finished, but in its current state the hallway seemed to drop off sharply into nothingness.

I'd just stepped closer to investigate when a sound made me

freeze. It was a strange, melodic song, drifting through the foyer. It tingled up my spine, sweet and soaring, like fairies dancing on my vertebrae. A weird mental image, but nonetheless true. I turned to find the source. My feet followed, eager to hear more, desperate to get closer to that beautiful song. I didn't understand the words, but it didn't matter. The tune struck deeper than lyrics. Like a perfect symphony, tugging at my heartstrings, speaking to my very soul.

Whispers fluttered around my head, soft and inviting, saying, "Come to us. Be with us. Feel our warmth."

I giggled, which I almost never did. "I can't see you."

"We are here. Follow us. Follow our song," the whimsical, feminine voices urged. They spoke with a hint of melodic laughter that made me smile. All of my anxiety melted away as the song penetrated further into the fiber of my being. It lilted in my cells, turning my blood to pure magic. I wanted more. I wanted to be nearer to that sweet sound until I was part of it. Thoughts of the outside world disappeared. There was only me, and the song, and nothing else.

I looked upward as a different light dispersed the crackle of my Fire. No... lights, plural, glowing and hypnotic, floating merrily in the air. They moved effortlessly, flowing to the gentle current of the music. Dancing. And I wanted to dance with them. In the back of my mind, I recognized the trailing orbs. But those memories didn't mean anything anymore. Now, I understood why the glowing lights had appeared when Persie was having a panic attack. They'd wanted me to come to them, to hear this secret song. I had missed out. But I wouldn't miss out again. They were calling to me, and I had every intention of answering.

"Do you see us?" the voices susurrated.

I nodded. "I see you."

"Then come. We are waiting." The twinkling lights with their colorful comet-tails flitted away, toward the black sphere that I'd feared so much: the skeleton of the new Repository. I went after them, no longer afraid. I had nothing to be scared of, not with these lights leading me. They were pure radiance. Pure goodness. It resonated inside of me, filling me with giddiness. I felt like I could take flight.

The lights paused now and again, checking to see that I was following. It made me smile. They cared. They'd been waiting for me, and I couldn't let them down. All the while, their song urged me to keep putting one foot in front of the other. I didn't even flinch when I stepped out onto the rickety walkway that led into the center of the eerie black sphere. If anything, the percussion of my shoes on the metal added to the melody, punctuating it perfectly.

"Don't go without me," I pleaded, suddenly afraid they might vanish.

The orbs twisted in a spiral, playful and hypnotic. "We would not. We have been waiting. We want you to be where we are."

At the end of the walkway, the orbs dove downward and disappeared into the darkness below. Frantic that I might lose them, I didn't hesitate. I jumped. Sure enough, I spotted the twinkling lights dancing beneath me and smiled. *I'm coming to you.* Moments before I hit the bottom curve of the sphere, a hazy instinct encouraged me to release a blast of Air to cushion my fall.

"You are wonderful," the glowing lights cooed. "You will be welcomed."

I dispersed the Air and stood tall, bathing in their radiance. I'd never felt so alive. Their song continued and my lips moved along, as though I'd finally learned the haunting lyrics. Then the twinkling orbs swooshed around my head in a circle before zipping forward. My eyes trailed them longingly as they evaporated through a door. Some small, distant part of me knew the door shouldn't exist, but it didn't perturb me. It seemed to be standing on its own, with no walls to support it, floating an inch or so above the curve of the sphere. It thrummed with energy and light.

"Wait for me!" I called, walking toward the door.

"We are here. We are waiting," they replied from behind it.

I reached for the handle and swung the door wide. Waves of light rushed out in a blissful torrent, warm and inviting, like the gates to heaven itself. All I had to do was step forward, and I could join the twinkly lights in their joy and hear that beautiful song again. I didn't even need to think about it. Smiling in the ocean of warming illumination, I did just that.

And I disappeared into the light, just like the orbs before me.

TWENTY

Persie

Morning came, the bright sunlight mocking me with its yellow cheer as it slid through my pale beige curtains. I'd tried to sleep because there was nothing else to do, but it hadn't come. I'd showered at around three in the morning, but that hadn't helped, either. The cracks in the mirror and the decimated soap just reminded me of my failure with the pixies. My wet hair soaking the pillow, I'd tossed and turned, checking my phone every five minutes for news from Genie. But her radio silence continued, and the hexed room prevented me from going to find her.

Checking the clock and wincing at the harsh blue light, I saw that it was 6:03. After dialing Genie's number for the billionth time, I held the phone to my ear, willing it to go through... only to get the same voicemail recording: "Sorry, I can't come to the phone right now. Leave a message, and I'll get back to you as soon as I can. Thanks, bye!"

Her chipper tone made me all the more desperate to reach her. Worst-case scenarios tumbled through my head. What if Victoria had hexed her into her room, too? What if she was hiding out, unable to get in touch? What if the person responsible for these kidnappings had taken her? I couldn't stomach that last one. As bitter ironies went, that would have been the cruel icing on top of this rancid cake.

I tapped the phone against my chin, trying to come up with something. Anything. I thought about calling Nathan, but I didn't have his number. Even in this modern age of technology, I had no way of getting in touch with anyone outside this door. I could've called my mom, but that would've left me with a *lot* of explaining to do, and frankly, I didn't want to cross Victoria again. It would guarantee me a ticket out of there for sure if I went against her wishes a third time. Oh, and there was the big fat fact that it wouldn't have worked, even if I'd wanted to do that, since she'd blocked outside calls from coming in or going out. She clearly wanted to keep this inside the Institute, to avoid an external scandal.

Do you have any idea what damage this could do to my family name? That was what Charlotte had said, but I sensed it went deeper than that. It wasn't just the Basani name at stake, but the entire Institute. Magical authorities would have to get involved, and they'd be forced to assess the safety of this place and the students therein. It could get closed down. And that would all be because of me, if I opened my mouth and spilled the beans to the wrong people. But where did that leave me? Alone, with no one to talk to, that was where.

"This is ridiculous!" I yelled, punching a pillow. "Why couldn't you have picked someone else, you bastard! I liked my life! I didn't mind being ordinary! Why did it have to be me?!" This curse was merciless, without a single silver lining. I wondered how Echidna had endured it. How long had she lived, watching her creations get rounded up and put into glass boxes? I imagined it hadn't always been that way. Once upon a time, monsters must've roamed the Earth freely. It was only when the covens were created, and someone realized that Purge beasts could power them, that they'd lost their liberty.

You must've been so sad all the time. Perhaps she'd considered it a blessing when Tobe put her on ice, so she wouldn't have to stand by and watch anymore. I'd never expected to sympathize with my predecessor, but it was hard not to, given the circumstances—and I'd only had this curse for a short time.

What is wrong, my Persephone? That voice echoed in my head, making me jolt in surprise. It came through bright and clear this time. A direct line from Leviathan himself—not like before, when he'd told me to sing. I didn't know whether to laugh or cry. It paid to be careful what you wished for. Had I wanted someone to speak to so badly that I'd opened up a telepathic link to Leviathan?

I shook my head. *Is this a trick? You can't be in my head—you're at the SDC. I went away so you couldn't do this anymore.*

I felt your pain and came to ease it. You should not suffer like this. His words were alarmingly soft and soothing. Exactly what I needed, but from the wrong person.

I picked up the pillow and wrapped it around my head, like that would do any good. *This isn't possible. You're an ocean away.*

I pressed my hands harder against my ears, pushing further into the pillow. None of this made any sense. When he'd told me to sing, that voice had been far away, like a message that had been left some time ago. But this came through crystal clear and gut-wrenchingly present. Unless... everyone had been wrong about how far our connection could reach. Like the Purges, maybe it took extreme emotion to get the link to work like this, my anguish and misery somehow forcing the transmission across greater distances. The possibility stunned me for a second, equal parts terrifying and incredible.

Do you want me to leave? He let the words linger in my skull, putting the ball firmly in my court. Part of me wondered if he would actually go, if I told him to.

I'm not sure, I replied. He might have been the monster who'd done this to me, but he was the only person I had right then. And, sometimes, something was better than nothing.

He chuckled quietly. *Then I will stay until you decide.*

I didn't know what to talk to him about. He wanted to know if I was okay, but he likely already knew the answer, or he wouldn't have struck up a telepathic conversation in the middle of a nervous breakdown. So, I did the only thing I could do. I put the pillow back down and watched the sunrise, the vivid orange and sunflower yellow splintering the aquamarine sky.

What are you doing, my Persephone? he asked.

I shrugged, even though he couldn't see me. *Watching the sun come up and fretting about my friend and the pixies I Purged.*

He made a noise of intrigue. *Pixies? How thrilling. I have not seen their kind in many a year.*

So everyone keeps saying. I sighed, closing my eyes to the brightness.

You do not care for them?

No... I do. That's why I'm sitting here, locked in a room. Eyes squeezing tighter, enveloping me in a self-darkened world, a few questions popped into my head. Ones only he would be able to answer. *Is there a reason I didn't Purge for five days?*

I thought I heard him shrug. *Your ability does not want to kill you. It wants you to succeed. It was likely allowing you to recover from your last Purge.*

Oh, so it played nice then it made me Purge a horde. I puffed air between my teeth. *Not what I'd call considerate.*

Has it killed you? Has it destroyed you? As you are speaking, I think not, he replied with a muffled chuckle. He was clearly enjoying himself.

Another question pressed at the forefront of my mind. *Would there be a reason a monster couldn't turn into black mist if I held it in my hands? I caught one and it was like it... couldn't get away, but the ones I didn't get a hold of had no problem misting out of reach.*

You created them. Your touch is powerful. They may feel dutybound to maintain their physical form if you make contact with one, until you release them again, he explained. *Although perhaps it would be better if you told me everything. I must have full understanding of these developments.*

I flopped back on the bed and stared up at the ceiling while I told him the whole story. I had nothing better to do, and part of me hoped he might be able to give me some more advice, or a snippet of information that would help in the grander scheme of things. I wouldn't be able to convince Victoria, of course, but it might clear things up, once and for all, in my own mind. If I knew my path was just, it'd spur me to continue. Twisting the sheets around my index finger, I decided to add the bit about the glass-box dream to explain why I was constantly on edge.

A perplexing thought came to me, halfway through the story. *Hang on... Did you have something to do with that dream? If you did, you can leave my head right now and never come back!* He'd put dreams into my head before, after all.

Leviathan sighed, as though he were sad. *I did not. You may choose to disbelieve me, but I assure you I had no part in it. I give only pleasant dreams that I construct carefully. Fear created this. I understand the feeling within it—it is your worst nightmare, literally and figuratively. And your fears are justified. No one else can understand your situation; no one but me. People are terrified of what they cannot comprehend. They choose to imprison it, instead.*

He needed a lesson or two in how to be comforting. I didn't want to hear that my loved ones could turn against me, or that my fears were justified. I wanted him to tell me that it meant nothing—just an anxiety dream that had no basis whatsoever in reality. But this was Leviathan talking, and he had all the subtlety of a bull in a china shop. Plus, I didn't know if I actually believed him. He sounded sincere, but that didn't prove a whole lot.

I frowned. *How come you didn't try to talk to me after I had the nightmare, then? I was pretty freaked out the first time it came.*

I did not know if this would work. But it did and I am pleased. It sounded bizarre, but I could've sworn I heard him smiling. I could picture it, his razor-sharp rows of teeth crammed together in a grin. *Nor do I always know if such a visit would be welcomed. I had a sense it might be, on this occasion.*

I snorted. *You mean you'd like to think that.*

Yes. He sounded sad again. I wasn't sure what to do with sad Leviathan. I was so used to cocky, irritating, in-your-face Leviathan. *But I think you will be pleased that I contacted you.*

Oh? Why's that? Did he have some information for me? I sat up sharply and perched on the edge of the bed, leaning forward as if he were actually there. I could've used a breakthrough, right about then.

I know where your magicals have gone.

My heart hammered in my chest. *You do?*

There is ancient magic where the Institute rests. It predates even the ruins that the Institute scavenged. His tone took on a bitter note. *Magic of the Primus Anglicus, the Celtic contingent, if you will. Monsters know of it. It is part of why they despise the Institute, for it sits on sacred ground. Namely, the doorway to the land of Tír na nÓg, a mythical gateway. Though it is more frequently referred to, by our kind, as the Door to Nowhere.*

Why do you call it that? I felt like I already knew, but my exhausted brain needed it spelled out.

He laughed coldly. *Because of the many people who walk through it and do not come back. The magic of the Door has been dormant for a long time because of the Institute. It needed awakening, a spark of raw Chaos to ignite it. You have awakened it, my Persephone.* He sucked in a deep breath, as though the prospect thrilled him. *I can feel the Door to Nowhere through you. My Persephone, what a wonder you are.*

What? Are you saying that this is all my—

But at that moment, Victoria burst into the room, the door slamming into the wall with a bang as it opened, and the connection dissipated. She crossed to the center of the room and paused there, stiff and straight with purpose. Heavy silence blanketed the bedroom, and I found no hint of softness in her eyes. She stared at me, the silence getting thicker and more suffocating by the moment.

I had nowhere to run to… and the head huntswoman looked truly, madly furious.

This is about to get worse, isn't it?

TWENTY-ONE

Persie

"I need answers." Victoria didn't bother with any niceties. "Now."

I looked up at her, my mind still fuzzy from the connection to Leviathan. "I've told you everything I know, Ms. Jules. What else is there?"

We'd already gone in several circles during this interview-slash-interrogation. And it looked like the record would keep skipping, until I could verify what Leviathan had told me about this weird doorway and show, once and for all, that the pixies had no part in the disappearances. But it wasn't as if I could just go ahead and tell her that she'd walked in and cut off a mental call from the ancient monster who'd caused all this. That would just add a layer of fault to the trifle of blame already jiggling over my head.

Victoria sucked in a sharp breath. "I need to know everything about these pixies. Nathan has done his best, but there's not enough lore to go on, and the records from the Cornish coven were destroyed in a fire some years ago." She paced uneasily, reminding me a little of my mom. I sensed it was taking all of her willpower to stay calm.

"I've told you everything!" I insisted, fidgeting with the bedsheets.

Victoria shot me a dark look. "I don't think that's true, Persie."

"Then I'm going to need you to be more precise." I wasn't deliberately being sassy, but she was more or less asking me to read her mind.

"Did anyone ask you to do this? Did someone speak to you before you came to the Institute? Did someone put the idea of coming here in your head, or did it happen organically?"

I said nothing, thinking… Did she mean Leviathan?

She paused, her brow furrowing. "Can you remember anything else from the evening you Purged? Were you aware you could Purge extinct monsters, prior to coming here?"

I stared at her. "No! Of course not!"

"I think *you* ought to be more precise," she replied coolly.

"Nobody put the idea of coming here in my head." I shuffled nervously at the edge of the bed, trying to figure out where she was going with all this. "As for the evening I Purged—I got sick, same as every other time. There wasn't anything different, apart from the fact that I expelled a bunch of monsters instead of one. And no, I have no idea what I'm going to Purge before it happens."

Victoria went to my desk and absently picked up a few items. "But you understand where your ability comes from, don't you? You were the one who told me about it."

So she did think Leviathan had a part in this. Being vague about it didn't minimize the accusation, that, somehow, the monster had prodded me into this Institute and made me release an army of pixies. But for what purpose? Did she think he wanted to punish the hunters because of the nature of their job? Was I supposed to be the conduit in this scenario?

"Leviathan doesn't have any say in what I do, if that's what you're getting at." I stood, anger rocketing through me. "He gave me this ability, sure, but that's where it ends. I'm not his spy or his puppet. He's frozen in a glass box on the other side of the Atlantic."

Which doesn't stop him from whispering in my head, but still... He didn't control me. He'd tried that in a dreamworld, and it hadn't worked. My subconscious might have slipped momentarily, but his influence over me was nowhere near as potent as he would have liked. And I wasn't going to let anyone else tell me otherwise.

"If I had control over the pixies, do you think they'd still be out there?" I waved a wild hand around me. "They don't listen to me! They might, if you'd let me try and speak to one of the ones I captured, but you had your hunters take them away. So, that's out of the question, isn't it?"

Victoria looked unconvinced by my outburst. "And what if *you're* not the one with control over them? What if you're not even in control of yourself?"

"Leviathan? Tobe has him under lock and key, and even if he could contact me, he still wouldn't have a say in what I do. My decisions are my own." I shivered with anger, a chill prickling up the back of my neck. "And he can't bend monsters to his will, either. If he could, he wouldn't have been trapped all these years. He'd have just 'controlled' the other monsters in the Bestiary and staged a mass breakout. Do you hear sirens? Have you heard about any high alerts from the SDC? No, because there's nothing going on. Leviathan has no power as long as he's imprisoned."

A subtle movement drew my eye toward the door, making my heart jolt—a pixie had snuck in during the conversation, fluttering up to one of the bookshelves. This pixie looked bulkier than the she-pixie I'd first caught—instinct told me I was looking at a male of the species. His coloring was darker, with navy blue wings and emerald green banding across his body. He wore a nutshell hat on his head and was covered in dark red spots that pulsated gently, his dark eyes fixed on me from between two books. I tried to pretend I couldn't see him, for his sake. Victoria would have had him in a puzzle box faster than he could say "I'm innocent!"

Victoria plucked up a sketchbook and flipped through the pages. My fingertips itched to snatch it back. She might as well have been looking through my diary, peering into my innermost secrets. But I resisted; I was already in trouble.

"I have to do my job, Persie. I don't like interrogating you, but nothing like this has ever happened before during my entire tenure at the Institute. We have fifteen people missing now, and I have to suspect foul play. And, since we have untold pixies still on the loose, it follows that they're our top suspect—our only suspect, actually. My people are in grave danger, and I have to see them rescued as soon as possible, which means I have to pursue every avenue."

Fifteen?! The number had shot up while I'd been hexed into this room. All this time, I could've been out there, getting the pixies to help. We might've stopped that number from getting out of hand. Victoria and her hunters had prevented that possibility. I could only imagine the authoritarian state out there, right now. Hunters stationed in every hallway, armed with magic. The corridors would be deserted, and those still stuck in their rooms would probably be on the verge of mental breakdowns. With no way to get in touch with the outside world, the Institute had started to feel very isolated and frightening, indeed.

I side-eyed the pixie, and he shook his head solemnly. He pressed a tiny hand to his chest, and the pulsating red spots turned blue, as though he was sad. This gesture confirmed what I'd already deduced —these creatures were sentient and playful, and nowhere close to evil. Maybe Leviathan hadn't been pulling my leg about this Door to Nowhere business. It meant that we were at the center of a very different, much scarier kind of mess, but it also meant that I was right about the pixies' innocence. Still, I didn't want to add that idea to the mix until I had evidence.

"I'm not disagreeing that it's foul play, but Nathan knows plenty about the pixies. I'm willing to bet he doesn't think they're responsible, either." I moved to the center of the room, so I could see easily both Victoria and the pixie. "You said he did his best, but the truth is that he just didn't give you the black-and-white guilty verdict that you wanted from him."

Victoria's right eyebrow twitched. "He found enough to maintain the theory. Accounts of tricks going awry. Vengeful schemes."

The pixie shook a clenched fist at the head huntswoman from between the two books and received a warning look from me. He sank back into the shadows with a furious expression on his tiny face, squatting down where I couldn't see him anymore. I had to clear my throat loudly to cover the quiet grumblings from the bookshelf. Victoria definitely wouldn't have been happy to hear the crude sentiments coming out of the pixie's sharp-toothed mouth.

"That's nonsense and you know it!" I shot back. "Fifteen disappearances is more than 'tricks going awry,' and far beyond the scope of anything Nathan could have found."

Victoria turned her back to me, her eyes presumably fixed on the horizon. "For the safety of the Institute, you will continue to stay under lockdown until further notice. We may not *know* the pixies are guilty, but there *is* enough evidence to consider the creatures hostile and dangerous."

Another round of savage grumbling came from the bookshelf, causing me to feign a full-blown coughing attack. Victoria didn't even turn to check that I was okay.

I lifted an angry finger to my lips and hoped the pixie understood. He stuck out his bright blue tongue but retreated back into the books, sulking. And not a moment too soon. Victoria turned back around, and I made some dumbass attempt to pretend I was rubbing my lips. "It's not them, Victoria. You're making a mistake." I put my hands behind my back to avoid any more awkward charades.

But a question lingered, hot and spiny and horrible inside my head. If what Leviathan had said about my ability was true, then all of this was my fault. It might not have been the pixies, but I'd sure as heck done something to get this doorway open. And that doorway had sucked the missing magicals right into it, somehow. Leviathan had just flipped me out of the frying pan and into the proverbial flames of guilt.

Maybe he's lying. Maybe it's a game he's playing. The strange, Irish-named place had sounded real enough, but the Door to Nowhere had a distinctly made-up, kid's story vibe to it. And it seemed like the kind of thing that the Institute would know about, or that someone would have read in a book somewhere. They wouldn't just build something on top of a powerful, mythical gateway... would they? That was just asking for trouble.

But a conflicting notion nagged at the back of my mind. What if he *wasn't* lying? What if this doorway existed, and I'd opened it, and that was where the magicals had gone?

I decided to go with it, just in case.

"The Door to Nowhere is responsible for this. The Basanis built this Institute on sacred ground, and now the magical powers that be are pissed. I don't know why they've chosen now to take their revenge, but it's happening."

Another slight omission of the truth. Leviathan had told me I was somehow responsible, but I didn't think it wise to implicate myself when I was already implicated for something else. If I'd somehow opened the Door, maybe I was the only one who could get the missing people back and close it again. If not, people would keep on vanishing and the pixies would keep on getting blamed. If all the pixies were captured and people continued to disappear, Victoria's theory would grind to a halt. But I didn't want it to get that far—no one should have to suffer for Victoria's stubbornness.

Victoria laughed. "That is a fairytale, Persie. An ancient legend that has no basis in reality whatsoever. Do you know how many places in Ireland claim to be the gateway to the land of Tír na nÓg? There are entire Internet pages dedicated to it. If you believe in that, I strongly urge you to avoid toadstool rings. As for the idea that the Institute is built on such a place," she continued, opening her arms to indicate the facility, "that isn't even mentioned in the most thorough of Internet chatrooms. I think there's one nod to it in an old text somewhere, but that manuscript also posits the theory that Finn McCool threw a rock that turned into an island. So, I'll let you be the judge of how reliable that source is."

"There's truth in legends, Ms. Jules." Someone had told me that, my mom or Uncle Finch, or maybe Melody. Atlantis had been nothing but a legend for thousands of years, but it had been at the bottom of the ocean the whole time, as real as the surface world.

"Not this one." Victoria walked to the door, prompting the pixie to disappear in a puff of green smoke. I prayed she hadn't seen it wafting across my books. "Stop looking for other culprits, Persie, when the truth is staring you in the face. I know it's hard for you to accept because these pixies are yours, but you need to come to terms with it. The simplest explanation is likely the right one. Pixies have been Purged for the first time in centuries. Fifteen people have gone missing so far." She paused and hit me with a solemn stare. "And among them is your friend, Genie Vertis."

After dropping that bombshell, she strode out and closed the door behind her.

TWENTY-TWO

Persie

Genie can't be missing! No... no, no, no. She can't!

An hour later, my thoughts were still leaping up and plunging low, leaving me with mental whiplash. I spun around and around in an endless vortex of panic and fury, fearing the worst— that 'missing' meant something else. That it meant gone, in the most final sense of the word: dead, or trapped, or hurt, or being tortured in some place I couldn't reach her. As the terrifying possibilities kept coming, my nerves sang at fever pitch, making my skin crawl and my head hurt. I paced, I sat down, I leapt up, I paced some more. I wanted to scratch at the walls and kick down the door, just to get out and *do* something for my friend, in case it wasn't too late to help her.

The cold manner in which Victoria had given me the news made me want to turn pixie and break everything in my room. Maybe if I set fire to the rug and the alarms went off, someone would come and let me out. But I had no means of starting a fire. The hunters had taken my lighter and anything remotely sharp when they'd locked me in here. And, to add insult to injury, Victoria had somehow taken my phone when I wasn't looking, so I couldn't have called the SDC even if she hadn't put a block on outside communication.

Storming over to the door for the hundredth time that hour, I battered it as hard as I could. "Let me out of here! My friend's in danger! LET ME OUT!" I heard footsteps in the hallway and a burst of cruel laughter, but nobody came to open the door. Like Einstein (or maybe someone else, no one knew for sure) said, this was the very definition of insanity: doing the same thing over and over again and expecting different results.

I felt insane, and hopeless.

They're treating me like a monster. My room wasn't a glass box, but still… There were four walls and no way out, so what was the difference? And I was stuck in here "for my own safety, and everyone else's." Just like in the nightmare. Only, Genie's safety was on the line, and me being imprisoned wouldn't do a damn thing to get her back.

If I *could* get her back.

I slid down the door and ended up hunched on the floor, my knees drawn up to my chin. My body shivered violently, though the radiators were on full blast. My throat tightened with each breath I tried to take, my nails raking against the wooden floor and my head careening into panic mode. If I wasn't careful, soon enough I wouldn't be the only one in this box. Panic led to Purges. I needed to get that on a T-shirt.

Why isn't anyone rebelling against this? I leaned my head back against the solid door, tapping my fingers against my knees and trying to distract the panic attack. If there were fifteen people missing, how come there weren't parents swarming this place? Maybe not enough days had gone by for parents to be worried about not hearing from their children, since everyone was an adult here. Plus, since Victoria had blocked phone signals from getting out in case someone attempted to make this an external problem, it wasn't like authorities could be informed on the sly. She'd been so insistent about keeping it within these walls, and it looked like she was getting her wish. But that seemed so underhanded. Perhaps the truth was simpler—that, even if they could call out, everyone here was more afraid of Victoria than they were of whatever was taking the magicals.

I'm not doing so well, Genie. I scrunched up my eyes and remembered everything she'd taught me. I pictured us on the bench, just before seeing those curious orbs of light for the first time. What had she told me to do? *That's right... deep breaths, focus on textures, root yourself in reality.* I pretended she was there with me, inhaling for five, holding for five, exhaling for five. I went through the motions with my eyes closed. The first few breathing patterns were difficult, my lungs not quite filling, and a drowning sensation made my head throb during every hold. But, somewhere in the back of my mind, I knew it was only the panic attack talking. It was all in my head.

A sound, like a rush of air, made my eyes open. The pixie with the walnut shell hat puffed back into existence, right where he'd cussed out Victoria on my bookshelf. He grinned at me, making a mockery out of my panic attack by flopping about between the books, gasping dramatically and beating on his small chest. An involuntary burst of laughter shot out of me, startling the pixie. He stared at me as though I were a crazy woman, before deciding to join me in a fit of hysterics. He cackled, I cackled, until the room filled with wheezing, manic laughter.

Miraculously, it seemed to stop the panic attack in its tracks. The drowning sensation ebbed, though I still felt breathless from the laughing. The shivers subsided, my throat relaxed, and the anxiety drained from my body, slowly but surely. Sunlight dappled my desk, and through the window I saw an azure sky with a few wisps of cloud drifting by. Thanks to the pixie's intervention, everything suddenly seemed brighter, outside and in. Happiness swelled in my chest and flowed through my limbs until I was so full of euphoria that I felt like I could've broken down the door like a superhero.

Gathering all of my newfound elation into my muscles, I jumped to my feet and yanked on the door handle with all my might. I tugged and tugged, refusing to give up, while the pixie mimed my actions, grunting and pounding on a book like a gorilla. He didn't make me look nearly as heroic as I'd have hoped. To my shock, as I braced my foot against the wood and heaved harder than ever before, the door swung wide, sending me flying. With a yelp, the pixie puffed back into greenish smoke, and I hit the hard floor with a thud, seeing stars.

"Ow," I muttered, in disbelief that I'd managed to break open the door.

"Goodness, I'm so sorry!" A figure leaned over me, helping me into sitting position. "I didn't think you'd be behind the door." It was Nathan, crouching in front of me.

I blinked in confusion as the door closed behind him. "What are you doing here?" I asked, realizing with embarrassment that I hadn't opened the door at all—I'd just been in the way as Nathan had pushed it open from the outside. And I already had the headache to prove it.

"I snuck past the guards stationed in the corridor." He offered me his hand, pulling me to my feet. I swayed for a moment, waiting for the dizziness to pass. "I heard what happened and knew I had to see you. Locking you up like this is nonsensical at best, cruel at worst. But... there's something I have to tell you."

I sighed. "That Genie's missing?"

"Ah, so you were told, at least." He looked as worried as I felt, his mouth twisted into a grimace. "Whatever is taking these people, it has escalated rapidly. If we don't find out who or what is doing it soon, the whole population of the Institute might vanish."

My stomach plummeted. "You think it's that serious?"

"I do, Persie. I realize it sounds extreme, but Victoria and the hunters aren't willing to listen to other options, and that gives me very real concerns for the future of this place." He adjusted his glasses. "I've tried to warn them that they may be leading us down the garden path, but their pride and stubbornness is clouding their judgment."

I breathed a sigh of half-relief, half-terror. "You're probably the only person in this place who agrees with me."

"The one thing I know for certain is that the missing people were taken by the same thing." He produced a strange-looking magnifying glass from his pocket, with a crimson lens that shone with flecks of black and gold in the sunlight. "Do you know what this is?"

I shook my head.

"The lens is made of specterglass, which allows the naked eye to see the residual trails of spirits or ancient creatures who have lived long enough to make that sort of mark in Chaos. I dug it out of my personal collection because I hoped it might reveal the pixie trails, what with them being formerly extinct and all."

He weighed the tool in his hands. "Now, the trails don't last long, but I *have* noticed a distinct recurrence—pale, milky-white streaks along the walls and ceilings. They disappear after a minute or so, but I've managed to spot several. I also shone the glass on that she-pixie you brought to the Repository, but I couldn't see anything other than a few tiny, glittery red specks."

"Have you told Victoria?" I pressed. This specterglass opened up brand-new possibilities, and this was exactly the kind of evidence the head huntswoman needed to see, since she obviously needed proof.

Nathan nodded sadly. "I did, and she told me it wasn't reliable. She explained that there are countless ghosts inside the Institute— spirits of dead hunters and warriors from the old castle that was here before. She reasoned that the white trails came from them, and it would only be a valid abduction theory if we had a poltergeist. Which, of course, we don't, or they would've made themselves known long before now."

"And a poltergeist would've made a lot more mess," I added. My Uncle Finch had told me all about his run-in with Ponce de León during his search for the Fountain of Youth.

"So, circling back to the main question here—what's doing this? It has to be something vaguely spiritual, or the specterglass wouldn't have picked it up." Nathan slipped the item back into his pocket. The poor guy looked exhausted.

I fixed him with a stern gaze, about to reveal the secret of the Door to Nowhere. Before I could say a word, however, the pixie burst back out into existence, apparently realizing it was safe. Everything I'd wanted to say melted off my tongue at the sight of him. Maybe we didn't have to bandy theories about anymore. Nathan spotted the pixie at the same time I did and turned very slowly toward me, as if the slightest sudden movement might spook the little monster.

"I've got an idea," he whispered.

"What if I try to talk to him?" I prompted.

He smiled. "Great minds think alike."

"He showed up before, but I think you frightened him when you came in. If he's hanging around, there must be a reason, and I don't think it stops at mocking the heck out of me."

I glanced back at the pixie, trying to think of the best way to approach him. After what the Institute had put his people through, he had no reason to trust me. But I *had* brought him and the other pixies into being, and he had laughed with me, so maybe that earned me some brownie points.

Nathan frowned. "He? Not to be rude, but how can you tell?"

"He's bulkier than the she-pixie, and his coloring is different," I replied, taking a step toward the bookshelf. Carefully, I put out my hand. "Do you understand me?"

The pixie eyed me curiously, before giving a loud trill and a nod of his head. Fluttering his navy wings, he floated down from the bookshelf and landed on my shoulder, ignoring my hand completely. It was a little more in-my-face than I'd have preferred, but beggars couldn't be choosers.

Folding his arms across his frog-like chest, he marched up and down the length of my arm, chattering furiously and growling every few seconds. I had no clue what he was trying to say, but I guessed he was peeved.

"Can we rein it in for a second?" I asked. "I've got some questions for you."

The pixie stopped abruptly. Whirling around, he half-leapt, half-flew up to my face and pushed down on the flat of my nose, like a person might do to a dog that wasn't paying attention. Squeaking and babbling, he flailed his free hand wildly. I didn't speak his language, but I understood perfectly: he'd talk on his own terms, and he'd answer how he damn well pleased.

"Okay, okay, I'm sorry!" Up close, his black eyes were kind of threatening. "Please, if it's not too much trouble, would you answer some of my questions? I want to help you. I want to stop the hunters from trying to catch you."

The pixie muttered under his breath and stepped away, dropping to sit on my shoulder and swing his tiny legs. He made a grumbling sound of affirmation and flicked his wrist, which I guessed meant "Go ahead, idiot." I wanted to laugh, but I imagined he wouldn't take kindly to that. Polite caution seemed to be the best way forward.

"You heard what the head huntswoman said earlier, didn't you?" I said.

The pixie erupted into another tiny barrage of rage, punching the air and kicking out his legs. His pulsating spots turned bright red—a warning sign, and I totally understood where he was coming from. If I had pulsating spots, they'd be flashing furious, fire engine red right now.

I chuckled. "So, I take it that means you pixies are definitely not responsible, then?"

The pixie shot me a withering look and rolled his eyes. He pressed his hand to his chest, as he had done earlier, and the spots turned a shade of warm pink. The color wasn't as easy to decipher as red or blue, but it made me feel strangely comforted, as though I was... loved.

"You want to be friendly?" I offered.

The pixie nodded and gave a sad chirrup. A second later, he exploded into a fresh tirade, waltzing up and down my arm in a mocking imitation of Victoria, his arms behind his back and his chest puffed out, babbling in a high-pitched tone and sashaying as though his life depended on it. Nathan stifled a snort, which drew a pleased grin from the pixie.

"Do you know where the missing magicals might be?" I asked, before he could start sashaying again. I realized I was smiling... because of him. Aside from Leviathan, I'd never been able to hold a conversation with a Purge beast. Sure, this might not have been a simple back and forth, but he understood me, and I understood him. Mostly. It felt as though some kind of bridge had been crossed, bringing me a little bit closer to understanding the nature of monsters. At least, these ones. And the most ironic part was that I hadn't intended to get to know them. Before I'd come to the Institute, my goal had been control, but I was beginning to think I'd misunderstood what "control" could mean.

The pixie took off his walnut shell hat and scratched his head. Then, very decisively, he shook his head. My heart sank, only to leap again when the pixie held up his index finger. He pointed at himself then swooshed his arms in a circle, chattering the whole time.

"You think other pixies might know?" I prompted.

He grinned and nodded.

Thrilled to have a potential lead, I pressed on, lowering my voice so Nathan couldn't hear. "Could it have something to do with the Door to Nowhere?"

A dark expression drifted across the pixie's face. He lifted a finger to his lips and hovered terrifyingly close to my face, wings fluttering. Almost nose to nose, he lurched at me with spread arms and unleashed an almighty shriek that nearly made me crap my pants. He collapsed back onto my shoulder a second later, cackling to himself.

"Not funny!" I barked, but the pixie kept howling with laughter. "Answer the question!"

He shrugged, making the same circle gesture as before: he had no idea. I'd have to ask the rest of the pixies. I had hoped for a quicker solution so we could get straight to the saving-my-friend-from-a-dangerous-mystical-gateway part of the evening, but if it eventually led to Genie and the others, then I supposed we'd need more input from these funny little pests first.

I turned to Nathan. "I'm guessing you've got an exit strategy? You got in, so you can get us out of here, right?"

"Getting in was actually the easy part." He lowered his gaze, his tone apprehensive. "The hexes prevent any non-authorized personnel from leaving, and we'd both be on that list. So would the pixie."

I frowned. "But the pixie left once already."

The pixie snorted and started running through a rapid charade of what had happened. He flew back up to the bookshelf and puffed out his cheeks like a bullfrog. Snapping out his arms, he ducked behind one of the books, then jumped back into view. He did this again and again until I understood what he was trying to say.

"You tried to get out, but the hexes stopped you?"

He nodded furiously.

I turned to Nathan. "Would a puzzle box work?"

"For the pixie, yes. For us—we don't have one big enough."

He'd made a joke, and Genie had missed it. I'd have to tell her that Mr. Humorless had some decent dad jokes. *When I see her again.*

"Can you deal with that?" I whispered, tilting my head discreetly in the pixie's direction.

He nodded. "No problem."

Behind his back, he slipped a puzzle box out of his pocket. Charging it with a press of the harp button, he hurled the entire thing at the bookshelf. The puzzle box sped through the air toward the pixie, giving the creature just enough time to screech at Nathan in disgust before he evaporated into a stream of black mist. As the puzzle box clattered to the ground, the black mist went with it, sucked inside the device until there was nothing left. The lid snapped shut and I lunged at the box, twisting the designs to make sure the pixie stayed put. He'd be free again soon, and I knew I'd get another earful for putting him there in the first place, but necessity called for it.

"He's going to beat you to a pulp for this." I brandished the box at Nathan.

He chuckled nervously. "Not if he gets to you first. Anyway, that's the least of our worries."

"Right, we need to figure out an escape route." I narrowed my eyes at him. "You *were* planning on taking me with you, weren't you?"

He looked affronted as he pocketed the puzzle box. "I'd have just spoken to you through the door if I wasn't." His eyes surveyed said door, his fingertips reaching out to touch the smooth wood. "And we need to hurry, before anyone else goes missing... or something worse happens."

I'd said it before myself. But in my short time at the Institute, I'd learned categorically that things could always get worse.

TWENTY-THREE

Persie

Nathan closed his eyes and let his hands move across the doorway and the walls, thorough and calm. His mouth moved as he did so, whispering a spell: "*Ut revelare speciem adsumendum. Ostende mihi viam. Quod patet iter. Fiat lux. Ut revelare speciem adsumendum. Veritatem revelare.*" My Latin had never been great, but I guessed he was trying to figure out the locations of the hexes that held us prisoner.

Sure enough, on the fifth repetition, a ripple thrummed across my bedroom. Sigils just in front of the walls lit up like the Fourth of July, spaced at sporadic intervals. Some glowed amber, pulsing steadily, and some carried a deep red. Others were a stark, bold green that reminded me of Celtic knots, the strands of the hexwork intricately folding in on themselves. Two were a juddering violet, the edges crackling and fizzing with energy, too volatile to hold a defined shape.

"I've never seen these hex designs before," I marveled. "They're sort of… beautiful."

Nathan laughed. "That's dangerous talk, finding imprisonment hexes pretty, though it makes it easier to unravel these things when you can actually see them."

"Where did you learn this?" I sat on the bed and watched him work. His palms covered each hex and unraveled them on impact, almost like he was plucking them away. His fingers were elegant and fluid, and utterly mesmerizing to behold. Watching him distracted me from the fact that my best friend was out there somewhere, potentially trapped in some insane doorway that I'd accidentally opened. I had no clue what was on the other side of that door, and the not-knowing frightened me more than anything else. More than banshees, more than Leviathan, more than Victoria. I tried to think of this as a recon mission so I could fill Genie in on some Nathan details when I rescued her, because I *would* be rescuing her. One way or another.

Nathan set to work on the amber hexes, which fell apart at the touch of his fingertips and a further whisper from his lips. *"Separabunt necessitudines. Discoperiet nodum. Quod sit potentiam perdidit. Frange est. Frange vincula. Fiat."* They must have been the weaker ones, judging by how rapidly they unraveled. The amber threads unlooped, as though invisible hands were tugging the strands free, the entire thing disappearing in a puff of golden smoke as it finished undoing itself.

"You're good at this," I encouraged.

He smiled and moved on to the rusty red designs. "I've had a long time to study."

"You can find out how to do this in books?" I had to keep asking questions to stop myself from toppling into an abyss of fear for Genie. And I really didn't want Nathan to see me have a panic attack.

"You can, but not these specific spells." He continued humoring me while he dispensed with the first few reddish hexes, altering the unraveling spell ever so slightly. "You know what a Grimoire is, yes?"

I laughed coolly. "I might not have magic of my own, but I *did* grow up in a coven."

"I'll take that as a yes, then. Apologies if I insulted you—it always pays to understand the knowledge people have before bombarding them with things they may not know." Beads of sweat trickled down his face as he delicately untwined the last of the red hexwork, deft and precise. "Well, these anti-hex spells came from my father's Grimoire."

"He must've been very powerful," I said. "Or did he just have a penchant for hexes?"

Nathan wiped his brow with the back of his sleeve. "I didn't know him very well, so I couldn't say. Maybe both, maybe neither."

"Oh… I'm sorry. Is he… uh… no longer with us?"

Nathan shrugged and began working on the green hexes. "Again, I couldn't say. He took off when I was three, leaving nothing but a Grimoire to remember him by. My mom gave it to me when I was twelve or so, but before that she hadn't said much about him, and I didn't ask." His Chaos untied the Celtic knots smoothly, but I could see the strain of it on his brow. "I have vague memories of his face from when I was little, but you can't trust the human brain with such things. It's more likely that I've put together an impression in my mind of what I think he looks like."

"Did you ever try to find him?" As a daughter of still-married parents, I found it difficult to put myself in his shoes. If it were me, I would've wanted to find them. But I knew that wasn't the case for everyone, depending on the circumstances of a parent's departure.

Nathan paused and sucked in a heavy breath, his hands still sparking as he worked on the glittering green hexes. "I thought about it, then realized there wasn't much point. He wouldn't have left if he wanted to be found. And I had no need for a father figure. My mum had no trouble filling the gap."

"You said 'mum.' I thought you were American?"

"Canadian, actually, but my mum is born and bred Republic of Ireland. Hence the 'O'Hara' part. My parents never married, and I guess he didn't care if I took his name or not." He closed his eyes, as if he were thinking of her. "We moved to Canada about a year after he walked out. Mum had family there, and I think she wanted to put distance between us and the place where she'd been with him, you know? I don't think it ended well, but I didn't understand that until I was much older. And now I'm back here, in the homeland." He chuckled and got back to work on the last green hex.

I was intrigued to learn more about the calm and collected researcher. It proved the theory that you couldn't tell much about a person just from looking at them. "Who was he?"

Nathan's eyes darkened, as if it was painful to remember. "He wasn't anyone. He certainly proved that when he left. Just a guy, passing through our lives, who never intended to stay." His breath caught in his throat, and I knew the Q&A session had come to an end.

I was looking for a distraction, but I didn't need to dredge up all of Nathan's bad memories while I was at it. Still, I was glad his dad had left him that Grimoire, or we wouldn't have gotten out of here anytime soon.

I focused on Nathan's spellcasting instead of idle babbling as he turned his attention to the sparking purple hexes. They called for a very different spell, Chaos streaming out of his palms in crackling strands that were tangibly more powerful. As he chanted, a sliver of lavender light flowed out of his skin and pooled in his hands. Finger-like fronds of the light slithered out and sank into the frenetic balls of purple hexwork. With every thrum of his Chaos strands, a piece came undone, like he was trying to undo the knots in a huge ball of wool. And I stared, transfixed by his power and skill. He had hidden talents beneath the stiff upper lip and the tweed.

Finally, with one exhausting stream of Chaos, he broke apart the entire thing and the rest of the purple hexes collapsed with it, as though they were all connected. Sweating profusely, he looked back at me.

"Shall we?" He dug a stick of chalk out of his pocket. I knew this wasn't any ordinary chalk—my mom and dad each carried a similar item.

I nodded. "Where to first?"

"The Repository. We need to get more of the pixies to help us before we can make our move." He sketched a doorway into the wall and whispered the Aperi Si Ostium spell. The lines fizzled like a lit fuse, bringing it into being.

"One of them has to know where this doorway is," I muttered.

He turned. "Doorway?"

"I… had a thought about where the missing people might have gone. Let's just say a little birdie told me about it." I fidgeted, hoping he wouldn't ask for details. Trying to explain to someone, even a monster enthusiast, that I could speak to Leviathan across oceans would take more time than we had. "They mentioned the Door to Nowhere. That's what I asked the pixie about. He didn't seem to know anything, but he said the other pixies might."

"The Door to Nowhere…" He pulled open the chalk doorway as he spoke. "I haven't heard about that in many moons. It's thought to be a mystical gateway to the land of Tír na nÓg, if memory serves, and there's lots of speculation about where it might be. But why would you think it's here?"

"Like I said, a birdie told me." My cheeks burned. "And that birdie was very certain about it. They said that the Institute was built on top of it, and that... uh... something must've awoken the magic, hence the gateway opening and swallowing up magicals."

His eyes widened. "Those trails! The ones I saw through the specterglass! They might be residual spirits of those who were trapped there before. Gateways work both ways—things go in, things come out." He nodded eagerly. "That would make perfect sense! And do you know what else is useful?"

"What?" I asked nervously.

"Monsters are like truffle-sniffing pigs when it comes to dense concentrations of magic. I think the pixies might be able to lead us right to it. With the right persuasion." He grinned broadly, his eyes hopeful.

I walked to the chalk-door. "Then we probably shouldn't put any more of them in puzzle boxes."

As it turned out, trying to persuade pixies to do anything at all was like wrangling slippery eels. We'd arrived at the Repository through the chalk-door to find the place empty of hunters, and with our puzzle box pixie in tow, we had the perfect opportunity to make peace offerings to my Purges. Except they weren't playing ball.

Twenty of them bounced around in their respective glass boxes —five apiece, aside from one that had four, plus the one where we'd put the first pixie. She had her own private domain, which secretly pleased me. As for the rest, they zoomed from curved wall to curved wall, flat out ignoring Nathan and me. One had fallen asleep at the bottom of an orb, while the other four made every valiant and mischievous attempt to wake her—at least, I thought it was a her. Divebombing her, prodding her, elbowing her in the stomach, and hurling their nutshell helmets at her, yet she somehow managed to sleep through the entire thing, snoring softly.

"Hey!" I banged on one of the orbs. The five pixies inside whirled around at the same time, black eyes glinting. And then, to my horror, they all turned around and flew backward toward the glass, mooning me through the orb. Once they were satisfied they'd shocked me enough, they somersaulted back through the air, cackling like hyenas. One of them pointed at me, opening his eyes wide in alarm, mimicking my reaction. The other four collapsed into hysterics, and I realized I'd have to work a lot harder to get these pixies to focus.

I moved to a different orb. "We were just wondering if we could talk to you for a second?"

A she-pixie approached the glass and lifted her bird skull helmet like it was a visor.

"Does this mean you'll talk?" My hopes rose, only for them to be dashed when she trilled back, mimicking the tone of my voice. Her compadre, another she-pixie, proceeded to fall to the floor and recreate a blow-by-blow of my Purge. She even managed to form some black mist from her own body, which I had to give her credit for.

"Come on! I'm trying to help you here!" I said, but they weren't paying attention. I'd put them in these orbs, and they were going to mess around and ignore me as payback. Frantically, I tried to remember the song that I'd sung by the dumpsters, but the words wouldn't come to me. It stayed stubbornly on the tip of my tongue, just out of reach.

Nathan sighed. "I don't think they want to listen, and who could blame them?"

The only one who didn't seem to be having a whale of a time was the she-pixie I'd first caught. She sat at the bottom of her orb with her back to the glass, her little shoulders hunched. Her wings lay drooped against her, her body language so sad I wanted to free her right then and there and beg forgiveness.

Then, I had a eureka moment. "What if we were to free them, and earn their trust that way?"

Nathan looked at me as if I'd lost my marbles. "*Free* them? What if they escape? I just watched one puff back into existence, which means they might try puffing off, if you get what I'm trying to say?"

"But 'puffing off' doesn't mean much. It just turns them invisible, so they can try and make an escape on the sly. It doesn't mean they can pass through walls." My sixth monster sense seemed to be tingling again, giving me an idea of what they could and couldn't do. "If we close the doors and get prepared with puzzle boxes, they can puff as much as they like—they won't be able to get out. And if we want them to talk, we can't keep them cooped up like this. They've made that blatantly obvious."

I watched a duo of male pixies in the middle of a brawl, slapping and biting the heck out of each other. They broke apart a few seconds later, putting their arms around each other and laughing as though nothing had happened.

Nathan went quiet for a while. "Okay... let's do it."

"Really?"

"It's the best idea we've got, even if it might get me fired."

Straightening up, he ran to the far side of the Repository and closed the doors. On his way back, he grabbed an armload of puzzle boxes and dumped them on the ground in front of me before zipping off to his study. I had no idea what he needed from there, but all became clear when he ran back, beaming from ear to ear, with a cup, a carton of milk, and a basket of strawberries in his hands.

I laughed, despite my growing anxiety. "You remembered."

"Milk and sweet fruit. If anything's going to grab their attention, it's this." He set to work, pouring a cupful of milk and putting out the strawberries. I glanced from him to the pixies and back again, wondering if this was the worst plan I'd ever hatched. So much could go wrong. Then again, I didn't like the sight of the pixies in those glass orbs. I knew it was Institute protocol, and Victoria would flip her lid if she found out they'd all escaped, but if the pixies listened... if they could just give us an indication of where the missing magicals might be, then it would be worth the head huntswoman's rage. And if the pixies could exonerate themselves in her eyes while they were at it, even better.

"Are you sure you want to do this?" Nathan approached the first orb full of pixies.

I shook my head. "No, but I still think it's our best shot."

"Okay, then, brace yourself." He opened the puzzle box with the pixie inside first, then lifted the lid on the first orb, then the second, then the third, then the fourth. And, finally, the opened the last one, with the solitary she-pixie inside.

In a collective flurry, the pixies erupted from their prisons. They flew up and up with their gossamer wings until I worried they might disappear through the roof, only to hurtle back down the millisecond they spotted the cup of milk. A cascade of brightly colored monsters made an aerial assault on the dairy goodness, one of them diving right into the cup and splashing around in the milk. Four others spied the carton that Nathan had put down and snatched it for themselves. Cheering and chanting, they hauled the milk carton away and went to town, scooping up handfuls and guzzling down every drop.

The strawberry situation quickly turned into a bloodbath. Well, it looked like a bloodbath. Smushed fruit everywhere, smeared on their hungry little faces and all over their tiny frames. Two she-pixies ripped off the green tops and plopped them on their heads, using them as fetching hats. A moment later, they devoured a strawberry between them like piranhas gnawing a whole duck down to the bone.

"Excuse me?" I sank to my knees and tried to get their attention. "Would you be willing to talk now? We need your help with something, and it's urgent."

I might as well have been talking to myself.

Over the cup of milk, a fight broke out. A trio of pixies squawking and squabbling, trying to pull the cup toward them in a three-way tug of war. Meanwhile, a fourth pixie still swished and swam about in the milk, happy as a clam. Pixies battled for the prime spot atop the milk carton, shoving each other out of the way to get to it. A she-pixie slapped another so hard across the face that he fell to the ground for a moment before shaking his head and getting back up. He tackled her from the top of the carton, and the two of them wound up in the strawberry basket, where they seemed intent on making jam out of what was left.

"This is useless! They don't care!" I hissed to Nathan. We were running out of time to save my best friend, and these punks were too busy fighting over milk and strawberries. I wanted to grab them and knock their heads together.

Instead, I sat back on my haunches and let the frustration wash over me. Bitter tears welled in my eyes, trickling down my cheeks and onto the floor. One of the little ingrates even dared to dip a finger into the small puddle and taste my tears. I would've flicked him away, but it wouldn't help. We'd let them out, and they didn't give a crap what we wanted.

Why should they? No one in the Institute cared about what they wanted. They were just returning the favor.

I was so absorbed in my misery that I didn't notice the she-pixie I'd first caught finally emerge from her orb, as though she'd been observing the situation. For a moment, she was just a flutter in the corner of my eye. Then, she shot upward to meet with the puzzle-box pixie, who was chomping contentedly on a strawberry. He dropped it the moment he saw the she-pixie, and the two of them hovered there for a moment. Their loud chatter and the falling strawberry drew my attention away from my tears. They jabbed bony fingers at me, babbling animatedly, and performed some less-than-flattering charades. Finally, it seemed they'd made some kind of decision. Both creatures nodded to one another and hurtled to the ground.

The she-pixie landed by the milk, while the other one landed by the strawberries. There, in a display of pure rage that I could only have described as jaw-dropping, the two pixies set about terrorizing the others into obedience. Slaps, bites, irate shrieks and yelps, and a lot of angry gesturing and shoving. Every so often, the two additions pointed up toward me, their chatter becoming even more incensed, as if they were reprimanding the others for not listening to me.

Nathan knelt beside me, observing the telling-off of a lifetime. "They have a hierarchy. Fascinating."

"What do you mean?" I whispered, not wanting to disturb them. The she-pixie and the one from my bedroom were in the middle of corralling the rest into the center of the floor, right in front of Nathan and me. I didn't dare laugh, but the others looked so put out, their wings drooping and their heads bowed as they shuffled forward, ashamed and humbled. It was made funnier by the fact that most of them were doused in milk or smothered with strawberries.

Nathan gestured to the two he'd freed last. "They operate as a group, socially connected to one another. These two are clearly fond of you, and they're getting the rest to accept you."

"They are?" I smiled down at the tiny beasts.

"It looks like it."

Just then, the fearsome she-pixie tiptoed forward and tugged the bottom of Nathan's tweed jacket. She sniffed it, then beckoned for the others to do the same. He froze, evidently less confident about the pixies' intentions than he'd been a moment ago. After all twenty-one had done their smell test, the she-pixie patted her chest frantically. Immediately, the whole flock "oohed," as if they understood something that Nathan and I didn't. She then pointed to me and chattered loudly, wrapping her arms around herself and grinning manically. The male pixie who'd come out of the puzzle box nodded and copied her movements, getting them to sniff my knees. I'd never felt less comfortable in my life than I did as a gang of pixies took a whiff of me. The pixies "oohed" again when the male pixie beat his chest, smiling proudly.

"I'm not sure why they're sniffing us, though." Nathan chuckled, looking remarkably chipper about this entire thing.

I smiled, my heart softening like a marshmallow. "They recognize our smell. They're showing the others that they know us, and we're not going to hurt them." I pointed to his tweed jacket. "This is the jacket I wrapped her up in, back in your room, and I'm still wearing the clothes that the 'poofing' pixie met me in. That's why they're sniffing."

The she-pixie muttered something and made a retching sound. Her wrangling colleague nodded and performed his Victoria impression again, before gesturing at us and shaking his head. The other nineteen pixies eyed us with new intrigue, chirruping excitedly amongst themselves. A few of the she-pixies batted their eyelashes at Nathan, pretending to smooth down imaginary lapels the way he'd just done.

"I think we just made some new friends," Nathan whispered nervously.

I giggled, laughter bubbling up the back of my throat. "You're right. I think we did."

At the sound of my joy, the pixies burst into cackles, nudging each other and hopping gleefully from foot to foot. A few of them even scooped the strawberry goop off their faces and offered it to

Nathan and me. After we politely declined, they gobbled it up themselves, clearly relieved we hadn't accepted. But it felt like a good start to a good relationship.

Now that I had their attention, I stood a chance of getting their help. And that brought me one step closer to finding a way to rescue Genie and the other missing magicals. As terrible ideas went, this might've been my best one yet.

TWENTY-FOUR

Persie

W ith the she-pixie and her male counterpart cracking the whip, I addressed the now-attentive creatures. "Do you know where the missing magicals have gone?"

Chattering whispers did the rounds, each pixie turning to the next, and the next, until they had formed some kind of collaborative answer for me. But the she-pixie seemed to have taken on the role of spokesperson. She stepped forward and cleared her throat, then began chirruping a mile a minute in high-pitched pixie-speak.

"Whoa, whoa, whoa." I put up my palms to stop her. "I'm sure what you're saying is super helpful, but I don't understand. Can you make it… simpler?"

The she-pixie rolled her eyes and gave a sarcastic nod.

My heart leapt. "You know where they were taken?" I paused, realizing I might have jumped the gun. "Or are you saying you can make it simpler?"

She tilted her head from side to side, which muddied my understanding even more.

My temper flared, but I had to keep the wheels greased. "Let me ask in a different way. Do you know anything about the missing magicals? Or anything about a magic door?"

I struggled to suppress the snap in my tone. My friend was waiting for me out there, and I needed to get to her ASAP. I didn't have time to decipher pixie hijinks, but I also couldn't do this without them.

The pixie tapped a slim finger against her chin, then jabbed it in the air as if she'd had a lightbulb moment. She ran into open space and began what could only be described as a mind-boggling interpretive dance—definitely one for the contemporary crowd. Smoothing down her mossy mass of hair, she sauntered a few paces forward and then lifted her head in melodramatic awe. Her black eyes widened until they took up most of her small face, and then she dropped her jaw comedically and released an excited "aaaah." She switched to a zombie shuffle, her arms trawling sluggishly through the air as if she were trying to catch something. Mimed to perfection, she opened up an imaginary door and stepped inside.

I might not have understood the rest, but I understood that.

"There *is* a magic door?" Nathan's jaw dropped just as comically as the she-pixie's had.

The pixie took a bow and drank in the rapturous applause of her fellows, clasping her hands together and shaking them from side to side. I added a few lackluster claps, so as not to seem rude. Useful though the charade had been, we really didn't have time for more amateur dramatics.

"Can you take us to it?" I failed to disguise the pleading in my voice.

The she-pixie gestured around and shot me a look that said, "Well, duh. Why else would I have asked everyone what they know?"

"Point taken." I smiled apologetically. "Please, guide us there. My friend is one of the people missing, and I need to get her back."

The entire squadron of pixies gasped and shook their heads,

chattering ominously. I even saw one of them pretend to tie a noose and hang themselves with it. The gesture felt like a knife to the gut. I didn't need to understand their language to get the picture—if Genie had entered that doorway, then she was obviously in a lot of trouble. All the more reason to get going.

The she-pixie held up her hands and drew a square shape. Her eyes narrowed in annoyance, and she shook her head vehemently, giving one loud, high-pitched squawk that definitely sounded like "NO!"

"You don't want us to put you in puzzle boxes?"

She nodded, repeating the singular squawk.

I cast a look at Nathan. "What do you say?"

"I say we let them go free-range. They're helping us, after all." Nathan looked pointedly at the assembled crowd. "But you *have* to stay out of sight. Can you do that?"

The pixies snorted and puffed out their chests proudly, and a few polished their fingernails against their shoulders: "easy peasy lemon squeezy." They'd given the hunters the runaround for days without getting spotted, and they had us to help cause any necessary diversions if hunters happened upon us. And why shouldn't they get to come with us as equals? They were doing *us* a favor, not the other way around. And the pressure was mounting by the second.

"Just keep as close as you can, and stay hidden," I warned. To the she-pixie, I said, "You can lead us there, but don't take any chances. If you see a hunter, take cover, and only come out again when it's safe."

She lifted her hand to her temple in a salute. No sooner had she done that than the entire crew took off into the air, fluttering all the way up to the ceiling. The she-pixie surged upward last and flew past the others to take her position at the head of the aerial squadron. Once there, she beckoned for Nathan and me to follow before waiting by the closed Repository doors. Nathan and I gave each other an encouraging nod and jumped to our feet, racing across the marble floor. He did the honors of opening the towering doors, and all of us ducked out into the hallway beyond.

I scoured left and right to make sure there were no hunters around as the pixies blended into the shadows overhead. I glanced up and saw how their colored banding and vibrant wings darkened until they were entirely camouflaged. Now I understood why they'd given everyone hunting them such a headache; like cuttlefish, they could alter their skin to fit their surroundings, making them trickier to find than a needle in a stack of pins. The only one who stayed vaguely visible was the she-pixie, who I decided, then and there, to name Boudicca.

I'd read about the ancient Iceni queen in the Institute's entrance hall, on a plaque beside a gold torc, a thick metal necklace, that had belonged to her. A rumored Celtic magical of the Primus Anglicus, she'd led an uprising against the Romans. Like the she-pixie, the original Boudicca was said to have wild hair, a harsh voice, and a piercing glare.

"Why are you smiling?" Nathan whispered, looking at me as though I'd lost my marbles.

I pointed up to the leader. "I named her."

"Oh?"

"Boudicca. Queen of the Pixies." I slowed my pace to match hers as we approached an intersection of hallways. She stopped, looking both directions for the enemy.

Nathan laughed. "I think she'd like that."

"Me too." I quickened my pace again as Boudicca took a left. *Where were we going?* There wasn't anything up there aside from the new wing, which hadn't been built yet. But I wasn't about to argue with her. She could sense high concentrations of magic, and I couldn't.

Nathan side-eyed me. "Do you think she might have her wires crossed?"

"I'm not sure. Is there an annex up here that I don't know about?" I whispered back.

"There are private studies and offices, and a chapel which has an exit to the back gardens. Maybe that's where she's leading us. It would be the quickest way." He frowned, evidently deep in thought. "I suppose it depends where this doorway is. Did your little birdie happen to mention how far down it was buried beneath the Institute?"

I shook my head. "My little birdie is never that detailed."

The day Leviathan gave me information that wasn't peppered with gaping holes would be the day his glass box properly froze over again. All he'd told me about the door was to "look into it." I'd done that, and I'd hardly learned anything. Oh, he must've been killing himself with laughter, knowing my only option was to ask the pixies for help, that we'd have to resort to a bevy of hilarious charades to communicate.

"It's Leviathan, right?" Nathan asked as we continued to walk, following Boudicca's fluttering wings. Some of her motley crew were acting up, wiping the last of the strawberry goop off their faces and smearing the jammy blobs across the nearest available canvas—rafters, the tops of the high windows, the wall. I didn't get to focus on it much, since Nathan had dropped that doozy of a question on me.

"Huh?" My throat closed up.

Nathan looked half-excited, half-sorry, an expression he seemed to have perfected. "The little birdie is Leviathan. He gave you this ability, didn't he?"

"H-how could you possibly know that?" I blurted out, my hands turning clammy with cold sweat. No one, other than Victoria, was supposed to know where my ability had come from. Chaos, if the rest of the Institute found out... They'd make accusations like the head huntswoman had, claiming I was in cahoots with an ancient monster who wanted to make mankind suffer for centuries of injustice against him and his kind.

Stop panicking. Even Victoria doesn't know the part about turning the world into monster paradise or him making me his queen. I served myself a swift reminder of the facts before the stress could take hold and bring on another unwanted Purge. Learning to control my emotions was my best defense against this ability. I needed to stop with the knee-jerk, paranoid reactions, before they got even more out of hand. My cousin Diana would've called me a "typical Pisces." I didn't necessarily believe in that stuff, but my emotions really did have an iron grip over me. One I'd have to loosen, if I wanted to get ahead of my curse.

Nathan smiled reassuringly. "Relax. No judgment here, remember?" He gave me a light knock in the arm. "Victoria mentioned it to me, in private, after she caught me trying to catch pixies in the Repository. She hasn't told anyone else, but she knows about my research into ancient monsters. I think she wondered if I knew of anything that might be helpful to you."

My panic turned into a fleeting glimmer of hope. "Do you?"

"I can only tell you what I told her: that I will look into it, and let you know if I find something worthwhile," he replied. A few of the pixies at the back of Boudicca's aerial squadron shoved each other for a better spot in the line-up, earning a sharp hiss from their gutsy leader. I wouldn't have wanted to get on her bad side, either.

"Could you maybe tell me before you tell her?" I said. "Give me a grace period, to see if I can do anything with it?"

"It's your ability, and your connection to Leviathan. It would be wrong of me to do otherwise. I swear on my integrity as an academic that I will come to you first. After all, you have more insight on this matter than anyone else."

"Thank you," I said, relieved.

He chuckled softly. "Might I ask a favor in return?"

"That depends..." I eyed him curiously. "If you're going to ask me to set you up on a date with Genie after we've got her back safe and sound, I can't make that sort of promise. I can put in a good word, but it'll be up to her."

He froze mid-step and turned to face me. "A... date?" His cheeks burned beet red. "Chaos help me, have I really been so obvious?"

I shrugged, smiling.

"She's just... intriguing. I've never met anyone like her, and nor do I think I've ever had anyone keep me on my toes in quite the same fashion. I'm genuinely worried I might end up with some kind of repetitive-strain injury in my feet." He smacked himself on the forehead, shaking his head at himself. "And now I've just gone and babbled all of that to you. That wasn't even what I was going to ask."

"Is it even okay for students and aides to date?" The prospect of a maybe-romance was a welcome distraction from monstrous, worst-case scenarios. I reminded myself that we'd rescue Genie, and everything would be all right again.

He swallowed audibly. "It is, but that's really not what I was going to ask." He looked down at the ground. "I'm just so worried for her welfare... I didn't mean for all that to come out. Please, I'd appreciate if you forgot I said anything."

"Forget you said what?" I gave him a conspiratorial smile to let him know I didn't plan to breathe a word. Girl code maintained that I would have to, but he didn't need to stress himself out over that. Besides, we didn't even have Genie back yet.

I glanced up and realized that Boudicca had stopped and was waving her hands wildly. And probably had been for a while, judging by her annoyed expression.

"Crap. We'll have to talk about this later, or we'll lose the pixies."

"Of course."

We carried on up the corridor from the Repository toward the point where it branched off to the right. Above, Boudicca did a rude mime that made it clear she wanted to strangle the life out of me before fluttering onward.

"What's the favor?" I asked Nathan, keeping an eye on the pixies.

Nathan looked up. "Ah, well, I was hoping you might be willing to tell me more about what Leviathan is like from a personal perspective. Anecdotes from your mother and her friends, from their experience with Echidna, would also be welcome."

I mustered a halfhearted snort. "Would a page full of curse words do?"

"There must be hidden depths to him, even if they are—"

He came to a stop, eyes locked on Boudicca. She was waving maniacally from behind a rafter, her tiny colored dots flashing a red warning through the shadows. I frowned in confusion. Did she not want us talking to each other?

Everything became clear as Charlotte rounded the corner, carrying one of the heavy metal folders that I'd seen during my exam—the folders that connected to the wider magical world through the Krieger Detection Technology, or the KDT, as it was more commonly known. She must have been using one of those private offices that Nathan had mentioned, and we'd been too busy talking about Genie to hear the door close. Seeing us, she halted abruptly, looking from Nathan to me, then back again.

"You're not supposed to be out here! Victoria put you on hexed lockdown!" She cast a conflicted look at Nathan. "And you... you should have stopped her. I remember what you said in the orchard, Persie, but I can't allow this. I'm sorry, but I'm going to have to hold you here and call for Victoria." She dumped the folder on the floor with an echoing bang and raised her hands.

Finally, I'd get to see the famous Charlotte Basani in action—just not in the way I'd imagined. White sparks glittered around her fingertips, and I knew what was about to go down—the same thing happened when my mom got ready to use her Telekinesis.

Here we had a classic preemptive strike (apparently, I had learned something in Hosseini's class), and I dealt with those the pacifist's way—by ducking and rolling. Silvery strands shot out of her palms, and I made my escape, diving under the Telekinetic trajectories. I hit the floor hard, a jolt of pain shooting through my knee, which had absorbed the shock.

"Charlotte, enough!" Nathan stepped between us. "You may be Shailene's daughter, but that doesn't give you the right to attack us. What we're doing does not concern you, and Persie and I will deal with Victoria once we're finished."

Charlotte didn't listen. Instead, she shot a strand of Telekinesis toward him. It took him by surprise, snaking around his waist. He lifted his palms to retaliate, but she flicked her wrist and threw him against the nearest wall before he had the chance to do anything. I grimaced as I heard the thud.

Meanwhile, my hand clawed for the metal folder she'd dropped. I grabbed it before she could aim a fresh round of Telekinesis at me and hurled it at her head with all my might. She ducked, whirling around to watch it skid down the hallway behind her. I didn't waste any time. Jumping up, I raced toward Nathan, helping him up.

He groaned. "We need to get... out of here. We can't... save Genie, if she turns us in... to Victoria."

"Way ahead of you." At least, I'd thought I was, but Charlotte was facing me again, her hands raised and ready for more.

"If you're not going to come quietly, that causes a few problems for me," she said. Closing her eyes, she slammed her palms into her chest, sending green ripples down her body.

Nathan sighed. "Ah, crap."

"What?" I whispered, trying to hurry him away from the scene.

"Charlotte's best attack." He dropped to the floor and pressed his palms into the ground, presumably preparing some kind of Earth-based defensive maneuvers. Beneath my feet, I felt a rumble growing. The polished concrete splintered just in front of Charlotte's feet, and out slithered a tangle of vines. They crept up Charlotte's legs, wrapping around her.

It took a second for me to understand what was happening when her body began to transform. Her face morphed into a mask of pain as her shoulders broadened. She lengthened right in front of us, growing two feet taller. Her skin rippled, and thick brown hair sprouted rapidly. Muscles that hadn't been there before bulged out, and I stared in disbelief as a snout formed and huge claws protruded from newly-born paws. It took less than twenty seconds for the process to complete, leaving Nathan and me standing in front of a freaking grizzly bear. The only thing that hadn't changed were her hazel eyes, which glinted at us with very human anger.

"She's… she's…" I remembered vaguely that she was a Bestia, but I hadn't fully understood what that entailed until now. With a growl that shook the walls, she clawed away the constricting vines like tissue paper. And that meant nothing was holding her back from a full-on grizzly charge. Surely she didn't intend to maul us?

"We need to run!" Nathan urged. "I could hit her with everything I have and it wouldn't bother her in the slightest, not in this state."

Just as we were about to whip around and flee, my own beasts reminded us that they were there. A divebombing unit of twenty-plus pixies plummeted from the ceiling, shrieking a deafening war cry. The bear looked up in bemusement as the creatures struck. Two of them went straight for the eyes, coming in for a dropkick with their tiny legs extended. The bear's massive paws flailed in front of her face, trying to fend them off, but there were two more right behind, prepared and willing to temporarily blind Charlotte. A distraction crew circled her, tugging at her fur and generally trying to piss her off by socking her in the jaw and yanking on her ears.

Meanwhile, two smaller groups had materialized curtain ties from who-knew-where. One team wrapped the velvet cords around her legs, crossing over one another in perfect unison as they pulled the cords tighter and tighter, like something out of a cartoon. The other team did the same with her arms, binding them to her sides.

I wanted to give them a standing ovation as the bear came crashing down like a bowling pin. Charlotte roared as the distraction crew jumped on her head, dancing a jig and elbow-dropping into her fur, while others pulled at her bear ears, basically ensuring she kept her head down. Boudicca walked across the bear's head, all the way down to the tip of her snout, lifting her hand in a salute before gesturing wildly at the now-clear hallway.

"Sorry, Charlotte." Grabbing Nathan's arm, I pulled him past her. "I didn't want you to get involved in this," I said to bear-Charlotte. "But you wouldn't listen. You'll understand soon. I'm doing this to save both of our best friends."

If the pixies were right, then we'd be able to solve the mystery of the missing magicals before the night was over. I just prayed I wouldn't be getting expelled for letting a horde of free-range pixies loose on a Basani-Bear.

She attacked first. She's the one who should be reprimanded. Defiant, I let go of Nathan's arm and tore along the corridor, though I still had no idea where we were going. Once Charlotte broke out of her bonds, she'd probably go straight to Victoria and we'd be on the hunters' most-wanted list, but we'd have to handle that after we saved Genie. I couldn't waste this window of time worrying about what *might* happen, not with my friend in peril.

The farther we ran, the closer we got to the unfinished part of the Institute. But that couldn't be right. Boudicca landed on my shoulder and pointed forward as if I were her majestic steed. I glanced at her as I ran and she grinned back, her pulsating spots turning a vibrant shade of golden yellow—the color of friendship and triumph. Beside me, pixies crowded Nathan's shoulders and head, enjoying a free ride. The rest flew above us as an aerial entourage, no longer worried about hiding in the shadows. Boudicca had spotted Charlotte long before we did, and I wondered if they had a way of sensing the hunters.

"Are we going to the new wing?" I asked Boudicca.

She nodded solemnly and swirled her hands over each other, as if trying to explain the unknown power that awaited us there. Her pulsating spots changed to a dark, foreboding purple. Knowing my color palettes had been a Godsend for breaking through language barriers with these pixies. They wore their hearts on their sleeves, literally.

Sprinting onward, we pounded the polished concrete until we came to the stunning, half-formed entrance to the new wing. The darkness dulled the colors of the stained glass, giving the wing a gloomy feel, as though it didn't want us to enter. Nothing penetrated the dense black beyond the archway. No workman's lights, no fireballs, just endless shadow.

"In here?" Nathan asked his freeloaders.

The pixies jittered, trying to tuck under the lapels of his jacket, and hide behind his ears and his neck. A few slipped into his pockets, and one managed to fold itself under his leonine locks, trembling against his scalp.

I shuddered, strengthened only by Boudicca's steadfast face. "I think we can take that as a yes."

With a deep breath, I put my best foot forward and stepped into the breach. It might've sounded dramatic, but it felt even more dramatic. The moment I entered the half-constructed foyer, the shadows seemed to close in and darken further, reminding me of that endless, tarry black substance I'd been trapped in at the start of my nightmare. Had that been an omen of this? I couldn't see Nathan or Boudicca anymore, which supported the impression that I was entirely alone in a world of impermeable black.

"Nathan?" I whispered.

"I'm here," he replied from nearby, though the reverb made it sound like his voice was coming from everywhere at once. "I can't see a thing," he whispered.

"Me neither." I reached out, swishing my arms in front of me and hitting only air. "Can you find my voice?"

"I'm not sure." His tone was concerned, but not afraid, and that was comforting.

"Do you have a lighter, or some kind of light spell we could use?" I all but begged. A moment longer in this darkness and I'd lose my mind. My breaths had already become ragged, and if I couldn't fight it, the cold sweats would follow. And then, the inevitable.

Just then, I felt tiny hands on my face and heard a soft hush from Boudicca. She smoothed her palm across my cheek, small as a dime, and whispered in her pixie dialect. The words made no sense, but the sentiment did. Boudicca—the pixie I'd put in a glass orb—had sensed my terror and was trying to comfort me. Through the dark, I saw her pulsating spots glowing white.

"Thank you," I murmured, feeling my breaths slow with every stroke of her small hand.

She giggled and chattered something that sounded like: "No problem."

"Persie," Nathan hissed. "Do you see that?"

"What?" I whipped my head around, my eyes focusing on lights heading in our direction. I nearly shrieked, thinking they were hunters' flashlights. But then I noticed the colors, burning bright at the center, encircled by a gaseous halo. Purples, pinks, greens, blues, yellows, all bobbing toward us. They'd come from somewhere within the unfinished sphere of the new Repository, though I had no idea which way I was even facing.

I smiled as they illuminated the dark of the foyer, chasing the shadows back into the corners where they could lurk all they liked without bothering us. They were beautiful, like magical, dancing wisps. Just looking at them made my insides warm and happy.

"The orbs came back," I thought aloud, ignoring a frantic chirp from Boudicca. Her tiny hands tried to grab my face, but I was too fascinated by the lights to turn away. "Do you remember them, Nathan?"

He stood beside me, looking up. "I do. They were in here last time, weren't they? I... didn't realize how astonishing they were. I expect you have to see them in the dark to fully appreciate their beauty."

"Didn't you say they might be spirits of dead hunters?" I whispered, not wanting to disturb the wisps as they spiraled around each other and danced off in different directions, putting on a show just for us.

"Hmm?" Nathan appeared just as captivated as I was. "Oh, yes, something to... uh, that effect. They might be the remnants of... What did you say again?"

"Dead hunters' spirits," I replied.

"Yes, they might be remnants of... a dead hunter's magic, though I can't think who they would belong to." He giggled, his eyes wide as saucers. "They would have had to be... What was I saying? Um... exceptionally powerful to leave such wondrous fragments behind. And I can't think... I can't think... of anyone who would have fit such a bill recently. Maybe not even in the... the Institute's history."

Grinning idiotically at the floating lights, I looked around in wonder as music began to play, melodic and sweet with an undercurrent of sadness that brought tears to my eyes. I could almost envision a chorus of angels, cheesy as it sounded. But music inspired imagination, and I'd never heard a sweeter or sadder song in my whole life.

"Tell me you can hear that?" Nathan sighed, his eyes wet.

I nodded dumbly. "It's incredible. Do you know what they're saying?"

"It's an old variation of Gaelic..." He hummed quietly, trying to find the melody. "But even my ordinary Gaelic is *very* rusty. I can only make out something to do with a broken heart and... eternal longing, perhaps? But it might be a stomachache."

Persephone? A not-so-melodic voice cut through my charmed thoughts. *Persephone, can you hear me?*

Not now! You're ruining it!

Ruining what? He sounded bemused.

The pretty lights and the beautiful music. It's... the most incredible thing I've ever heard. I watched the lights flow balletically through the air, moving in time to the slow, bittersweet song. *I'd appreciate it if you could get out of my head so I can keep on enjoying it. Why are you in my head, anyway?* Weirdly, I wasn't upset that Leviathan had made contact.

The music is why I came. Your fascination with it. His tone carried a hint of concern, which annoyed me.

Oh, so I can't be happy or angry or sad without you showing up unannounced? Are there any emotions I can feel without you butting in?

He chuckled softly. *Your emotions are erratic. That is why I am here. There is something amiss.* His laughter faded. *Tell me about the lights and music.*

I don't know. They just appeared, but I've seen them before—they're these gaseous, floaty orbs, a bit like small, colorful comets. There wasn't any music last time, though, I explained. I wished he'd buzz off so I could hear the music properly without him taking up headspace.

Ah... A note of surprise punctuated the sound.

I rolled my eyes. *Ah? What does that mean?*

They sound like Will-o'-the-Wisps. I have heard of them, but they have never interested me enough to warrant my full attention. He paused. *Now, however... Perhaps they have earned my curiosity.*

I tried to hide my excitement in case Nathan noticed, but I quickly realized he was too transfixed by the lights to even remember that I was here. The hiding pixies had come out to slap some sense into him, the one in his hair tugging on his locks, but he didn't pay them any mind. I didn't blame him. Who would want to be distracted from such a remarkable display? I definitely didn't, but I had a nuisance in my noggin that wouldn't go away until he'd done whatever it was he'd come to do, and I was anxious to return to the light show.

Are you going to leave me hanging? I asked.

He laughed. *You know I would never do that, my Persephone. Will-o'-the-Wisps are elemental spirits. The lights themselves are candles of the dead. The spirits hold the candles, and they are the ones who sing, but you cannot see the bearers with the naked eye. They may appear to some as hazy figures. I am surprised you are not able to see them.* He made a sound, as though he was slightly disappointed by this fact.

Sorry that I'm not some almighty Mother of Monsters, I spat, becoming more and more frustrated by his voice. It was like hearing three songs at once, all the notes clamoring in my head and making my nerves bristle. Besides, last time we'd spoken, he'd told me about a Door to Nowhere, not elemental spirits or wisps. It sounded like he was making it up as he went along, trying to keep my attention.

Anyway, that is by the by, Leviathan continued. *The candles of the dead and the song of the spirits hypnotize people in order to lead them astray. Usually, it is to lead them from safe paths into bogs and marshland, to claim more spirits for themselves. However, it seems they have diversified.*

"Will you not listen to us?" whispered a soft voice, ethereal and sad. Almost as if they were pleading with me. "Please, hear our song. We sing it for you."

I nodded slowly. "I'm listening." The moment I spoke, the connection severed and Leviathan vamoosed out of my head, just as I'd wanted. Now, I could give all of my focus to the hypnotic wisps, just as *they* wanted. I'd come all this way; the least I could do was listen.

"Will you follow us, sweet lady?" the voice whispered again, gentle and warm. "Will you come to us? We can sing to you there. We sing for you."

I smiled shyly. "For me?"

"For me?" Nathan parroted.

"Only for you. Will you follow us?" The lights floated toward the dense black of the new Repository sphere, and my feet did the talking. I stepped forward automatically, eager to go wherever the Wisps were going. Beside me, Nathan did the same.

"I'll follow," I replied dreamily, desperate not to lose sight of them.

I'd walked a few paces when Boudicca put her fingers to her lips and gave the loudest whistle my eardrums had ever heard. En masse, the pixies surged toward the Wisps. The pixies' pulsating lights burned with blinding brightness for a few seconds, the sudden ferocity chasing the Wisps away down the central walkway of the sphere and into the darkness below. The moment they disappeared, taking their heartbreaking song with them, I snapped out of whatever trance they'd put me in. It was like waking up after a long, strange dream, and finding that you'd sleepwalked into the kitchen for no reason.

I blinked. "Nathan? Are you okay?"

"I was just about to ask you the same thing," he replied, concerned. "Did they just... hypnotize us?"

I nodded. "And the pixies saved our behinds." The pieces were slowly making sense. "I've got a feeling that, if we'd followed them, we'd have ended up in the same situation as the missing magicals.

That's why there were no signs of a struggle: no one *did* struggle. They came here of their own accord, because of the Will-o'-the-Wisps."

Nathan's face was marginally visible in the light of the glowing pixies who'd come back to roost. "Pardon?"

"They're Will-o'-the-Wisps," I said, fixing him with a stern gaze. Weren't we almost trapped like everyone else, and wasn't he supposed to be a genius in this subject? "Do you know anything about them?"

"Yes. They are thought to be controlled by..." He trailed off, looking at the pixies on his shoulder.

"By?" I prompted.

He cleared his throat, his eyes wide. "Pixies."

Boudicca leapt to the defense of her people, chattering loudly, jabbing and pointing like there was no tomorrow. I got the feeling she disagreed with Nathan, and I wished more than ever that I had a way to understand exactly what my Purge beasts were saying. It would've made this so much easier.

"Calm down," I urged Boudicca. "Explain it slowly, so I can get the gist."

She turned her pulsating spots to a sad shade of blue and began to act out the message she was trying to get across. First, she pointed at me and pretended to walk across my shoulder, shivering and hunched, her expression scared. Then, she pointed to herself and lifted up off my shoulder, gesturing and beckoning as though she were leading me somewhere. For her next act, she dropped suddenly to the floor, as if she were dead, and turned her spots purple. She rose up with her arms outstretched, like a resurrected mummy, and returned to her second performance of guiding me somewhere. Then, things turned bad again as Boudicca began snickering and tiptoeing through the air, leading me, presumably, down the wrong path.

"The Wisps are spirits of lost souls?" I said. Boudicca nodded vigorously. "Who haven't been able... to cross to the afterlife?" She nodded again, flashing her purple spots. "But how did they end up like this, causing trouble? They aren't poltergeists." Boudicca grumbled something rude in pixie and flashed her purple spots more frantically.

Nathan cleared his throat. "I think she's trying to say that they were brought into being with some kind of Necromancy. Purple is the color of Necromancy."

Boudicca took off and hurtled toward Nathan's face, landing a huge smacker on his nose. She flew back again, smoothing down her hair with sudden bashfulness. In fairness, poor Nathan looked stunned, and maybe a little horrified.

"I guess that means you were right," I said, chuckling nervously. "Did you bring them into being? I didn't know you were Necromancers."

Boudicca gestured, and then swept her hands through the air in a cross.

I arched a confused eyebrow. "You were, but you're not anymore?"

She grinned and nodded, before motioning in the direction of where the Wisps had disappeared. I tried to remember the rest of the scenes that she'd played out so I could put together a timeline of events in my head.

"So, you brought them into being with Necromancy and gave them the task that you'd been doing of guiding travelers? Only, they... stopped doing what you told them to, and started leading people astray instead?" I was really wading through some wild speculation here. "And that's when you had your Necromancy abilities taken away from you?"

Boudicca punched the air and nodded effusively. She held up her index finger and added one last scene. Miming to perfection, she signed out a doorway, then pretended to get sucked through, shaking her fists as her spots flashed red with anger.

"They got trapped behind the Door to Nowhere because they were disobeying?" I guessed.

She grinned and gave me a thumbs-up. But she wasn't quite done. Flying right up to my face, she tapped my forehead. And I had a horrible feeling I understood exactly what she was trying to say this time.

I lowered my voice, so Nathan wouldn't hear. "I opened the Door to Nowhere by Purging you?"

She tilted her head from side to side and tapped my forehead again.

"I opened it by coming here?" I asked.

No matter which way I swung it, I was responsible for this. The pixies hadn't stolen anyone directly, and neither had I, but our joint actions had caused a chain reaction that had opened up this mysterious door.

She repeated the head tilt.

I sighed, exasperated. "You don't know why the Door is open?"

She nodded and pressed her bony finger between my brows.

"You don't know, but you think it has something to do with me?"

Her black eyes widened in apology as she gave one last, slow nod. I really hadn't wanted Leviathan to be right... about any of it. The Door to Nowhere was real, and I'd played a part in unlocking it so the Wisps could get out and wreak havoc. He might have had incorrect information about the Wisps, but he'd been on the right track. Maybe, if he wasn't so arrogant, he would've paid attention to beasts who hadn't warranted his attention, and I'd have been spared this lesson in advanced charades. But I couldn't change that now. I couldn't change any of it.

"Is everything all right?" Nathan stepped into my hazy view.

I tried to rally my nerve, for his sake. "I think so. Those Wisps were trapped beyond the Door to Nowhere, and now it's open. They're leading people off the path and through the Door, because that's what they do. It's real, and it's here, and I'm guessing it's down at the bottom of the sphere, since that's where the Wisps went."

"But... there has never been any connection between Will-o'-the-Wisps and the Door. Both show up in ancient texts, but never together. And, like I said before, the gateway has only been mentioned once as being anywhere near here." He scratched his head. "This doesn't make any sense."

"It doesn't have to. Not everything is written down in books, Nathan. Sometimes, there are things in this world so great that they have to be kept secret at all costs." A lump formed in my throat as the feeling of responsibility built in my chest, the pressure immense. "All I know is, something happened here. Something stirred this place into reacting."

Nathan's eyes opened wide. "It's the construction! If the Door is down there, it must've been unearthed when they started building the foundations. They didn't begin on the sphere too long ago—maybe a week before you arrived—so, if we add a bit of wait time for the gateway to gather energy from... some unknown source, then the timeline would fit!"

Nathan O'Hara. You really are one of the good ones. In the space of one theory, he'd managed the impossible—he'd taken the weight of all of this off my guilt-ridden shoulders and displaced it elsewhere. Thanks to Leviathan—and Boudicca, to a lesser extent—I'd been so sure that this was my fault. Instead, it appeared this might be a hideous coincidence, after all. The Door needed bestial energy, that was what Leviathan said. Well, the Institute had an entire Repository just waiting to be sapped as an energy source. And all of that would've begun a week before I arrived. Sure, I might've added a little bit of juice, but only once the ball was already rolling. Tentative relief washed over me as I hoped, with all my heart, that Nathan's theory was right.

"Can I ask you one thing?" I straightened, dragging my confidence with the rest of me.

Nathan nodded. "Of course."

"Have any of the beasts in the Repository seemed sluggish or weird lately? You know, around the time the foundations for the sphere were dug?" I wanted one last piece of evidence to exonerate me.

He rubbed his stubbled chin in thought. "Now that you mention it... yes, they've been more lethargic, and less inclined to emerge from their mist. I thought it had to do with the changing seasons and the particularly awful weather we've been having, as Purge beasts can be very sensitive to atmospheric pressure."

"Do you think the Door might've been sapping their energy?" I put it out there and prayed.

He squinted, thinking. "I don't see why not. It certainly fits the timeline."

Thank Chaos! Thank freaking Chaos! That meant it wasn't the pixies, it might've had very little to do with me, and I could stop feeling like everyone who'd gone missing had marched off to a terrible fate because I'd had the audacity to come to the Institute. A nagging thought in the back of my head reminded me of the other missing magicals, the ones out there in the wider world, disappearing each month. The Door couldn't have had anything to do with that.

"Then let's find this Door." I steeled myself, letting the pixies light the treacherous path down the central walkway. They didn't provide much light, the equivalent of cat's eyes reflecting at the side of the road, but it was enough to avoid tumbling to a tragic death.

Nathan followed me toward the middle of the sphere only to veer off and pause at the sheer lip of the suspended walkway, staring into the abyss below. A pole, which would one day have glass orbs clinging to it like in the Repository, stood within arm's reach, though we'd have to lean out at 45-degrees to grab it.

He cast me an anxious smile. "I wanted to be a firefighter when I was little. I guess now I'll finally find out if it would have worked out."

"You're going to go first?"

He gulped and reached for the pole, his toes barely hanging onto the walkway. "Looks like it." He grabbed onto the pole and swung his torso toward it, and his legs followed. He clung koala-style for a moment, frozen. A second later, he whooshed downward, with a horde of pixies hot on his heels, and disappeared from view.

Taking a deep breath, I approached the spot where he'd stood. Boudicca plopped onto a sitting position on my shoulder and gripped my T-shirt with both hands. Why she didn't fly down with the others, I had no clue, but I liked having her with me.

"Hold on, Genie," I whispered, wishing my words would somehow find her.

I leaned out past the point of no return and grabbed the pole, then froze, half on the walkway and half off. Finally, I wrapped my legs around the pole, as Nathan had done, and clung there for a few seconds. It was always a mistake to look down, but the fact that I couldn't see a damn thing down there made it ten times worse. Genie had saved my behind more than once. Now, it was my turn to reciprocate.

Squeezing my eyes shut, I loosened my grip and plummeted into the unknown.

TWENTY-FIVE

Genie

Did I fall asleep? Bright light burned through my eyelids. Closed eyelids. I could see all the little veins crisscrossing over the thin skin. I must've fallen asleep at some point, though I didn't remember dropping off. And why was the sun shining in my face? Ireland hadn't seen more than an hour of strong sunshine since I'd arrived.

I groaned, cracking my eyes open. I was in the new wing somewhere, and one of the hunters was shining a flashlight in my face, asking why I was somewhere I shouldn't have been. There were nearby voices—other hunters, probably—but I couldn't make out what they were saying.

But then my eyes adjusted to the light, and I froze. The new wing, I realized, was long gone, and... oh, man, was I not in Kansas anymore.

I lay on a sloping hill that led down to a purple stream, and the grass was the silvery white of fresh winter frost. The colors were all wrong. Bright, red-trunked trees grew white leaves, copses of pale purple bushes carried alarming bright blue fruit, and above stretched a sunless pink sky with pastel yellow clouds. There were moving clouds, but no wind. There was light, but no sun. There was definitely supposed to be a sun. Everyone knew that.

What the hell happened to me? My body was shaking, but not from the cold. It was the shock of jolting out of my happy daze into whatever this was supposed to be. Presumably not the real world anymore.

I squinted as I noticed hovering lights by the stream. They bobbed around in a familiar way. Little gassy balls of color, playing with one another. Where had I seen that before? My mind felt like it'd been stuffed with cotton balls, and the trippy landscape wasn't helping.

You followed them here... It was coming back in hazy bursts, like a half-remembered dream. Only *this* was the part that felt like a dream. I remembered being in the new wing and hearing that song... A mesmerizing tune that pulled me through a door of light. I realized, with a stomach lurch, that this must have been where it led to. A hidden world. And, if it was hidden, who the heck was going to find me?

I lifted my hand to my brow, blocking out the light that seemed to be everywhere at once. It took just half a second to spot another person... and another, and another. Quite a lot of people, actually, all scattered across the sloping hills, tucked under the weird trees, or sitting by the stream as if everything was totally cool. But they didn't seem very... with it. They were all staring into space, their lips moving in a steady rhythm. The whisper of the cumulative voices drifted across the hidden realm like wind.

Getting up, I dusted off the back of my jeans. A silver, glittery residue clung to my palms, so I wiped harder, sending cascades of powder floating to the floor. Sort of like snow, but not. Sort of like frost, but not.

Trying my best to ignore the bizarreness, I set off to explore.

Every footfall made the grass crunch, leaving my distinct footprints. I saw more of these tracks trailing the hills, where people had obviously gone a-wandering. So, why wasn't anyone walking now? It looked like someone had arranged them in this world the way they wanted them, like dolls or mannequins, then abandoned them. And not one of them seemed to be aware of their surroundings.

Edging down the slope, I spotted a familiar face standing on the stream bank. Dark hair, sourpuss face, fancy clothes—oh yeah, I remembered this girl. Xanthippe. The first to go missing, and the first to launch a discriminatory tirade at me. Gritting my teeth for the anticipated cry of "Get away from me, filthy Atlantean," I headed toward her. But she didn't even turn when I touched her arm.

"Xanthippe?" I shook her arm, this time. "Hey, Xanthippe!"

Her eyes stayed fixed on something in the distance as her mouth moved, whispering words I had to lean close to hear. "I'll follow you. I'm here. I want to hear the music." I waited for her to snap out of it, but she just kept repeating those three sentences, stuck on a loop. Her eyes were zoned out, entranced.

"Xanthippe!" I screamed in her ear, yanking on her arm. But every time I pulled her, she moved right back into her autopilot position.

Okay, this is freaking me out. I scanned the rest of the people, in search of more familiar faces. There must've been thousands of people scattered to the four corners of this place. Some wore modern clothes, so I guessed those were Institute people. However, they were a distinct minority. The rest, from what I could tell, were either re-enactment enthusiasts or... or what? Was it possible that they were actually from an ancient time? Old-timey jerkins and bloomer-looking pants stopped mid-calf. Long cloaks and men in plate armor. Hunched elderly folks in threadbare dresses and tunics.

One of the armored men wasn't too far away—twenty yards or so. Making a decision, I left Xanthippe to her mantra and made a beeline for the soldier. The glowing orbs closest to him winged away, not wanting to be close to me. I didn't mind that one bit; I didn't want to be close to them either. The soldier was less frozen than some of the others, doing a kind of box-step on replay. I gave his sword a wide berth as I approached.

"Hello?" I patted him awkwardly on the back. "Can you hear me?"

The soldier continued to box-step, his chainmail clattering with each move, all the while speaking in an accent so thick, I wasn't even sure he was speaking English. "*Leanfaidh mé thú. Táim ag teacht. Fan liom. Leanfaidh mé thú. Táim ag teacht. Fan liom. Leanfaidh mé thú. Táim ag teacht. Fan liom.*"

After a few repetitions, I realized it wasn't English at all. It sounded Gaelic, but it might as well have been gobbledygook to me. His eyes had the same glazed sheen as Xanthippe's.

"Am I dead?" Finch and Harley had comforted Persie and me with tales of the afterlife. They'd categorically confirmed its existence, after Persie had had a nightmare about dying. But even they didn't know what lay in the great beyond, behind the proverbial veil. They knew it existed, because they'd had passed loved ones communicate with them, but there was still no roadmap. Maybe I'd found it. Maybe that was where the door really led.

If this was heaven, it wasn't for me. And the floating orbs whizzing around made poor and slightly unnerving angels.

Determined to push away my increasing terror, I stepped away from the soldier and headed for a duo of elderly folks, an old man and woman, both drowning in dirty cloaks. Beneath, they wore a tunic and a dress, respectively. The woman carried a basket, while the man had his arm around her, and both had muddied, bare feet. Like they'd walked into a bog. Another strange detail. Where, here, could they have gotten their feet so filthy? The grass couldn't be drier—it crunched, for Pete's sake.

This time, I stepped right in front of them. "Excuse me?"

They stared right through me, both chanting the same mantra under their breaths: "I'll follow you. I'm coming. Wait for us."

"Who are you following?" I asked helplessly.

The same words repeated back.

"Someone else has to be awake!" I snapped, my nerves jangling. "Hey! HEY! Can anyone hear me? Where the heck are we?!"

Why was I the only conscious person here? Was I supposed to be like them, a glitching statue? A blood-chilling thought snuck into my head. What if I *would* end up like them? Was it only a matter of time? I had no idea how long I'd even been here.

I decided I'd find someone in modern clothing. Maybe they wouldn't be as stuck as the others. But then I heard, behind me, a crunch of the silver grass. I whirled around, and there, approaching on the opposite side of the riverbank, was a man, and he was looking at me. A conscious, mobile, non-hypnotized man. He was dressed in old-fashioned clothing, too—black leather pants tucked into high boots, and an elegant jacket that split into coattails at the back. Brass buttons went all the way up to his high collar, and he carried a riding crop in his left hand.

Neither of us moved. He simply watched me with a sullen expression on his face. Sad and bitter.

"Hey! You!" I broke into a run, heading for the riverbank. He didn't take his eyes off me. The closer I got, the more miserable he appeared. His shoulders were hunched and his red hair was all mussed, as though he'd been running anxious hands through it for hundreds of years. His mouth was set in a grim, melancholy line. Still, he didn't answer. Had he forgotten how to speak? I supposed that could happen, if he'd been here long enough with no one to talk to. Or, worse still, perhaps he thought I was a figment of his imagination, so there was no use talking to me. I knew I'd go bonkers if I was trapped here alone.

Coming to a halt on my side of the river, I waved to him. "Can you hear me? Can you understand me?" He tilted his head, but his mood didn't improve.

He didn't say a word. In fact, the cheeky bastard turned his head away from me.

"Hey! I'm talking to you!" I glanced down at the river. A bit of Air would launch me clean over this thing. However, when I tried to release my Chaos... nothing happened. A few pathetic sparks sputtered out, nothing more. Puzzled, I tested my invisibility spell instead. Sure enough, the shield of green slid over me. I let it slough away again, not wanting to go through the burning pains for the sake of an experiment.

Well, that's weird... and probably not good. Wherever I was, it seemed to have some kind of ability dampener on it. Hexes and spells worked, but not innate powers. Still, I had to cross this freaking water. Even if I had to do it the hard way.

Sadly, I had no 'walking on water' spells up my sleeve. I didn't love the idea of the water being purple, but it didn't look too deep. And it was totally clear, revealing every rock and shiny pebble below the surface.

Keeping my gaze locked on the guy, I clambered into the water. My body braced for the shock of cold wet, but it didn't come. The stream felt like I'd stepped into the Goldilocks of baths. Not too hot, not too cold. It did, however, have a bit of a current. I used my hands like paddles to help me cross.

I was halfway—a few more steps and I'd be there. *The other side of the water. That's where I'll find answers.* I slipped on a smooth stone on the riverbed, and as I regained my footing, I saw the man whisper something. The precise words were lost over the babbling rush of the water.

I thought I'd try again. "Hello?"

He turned his back on me and walked back toward the white-leafed tree behind him.

"Hey! Would you just... wait!" I swallowed the despair in my voice. "I need to—"

My words died on my lips as I noticed something else coming toward me at breakneck speed: all of the glowing lights that had been hovering around, minding their own business... Well, they weren't minding their own business anymore. Whatever that man had whispered, these orbs had heard. And now, they were coming for me. Fifty or more of them, rocketing through the air.

Panic set in. Scooping my hands through the water as fast as possible, I struggled to cross the riverbed. But I was still at the center, where the current was strongest. Leaning forward, I forced my thighs to power through. If that guy thought he could send a horde of... aggressive lights after me and not get an earful, he was sorely mistaken.

I ran through the water, keeping my eyes fixed on sweet, dry ground. After clawing with all my might to haul my body out, I collapsed onto the crunchy grass... just as the orbs descended. They spiraled around me, blocking my view of the tree and the man. I turned this way and that, looking for an escape, but they only whizzed faster and faster, overwhelming my senses until all I saw was bright, blinding light.

And then, I saw nothing at all.

TWENTY-SIX

Persie

L anding on my butt with an unexpected thud that ricocheted up my spine, I reached the end of the fireman's pole. A soft, gauzy light made the eerie darkness down here marginally less terrifying. At first, I thought it was coming from the pixies, or that the Wisps had come back. But then, I saw it—the faint outline of a doorway, hovering just above solid ground—four glowing lines that formed a rectangle.

Nathan reached down and grabbed my arm, pulling me to my feet. "Are you hurt?"

"I'll have a nasty bruise, but it'll heal."

I observed the doorway, taking it in. There wasn't a handle or solid wood or… anything. Just a glowing outline.

Nathan nodded. "Same here." Like me, he was staring at the rectangle. "I think we found it."

"But how do we get in?" I stepped toward it, half-expecting it to open in welcome. But nothing happened. Without the Wisps leading us, maybe we weren't allowed to enter. And that wouldn't do at all, not with Genie on the other side.

If she's still alive... My heart clenched and my breath hitched. The Wisps led souls off the beaten path for the sake of adding more spirits to their guiding legions. What if I was already too late? What if she'd turned into a shadowy soul, wielding a candle to lead more people astray? Perhaps, now that the door had been opened again, their deadly cycle had been triggered. There was no way of knowing.

I looked at Nathan in desperation. "Can you get us through? Did your father have any spells in his Grimoire that could work for this? Otherwise, we're going to have to let the Wisps hypnotize us again, and that's not going to end well. We need to get in without our brains being mush."

He took off his glasses and wiped the lenses, his mouth twisting in a thoughtful grimace. "There might be something I can use, but it's not from my father's Grimoire. I may be wrong, but the Wisps might be the only ones who can go in and out without any trouble, if this *is* their domain. There's an ancient manuscript in the Theorem Complex that might have what I need, but it'd be a huge risk to go up there and try to find it. We've already put Charlotte on the warpath, and there will undoubtedly be hunters searching the libraries. Also, I'm not sure how good I'll be at shimmying up a pole."

No, no, no, no, no! I refused to accept that we'd fallen at the last hurdle, so close to finding Genie. Fortunately, I still had one option left—a dangerous mission for my pixie friends. They'd already shown how skilled they could be with camouflage, but there would be no assurances that they wouldn't be caught, especially with hunters on the prowl. Still, if I could prove they weren't responsible by getting everyone back, then maybe it would only be a temporary sentence for any captured critters.

I looked at Boudicca, still perched on my shoulder. "I need you to do something for me, but I'm going to need *all* of you. Can you gather the others?"

Boudicca eyed me warily for a few seconds, but she must've seen the despair in my eyes, because a moment later she hopped off my shoulder and landed on the floor. Squeaking sternly, she beckoned for the other pixies to join her on the ground. They obeyed immediately, abandoning Nathan for their rightful leader. Gesticulating furiously, she looked around at her brethren. And then, wordlessly, they gave a collective nod of understanding.

"What are they doing?" Nathan whispered, in awe of the creatures.

I watched them hopefully. "I think they're… gathering their forces."

In unison, the pixies lifted their arms and started to step side-to-side, their cuttlefish dots pulsing in an identical rhythm, rotating through the whole rainbow of colors. They moved their arms up and down, keeping the same side-step rhythm, and began to chant something ancient and mesmerizing, sending a message through the Institute to the remaining pixies-in-hiding. I *felt* it reaching out, my monster sense tingling, letting me know the purpose in their sounds and movements.

"They have rituals, they communicate, they show compassion." Nathan adjusted his spectacles, peering closer. Even I knew this was special, and I didn't know nearly as much about monsters. "How can anyone suggest that they aren't sentient beings with souls and conscious thought?"

I nodded. "I'm right in that boat with you."

Within minutes, all the pixies from my Purge fluttered down to the bottom of the sphere on dragonfly wings, greeting their fellow creatures with hugs and mischievous slaps on the back. A chubbier pixie with three tiny feathers sticking out of his mossy hair dove into a display of chirps and squeaks, pretending to be, from what I could tell, a hunter trying to chase him. He leapt over imaginary obstacles and stuck out his tongue, waggling his behind at the make-believe hunter before puffing out his chest proudly.

Boudicca smacked him on the back of the head to get him to shut up, and he immediately quieted. Now that she had the floor to herself, she spoke to the newcomers in her punctuated chirps, which I'd come to appreciate the sound of. They stared at Nathan and me with bewildered eyes, as if to say: "But aren't these guys the enemy?" As Boudicca explained, though, they began "oohing" and "ahhing."

When that was done, she turned to me with a look of "so, now that I've got everyone here, would you mind explaining why?"

I knelt, as it seemed like the polite thing to do, and the pixie army looked back at me solemnly. "There's a book that we need from the main library, and we'd like you to retrieve it. It's a risky mission, and there's a chance that some of you will get caught, but we need that book to clear your names of wrongdoing." I nodded to the doorway. "Hopefully, it'll help us get inside there."

There was a roar of outrage and general dissent from the gathered group, and some disdainful stares were cast in our direction. Some pointed at me, shaking their heads and tiny fists. I was asking a lot, and I didn't want any of the pixies to end up in a glass orb or dead under Victoria's code red order, but this was the only way we could get through the doorway. It was all in the pixies' hands.

Boudicca folded her arms across her chest and marched back and forth in front of me, visibly contemplating the dire situation. As any wartime general knew, there came a time when sacrifices had to be made and dangers had to be faced. She unleashed a massive sigh before whirling to face the others—now a forty-strong horde. She pointed at me and chirped, like a very stern sparrow telling off her pesky offspring. The other pixies grumbled their displeasure, and Boudicca took her chirping up a notch, her cuttlefish spots turning red as her hands waggled furiously. My monster sense suggested she wasn't peeved at me, which was nice. Gradually, the dissent subsided, and the pixies gave a stadium wave of reluctant nods. Boudicca was the queen bee, after all, and whatever she decided, the hive was expected to follow.

"Is that a yes?" I looked to Boudicca.

She grinned with her needle-sharp teeth and gave a prideful nod.

"It's on the third level, on the right-hand side of the library, as you enter. It'll be in a section marked 'Rare Manuscripts,'" Nathan said, kneeling beside me. "There should be a Kelpie carved into the wooden post just next to it. It'll be a few books to the left of the Kelpie. It's called *A Complete History of Wisps and Legends*."

I cast him an intrigued side-eye. "Have you memorized the place?"

"It's part of the job." He smiled back, proud.

Boudicca let out a high-pitched war cry, shooting her arms upward like a real queen ordering her army into battle. As one, the pixies spread their colorful wings, fluttering them with the speed of hummingbirds as they ascended and disappeared into the darkness above. Boudicca was the last to leave, leaping into the air and winging her way toward me, for a brief moment. Flying right up to my face, she leaned in and planted a tiny kiss on my forehead, cackling to herself as she spun around and ascended to catch up with her motley crew.

As I watched her go, silently wishing them luck. I felt a little lonely, like I'd lost another friend to this Wisp calamity. I guessed the mini-kiss had been her way of saying 'au revoir'—goodbye, until we meet again. I just hoped the reunion wouldn't be too far away.

"Do you think they'll come back?" I whispered to Nathan. We were alone, with no way to get back to the walkway unless we wanted to clamber back up as though we were on some military assault course. Well, not unless Nathan had a trick up his sleeve for that.

Nathan smiled strangely, as if he knew something I didn't. "I think they will."

"What makes you say that? If I were them, I'd amscray." I hated to admit it, but it was true.

"They like you, that's why. You brought them back to life. Gratitude creates a very strong bond," he replied. "It's similar to resurrection, in a way. Necromancers have had their share of good and bad eggs throughout their history, but those who used it for good—to prevent tragedy... Well, they tend to be bonded for life with those they saved. You gave that to the pixies and, what's more, they know you respect them."

I thought about Astrid, back at the SDC. Her father, Alton Waterhouse, had been a Necromancer, and he'd used his abilities more than once to save the life of his daughter. Purging pixies didn't feel quite as emotionally loaded as that—it wasn't a split-second, life-or-death decision that I'd consciously made. But it *was* becoming more life or death thanks to Victoria's code red, lethal force order. In essence, they wouldn't be here if it wasn't for me, and I was so glad they were.

I laughed awkwardly. "I can't help it. They won me over."

"Monsters do that, if you take the time to get to know them." Nathan sighed. "That's why it's always so hard to let them go when the message comes that they need exporting to the Bestiary."

I released a breath, realizing I'd been holding it in. Nathan was saying things that I hadn't dared to, and it felt validating to have a kindred spirit in this place. "How do you stand it?"

Nathan frowned, as though the question had thrown him. "I suppose... because I have to. At least by being with them, I have some control over their care, and I can learn more about each one." He lowered his gaze to the floor. "Besides, if it wasn't me, it might be someone who doesn't care at all."

We stood in silence, both of us engrossed in our thoughts as we waited for the pixies to return with the book. I still wasn't convinced they'd come back, but I had to hope that their desire to be exonerated was stronger than their desire to escape. Nathan's words had perplexed and intrigued me. Did the pixies really like me, or was he just blowing sunshine at me? Truthfully, my heart had developed a soft spot for them, too, despite their mischievousness.

Some twenty minutes later, a faint buzzing sound drew my gaze upward. The squadron of pixies descended in formation, a small cluster of them carrying Nathan's book. I tried to count the pixies, but I had no idea how many I'd actually Purged in the first place.

"Is everyone here?" I asked Boudicca as she made a grand entrance on my shoulder, flourishing her beautiful wings.

She beamed and pretended to count everyone off on her tiny fingers before shaking a triumphant fist in the air. I guessed that meant they were all present and accounted for, and my lungs took an easier breath. None had been captured during the mission, and they sure looked smug about it.

Grinning through her pin-sharp teeth, she swept a hand toward the book: *ta-da*. My eyes sought it out eagerly, only for my hopes to deflate as I realized what they'd brought: *The Ladybird Book of Irish Myths and Legends*. A kids' book, more pictures than words, and definitely not what I'd asked for.

To make matters worse, the splinter cell who'd carried it was squabbling over who got to bring it to me. As each clawed for a corner, the book flew open to reveal a painstakingly detailed illustration of a leprechaun sitting under a dock leaf, dressed in green with ginger hair and a pipe in his mouth. As the rabble battled over the book and one of the pixies seized the corner of the page and pulled, the illustrated leprechaun ripped right in two. The pixies fought over the remaining pages, pulling the paper apart.

I didn't know whether to laugh or cry as they scampered toward me with eager faces, each of them brandishing an armful of shredded pages like it was the best gift in the world.

"This isn't the right book," I muttered apologetically, and the pixies looked crestfallen. "And books aren't all that helpful if you tear them up, just FYI."

They'd done their best, book-mutilation aside, but the language barrier was proving difficult to overcome. The pixies were wild, despite my unique connection with them.

Nathan huffed out a sigh. "Without going with them myself, I don't see how we're going to get this book." He brushed a hand through his hair, and a throng of she-pixies swooned. Boudicca glared at them, as though she'd already staked a claim. "Although, I'm somewhat glad they didn't bring the right one, otherwise I'd be looking at the pieces of a rare manuscript right now."

"Then we need to come up with another game plan, and we need to do it—"

I was interrupted by a sudden, blinding pain that cut through my skull like a white-hot blade, severing the sentence before I could finish. My knees buckled and I toppled forward, unable to move a single muscle to break my fall. The pixies shrieked and swarmed, trying to catch me, and the ground rushed up to meet my face. A moment before I hit the deck, the lights went out in my world, and everything disappeared into darkness.

TWENTY-SEVEN

Persie

I opened my eyes to nothing at all, a dull throb pinballing back and forth between my temples. My cheek rested on something hard and cold and smooth, presumably the floor where I'd fallen flat on my face at the bottom of the sphere.

Did something hit me? I struggled to recall what had happened. I remembered vague panic about the book, and then blackness. I squinted into the gloom, confused, trying to find Nathan and the pixies. They had to be nearby. They wouldn't have just left me alone, unless… unless the Wisps had come back and taken Nathan. Still, that didn't explain why Boudicca and the rest of the pixies would've left me. They'd had a chance to run away, and they hadn't. Had I been out for hours? Days?

"Hello?" I called out. My voice echoed back strangely, as though it were bouncing off nearby walls. I hauled my body into a sitting position, frowning into the darkness. "Is anyone here?" The soundwaves spread out, creating a peculiar effect. It was as though I could see them, bouncing off invisible barriers that surrounded me on all sides. Bright ripples of bluish light suddenly shimmered across the unseen barriers, turning them into solid walls. And not just any walls.

Glass walls. I recognized them immediately.

No... I scrambled to my feet and ran for the glass, launching myself at it with my full weight. A clang echoed back, but the impact made no difference. Panic took over, sending me into a blind fury. Someone from the Institute had trapped me. I'd disobeyed Victoria, and she'd sent her minions to bash me on the head and take me out. And this was my punishment—the glass box that I'd feared since I Purged the hydra on my birthday. It wasn't exactly the same as the glass box from my nightmare. It felt far more real, thanks to the pounding in my head, the ache in my bones, and the biting cold of the glass against my cheek. Details too concrete to be part of a dream. Plus, there were no familiar spectators standing outside the box, watching me. Beyond the pane lay nothing but endless dark.

My heart hammered harder as understanding dawned. That was why Nathan and the pixies weren't with me. They'd been taken away, too. Maybe they were suffering a similar fate, somewhere else in the Institute. And Genie was still out there somewhere, needing my help.

"Let me out! I know who's doing this! Please believe me! Please!" I screamed, pounding the glass until my already-tender knuckles swelled anew, reigniting old injuries. "My friend is in danger! Please, you have to let me out of here! I can't... I can't breathe!"

I slammed my hands, knees, arms, fists, hips, and feet into the glass in a violent cycle, until everything hurt. Even then, I didn't stop. I couldn't stop, not until someone let me out. If I paused for even a second, the claustrophobia would take over, and there would be no coming back from that.

"Persephone?" A cold touch trailed across the back of my neck, and the shadows within the box shifted.

I whipped around, panting. "Leviathan?" Just like in the nightmare, he'd come to comfort me in my darkest hour. But I didn't want him here. I didn't want him anywhere near me. "Where am I? And what the hell is going on?"

He emerged from the thick, black smoke, coiling his scaly tail beneath him to prop up his humanoid torso. His glowing angler-fish appendage shone with a warm yellow light, but I'd learned my lesson about that. I turned my face to the side in case it drew me in again.

"Apologies, Persephone." He bowed his head. "I did not mean to startle you."

"Then don't creep up on me, and don't touch me!" I snapped. My chest felt like a ten-ton weight had been dropped on it. "I think you should start answering my questions, *now*."

His striking eyes observed me with... concern. "You must relax, Persephone. I intend no harm. You are safe with me." The end of his tail flicked, making the scales shimmer with a teal sheen. "I am sorry to have to contact you in this manner."

"Wait..." I froze. "So, this *is* a dream?" I didn't know what emotion I was meant to have. I felt numb and overwhelmed all at once, my mind a seething mass of panic and confusion.

"Yes and no. It is more of an astral projection," he explained. "It was necessary."

Anger sliced through me, finally fixing me on one emotion in particular. "Necessary?! I thought I'd been locked in a freaking prison cell, Leviathan! I thought Victoria had thrown away the key! Because of you!"

He had the decency to look sheepish. "I was worried."

"You should be more worried that I'll cave your head in, after you pulled a stunt like this!" I shot back, livid. I'd told him about the nightmare, and now he was using my worst fears against me simply because he wanted to. I had no right to be surprised. I'd given him ammunition—of course he was going to hurl it back at me.

He snickered softly. "You are angry. You should not be. I was worried that you might be stepping into danger you cannot handle. You do not have all the knowledge required to succeed."

"And whose fault is that?" I really wanted to hit him, but I had a feeling my knuckles would shatter if I tried to punch his armor plating. "You had every chance to give me more information, and you chose to be all vague and 'disinterested.' I've had to figure things out for myself, and we were *about* to get more intel when you decided to play this... telepathy trick on me."

"I highly doubt that," he replied coolly.

I narrowed my eyes at him. "Then start talking. Tell me what I need to know about the Door to Nowhere. You can begin with how to open the damn thing."

He laughed, his silvery eyes glinting with mischief. "You do not know me very well, do you? I would not make it that easy." He lunged forward on his coils, but I didn't flinch. "I will not rule with a weak queen at my side. You must prove that you are worthy of my gifts. I must see your value. You say you have had to figure things out for yourself, but I see no evidence. You have sought aid at every turn."

"I. Don't. Want. Your. Gifts!" I punctuated each word with a palm to the glass. In all my life, no one had aggravated me more than Leviathan. How could he stand there and spout all this bull about me not doing things for myself? Yes, I'd had help, but that didn't minimize what I'd managed to achieve so far. And he was one to talk —his mind would still be in deep freeze along with his body if it weren't for me, which didn't make me feel good, but it was still the hypocritical truth.

Mom always said that the sign of a true fighter was one who knew when to share the load, which she'd learned the hard way. I wouldn't let him make me feel guilty about accepting help when I really needed it, like getting out of my bedroom thanks to Nathan.

Nor would I let him belittle what I'd done myself. I'd been the one to figure out the pixies weren't responsible, and I'd managed to coax them into joining forces with me. As self-sufficient victories went, mine weren't half bad. And my shared victories weren't bad, either. Besides, I didn't care what he thought of me, and I definitely didn't want to be his freaking queen! All I cared about was rescuing my friend and exonerating my Purge pixies.

Leviathan chuckled. "And yet, you have grown to admire the creatures you birthed. If you were to suddenly find yourself without your new gift, you would feel its absence. That is enough for me. For now." He pulled back, giving me space from his rotting fish breath. "As for information... the best I can do is point you in the right direction. You will find what you are looking for in the new wing of the Institute. That much I heard from your pixie friends."

"What?" That didn't make sense. How could he have heard it from the pixies?

"I can now communicate with others of my kind. All thanks to you, and my link to you." He sighed wistfully. "Our bond has turned you into a telepathic satellite dish, of sorts. I hear messages and thoughts from my kind as they bounce off you and reach me—in a way that's never happened before. Since the Institute is full of monsters, I can hear a great deal. Now I know the lay of the enemy terrain."

What's he going to do with that sort of intel? I didn't dare ask. As long as he remained in his box, there wasn't anything he could do in the outside world... right? I doubted he could manipulate the monsters through this link, or he would've done it already to break himself loose. Still, the idea of being his cellphone tower, with thoughts pinging off me and back to him... It didn't sit well with me at all. He didn't deserve an outlet to the wider world. He'd shown he couldn't be trusted with it.

I squinted at him, deciding what to say next. "I'm already in the new wing. That's what I was trying to tell you earlier." I allowed myself a small smirk as his eyes widened in surprise. "I told you I was capable."

"You are already there?" He sounded baffled and intrigued. "How did you figure that out?"

"Oh, now you want me to spill the beans?" I grumbled, not wanting to tell him anything. And yet, if he could hear monsters talking now, maybe he had intel that he'd be willing to cough up, now that he knew I'd gotten here without him.

He laughed. "Have you developed a means of conversing with the pixies? Has such a power come to you already?"

"We have an... understanding of sorts." I refused to let him be smug over the fact that we were mostly talking in charades and mime performances. But I should have known better than to try and pull the wool over his eyes.

"They will not listen, will they?"

"They *listen*," I shot back stubbornly.

He nodded in thought. "Yet they do not understand you fully. Is that right?"

"They get mixed up sometimes, that's all." I thought of the children's book and grimaced, though I tried to cover the expression as quickly as possible. "But they're doing their best, and they're helping me, which is more than I can say about you and your vague comments." I also felt an urge to defend them. They weren't stupid, by any means. There was just a bit of an issue with their love of destruction.

Leviathan smiled. "You continue to impress me."

"I'm not doing anything to impress you. I'm doing this to save my friend," I retorted. I didn't plan on ever becoming his evil queen, so he could stuff that.

"Nevertheless, I am pleasantly surprised by the warmth you are showing toward these creatures. And your ability to reach the crossroads you are at, without my assistance. In return, I will grant you a valuable piece of information." He lunged nearer, coming disgustingly close to my ear. There, he whispered a single word: "*Inwalla.*"

My brow furrowed. "Is that supposed to mean something?"

"It will mean everything to you." He pulled back, all smugness and arrogance. "It is how you will get the pixies to obey. They will understand every detail of your instruction. No more mishaps. No more accidents. It is an ancient word of the Primus Anglicus; the only word they will listen to."

"*Inwalla?* That's all I need to get them to understand?" It seemed too easy, and with Leviathan, that was never a good thing.

"Yes," he said simply. "However, I would urge you to be careful. You are entering a perilous unknown. Even I know very little about the Door to Nowhere and the land beyond it. It is hallowed ground, and the spirits are uneasy."

I saw an opportunity to give him a few home-truths. "But not because of me, like you implied. You said I was the one who caused all of this by opening the gateway, but that's not true, is it? It opened because they built the foundations of the new wing too deep and stirred the gateway back into life."

He pressed a palm to his chest. "More and more remarkable with every encounter. What a wonder you are." His eyes twinkled, his angler-fish bulb flashing a sultry pink. I realized he might've made his earlier digs about my apparent uselessness to manipulate me. Bastard. "I know you have been worried. I have heard your fears. I wanted to see if you could bear the weight of such responsibility, and you did. You did not crumble. You feared you would, yes, but you did not."

How does he know that? Dread bubbled in my stomach. I hadn't told him it concerned me, though I supposed you wouldn't have to be a genius to figure that out. And yet, his certainty made me nauseous. Could he... read my thoughts when we were linked like this? I suddenly felt very exposed and vulnerable, my mind open for him to scoop out the highlights. It set a dangerous precedent. If he'd listened to my fears without me knowing, then what else could he hear?

"I do not delve too deep," he said, as though he *had* heard everything I'd just thought. He laughed, without so much as a hint of malevolence. "I skim the surface so I can sense how you are feeling. I would not intrude where I am not welcome. A person's mind is a locked box that should never be opened, unless the key is given. I reach only for your emotions. I do so because I wish to know your state. I do not like when you suffer."

"Then why play games, why manipulate me into feeling guilty?" I felt breathless again, panicky. He'd allowed me to believe that I'd been the catalyst to these kidnappings. If that wasn't suffering, I didn't know what was.

He sighed. "Truthfully, I did not know about the new wing until after we spoke last. I said only what I thought to be true at the time. And I would have remedied your feeling of guilt during this meeting, but you had already figured it out yourself." His voice turned soft and caring, which unsettled me more than his cool-as-a-cucumber act.

I could hate Leviathan. Hate was easy because he'd caused me so much upset. But to think he might actually be on my side, trying to help me through this in his own twisted way... That was harder to swallow. He was trying to get me to stand on my own two feet, like I'd wanted. And that notion boggled my mind.

Crap, can he hear all of this? I peered at him, but he showed no sign that he'd invaded my private thoughts. Maybe he really meant it. The idea alone sounded insane: it suggested he had some sort of moral compass. But if he *had* read my mind at that moment, he wouldn't have been able to resist a dig at my expense.

"What lies beyond that door is likely treacherous," he said

instead. "It is a mystery. No one has ever come back from it. So, you must be cautious. Do not be foolish and get yourself trapped there, too. Take pains. Gain insight. Have courage. Never try to be a hero, for heroes have a tendency to die gloriously."

I nodded uncertainly. "Then I need to get back to the real world, where I can make a difference. Genie needs me, now more than ever. And I will figure this out, because that's what I do, even if you 'highly doubt' it."

He laughed and reached out his hand, pausing just shy of my cheek. "Ah yes, the Atlantean firecracker. By all means, return and rescue the wench. That girl has grown on me in recent years. She is a good friend to you. And you will need good friends, later…"

Before I could ask what the heck that was supposed to mean, a blinding pain tore through my skull, and the shadows and the box and Leviathan's eerie eyes vanished. This time, at least, I knew where I would wake up.

TWENTY-EIGHT

Persie

"Persie?" Someone shook my shoulders. "Persie? Can you hear me?"

My eyes opened slowly to the hazy glow at the bottom of the sphere and Boudicca staring at me upside down from where she stood on my forehead. Nathan loomed over me, his expression deeply concerned.

"I'm okay," I croaked. "How long was I out?" My head still throbbed, but I could handle that. Although Leviathan might've given me a heart attack by choosing the worst possible time for a telepathic visit, at least I'd come away with something useful: *Inwalla*.

"Ten minutes or so." He helped me sit up, and I discovered that all of the pixies had formed a protective circle around me. A murmur of relief rippled through the creatures, some of them wiping their brows with their usual brand of melodrama. "What happened? You were talking, and then you just… keeled over."

Only ten minutes? It had felt a lot longer.

"I'm not sure," I lied. "I think it was an aftershock symptom of my last Purge. But I'm fine now." I couldn't bring myself to explain about the glass box or how real it had felt. I knew Nathan would've understood, and that he wouldn't have judged me for it—he already knew, to some extent, about Leviathan's mental visits. However, there was a huge difference between Leviathan talking to me and him being able to take control of my mind long enough to drag me out of reality and into… wherever we'd been. Nathan didn't need to know all that, not right then. We had plenty of other concerns on our collective plate.

Nathan squinted, as though he only half-believed me. "Does that happen often?"

"It's mostly headaches and residual pains, but I did Purge a bunch of creatures at once this time, so the aftereffects are more intense. Honestly, I'm fine now."

Nathan sighed with relief. "Thank goodness for that. You had me worried." I stared at the phone in his hand, which he hurriedly slipped back into his pocket. He gave me a solemn look and said, "I was about five seconds away from sending the pixies off to hide and calling for help. To tell you the truth, I didn't know if you were going to wake up."

"Then… thank you for waiting." I meant it. If Nathan had phoned Victoria, it would've been game over, and the useful information Leviathan had given me would have been worthless. Nathan got to his feet and dusted himself off, taking a moment to gather himself. He looked rattled, and I had an opportunity while Nathan walked a short distance away, just out of earshot, to pace off his lingering nerves.

"*Inwalla*," I whispered.

The pixies all whipped around to face me, staring in wonder at the person who'd spoken their sacred word. A moment later, they shivered as though a bolt of electricity had shot amongst them all: a magical current running through the pixie circuit. With no need for further prompting, they marched forward into formation and stood at attention, falling into line like an army. Boudicca stood at the front, her shoulders back, arms straight, ready to take orders.

Nathan gawped at the scene. "What are they doing?"

"They're obeying." I smiled, thrilled that the word had worked. "And we've probably only got one more shot at this before some pixies gets caught, so cross your fingers." I focused on Boudicca. "Can you send a team to bring us the book we need? *A Complete History of Wisps and Legends.*" I repeated the instructions that Nathan had previously given and prayed they wouldn't bring back another kiddy book.

As she listened, Boudicca's eyes swam with a swirling galaxy of purples and pinks, flecked with silvery stars, as though she were hypnotized. An undercurrent of guilt ran through me as it occurred to me that I was following a very Wispy path here—in a way, I too was using the pixies for my own benefit, like the rest of the magical world used beasts. And I had her under a control that I didn't fully understand. *The difference was,* I told myself, *I care what happens to them, and I'll do what I can to repay them for their help.*

Once I finished explaining what I needed, Boudicca turned to the others and relayed the message, thin strands of pinkish light flowing from her temples and into the temples of the others, until everyone understood. She pointed to a quintet of pixies, who immediately took flight and vanished into the overhead gloom.

"How did you do that?" Nathan frowned at me.

I shrugged. "Maybe they're finally listening to the one who brought them back into existence."

"It's unlike anything I've ever seen." He observed the now-uniform squad of pixies, no doubt trying to commit every quirk and behavior to memory. As a researcher, his lack of pen and paper must've been killing him.

Ten minutes later, heralded by a bumblebee-like drone, the

quintet of pixies returned. This time, the results looked more promising. They bore a hefty tome bound in red leather, stained and pocked by time and rough handling. The weight made them fly awkwardly, and I heard their groans as they got closer. Moments before they landed, Nathan lunged toward them and pulled the book from their hands, clearly terrified they would tear this treasured item to pieces, too. The quintet eyed him with disapproval, pouting and muttering under their breaths. I still couldn't understand what they were saying, but I could grasp their meaning with a touch more specificity, and I sensed they weren't too pleased with Nathan's snatch-and-grab, or the inference that they'd rip the book apart.

"He's just careful about these things. Don't take any offense," I said to the returning group. Now that I had them under the influence of their sacred word, they looked at me with understanding, their eyes swirling with that same mesmerized galaxy of color. I guessed the translation from my language to theirs happened somewhere in that space. They glanced at Nathan and giggled, pretending to flip through books of their own and pushing imaginary glasses up the bridges of their noses.

Nathan didn't notice their mockery. "This is it!" he said, rifling frantically through the pages. "Now, where's the part that might help us... I know it's around the end somewhere."

I peered over his shoulder. To my surprise, the words were handwritten. Elaborate Celtic lettering graced every page. I had no idea what he was looking for, so I stood by as a hopeful observer while he did the hard work. The words were so crammed together and faded that I couldn't believe he was reading it.

"Yes. This is the bit." He ran his fingertip beneath a section of text. "*Coinníonn neart an déantóra an Uacht le chéile,*" he murmured in Gaelic, the language of Ireland and its Celtic heritage.

I looked at him. "Huh?"

"Now, as you know, my Gaelic isn't great, but I think it's something along the lines of 'The maker's strength holds the Will together.' I'm guessing that 'Will' is referring to the Wisps." Nathan scanned a portion of text beneath. "Yes, and here it says that 'they reside in a different realm—an interdimensional pocket enveloped in secrecy. This realm is thought to have been created naturally or, at best, accidentally.'"

"But we know it wasn't," I chimed in. "The pixies said it was created to imprison the Wisps after they disobeyed their missive."

Nathan's eyebrows knitted together. "That may explain this next part. It says that the Wisps were thought to have been expelled about a thousand years ago by a Primus Anglicus by the name of Fergus McLeod. No one knows why for sure, but it's speculated that he was punishing them for leading people astray."

Boudicca yelped suddenly, nodding so hard I worried her head might fall off.

"Did he forge the gateway? Is he the one who trapped the Wisps and took away your Necromancy?" I held out my arm, and she hopped onto it. She squeaked enthusiastically and began a one-woman show. She knelt in prayer before leaping into the air and pretending to be some kind of higher being, floating down to... answer that prayer?

"Fergus McLeod summoned a Child of Chaos to help with the Wisps?" I asked. "And that Child took away your Necromancy and helped Fergus forge the gateway?"

Boudicca grinned and clapped. From what I could remember of Mom's and Uncle Finch's Child of Chaos lectures, they probably would've been in their otherworlds by then, but still at liberty to help the Primus Anglicus here and there. It was only when the bloodlines got watered down that the rules had tightened. And since it had been a life and death matter, and wayward spirits misbehaving was against Chaos's rules, I guessed the Children of Chaos had no choice but to get involved.

Nathan nodded thoughtfully. "That would explain why it's such a powerful gateway. If these Wisps are spirits of the dead, then it would be tantamount to creating a separate afterlife in that interdimensional bubble. As you can imagine, the energy required would be enormous, but child's play for... well, a Child."

"Wait... a separate afterlife?" That chilled me, for one terrifying reason. "Do you think people die instantly, when they go in there? Do they become spirits, too?"

Nathan flicked back through the book, his mouth scrunching up in concern. "Here's something." He swallowed loudly, as though trying to force down a lump in his throat. "It says: all that enters is held under the maker's rule. No soul may leave unless bidden. No Chaos may leave unless instructed. Corporeal beings should not set foot in such a world, lest they find themselves confined, their bodies turning to spiritual matter with the passage of time."

I gulped. "Any suggestion of how long a person has in there before they start to turn?"

"No." He shook his head grimly. "But we shouldn't assume they have decades. We should work on the assumption that they don't have long, because I'm not risking everyone coming out... dead."

Neither am I. My nerves amped up with the thought of Genie being trapped in there, only to turn to dust or something if we managed to get her out. Surely, it couldn't be an instantaneous thing? I had to hope it wasn't, because losing Genie was something I knew I would never recover from. Never. She wasn't just a friend. She was more like a sister, and I refused to walk this life without her.

"Does it mention what happened to Fergus?" He was the key to this, the supposed 'ruler' of the realm behind that door. The more I knew about him, the better prepared I would be to break into his world and get back what belonged to us.

He pored over the pages some more. "It says he disappeared one day without a trace. Some believe that the Wisps took him with them when they were sucked through the gateway. Although it might've been the cost of building the gateway in the first place, his sacrifice to the Children for ridding the world of these disobedient spirits. A gatekeeper of sorts, though I'd say he's not doing his job properly, since they've managed to sneak out again."

"What about the Door itself? Any way we can open it without the Wisps?" Theorizing as to how it had been created was all well and good, but getting through was more important. Genie was still in there, somewhere.

Nathan licked his finger and turned the page. "I'll need a few more minutes and a bit more light."

He got what he asked for, sooner than either of us expected. Just then, the Door to Nowhere flew open and searing white light spilled out into the darkness of the sphere, setting it ablaze. The gaseous Wisps pummeled out with a vengeance, and in greater numbers, determined to hypnotize us this time. They were less like floating ballet dancers this time and more like angry hornets buzzing around our heads, stingers out and eager to strike.

I covered my head with my hands as a group hurtled toward me, swirling around and around in a dizzying spectacle. They weren't trying to hypnotize us; they were going for harder, more violent tactics. Aiming to weaken us or bring us to submission, maybe, before they hit us with their siren song again. Another cluster gunned for Nathan, whizzing so close to his face that they left a streak of colorful dust across his nose. They really weren't taking any prisoners this time. Even the light coming off them was noticeably hot. Every time they swung close to my face, I felt it, as if I'd gotten too near a naked flame.

My skin stung and my eyes throbbed from the unbearable brightness but trying to look away or protect myself did no good. They could slide through the narrowest gap and force their way into my field of vision. Their glow burned through my lids, even when I tried to close my eyes.

Boudicca shrieked a battle cry, and the pixies launched into action. Some tackled the Wisps head on, somehow able to grasp the apparently solid center of the gaseous orbs. Others fought fire with fire, pumping up the intensity of their pulsating lights to chase away the fierce glow of the Wisps. I didn't know where to look or how to help, but it felt like being stuck right in the middle of a firework display. No, it was more like being caught in the middle of a firework explosion. Shards of light erupted in every direction, glinting purple and red and blue and orange, fizzing to their demise on the floor.

"Here." Nathan scurried over and covered both of our heads with his jacket, sheltering us in darkness. But I could still see the flashes of vivid color through the dense fabric and hear the howls of the pixies as they gave the Wisps hell.

"Shouldn't we do something?" I whispered.

Nathan shifted to peek out beneath the edge of his jacket. "I don't know what we can do. But it looks like the pixies have it covered."

I took a peek for myself. "Remind me never to get on their bad side."

The pixies worked in focused units, like a well-oiled machine. I watched a trio literally drag a Wisp to the ground, where they stomped on the glowing orb until the brighter flame in the center sputtered out completely. The message seemed to spread through the rest of the pixies, and soon they were all trying to drag the Wisps downward. The firefight of light on light continued amongst those that remained airborne, rainbow sparks cascading down like colored rain. It might've been the most brutal and beautiful fight I'd ever seen. And the pixies were winning.

A sound pierced the air, soft and sorrowful, and totally incongruous with the battle taking place. Words drifted around me, clear despite the jacket and the bellows and screeches of the pixies. A song I knew, but slightly different—sadder than when we'd heard it in the foyer of the new wing. The Wisps began to pull back toward the Door, called to retreat by the bittersweet music.

"Whatever you do, don't listen to it," Nathan urged, sticking his fingers in his ears.

I pulled back the jacket, much to his horror. "Maybe we have to."

"We can't, or we'll end up trapped inside." He tried to flip the jacket back over my head, but I brushed it away.

"Then we should go now, before we're hypnotized," I said, knowing our window of opportunity would close rapidly once the Wisps were back over the threshold. It had to be now. "It's open, and that's where we need to go." I grinned at the hovering pixies, who'd paused to let the enemy retreat. "Besides, we've got a whole cavalry with us."

Nathan grimaced. "I'm not one for heroism. I'm happier with my books." He stood and threw his jacket to the ground, like it was some kind of metaphor for his fear. "But these people need us, and I won't let them down. Otherwise, I might as well have become a Librarian."

"You'd be surprised what a Librarian can do." I grinned, thinking of Melody and wishing she were here. She'd have been able to get us out of this in no time, but I doubted a call would get out to her, even if Victoria's hunters hadn't nabbed my phone. "Come on. It's now or never."

I jumped up and approached the fizzling door, knowing we were moments away from missing our shot. That sweet song continued to ripple outward as the pixies swarmed around me defensively, Boudicca landing on the top of my head.

Taking a courageous breath, and remembering Leviathan's

words about being careful, I stepped into the light. Nathan followed, and the two of us emerged into the weird and overwhelming world beyond. My feet hit the ground instantly, Nathan beside me. I allowed myself a moment to feel stunned, then I took in my surroundings.

The realm of the Wisps was a confusing collision of the familiar and the strange—like Earth, with gravity and breathable air, but like it had been dipped in the palette of a different planet, with silvered blades of grass that sparkled like a winter's morning, and blood-red trees that sprouted pure white leaves. Rolling, pale hills stretched for miles toward a bruised-purple horizon. Warm ambient lighting blanketed the peculiar world, like it was golden hour in San Diego, although there was no sun to tell the time of day or to explain how there could be so much light in the sky.

Weirder still, this pocket within an interdimensional pocket was full of people clothed in period dress, from dozens of different centuries. But they didn't seem to notice that two strangers had just materialized, nor did they seem to be aware of those around them. They all seemed... hypnotized, standing around like they were waiting for something important. Perhaps they were focused on the singing, although it wasn't clear where the voice was coming from. It seemed to be everywhere and nowhere all at once, much like the light.

"This is supposed to be a prison?" I wondered, gasping.

Nathan's eyes widened. "I have no idea what this is supposed to be."

I heard a sound like Velcro ripping and, turning, I saw the four lines of the Door beginning to fade as the gateway sealed itself off. One thing was for certain—there was no going back now.

And we'd left our one lifeline behind. The book.

TWENTY-NINE

Persie

"Who are all these people?" I murmured. They looked solid, not like the hazy spirits I'd expected. Wisps floated about, zigging and zagging more animatedly than they'd done in the Institute. I supposed they didn't have to put on a pretense here in their own realm. After all, if we were standing on their turf, they'd already done their job.

Nathan shook his head slowly. "I'm not sure. They're not from our time, that much I can say." His eyebrows raised. "Except for those people."

I followed his eyes across the slopes of the nearby silvered hills, where individuals in modern clothing stood in groups. Without waiting, I hurried toward them with my aerial fleet of pixies flocking me, hoping someone might have seen Genie.

"Wait!" Nathan called, chasing after me. My boots crunched against the strange grass, and my senses filled with the metallic aroma of ozone. It reminded me of being by the sea, although I couldn't see one. Clearly there were some odd atmospheric forces at work here, but that didn't concern me right then. Getting my friend and the others out of here was the only thing I cared about.

I paused beside a youngish guy in jeans and a T-shirt, his eyes fixed dead ahead on the expansive hills and purple sky beyond. He was chattering to himself, saying, "I have to remember to do my laundry. Mom will be mad if I don't. I should call her and let her know I'm okay." I waited for him to acknowledge me, but he didn't. He just repeated the same sentences over and over again, caught in a glitch.

"Do you recognize this guy?" I whispered to Nathan.

He nodded. "That's David Harper. He was the seventh person to go missing, I think." He approached the entranced man. "David? Can you hear me?"

But either David couldn't, or he had forgotten how to reply. He wouldn't even turn to look at us, his eyes out of focus like he was sleepwalking.

"What happened to him?" I tried to shake him by the shoulder, but he seemed unaware of that, too. Nothing was going to get through to him.

"I don't know," Nathan replied anxiously. "However, I think it's highly likely that everyone we're seeing here are the people that the Wisps have drawn to this place. Possibly over the span of a thousand years or so."

I hit him with a confused look. "How can that be? I thought the Wisps were trapped here, with no way out until the Institute accidentally opened the gateway."

"They must've found a way to slip out from time to time. And they wasted no time enticing as many people as possible." Nathan visibly shuddered. "As you're already aware, Ireland is rich in natural Chaos. Perhaps, when monsters came near, it allowed the gateway to temporarily open."

"Well, we already knew the Wisps were sneaky." I set off to

explore, determined to find my friend. Genie was around somewhere and I wouldn't rest until I found her, even if I had to travel to
the very edges of this interdimensional pocket.

Hiking up and down the hills with my pixie entourage, peering
behind chalky bushes with ripe blue fruit and scouring the shade
beneath those strange blood-red trees, it didn't take long for frustration to set in. Not even the pixies, picking the blue fruit and hurling
it at each other, could lighten it. I'd counted around thirteen people
in modern clothing, and a lot more in period clothing, but Genie
wasn't among them. Part of me wondered if she'd managed to
escape somehow and was just lost in the real world, trying to find a
way back to the Institute.

But that smarted of wishful thinking. In truth, there was a higher
chance that something worse had happened to her. I'd seen those
Wisps turn violent. Maybe she hadn't wanted to play ball, and it had
landed her in trouble.

"There!" Nathan shouted sharply, yanking my arm and spinning
me around. "Over there!"

I squinted, not seeing her.

"On the riverbank, just in front of that tree." He jabbed a finger
toward the biggest tree on the horizon, which branched up and out
on the opposite bank of a crystalline, purplish river. I searched the
riverbank desperately, bracing for the worst.

And there she was. Genie, sitting in the silver grass, rocking
slowly back and forth with her knees tucked under her chin, her
eyes staring into the water. She looked so small and vulnerable that I
had to do a doubletake, confirming that it was, indeed, my best
friend. Seeing her like that was all the reason I needed to take off at
a full sprint, skidding to a halt only when I reached the water's edge.
The pixies stopped messing around with the fruit and flew after me,
careful not to let me out of their sight. I sensed their defensive
streak kicking in.

"Do you think it's safe to cross? What if it's acid, or something?" I turned back to Nathan as he caught up.

He eyed the river for a moment, breathing hard, before shaking his head. "It can't be. Look, Genie's jeans are still wet. She must've waded across."

"I really hope you're right." I swallowed hard. "Don't suppose you've got any Water abilities you could use, or a spell to carry us over?"

He hesitated. "I could try to build a land bridge." Lifting his palms, green sparks erupted and sputtered out almost immediately. "How odd..."

"Is something wrong?"

He stared at his hands like they were broken tools. "My Chaos doesn't seem to be working. Let me try something else—it won't help us cross, but I'd feel better knowing we weren't entirely vulnerable here." His mouth moved and a fizzing shield of light slid up his arm and over his body. A moment later, he dispensed with it.

"What's the consensus?" I asked nervously.

"Hexes and spells appear to work, but my Elemental abilities won't. It's very strange, for this interdimensional bubble to be so specifically preventative." He put his hands down. "It seems we will have to proceed without magical assistance."

I managed a quiet laugh. "Nothing new there."

Stepping into this world, I thought, was the bravest thing I'd ever done, and clambering down into unknown purple liquid was probably the second bravest—or second dumbest, depending on your perspective. I'd never done anything like this before. I could be quietly courageous at times, but transforming that into ballsy action had never really been my forte. Genie had always carried that flag. And now it was my turn to take it up.

I slipped into the water and waited for my skin to start sloughing away, or for tiny aquatic creatures to devour me. At the very least, I'd expected it to be cold, but it proved to be neither cold nor dangerous. Satisfied that I wouldn't dissolve, I pushed through the river with Nathan beside me, careful not to lose my footing and get swept away. Meanwhile, the pixies skated across the surface, cutting only faint lines through the water, like they were ice dancers. The current pulled slightly on my legs as I reached the center of the river, but my boots kept me rooted to the smooth, silty bed. Puffs of glitter rose in the silt, disturbed by my footfalls. Beautiful but unsettling, like everything else in this peculiar world.

Reaching the opposite side, I dug my fingernails into the dirt and heaved my body onto the bank. The pixies attempted to help, pulling on my hands and my wet shirt, but they didn't have the strength. *They could never have carried a person away, Victoria,* I thought to myself once more. Nathan jumped out with surprising agility and immediately helped me to my feet. Only when I'd grasped his arm to use as leverage did I see that the dirt beneath my fingertips wasn't the usual mucky brown. No, this dirt was blood-red—the same shade as the trees. I hastily wiped it away on my dark jeans. Maybe I didn't want to know.

"Genie!" I ran the rest of the way and knelt in front of her. "Genie? It's me, Persie." I grasped her face in my hands, trying to tilt her head back, but it was like her neck was made of solid steel. I couldn't get her to move an inch, let alone make her look at me. Her eyes carried that same glazed sheen as the others. I couldn't deny the truth sitting right in front of me—Genie had fallen under the same trance as everyone else.

"My father would hate to find out he was right, so I won't tell him," she whispered. "I don't want to go back to Atlantis—I want to be free to do whatever I want and go wherever I want, and love whoever I want. I don't want an arranged marriage with a puffed-up Atlantean who's never seen the outside world."

Nathan leaned in, his eyes glinting. "What did she say? Is she... getting married?"

"Not if she can help it," I replied, my heart breaking for Genie. She would've hated this, to be frozen and trapped in her own mind.

Nathan ruffled his hair, clearly irritated by this particular topic and torn between wanting to know more and wanting to stay focused on the situation at hand—de-hypnotizing Genie. "Is... is her father intending to marry her off?"

I sank back into a sitting position. "He's talked about it, and she's refused. But it's a huge custom in Atlantis, apparently, even for Atlanteans who've integrated. They're expected to marry one of their own kind for the sake of maintaining Primus Anglicus bloodlines, but she's never going to go willingly." My shoulders sagged. "That is, if we can even get her out of here."

"I'm pleased to hear that," he mumbled. "I've never liked the idea of arranged marriages, especially not for the sake of something as foolish as bloodlines. People should be allowed to love whomever they please." He turned his face away from me, his body hunched as though he wanted to shield his emotions from me. "And we will rescue her from this place, I assure you. There's a way. This can't have all been for nothing."

I reached for Genie's hand and tried to hold it, but I couldn't loosen a single finger of her iron grip. All the while, she repeated the same ideas in an endless cycle. Coming through the Door had only raised more questions. Why was she stuck thinking *these* particular things? Why was she stuck at all? Were the Wisps doing this? I couldn't see how it benefitted them, unless this was somehow a vengeful ploy to get back at the person who'd trapped *them* here. But Fergus McLeod had to be long dead by now. Unless he was stuck here, too, repeating his fears on a loop like Genie and the others.

"Genie?" I begged. "Genie, you have to snap out of this. I know you're still in there, and you have to be able to hear this, so just...

come back to me, Genie. Please, just fight whatever is doing this to you!" I tried to shake her, but she remained stubbornly fixed to the same spot. Even Boudicca had a go, flashing her pulsating lights in Genie's eyes to try and break her out of the trance. But nothing worked.

Then, the bone-white leaves overhead began to rustle loudly. That wouldn't have been strange, except... there wasn't any breeze to speak of. My head lifted, and I watched the leaves shake against some unknown, unfelt wind. And when I lowered my gaze back to Genie, I got the fright of my life. Her gray eyes were looking right at me, her expression blank and eerie.

"Uh... Persie." Nathan glanced over his shoulder, the color draining from his face. "I think we have a problem."

I followed his line of sight and my heart plummeted. "Yeah, that's not good."

Across the riverbank, the formerly hypnotized abductees were trudging slowly in our direction. A young woman in modern clothes reached the embankment and stepped right into the water without a moment's hesitation. My head whipped back around to find more abductees approaching in a zombie-like horde from our side of the river, all headed for Nathan and me.

"Genie, please, you have to—"

My words were cut short as she lunged for me. I managed to stagger backward just in time to avoid her clawing hands, but it wouldn't stop her for long. Everywhere I looked, abductees marched toward us, blocking off every exit. I thought about diving into the river and letting it sweep us all the way to the ends of the pocket, but who was to say there wouldn't be more waiting for us there?

Crap, crap, crap! I weighed my options, wondering if I could somehow coax out a Purge if I panicked hard enough. That would be a last resort, considering I had no control over what emerged.

Still, I could keep it in mind, if things really got desperate. The pixie Purge had turned out all right, after all.

As Genie lunged for me again, the pixies propelled themselves into defense mode. Boudicca led a battalion of six against my best friend, whizzing around her head and pulling her hair—but Genie's focus was unbreakable. All around me, the rest of the pixies set to work, trying to push back the encroaching zombie horde. They flashed their gaudy lights and scratched, scraped, punched, kicked, and clawed at the clueless enemy, but nothing they did made a difference. The zombies marched on, apathetic to the attack.

"Persie, quick!" Nathan grasped me by the elbow and dragged me closer to the tree trunk, away from Genie's intent hands. With a rough shove, he pushed me into a crouching position and joined me there. His palms went up, and scarlet sparks juddered out of his hands, spinning around us in a vortex as his mouth moved in a silent spell. The vortex gathered into a revolving ball of dark red, rippling with threads of silver and gold. He clamped his hands into fists and the ball responded, shooting out a shimmering dome of magical protection that slid around us and slammed into the ground with a hiss, singeing the grass where it hit.

I eyed the dome suspiciously. Through the reddish sheen, I could still see everything beyond, and the zombies were getting closer by the moment. "Another spell from the Grimoire? Tell me it's strong enough to keep these people from strangling us."

He panted. "It's a *very* strong one, which is why I don't use it too often. Not that I usually have a reason to." He tipped from a crouch to rest on his knees. "As you can see, it takes a lot out of me."

"If Genie could snap out of this trance, she's got a billion tricks like this up her sleeve." I saw Genie looking blankly at our hiding place. Evidently, we weren't *quite* invisible, as she began to approach our shelter. Before long, she was right outside the protective bubble, bumping against it and swiping at the shield to try and break through. The thud of each impact bounced the bubble around as though we were crouched inside a balloon, but it appeared to be holding.

The pixies! I suddenly remembered the rest of our party and scanned the Wisp realm for them. Fired up, they were still in a one-sided battle with the zombies, divebombing the listless abductees. A large group of pixies had managed to bring one of the zombies to a halt by heaving backward on the young woman's arms, legs, and hair, but she still made the motions as if she were moving forward.

I was about to turn back to Genie when I noticed the Wisps swarming—by the hundreds—and they were looking for a fight. Splitting in every direction, they launched their assault on the pixies. And my poor Purge beasts didn't see it coming.

Now on their home turf, the Wisps were strengthened in violence and fury. They outnumbered my creatures considerably, surrounding the pixies and powering up their central flames, building to that scorching heat that had stung my skin in the sphere. Then I heard the most heart-wrenching sound... the scream of a dying pixie. I searched desperately for the creature who'd made the sound, but there were too many Wisps, their light hiding the pixies' torment from me.

Another scream pierced the air, brimming with untold agony. They would all die, I realized, unless I did something.

"Let me out!" I yelled at Nathan. "They're killing them!"

Nathan dipped his chin to his chest. "I can't, Persie. If you go out there, they'll hurt you too."

A third scream shivered through the bubble, chilling me to the bone. I felt his last moments as though they were my own. I'd made the pixies, and I didn't want them to die for me. I couldn't just sit back and let them all get burned to a crisp while trying to protect me. I might not have been the bravest person in the world, but I wasn't a coward, either.

"Let me out of here, NOW!" I shouted.

Nathan's eyes hardened. "I won't do it, Persie. I'm sorry. I don't like this any more than you do, but I can't let you go out there."

"Listen to them, Nathan!" I was beside myself now, my voice cracking. "They're dying! Please, let me try. I have to try!"

"No," he said simply.

Frantic, I hammered on the inside of the bubble, causing the magical shield to spark. For a moment, it reminded me of my nightmare again, only this felt way worse. The helplessness came from a different place, heavy with the responsibility of the pixies' fate. "Stop! Please, stop!" I bellowed, tears streaming down my cheeks. "They haven't done anything wrong! Please, stop! They're only trying to protect me. They don't deserve to die! Please, please, please!"

I pounded harder on the bubble. "Please…" I slumped back on my haunches, holding my face in my hands. They weren't going to listen to me. Who was I kidding? I'd brought the pixies here; I'd done this to them, and now they were paying the ultimate price. I owed it to them to look, but I couldn't. It hurt too much.

"Persie…" Nathan nudged my arm.

I shrugged him off roughly. "I know, you won't let me out. You said already."

"That's not it. Look."

I peeked through my fingers, and my jaw dropped. The zombies had frozen in their tracks, and the Wisps had buzzed away like they were innocent little fairies who hadn't killed anyone I cared about. And, in the midst of it all, a man emerged from the crowd of zombies, striding right up to our protective bubble. He had a mane of fiery red hair that touched his shoulders, impossibly green eyes, and the outfit of some kind of soldier—a cavalryman, perhaps, judging by his battered leather riding boots and riding crop.

"You were not led to this place. What are you doing here?" he demanded in a thick Irish brogue. The words didn't sit comfortably on his tongue, as though he wasn't used to speaking.

Breathless, I asked a question in return. "Who the hell are you?"

His eyes narrowed, his mouth twisting in a scowl. "I'm Fergus McLeod."

THIRTY

Persie

"How?" Nathan maintained the protective bubble, muscling between me and this strange man who claimed to be Fergus McLeod. It made me wonder how secure these defenses were if he felt the need to act as a human shield.

The red-headed man turned up his nose. "What d'ye mean?"

"How can it be you? No offense, but you should be dead." Nathan discreetly pushed me further behind him. I appreciated the heroic sentiment, but I was more concerned about scanning the area for my pixies.

My heart wrenched as I saw the tiny bodies on the ground—far more than three. I counted twenty in total, prompting bile to rise up my throat. Only three had called out in their last moments, while the rest had died in stoic silence. Was it any wonder I'd felt their anguish and fear as though it was my own? The surviving half congregated around the fallen, bowing their heads and weeping quietly. I saw Boudicca among the living, crouching to press her tiny palm to the chest of one of the dead, and I breathed a small sigh of relief. Still, the guilt lingered for the ones who hadn't been so lucky.

Shouldn't the dead Purge beasts be turning back to smoke? I knew that was what happened to Purge beasts when they died, but the twenty pixies on the ground didn't seem to be transforming. Perhaps the realm we were in prevented it.

"I am dead," Fergus shot back, as if he thought we were idiots. "Do I look alive to ye?"

I turned to him. "Actually, yes."

"Well, I ain't. Me corporeal body turned te dust like bodies do, but me spirit stayed on. I bartered for it to stay in here, with them what forced my hand." Fergus glared at the Wisps in the distance, which seemed frightened of him. They darted out of sight when his gaze rested on a group, hiding wherever they could. "And this is me own personal paradise, or me own personal hell—depends on how ye look at it, I suppose."

Does that mean...? If he'd become a spirit, what about the others? Were they already dead, too, and we just couldn't tell? I shook away the thought, unwilling to accept it. My friend couldn't be dead. She looked so... solid, albeit dazed. Then again, Fergus didn't look dead, either. But he *was* moving around however he liked, instead of being stuck on a loop. Perhaps that meant he was the only truly dead person here, no longer bound by the endless cycle of thoughts that held the others captive. Or maybe I just didn't want to see the truth —that we'd arrived too late.

An idea came to me as I crept back toward the fizzing shield. "You don't like the Wisps much, do you?" I nudged Nathan and mouthed "specterglass" at him. He nodded back discreetly and dug into his jeans pocket for the lens.

"Don't matter whether I like 'em or not. I'm stuck with 'em." Fergus ground the end of his riding crop into his palm. "And they might not have brought ye here the proper way, which don't sit too well with me. But ye'll be joinin' us regardless, now yer here."

I looked to Genie, who stood as still as a statue. "No."

"Yer what now?" Fergus scowled at me, his emerald-green eyes glinting with annoyance. A band of Wisps came to hover on either side of him, like his own personal guard. If they were singing their hypnotic song, I couldn't hear them.

"I said no." I stood my ground, feeling defiance build in my chest. "Why would we want to stay here? This place isn't real. It's just an illusion that you asked some Child of Chaos to create a long time ago. And even you can't decide if it's a heaven or a hell. These people —*all* of these people—belong outside, in the real world. My friend belongs there, and you've got no right to keep anyone here."

Fergus eyeballed me. "Ye seem te know a lot, lass. I'd ask how, but it don't matter to me. Naught matters much in this place. That's why it's better for everyone." He swept his riding crop around at the motionless zombies, while two Wisps came closer to the protective shield. "People can be at peace here, not worryin' about who's goin' te bother 'em. A happy purgatory for folks who need a bit o' quiet."

"Purgatory isn't living, Fergus. Why don't you tell us why you're really doing this?" I nudged Nathan again, so we could use the specterglass to see who was truly dead and who wasn't. But he wasn't responding.

Turning slowly, I gasped at the sight of him. His eyes had glazed over, his mouth moving in a frightened whisper. "What if I can't make a difference?" he said. "What if I can't defy the order of things? What if I'm not doing enough to prevent future harm?"

No... The Wisps flanking Fergus must've launched a sneak attack at Nathan when I wasn't looking.

I grabbed Nathan by the shoulders and shook him hard, just as the defensive shield failed with a frazzled crackle of magical sparks —in his hypnotized state, he couldn't hold it anymore. "Nathan, don't listen to the Wisps! You have to ignore the music. Please!" I shook him so hard my own teeth chattered, but I refused to give in.

Fergus smirked in my periphery, giving a small nod of approval to the guardian Wisps. With his focus distracted for a second, it gave me the chance to palm the specterglass in Nathan's hand and slip it into my own pocket before Fergus noticed. I had to know, beyond a shadow of a doubt, what this Wisp trance did to people. And I prayed that when I looked through that lens, it wouldn't show me they were all dead. My heart wouldn't be able to take it.

"Why are you doing this?!" I screamed. "Give them back. Give them all back, or so help me, I'll rain monsters down on your little paradise until you can be certain it's hell."

I had enough panic coursing through my veins to make good on that promise, though I was surprised at the ferocity in my voice. It didn't sound like me talking. It sounded more like... No, I wasn't like him. I wasn't *anything* like him. I would not fall prey to Leviathan's will. This was about Genie and Nathan, and all the people Fergus had taken. Nothing more.

Fergus laughed coldly. "Aye, o' course ye will. And I'm Queen Mab." He whispered something, and the Wisps came spinning back. For someone who obviously loathed these beings, he seemed to rely a whole lot on their obedience. "Ye'll be a lot happier when ye stop fightin' it, lass. I suggest ye give in."

Not a chance. I didn't have useful abilities, but if the Wisps attacked, I'd do what I could to punch and swipe them back. Plus, I supposed I had my not-so secret weapon: the creatures I'd created. As if sensing my need for help, they rallied to my aid. The pixies might've been decimated, their number halved, but the remaining horde left their dead and hurled themselves into the air, coming to my defense. The Wisps wanted to take me, but I'd stopped hearing their music. The voices had to be singing somewhere, or Nathan wouldn't have fallen under their spell, but I was deaf to them. And I had no idea why. Was it Leviathan, somehow protecting me from afar? Or the pixies? Or had the Wisps' song just stopped working on me?

As the Wisps made their charge, the pixies formed a protective circle around me, their pulsating lights on full blast. They joined hands, forming a chain. A moment later, they lit up like a Christmas tree, chanting in their pixie tongue. Fizzing threads of dazzling purple light shot down their arms and into their neighbors', connecting them as one entity, with me in the center of their defensive ring. Their voices grew louder until an almighty explosion of violet-tinged energy surged from them in a juddering pulse, pushing the Wisps back. Nathan toppled like a domino, too, though it didn't seem to affect him. He kept right on repeating his mantra, curled on his side with that blank look in his eyes.

They've adapted. There might've been fewer pixies, but their strength didn't necessarily appear to depend on their number. Their survival instincts had kicked in, and they were stepping up their game to avoid a second round of decimation. It seemed they were willing to throw everything they had at these Wisps... and all to protect me. Why? Was there so much power in being their creator? I didn't know. But I did know that if we made it out of here alive, I would give the pixies what they deserved for this—their freedom.

"You asked a Child of Chaos to build this realm for you, to trap the Wisps. You obviously hate them, yet you use them to round up people for you," I ranted, trying to buy the pixies some time. Fergus clearly controlled the Wisps, and if I could keep him talking, perhaps he'd call them off. "You can't possibly believe this is the best place for anyone. Even you don't want to be here—I can see it in your face. I want to know why you're doing this."

He paused, and so did the Wisps. "Ain't it obvious?"

"If it were, would I be asking?" I retorted. So far, the plan to keep him talking was working.

"Color me surprised, since ye seem to know so much already." Sarcasm dripped from his tongue. "Aye, I did ask a Child o' Chaos for this world. I called te Gaia, and she answered. I did it for love, and I'd do it again, a thousand times over."

I frowned in confusion. "Love?"

"I asked her for the power te make this world—many centuries ago, now. I lose count—for me and me beloved, Lorelei. For years, I been waitin' for me love te come back. I lost her 'cause o' these Wisps, and I asked Gaia te punish 'em for it. She agreed, and now they're paying the price. They answer to me now. I get 'em to take people from around the gateway in the hopes that they'll bring me Lorelei too, someday." He sighed, showing a flicker of emotion for the first time. "Life, death, and everythin' in between ain't worth a damn thing without her."

"That doesn't make any sense." I kept my hand closed around the specterglass, waiting for the right moment. "Why would taking living people bring your love here? If you built this place a very long time ago, then she must be dead, too. If you loved her at all, you should wish she's in the afterlife, safe and sound. You should pack this whole thing up and join her there. Pass on to the next world, and free everyone else."

Fergus's expression hardened into pure rage. "She's lookin' for me! She'll follow me trail here, one o' these days!" He waved his riding crop as though it were some kind of magical wand and began to cry out. "*Bain an t-anam seo. Tóg gach duine nach leis an saol seo. Níl fáilte rompu anseo. Déan iad a dhíbirt ón saol seo. Níl mé ag iarraidh iad anseo.*"

Before I knew what was happening, my body lifted into the air. The pixies floated up with me, all of them flailing, battling the unexpected Telekinesis. But Nathan remained on the ground, having joined the zombie ranks in a way I hadn't. I guessed that meant he could stay.

Lightning fast, since I had no idea how much time I had left, I whipped the specterglass out of my pocket and lifted the lens to my eye. The image that came back made the breath rush out of my lungs. A hazy collection of white and red mist swirled into the human shape of Fergus, revealing his dead spirit. And where the gaseous orbs of the Wisps floated, another shape hovered beside each one. Human shapes. Arms outstretched, holding the death candles. These were the spirits that had been enlisted to guide people to safety in the afterlife—a task they'd spat on for their own hijinks, like Boudicca had told me. However, as I scanned the lens over the rest of the crowd, my heart lifted slightly. Those in modern dress, including Genie and Nathan, didn't have any mist at all, which I hoped meant they were still alive—they weren't touched by specter dust, or haze, or whatever this misty stuff was. *They're not dead. We're not too late.* But I couldn't say the same for the people in period clothing, from bygone eras. It was centuries too late for them.

I realized I might've spoken too soon. As Fergus flung the pixies and me across his pocket of paradise, the gateway roared open, and we sailed through it.

He was banning us from his personal heaven—maybe for good.

THIRTY-ONE

Persie

_____

The gateway spat us out into the bottom of the sphere, right back at square one. The twenty-strong band of pixies wheeled around and flew back at the now-closed Door to Nowhere, making rude gestures and hurling insults. I admired their spunk, but we had no time to waste on a gateway that would no longer open for us. It wasn't as though it had a handle I could push, and the pooling light had disappeared back into vacant darkness. We were in a race against the clock, before that specterglass showed something I didn't want to see—Genie, Nathan, and the other Institute abductees swirling in a death mist. I had no idea how long someone could exist in Fergus's world without losing their hold on the living world. Decades, years, days, weeks, hours? I couldn't risk delaying, either way.

But how do I get them out of there?

I stared at the thin, glowing outline of the doorway. It wasn't like I could borrow some C4 and blow it open. Leviathan's words came back to bug me—I had to be careful. But there was more to it than that. I had to be cautious, not just in the realm, but outside of it.

After all, what would happen to the people that were taken decades and even centuries ago, once they set foot outside of the eerie paradise? The dead pixies hadn't morphed back into Chaos mist to be returned from whence they came, but I would've bet good money that they would as soon as they were out of there. And that probably went for the other lost souls. If Fergus's physical body had rotted away in that place, leaving him as a spirit, it wasn't a huge stretch to think that the same might've happened to the older residents. They wouldn't last out here in the real world, because they didn't belong here anymore.

Does that mean I'd be killing them, in a way? I shivered uneasily, having a crisis of conscience. That kind of purgatory wasn't living, but it wasn't dying, either. And I'd be taking the choice away from the people who would likely die the moment they set foot outside. Or, perhaps, like Nathan had suggested, I couldn't defy the order of things. Maybe it was their time to pass on, and Fergus's realm was holding them back from that. It felt impossible to know which was the right way, but I had to save my friends. That part was clear. Plus, I had the added guilt of knowing that pixies had died for me, in there. The creatures I'd given life to couldn't pass on and return to Chaos, and I didn't want them stuck like that. Truthfully, I wasn't sure what happened to a Purge beast if it couldn't return to the Chaos stream after death.

"Did you think you could hide from me? Did you think I wouldn't find you?" A familiar voice cut through the silence, followed by the comedic squeak of someone sliding down the pole from above. A shadow descended, and I staggered back.

I clenched my jaw. "Not now, Charlotte. I'm busy."

"Busy causing problems." She hopped down onto the ground and raised her palms. "And I'm here to take you in."

I ducked a lasso of Telekinesis while the pixies regrouped around me. "Then why are you here on your own? I thought you'd have gone straight to Victoria!" It seemed odd that she hadn't brought a hunter entourage with her, so I decided to try and call her bluff. Maybe she wanted to take me to Victoria to get the glory, or maybe it was payback for toppling her in bear form.

"This is my family's Institute. *I* let you get away, so *I* have to clean up my mess." She lashed out with another lasso, and I kicked my leg out to avoid it slithering around my ankle. "Victoria has enough on her plate. After all you've said to me about fixing your own problems, I know you'll understand why I have to do this."

"Then, for Chaos's sake, would you listen for one freaking second! Our goal is the same!" I shouted. Boudicca led a quartet of badass she-pixies in a bombardment, all four of them slicing through the air, legs extended, preparing for their trademark dropkick.

Charlotte yelped in surprise when the pixies made contact. "I *knew* you were involved! I knew it!" She threw out two lassoes in an attempt to wrangle the pixies, but they were too fast. Boudicca managed to land a dropkick to her cheek, and two other she-pixies snatched up her hair and wound it around her eyes, blocking her vision. "Why are you doing this, Persie? Why are you getting these monsters to kidnap people?" she spluttered, trying to clear her hair out of her eyes.

"I'm not!" I resisted an eye roll. "They're on our side. That's what I'm trying to tell you, but you need to quiet the heck down so I can explain!"

My tone threw me—I rarely got this riled, and never with people I didn't know—but I was thin on patience these days. Fergus had already pissed me off, and now Charlotte was intent on getting on my bad side. If I showed weakness, she'd eat me alive, and I couldn't risk getting marched down to Victoria's office. No one would pay attention to the truth there, either.

Boudicca chattered something back at the remaining pixies and they swarmed around me, forming another defensive circle to protect me against Charlotte's Telekinesis. This time, however, it looked like they'd adapted yet again. They gripped hands and dove toward the floor, bright violet light sparking between them. An ancient chant rose up from them, and they rose with it, spinning faster and faster in their circle until a translucent veil of purplish Chaos rippled around me. These incredible little critters had built me a shield, to keep me safe from Charlotte.

"You're lying." Charlotte ducked and pulled her knotted hair away from her eyes, batting away the pixies who weren't forming the shield. They'd split into a defense group and an attack group. "You just want to protect your Purges. You're as bad as Nathan; just another monster lover."

As Boudicca and her warriors retreated inside my shield, Charlotte got to her feet. Her eyes widened in shock as she took in the pixies' protective shield.

"What... are they doing?" she said.

"They're defending me against you, because you attacked me. They aren't nasty creatures. They're kind, and they're loyal, and they don't deserve your hatred. It's not about loving monsters, it's about respecting them." I huffed out a sigh. "And they're trying to help. See, they know if I can't get you to hear me out, then the people who were taken won't be coming back again. And that will be on you."

"They're *protecting* you?" She looked as though she'd just found out the Earth was round. Evidently, this scenario didn't fit with her preconceived notions of what a monster should and shouldn't be.

I had to wonder just what kind of Monster History was being taught in this place. Hadn't they heard about the Battle for Elysium, where countless monsters had given their lives to save the world? Sure, Tobe had coaxed them into it, but they'd fought side by side with magicals. The same went for Murray and the gargoyles, when my uncle went to take down Davin Doncaster. By Finch's count,

Murray had chewed Davin up at least twice—all to help my family and their friends.

I glanced at Boudicca and she flashed me an encouraging grin, though it didn't quite reach her big eyes. After losing her people, I guessed it would take a while before her smiles were whole-hearted again. "The pixies didn't kidnap anyone. They've been helping me track down the real culprit, who just so happens to be behind that door." I gestured to the faint outline. "Do you remember those strange orbs we saw during orientation?"

Charlotte frowned and nodded slowly. "Yes. A prank or something."

"Not a prank. They're Will-o'-the-Wisps, and they're the ones doing this. They hypnotize people and guide them through that gateway, and then those people don't come back. I've just been through, but the guy who's running the show kicked me out because I didn't fall under the spell." I rattled off the words as fast as possible, not knowing how long I'd have her attention. I elaborated on what I'd seen in that mysterious realm, and told her everything I could about the Wisps, the Door to Nowhere, and Fergus freaking McLeod, until I ran out of breath.

"And now, I can't get back in to save everyone," I finished. "But if you take me to Victoria, you can kiss your friends goodbye, because she's not going to believe a word of this and they're going to stay lost and zombified in there. It doesn't fit with her story, but it's the truth. I swear on Genie's life."

For the longest time, Charlotte didn't say a word. She lowered her hands to her sides and paced, thinking. I hoped that was a good sign, but I'd seen how quickly Charlotte could turn—literally and figuratively. If she went into bear-mode, or worse, I didn't know how the pixies would fare.

Abruptly, she turned to me. "I read about Will-o'-the-Wisps once, but they haven't been seen in decades. Looks like extinct crea-

tures are popping up all over the place, thanks to you." Was that...
jealousy? Maybe? Her expression softened a touch. "Lucky for you,
I'm inclined to believe you, since I know you don't have the ability
to create Wisps. Only someone with Necromancy skills could do
that."

I nodded, hardly able to believe that she was listening. I knew
who the Necromancers were, but she didn't need to know that. *The
pixies did it, but they had their Necromancy stripped by a Child of Chaos
after the Wisps went rogue.* Still, that didn't mean they were responsible for this. That much, I *could* say. "After the Wisps were sucked
through the gateway, their actions were solely under Fergus's
control."

"It could've been me." She turned her gaze downward, her body
language stiffening with guilt. "I heard that music you spoke about—
only for a couple of seconds, when I was drifting off to sleep last
night, but still. I thought I imagined it."

I gave Boudicca a knowing look, and she instructed her pixies to
lower the shield wall. "You were probably too far gone, sleep-wise,
for the Wisps to influence you. They need you to see the lights and
hear the music fully, or the hypnosis doesn't work."

Charlotte was feeling guilty. Her best friend had been abducted,
and she hadn't. I knew exactly how she felt, like we'd narrowly
avoided a mine while our closest confidantes had stepped right onto
it. It hurt to know that they might've been able to avoid it, if only
we'd understood sooner.

"How do we fix it?" Charlotte's head snapped up, determination
replacing her guilty expression.

"We have to work together. And fast, or the Wisps will keep
taking people and nobody will be able to stop them. Now that the
gateway is open, they'll carry on until we can shut the Door for
good, or until it gets buried under a pile of rubble and earth again.
Saying that, we can't let it close until we've got everyone out. So, you

see the predicament we're in." I opened my mouth to say more, but at that moment the Door blasted open and the Wisps spun out in a frenzy, making a beeline for Charlotte.

After all, the pixies and I were tainted goods.

But my monster allies were prepared for all eventualities now and refused to be taken by surprise. Before the Wisps could get near Charlotte to start up the hypnosis trick, the pixies split into two bands of ten. They wasted no time creating the spinning shield of violet light around each of us, the vortex making the Wisps reel back in alarm. As the pixies' chanting grew to deafening levels and the glow of the shields intensified with the sound, the Wisps froze for a moment, unsure what to do next. A blast of fizzing energy erupted from the pixies, sending the Wisps flying back toward the Door. Evidently, they decided to cut their losses and run with their comet tails between their legs. But their quick retreat also caused the gateway to close again, shutting us off from those who needed rescue before we could even think about leaping through it.

With the Wisp wave held back, the pixies slowed their spinning and came to a stop. A handful hovered around drunkenly, holding tiny palms to their heads to ease their vertigo. Coming to my aid had taken its toll on them, but none complained. Instead, they giggled as they bumped dizzily into each other, while Boudicca kept one eye on the gateway.

Charlotte exhaled sharply, patting her body down to make sure she was intact. "Why did they do that?"

"Help you, you mean?" I smiled, knowing the Wisps had just put the icing on the cake. Now Charlotte *had* to believe that the pixies were innocent. They'd just saved her from a date with Fergus's paradise.

She nodded stiffly.

"Maybe they wanted you to see what I see," I replied. "That

there's not an evil bone in their bodies. A bunch of mischievous ones, sure, but they're far from evil."

Looking shaken, Charlotte fixed her gaze on Boudicca. "Thank you."

Boudicca chuckled and mimicked her voice, pretending to tremble like a wet dog. Charlotte frowned, like she didn't know what to make of the display, but I understood. This was Boudicca's way of saying, "Don't thank us yet. Thank us when you've told everyone that we're innocent."

"Don't worry, as long as you show the pixies respect, they won't mock you too much," I assured, laughing at—or more like *with*—Boudicca. The she-pixie winked at me and touched down on my shoulder. Perched there, she indicated a shadowy object on the floor. It took me a moment to figure out what it was: the book the pixies had stolen from the library. I plucked it up, cradling it in my arms like the precious treasure of knowledge I hoped it would be.

Charlotte approached warily. "What's that?"

"Nathan asked the pixies to fetch it. He thought it might be the answer to gaining entry, since we didn't have a Wisp to lead us through the gateway." I flipped through the pages to the section that had caught Nathan's attention before. But the words swam in front of my eyes, and they weren't written in English. "Can you read this? I think this was the line Nathan thought might be important."

Charlotte took the book from me and scanned the Gaelic. "What did he say it meant?"

"Uh... something like 'The maker's strength holds the Will together.' He thought it referred to the Wisps, and I guess the maker part has something to do with Fergus," I replied, thinking on my feet.

Charlotte shook her head. "His Gaelic never was very good. It's more like 'The maker's bones hold the Will together.' But... you made it sound like Fergus was alive? If that's the case, then his bones are inside that realm, and we're screwed."

"No, no, he's not alive!" I pretty much shrieked. "He looks like it, but he's not. I saw for myself with... um... a lens thing that Nathan had on him." I'd hesitated in case she started calling me a thief again, but I figured honesty would be the best policy with her. It would be up to her whether she believed me or not, though I'd done all right so far in winning her over.

"So, you think there's a chance the bones might be here, in the outside world?" Charlotte urged. "This is important, Persie. The bones are holding together the spell that created this interdimensional pocket. If we can't find them, we can't do anything."

I tapped my chin in thought. "He said his body had turned to dust, as all bodies do, but he didn't mention anything about his body decaying *inside* the realm." An idea came to me. "Maybe that's the price *he* paid to have the realm built, and to trap the Wisps inside. He had to die so he could be reunited with Lorelei's soul in their own private heaven."

Charlotte nodded, a smile turning up the corners of her lips. "What did you just say?"

"Uh... that's the price he paid? Or do you mean the reunited part?" She seemed to be having a lightbulb moment.

"Yes, that part!" I was still none-the-wiser. "There's another line here—though it's pretty smudged—that says, 'Only when destiny is fulfilled, and what remains is brought together will the Will break.' I think we're onto something!" She sounded excited. "The 'what remains is' part can also be translated as 'the remains are.' As in, the bones. If we want this to stop, we need to try something unorthodox —we'll need to find Fergus's bones and take them to this Lorelei woman, or whatever's left of her. Their bones need to be reunited. If they were in love, they might even be buried close to one another."

"That's all he wants, to be with his love again." I rolled with her idea, glad to have her sharp mind whirring. "If we give him what he wants, then the Will might disperse, and he might let everyone go. It might even close the gateway for good."

The pixies whizzed around excitedly, and Boudicca gave me a nod of approval. The thought of digging up bones didn't exactly fill me with joy, but if it brought Genie and Nathan and the others back, then I was more than happy to grab a shovel. The question was, how did we get out of the Institute without being spotted or sounding any alarms?

"Please tell me there's an escape route that won't get us caught?" I laid my hopes at Charlotte's feet.

She grinned. "I've been sneaking out of here since I was thirteen. I know back exits and secret passageways that even Victoria doesn't know about." Before I could argue, she stepped up to me and wrapped a firm arm around my waist. "Hold tight. This might be bumpy." Shooting a lasso of Telekinesis up to the rickety walkway overhead, she pulled us out of the sphere's gloomy depths as I clung for dear life, the pixies close behind.

Landing shakily on solid ground, I had no time to catch my breath as Charlotte sprinted off, out of the new wing. Then and there, I vowed to join Genie on her morning runs if I got her out of this, for the sake of my poor stamina. For now, I forced my legs to race after Charlotte, hoping my lungs didn't give out before we'd escaped.

I caught up to her in the hallway that led away from the new wing and fell into step at her side, until she came to a halt in front of a seemingly ordinary door. Taking out a set of keys, she turned one in the lock and swung the door wide. A grand study lay beyond, complete with seven white marble dragons identical to the ones in the main assembly hall, only smaller. Elegant golden drapes covered a floor-to-ceiling window, and every available stretch of wall space was filled with packed bookshelves. The tomes looked pricey and rare—a private collection for someone important. In the center of the room sat a desk of that same white marble, with a cream wing-back armchair behind it. And, sitting on the desktop, a plaque that read *"Shailene Basani, Founder."*

"I take it your mom isn't here at the moment?" I gulped, feeling like I was treading on sacred ground.

Charlotte laughed coolly. "You're kidding, right? My mom is never here unless there's some public show that she needs to put on a performance for." She headed for the back of the room and pulled aside a tapestry of a roaring, golden griffin, revealing a hidden door behind it.

Is that why you act so cold? I wondered. It might've been the most honest thing she'd revealed to me, and I didn't know what to do with that. Maybe being a Basani wasn't all it was cracked up to be. Kind of like being a Merlin. But where my mom shunned her fame, I guessed Shailene and Fay lapped theirs up, leaving Charlotte behind to bear the actual responsibility of the Institute's legacy. I remembered all the things Uncle Finch had told me about the twins. Maybe this place was just another shiny magazine cover to them—a feather they could put in their caps and forget about. Maybe Charlotte felt like that, too—that she was just another accolade, forgotten about when they moved on to the next big thing.

Taking out a smaller key, Charlotte unlocked the hidden door. Cold air whistled in, making me wish I had something warmer to wear. But there wasn't time to grab a coat, not with so much on the line.

I hesitated for a moment on the threshold, staring out at the beautiful night. The rain had stopped and a full moon shone ethereally, unhindered by cloud. Glittering specks lit the velvety dark blue sky and rolling hills stretched away before us, the calm sea off to the east.

Charlotte slipped out into the darkness and I followed her

uncertainly, glancing over my shoulder to find that most of the Institute had disappeared, leaving only an open doorway in the ruins of an old, imposing castle. With the Institute being inside an interdimensional bubble and all, I didn't know what else I'd expected. Charlotte hurriedly closed the door before taking off across the hills. She seemed to know where she was going, and so did the pixies.

Fifteen minutes later, we were trudging up a steep slope, my boots slipping and sliding in the mud from the day's downpour. At the top rested an old gray church, which looked about as old as the ruined castle in the distance behind us—the bare bones that the Institute's bubble was built around. Charlotte had already reached the top of the hill with the pixies, the motley crew waiting for me impatiently. Taking a deep breath, I leaned forward and upped the pace, until my thighs burned and sweat formed on the back of my neck. On the upside, at least I wasn't cold anymore.

"You're going to have to work on that, for training," Charlotte remarked, as I finally reached her. "The one thing you can rely on as a hunter, above all else, is stamina."

"Noted," I wheezed. The pixies snickered, one of them dropping to the ground and pretending to faint. "Yeah, hilarious. Thank you. Where are we, by the way?"

Charlotte turned toward the church. "St. Finnean's Chapel, though it's had a lot of names over the years. I figured this would be the best place to start looking, since it's a) the closest and b) the oldest one around here."

The graveyard was eerily beautiful in the moonlight, the silvery glow spilling across broken headstones which, in turn, were covered in bleached white lichen and tufts of brown moss. A willow tree stood watch on the far side, its rustling fronds bent like someone hunched with grief. I wondered how long it had been here, guarding this cemetery. If only it could speak, it might've told us the way to

Fergus McLeod's bones. And yet, I couldn't quite shake the feeling that it *was* watching and whispering, having seen us approach from the ruins.

"Some of these names are going to be hard to read." And I had no phone to see by, only moonlight and the glow of the pixies. Their illumination had amped up a notch, now that we were out in the open, as if their bodies instinctively responded to the darkness.

Charlotte shrugged. "It has to be here somewhere."

Letting ourselves in through a creaky iron gate, we set to work. I started at the top and Charlotte at the bottom, while the pixies flew around wherever they liked, all of us scanning the old headstones for the name Fergus McLeod. I scraped away layers of grime and moss, trying to spend as little time as possible at each grave. My mind wandered as I read the eroded inscriptions, thinking about who these people might've been, and what they'd done with their lives. Had they been happy? Had they died with regrets? Nobody spoke ill of the dead, especially not on gravestones, so I guessed no one would ever know what these people had been like when they were alive. After all, this cemetery was so old that I doubted anyone remembered these people.

Halfway down, the weeping willow caught my eye again. It stood out against the bare landscape as though it were trying to prove a point beyond mere guardianship. Intrigued by the whispering fronds, I headed toward it and parted the leafy curtains. Boudicca and her male counterpart fluttered in after me, shining their light on the darkened space within. A private world, almost, secret from the rest of the cemetery.

Is that...? I peered into the gloom and gasped as my eyes fell upon a solitary headstone. Boudicca hovered over it, shining her light on the words I'd been looking for: Fergus McLeod. The rest of the inscription had worn away over time; his name was barely legible, but I saw enough letters to know that this was the one. We'd found it.

"Charlotte!" I shouted. "It's here, under the willow!"

She erupted through the fronds a few seconds later, brandishing a spade and a pleased smirk. "I stole this from outside the church, but I think they'll forgive me. It's all for a good cause, right?" Her smile faded suddenly, as she turned away. "You'd better start digging. We've got Wisps incoming, and I don't think they're here for a group hug."

"Hold them off while I get the bones." I reached out for the spade, which she duly tossed at me before ducking back outside the shadowed confines of the willow. The pixies followed, leaving me alone in the darkness with no one but a dead guy for company.

My heartrate skyrocketed as I plunged the tip of the spade into the soft earth and plowed for my life, throwing heaps of soil and wriggling earthworms off to the side. Behind me, I heard the clash of pixies, Chaos, and Wisps. Shrieks and chants, blasts and explosions, and flashes of light permeated the cemetery. I tried to ignore it as I continued to excavate, using my foot to shove the spade deep into the ground. As it turned out, trying to dig through six feet of heavy, sodden soil was anything but easy, and the battle going on outside didn't help.

A lifetime of sweating and panting later, the spade finally clocked something solid. Frantic, and aware that I was now standing in a hole of earth on top of a rotting coffin that could give way at any moment, I cleared away the last of the dirt. Placing my legs to either side of the casket lid, I reached down and wrenched the wood away. It splintered and crumbled in my hands, but I didn't care.

Huh... I glanced down, expecting to see a skeleton. Instead, I found a threadbare sack. Swallowing the nausea in my throat, I tossed the bag up onto the side of the grave and pulled myself out. The groundskeepers would probably have something to say about a freshly dug grave in the morning, but there was nothing I could do about that. Heaving the bag over my shoulder, I ran through the willow fronds and into the Wisp battle.

"I've got them!" I yelled to Charlotte, who had a Wisp in her Telekinetic grasp.

"What about the other bones?"

Boudicca flew to me and squeaked desperately, gesturing away from the cemetery.

"Lorelei's bones aren't here?" I asked, feinting out of the way of an incoming Wisp.

She shook her head.

"Do you know where they are?"

She hopped up and down, nodding eagerly.

I gripped the sack of bones tighter. "I don't think they're here, Charlotte. The pixies can take us to them."

Charlotte groaned and squeezed the captured Wisp until it exploded into a shower of pink sparks. "Give me one second, and don't tell a soul about this. I promise you, neither of us will live it down. Oh, and try not to pull my mane too hard, or I'll kick you off."

While the pixies held the Wisps back, Charlotte toppled onto all fours and transformed into a recognizable shape: a long, rounded snout, flicking ears, and the mane that she'd warned me about, flowing in the breeze.

A... horse? Well, this wasn't going to be fun. If she thought my running was bad, she'd clearly never seen me try to ride a horse. But, with time trickling away, I didn't have a choice. I just had to get over the weirdness of climbing onto the back of someone who'd been human a few seconds ago.

"Here goes nothing." Clutching the sack, I scrambled onto Charlotte's back and held onto her mane as gently as possible. She reared up and kicked out at an encroaching Wisp, sending it spinning backward and almost making me fall off. It wasn't as though she had a saddle and a bridle to make this easier.

"Pixies! Show us the way!" I called, eager to be away from the Wisps and off this carousel before I got thrown off.

The pixies obeyed, and Charlotte followed, breaking into a terrifying gallop. As weird nights went, this one had just taken the top spot.

THIRTY-TWO

Persie

_____

Charlotte's hooves pounded along the dirt track, leading away from the church. The wind lashed at my face, stinging my eyes, and my legs ached from squeezing with all my might. If I loosened up for a second, I'd fall off, and I didn't like the idea of having a broken leg in the middle of nowhere. Who knew if this island even had a hospital nearby? And, as much as I hated it, this had to be the fastest way to get to wherever we were going.

Why won't you just buzz off? I glowered at the Wisps, who'd given chase. The pixies flanked us on all sides, forming a protective wall to keep the Wisps away. But those irritating orbs of light appeared to be getting more violent with each failed assault, coming back with a vengeance for their next attack.

Powering down the hillside, Charlotte came to a sharp stop beside the curve of a road, nearly throwing me over the top of her horsey head. I gripped tighter to her mane, gulping breaths of panicked air.

"What the heck, Charlotte?" I gasped.

She turned her head and, with her human eyes, cast me an apologetic look. I found out what she was sorry for shortly after, when she began Morphing back into her normal form. I realized just in time and jumped off, clutching the sack of bones to my chest. Shedding her horse skin, she stooped to catch her breath. Even in the darkness, I could see she looked pale, sweat beading on her brow.

"That's why I don't do that," she croaked. "I can never hold it for long. I just wanted to get us to the road, ahead of the Wisps."

Speaking of which, the Wisps were rushing down the slope of the hill, burning brightly. The pixies twisted around and hurtled back toward the oncoming Wisps in a phalanx of sorts—a square of rows, the frontline clasping hands to expel a massive blast of energy. The second line echoed the action as the front line moved to the back, throwing out a pulse that shook the ground beneath my feet. By the time it got to the third line, the Wisps were well and truly peeved. Rallying their forces, they combined into what could only be described as an uber-Wisp, the blaze of its light so intense that I could feel it from where I stood, a safe distance away.

As the two tribes collided, my heart wrenched. The two front lines of pixies howled in pain as the Wisps scorched them, while the back two lines fought valiantly with their own light, sending out a unified explosion of jarring energy that managed to send the uber-Wisp careening backward. But it was too late for those who'd gotten too close to the Wisps' pumped-up flame. Thin bodies tumbled from the air and landed in the damp grass, their vivid colors fading to a deathly white that made me scream.

"NO!" I yelled, but there was no Fergus to stop the Wisps this time. I whirled to face Charlotte. Her breaths had evened out, and she didn't look so pale anymore. "You have to help them, Charlotte. They'll die if you don't."

Charlotte straightened up. "I guess I owe them that much, for saving me earlier."

Lifting her palms, she stormed into the fray. The uber-Wisp had returned, pummeling my pixies with a breathtaking fury. The two remaining lines linked up their power, strands of bronzed fire throbbing between them all. They chanted, building up the inferno of their attack, and launched a fireball—twice as large as the Wisp— right at it. To my horror, the uber-Wisp dodged the projectile and swung forward, easily incinerating another row of pixies. They crumbled to dust, and my knees gave way.

"Don't kill them. Please, don't…"

My begging fell on deaf ears. The Wisps didn't care if it pained me; I wasn't the one giving the orders. And yet, I couldn't understand why they were trying to stand in our way. Surely this was what Fergus wanted, to reunite with Lorelei? Did he not understand what we were attempting to do for him? If it hadn't been for the fact that Genie and Nathan, and so many others, were still trapped in Fergus's realm, I'd have dumped his stupid bones right there. He'd killed my creatures. Why did he deserve to be reunited with his love?

That's how Leviathan would think. My brain served me a swift reminder that I wasn't spiteful or vengeful like the monster who'd given me this ability. But that didn't mean I couldn't hate Fergus's guts for what his Wisps had done to my pixies. This was for Genie, not for that cruel spirit.

"I've had just about enough of you lot." Charlotte clapped her palms together, unleashing a wave of Telekinesis that enveloped the uber-Wisp. It struggled to break free, but she'd pulled out the big guns. Her face scrunched under the pressure of holding the furious ball of light, a vein popping under the skin of her neck. With one guttural grunt, she hurled the uber-Wisp as far as her magical muscles allowed. It soared through the air, arcing like a true comet, and disappeared into the distance.

But the Wisps would be back. I knew that much.

Still red in the face, Charlotte ran back to me. A meager, devastating trio of pixies followed her. Two landed on her shoulders—a male and female, their pulsating spots blue with grief. And Boudicca came to rest on my shoulder, her head bowed as tiny, sparkling tears slid down her cheeks.

"I'm so sorry," I whispered, knowing it could never be enough.

She lifted her mournful gaze and came closer to my face, resting her small forehead against mine. If this was her forgiveness, I didn't deserve it. Too many of her kind had died for my sake, and I couldn't take that back.

"There's a car coming!" Charlotte hissed, dragging me behind the drystone wall that bordered the road. "Stay here, I'm going to... uh... commandeer it."

I opened my mouth to protest, but she'd already run to the road, waving her hands wildly. When I looked toward the spot where the pixies had fallen from the sky, there was nothing to see. They'd already returned to Chaos, unlike the pixies who still lay where they'd been cut down in Fergus's sick paradise.

The car screeched to a standstill and the driver got out: a middle-aged man, with salt-and-pepper hair and a kindly appearance. My entire body clenched as I waited to see what Charlotte would do. Rambling about a breakdown further up the dirt track, she got close enough to the guy to grab his temples. He looked startled for a split second before white light filtered through his skull and into his eyes, flowing from Charlotte's palms. I'd seen enough of my dad's work to know what I was seeing. She'd wiped his mind, which would leave him out cold for a while. Long enough for us to "commandeer" his vehicle, at any rate.

"Get in!" Charlotte yelled, dragging the poor driver off to the side of the road. I didn't agree with mind-wiping, as a rule, but saving the abductees had already called for gravedigging. Why not add another tally to this evening's morally gray behavior?

I ran to the waiting car and jumped in on the passenger side, balancing the sack of bones on my lap, while Charlotte finished hauling the driver to safety. After giving him a curiously gentle pat on the head, she darted back and slipped into the driver's seat.

"Seatbelts," she instructed, holding the wheel gingerly, like it was her first time.

I arched an eyebrow at her. "You've driven a car before, right?"

"In theory, yes." Her hand reached for the gearstick and ground it into first. "Well, that didn't sound healthy."

"Okay, let me rephrase. You've driven a stick before, right?" I grimaced as she put her foot down, the car bunny-hopping forward.

Frowning as she revved the engine, Charlotte cast me an apprehensive look. "Not exactly, but I know how it's supposed to work. In theory."

The car shot forward, making her yelp in surprise. Yanking the wheel sharply to the right, she spared us a head-on collision with the drystone wall and screeched into second gear way before the car was ready for it.

Undeterred, she pushed down on the accelerator until the car had no choice but to obey. Still, if this car didn't overheat or give up before we reached our destination, I knew we'd owe a debt to the automobile gods.

"I think you're supposed to change gear when it sounds like the car is about to explode," I suggested, the revving sound splitting my eardrums.

She shot me a dark look. "I know."

I watched as she rammed the gearstick into third, not too proud to try out my advice. Sure enough, the car settled into a more bearable sound, moving along the road without the startling lurch.

"Can you guide us?" I looked at Boudicca's forlorn face.

With none of her usual sass, she fluttered to the dashboard and pointed dead ahead. With her back turned, I could've sworn I saw her shoulders shaking. As for the other two pixies, they'd settled in the back, hugging one another.

As Charlotte picked up the pace, I realized there was one other factor we hadn't considered. While the road we started on was fine, with enough width for Charlotte to try her hand at drag racing, it quickly gave way to Irish country roads that might as well have been labelled "deathtrap." With drystone walls lining both sides, there was just enough room for the car, and shallow shoulders every so often so cars moving in the opposite direction could pass. Only, the lack of space hadn't done anything to slow Charlotte down. She sped along as though she were on a freaking freeway, giving me a coronary every time a curve came out of nowhere.

"Charlotte! Wall!" I braced against the dashboard as she made a hairpin turn down a very narrow road with walls on either side. I could only pray another car wouldn't come in the opposite direction.

"There's plenty of space," she replied confidently. But a squeal of metal on stone said otherwise, sending shivers down my spine as sparks erupted from the side of the car. "Okay, so not as much space as I thought. But at least I didn't lose the side mi—"

The mirror snapped off, dangling limply from its base.

I took a deep breath. "You were saying?"

"I've still got *one* wing mirror." She smiled, hauling the poor car into fourth as she barreled down the road. "Nobody needs more than one."

"The manufacturers, that driver, and I would all beg to differ." I slammed into the car door as Boudicca gestured right and Charlotte took it without even braking. Forget the car surviving, I wasn't convinced I would. I could see the headlines now: two young women, a sack of bones, and three pixies crash into a field of sheep. No survivors.

Charlotte chuckled. "Relax, Persie. I know what I'm doing. I'll get us there."

"In one piece?" I shot back.

"Not guaranteed, but you'll be mostly intact, unlike Mr. Bonejangles over there." She nodded to the sack, and I screamed.

"Watch the road!"

Her eyes flitted back. "Sorry. I forget how tricky these country lanes can be. Pretty though, in the daytime, and especially in the summer. If Victoria lets you stay, you should head out and take a walk sometime. It's good to get out of the Institute for a bit, whenever you can."

"*If?*" What was that supposed to mean? I'd explained everything with the pixies. Surely, she didn't think I'd get booted out once the truth was revealed.

Charlotte rolled her eyes. "Okay, so the pixies didn't kidnap anyone. We were wrong about that, but that doesn't mean you're out of the woods." A half-smile lifted the corner of her lips. "One of those little schmucks definitely screwed with my hair dryer, and I want revenge. Half a ton of talc puffed out of it this morning, and I had to take another shower to get it out. And I definitely saw one of the little buggers in my room."

I heard a snort from the backseat and turned to find the she-pixie grinning mischievously at the other pixie. I thought it best not to point out the culprit to Charlotte, not when we were so close to so many obstacles she could smash us into.

"Would you have my back, if Victoria wanted me gone?" I knew I might not like the answer, but I felt the frost thawing between us.

She tilted her head thoughtfully. "If you get me a new hair dryer, sure."

"Was that a joke?" I laughed, relaxing slightly.

"Do you know what, I think it was." Charlotte smirked, the two of us settling into an amicable silence as she continued to put my life and limb at risk, following Boudicca's rudimentary GPS.

About ten minutes of white-knuckle driving later, we sped past a signpost that read: Killeany. A small fishing village appeared below us, a few orange lights burning in the darkness. But Boudicca didn't want us to go down there. Instead, she led us around the village and up to a sparse promontory that overlooked the sea, which lay eerily flat and calm tonight, reflecting the moon above. Long grass susurrated in the icy wind, shrouding the bases of what appeared to be... headstones.

They protruded like watchmen, or chess pieces waiting to be moved, adorned with plain crosses, circular crosses, and no crosses at all. And in the center stood the pointed bookends of what might once have been a chapel, or a church.

"Is this it?" I looked to Boudicca, and she nodded.

Charlotte parked the car, and we got out. The sound of the sea whispered upward, giving the impression of murmuring ghosts. The shadows had a mind of their own, my heart pounding with every movement in the corner of my eye. It was easy to feel as though you were being watched here, with so many tombstones to hide behind. However, the only things chasing us were far behind, though catching up with every wasted second.

"Where's Lorelei's grave?" I urged, grabbing the sack of bones. At that moment, floating lights appeared on the horizon, gaining ground. We were fresh out of time.

Boudicca roused herself from her grief and fluttered off through the tombstones. I raced after her, wishing I'd brought the spade from St. Finnean's. I just hoped it wouldn't matter how closely the bones were buried to one another, as long as they were close enough. Besides, I had Charlotte with me this time. Maybe she could turn into an aardvark and help me out.

Tripping and stumbling over the stubs of ancient headstones, I chased Boudicca to the ruins of the church. She paused, hovering for a moment, as if trying to sense the right direction. And she'd need to be our eyes, because these headstones no longer bore any names at all.

She shot forward, landing in front of a small, curved stone tucked right up against the ruined wall of the church, then stamping her foot and pointing enthusiastically. I guessed she'd found the right spot, and not a moment too soon. The Wisps had arrived, but they seemed to have changed their tactics. No, it was more than that. They seemed to have learned from the pixies. Instead of surging forward to launch a direct assault, they spread out in a square around the graveyard. Shimmering feelers of gaseous light stretched between the orbs, until they were all connected. I felt the pulse of their power throbbing through the air, making my head ache and raising the hairs on the back of my neck. The scent of ozone overwhelmed my senses, stinging my nostrils.

"Get down!" Charlotte jumped on me, sending the two of us crashing into the dirt as the Wisps pummeled their unified energy into the center of the graveyard. As it collided in a deafening crash, a pillar of fire shot upward. In a scene that defied belief, I watched as brooding, indigo storm clouds charged in, conjured out of nowhere. A roll of terrifying thunder cracked, heralding the imminent tempest. Not a moment later, lightning forked down, striking a patch of grass not far from where we'd hit the ground, and I guessed the next strike would be more precise.

"We have to bury these bones, *now!*" I scrambled to my feet. "Charlotte, I need you to dig. Telekinesis, Bestia, whatever it takes."

Her eyes widened in terror as another fork of lightning shattered the darkness, striking the top of a headstone about ten yards away. I felt the rumble of the impact beneath the ground, and my stomach lurched. If we didn't hurry, we'd be toast.

"Charlotte!" I bellowed above the din, grabbing her by the hand. I had to be brave, because no one would be brave for me. "Dig!"

She shook her head, as if to get rid of the fear, and held out her hands. Green light rippled across her palms, Morphing them into the shovel-like hands of a giant mole. The rest of her stayed human, and she went to town on the soft earth, scooping great handfuls of dirt and flicking it over her shoulder. I joined her with my bare hands, raking at the soil with all the strength I had left.

As we dug furiously, the heavens opened on us. Unnaturally fat blobs of rain hurtled down, ice cold and drenching, turning the soil to slick mud. The pixies ducked for cover in a nest of ivy that clung to the wall of the ruined church. Those huge droplets were probably like water bombs to them. But Charlotte and I didn't stop. The Wisps could set their volatile storm on us, and we'd keep working until one of those forks of lightning stopped us.

"It's filling up!" Charlotte roared, as lightning crashed ever closer and rain filled the grave faster than we could dig. It was more swimming pool than hole.

Jumping into the grave itself, my feet slipping and sliding, I gathered the slimy sludge into my arms and dumped it to the side of the grave. "It doesn't matter! The bones just need to be buried together! I don't care if they're in six feet of water!"

"What about us?" She lay flat on her belly, half of her leaning into the hole where she carried on scooping and flicking, scooping and flicking, in endless motion. "Neither of us is six feet tall!"

"I can hold my breath!" I yelled back. "But you might have to fight them! Once they see we're close, they'll try to attack!"

She mopped her brow, smearing muck all over her face. "Why are they trying to stop us?"

"If the gateway shuts… they've got nowhere to go! They'll have to pass on!"

She nodded and dove back into the digging. "They think a half-life is better than an afterlife?!"

"Looks like it!" I couldn't see anything but murky water, filling the grave to the brim. But sudden logic gave me a thought—the water would've loosened the soil beneath by now. I could probably swim down and shove the bag of bones into the coffin with whatever was left of Lorelei. The idea of diving below the surface of that pool of death and decay didn't fill me with joy, but Genie would've done it. I had to swallow my fear and disgust and get it done, or my friend would never come home again. And I wouldn't have that resting on my conscience. It would destroy me.

"Watch my back, I'm going in." I grabbed the sack of bones and ducked under before Charlotte could stop me. As my head disappeared beneath the surface, the darkness overwhelmed everything. Shivering from the bitter cold that crept beneath my skin, I carried on, flipping upside down and dragging my hands along what I hoped was the bottom of the grave. My fingertips grazed something solid, just as a faint glow appeared in the water beside me. Boudicca, shining her light on the situation.

Grateful to have my pixie friend at my side, I looked down through blurry eyes, but couldn't see anything aside from shadowy shapes and floating detritus, while trying not to think of all the bacteria I was submerged in. I closed my eyes tight and used touch in place of sight again, until I felt that same firm something—definitely wooden—through the murk. I kicked my legs, aiming for that spot. I grappled until I found the edge of the lid and wrenched it upward, just enough to feed the neck of the sack into the gap. My lungs burned, desperate for air, but I couldn't surface yet. I pushed the whole bag inside before sliding the coffin lid closed again.

Grabbing the barely visible glow of Boudicca in my hand, I pushed up and broke the surface... just as the Wisps exploded in a massive flare of light that rivaled the lightning they'd brought down on us. Sparks rained down, and the storm receded as quickly as it had appeared.

Treading water, I felt a manic grin spread across my face. "We did it," I murmured. "Holy crap, we did it!"

THIRTY-THREE

Persie

M y eyes widened in alarm as the air around the grave crackled. I'd seen the Wisps explode, but what if I'd been mistaken? What if that had been another method of attack, and now they were being called back to pick up where they'd left off? I swam through the filthy water until a hand reached out to haul me from the grave. Charlotte's hand, back to normal, but slick from the rain and mud. I clung with all my might as she heaved me onto solid ground. I collapsed onto my back, gasping for breath.

"What's happening? I thought… it was over." I struggled to sit up, Boudicca and the two other pixies perching on my shoulders.

Charlotte eyed the fizzing air. The atmosphere prickled my skin, like the moment just before a storm hit. Only, the storm had gone… hadn't it?

"I don't know, but we should get back." She reached down and yanked me to my feet, the two of us holding onto one another as we staggered away from the danger zone.

Ducking behind a gravestone, I peered around the stone edge. I didn't have the energy to run from another assault, but I could hide.

My heart raced like a runaway train in my chest as bronze lines sparked to life, forming a glowing rectangle in the air, not unlike a chalk-door. Was someone coming to save us? Or capture us? Had Victoria figured out that we'd gone AWOL and sent her hunters to drag us back? I wasn't sure how she'd know our location, but maybe the weird storm had tipped her off.

A swirling, sparking energy appeared, filling in the outline of the doorway, and I braced for the worst. The energy burst outward and heavenly light spilled out onto the graveyard, the sound of mystical singing drifting over the slumbering souls of the dead. I jolted in surprise—I knew that song.

"Can you see any Wisps?" Charlotte whispered, peeking through a gap in the circular cross at the top of the headstone.

I shook my head, my fear morphing into a smile. "No... something far better."

Out of the gateway, people poured into the real world. Some were alone, some in couples holding tight to one another's hands. They wore the old-fashioned clothes I'd seen in Fergus's realm, the ancient wanderers imprisoned in his world, finally released. Feeling the icy wind on their faces, they paused and turned their faces to the night sky, marveling aloud at its beauty. It must have been a long time since they'd seen real stars. Smiles spread across their faces, and then, as a gust of sea air whistled across the graveyard, their bodies turned to dust, the gray flecks whisked away in a painless conclusion to their long imprisonment.

"They're free now," I said to myself, watching the gateway. It was bittersweet. The lives they might've lived had been stolen from them by Fergus and the Wisps, but at least they could be at peace now. Mother Earth and her elements would carry them gently to the next life, where, perhaps, they would be reunited with those who'd mourned them when they'd disappeared. There was beauty in that, no matter the circumstances.

A few minutes later, people in modern clothes filtered through the newly-positioned Door to Nowhere. It was the abductees from the Institute, all of them staring around in confusion. My heart lurched as wind chased the shadows across the cemetery, terrified that they would turn to dust, as well. But they didn't. They hadn't been in Fergus's world for long enough, their lives and bodies still intact.

Thank you, thank you, thank you! I didn't know who I was thanking, exactly. All I knew was that the relief coursing through my veins threatened to overwhelm me. My limbs jittered, my heart pumped erratically, my lungs were barely able to snatch a grateful breath.

"Where are we?" a young guy muttered, rubbing his head.

The girl beside him hugged herself, rubbing her arms to fend off the cold. "Beats me. Feels like we're still in Ireland, though."

"Xan!" Charlotte leapt out from behind the tombstone, scaring the girl half to death. I realized that this was the nasty sourpuss who'd insulted Genie in the banquet hall. She took a moment to recognize Charlotte and yelped in excitement. The two girls collided in a fierce hug, jumping around happily. I might not have liked Xanthippe at all, but Charlotte couldn't have been more over-joyed to see her. Watching them, I felt a pang in my chest. There were still two people who hadn't come out.

Where are you? Please... I just... need to see you. I waited.

And waited.

And then Genie and Nathan stumbled from the gateway. The last to go in, the last to come out. Genie tripped on a clump of dirt that Charlotte had chucked to the side of Lorelei's grave, and Nathan's arms shot out to catch her, pulling her away from a crash landing. She whirled into his arms, their eyes meeting for a lingering moment before she hastily unraveled herself.

No way am I letting you get the first hug, Nathan. Grinning, I sprinted from my hiding place and weaved through the group of returnees to get to my best friend. Nathan nodded at me, smiling, and Genie turned, her eyes flying wide when she saw me.

"Genie!" I cried, wrapping my arms around her. Her hands clasped me tight as we fell into an embrace, my exuberance almost knocking her over again. Fortunately, Nathan put up his hands to keep us from toppling over, before taking a few polite steps to the side.

"You had me so worried," I murmured, tears of relief trickling down my face. "I didn't know if I'd be able to get to you in time."

She smiled against my shoulder. "Did you free us?"

"With some unexpected help." I puffed out an almighty sigh, relishing the moment. "I can't believe I got you back. I didn't know if I'd be able to do it, but you're here, and everything's okay again."

"Thanks to you, it is." She gripped me tighter until I couldn't breathe. But I didn't care. "Look at what you did, Pers. Look at everyone who's safe because of you. You're every bit a freaking Merlin! Man, I'm so proud of you my head could burst."

My cheeks flushed with embarrassment. "I didn't do it alone. Nathan helped, and so did Charlotte and the pixies."

"Hey, every hero needs sidekicks." She laughed, rubbing my arms like a proud mom. "You did it! You seriously kicked butt, Persie! None of us would be standing here if you hadn't. If you didn't stink to high heaven, I'd smooch you right now!"

I looked at Nathan, over Genie's shoulder, and giggled as he took off his specs and wiped them on his polo shirt. The poor guy had never looked more uncomfortable. "I might've just swum through a grave, so sorry for the stench."

Genie pulled away. "I need to hear *all* of this story, down to the smallest detail." She arched a curious eyebrow. "Wait… did you say *Charlotte* helped?"

"You missed a lot." I looked at Nathan. "And there's a bunch you need filling in on."

"It sounds like it," he replied, placing his glasses back on his nose.

I was about to regale them when one final figure stepped out of the gateway—the man who'd caused this mess in the first place. Letting go of Genie, I stormed over to Fergus and drew my hand back, slapping my palm across his face with all the anger in my veins. But my hand went right through him, the uninterrupted momentum almost making me stumble. Rallying quickly, I blocked his path, determined to get an explanation even if I couldn't have the satisfaction of a soap-opera slap. However, as I came face to face with him, all the venting I'd planned got carried away in the wind, like the ashes of those who'd died in his realm. Tears streamed down his cheeks, his expression a confusing blend of happy and sad.

"Did ye do this, lass?" he asked, bowing his head.

I nodded slowly. "Yes."

"Then I owe ye a debt of gratitude. I never thought, for a moment, that ye'd do this after I hoofed ye out of me world like I did," he said softly, his breath hitching. "I never thought there were a soul alive who'd put me back where I belong. With her..." His green eyes sought out the headstone, though Lorelei's name had long been erased by the elements. "I know I'm dead as a doornail, but... ye've made me feel like I'm alive again, lass. She's calling me. I can hear her singin'—I've missed that sound, like ye wouldn't believe."

He tried to step forward, but I stood in the way. "Not so fast, Fergus. I've done something for you, now I want you to tell me everything. Starting with what's going to happen to this gateway."

Fergus wiped a tear from his cheek. "Me love died before she could get te the paradise I built fer us, so her soul never made it there. There ain't no point in it existin' now. Burn me bones—both our bones—and it'll destroy the gateway fer good. Them Wisps, too. They'll not bother no one again, and nor will I."

"Is that why the Wisps chased us?"

"Aye, they're crafty kippers. Tryin' te ruin me life, even after I died. I expect they could've brought me love's soul te me, if they'd wanted… but they knew what'd happen if they did." Fergus's eyes glinted with anger. "Well, now they'll get what's been comin' to 'em."

I sighed in frustration, still not understanding the whole story. "So, why trap them? Why not pass on when you died, where you'd have been reunited with Lorelei anyway? What if you've ruined that chance, by doing what you did?"

"I'll hope, with every piece of me blackened soul, that she and I will meet in the beyond. They say if a love's powerful enough, it'll happen. Ours were the strongest of all, and I ain't just sayin' that. Our paths crossed time and again like it were destiny, 'til we understood that it *were* fate what brought us together. As bairns, she saved me from drownin' in the sea. A few years after, I rescued her when her horse were boltin'. Then, she hid me when them witch hunters were after me, and I hid her when some rogue were wantin' a piece o' her. We tried te fight everythin' te be together—her father, my magic, a whole world what didn't want us united. I thought we'd finally be safe, in a world all our own. I were wrong." He lifted his head to the stars and blinked away fresh tears. "All these years, I've missed her more and more, until it ate up me innards and left me hollow."

"But how come your bones were outside your realm?" I'd seen the grave with my own eyes. Hell, I'd dug it up.

Fergus gave a bitter laugh. "It were the price I had te pay, in the end. The cost of heaven is always death, lass. But I didn't ever mean te live in my paradise as a spirit. Nah, that weren't the plan at all." His face fell, crumpling as a sob wracked his chest. "I were a Primus Anglicus—one o' the last. Me family name ain't written in no fancy books or aught, but it's true. Mine were a secret bloodline in a magical world, where folks thought we'd all been cut down. And that meant I were still able to beg a favor of the Children. I guess they thought they owed us a courtesy or two, since it were their watered-down magicals who were cullin' us left, right, and center."

Nathan stepped into the conversation, with Genie flanking me on the right. "Was Lorelei a magical?" he asked.

"Probably would've ended up the same way if she were, but no, she didn't have a drop o' magic in her, unless ye count the magic of her beauty, and her voice, and the love she gave me." He held his face in his hands, his shoulders shaking with the weight of centuries of grief. "Our love were thwarted from the off. Her da wouldn't let me near her, threatened te run me through if I came by again... But we met in secret, in a little glade that no one else knew. The gateway used te stand there, before time smothered it.

"Then, someone told a tale te her da, who were the ruler in these parts. They said I were a dabbler in devil worship and other evils." His mouth twisted into a grimace, teardrops running over his lip and into his mouth. "One night, the village elders came fer me, and I had te flee for me life, not knowin' who'd betrayed me. I left me love a message, tellin' her where te find me. That's when I begged the Children fer help, and Gaia answered. She gave me the power te build an eternal world, just fer me and Lorelei. I suppose she took pity, seein' a fool in love."

My heart sank. I could already guess the ending of his sad tale, but I wanted to hear it. "And Lorelei didn't get your message?"

"No... she got it." He crumpled to the ground, his body hunched over as he rocked back and forth, the memories clearly painful. "I waited and I waited, and I begged te Gaia te tell me where she was. And that's when I found out... It hurts te speak of it, even now." He sucked in a pained breath. "When she came after me, the Wisps led her off the path, and she drowned in the marshes what used te be around here. Te make it all the worse, Gaia told me that her soul would wander 'til it were found, because she'd died lost and alone.

I… got it wrong. I didn't understand, 'til now, what that meant. I didn't know it could be done like this."

I reached out to touch his arm, but my fingertips passed straight through. "You didn't know her bones had been recovered?"

He shook his head. "I thought all of her were lost, which is why I pleaded with Gaia te punish the Wisps fer what they'd done. I offered me life in return. She refused, but she'd already fueled up me power." He swallowed loudly. "I used a forbidden Sanguine spell te do it meself, and that cost me me life. I sucked those spirits into the world I'd created fer me and Lorelei, and I bound 'em te me, te do me biddin'. If I had te live in eternal suffering without me love, I wanted 'em to suffer, too." He paused. "More than that, I wanted 'em te find her lost soul. I hoped her soul might follow 'em one day, like she'd followed 'em off the path. I didn't realize she were already at peace… already found, just not by me." He fell apart, sobbing uncontrollably, whispering Lorelei's name under his breath and repeating the same two words as if he were stuck on one of those trance loops. The most heartbreaking words in the world, in this case: "I'm sorry."

"Then… she's been waiting for you, as long as you've been waiting for her." My throat tightened. I turned my head to the side, to brush away the tears that fell. Genie sniffled into her sleeve, and even Nathan turned away, overcome.

He lifted his head, his face a mass of misery. "Aye, and she's callin'. All this time, she's been callin' and I were too stubborn and lonely te hear." He closed his teary eyes. "Can't ye hear her? She used te sing when I fell asleep, strokin' me hair like I were a babe in her arms. If I existed another thousand years, I'd not forget that sound. That's me true heaven, lass. Her. Only her."

I couldn't even begin to imagine grief like that. The longing, the waiting, the loneliness of two star-crossed lovers who'd spent life and death missing each other, in both senses of the word. I let go of my anger, despite the awful things he'd done. Losing the love of your life was bound to make a person crazy, and he'd done it all in the hopes of Lorelei finding her way back to him. Besides, how could I stay angry at someone who looked so broken?

I turned to Genie. "Can you lift the casket out of the grave?"

"You bet I can," she murmured, her voice thick with emotion. Moving to the graveside, she stood and bowed her head, as though standing vigil at a funeral. Blue threads of Chaos spiraled from her body and plunged into the dirty water, her Water ability pulling the ancient casket from the bottom of the grave. It lifted higher still, until Genie brought it to rest on solid ground.

I went to help her, pushing off the lid to reveal the gray bones of two skeletons, now jumbled together, and the sack that I'd carried Fergus in. I glanced back at the abductees and noticed Charlotte a few yards away, her hands behind her back. Bronze energy spilled from her palms, creating a shield of some kind that seemed to be hiding us from the abductees.

I hate to say it, but I think I'm starting to like you, Charlotte. She had just as much reason to hate Fergus as I did, but she'd still allowed us some privacy to talk in peace. Maybe her moral compass swung true north more than I'd thought.

"I don't think I'll be able to get a fire going, with everything so wet." I gave Genie a discreet nudge. "Could you do the honors, and send these two back to each other?"

She covered her mouth as a sob escaped. "Who gets to have a love like that, man? Of *course*, I'm going to light these bones up." Vivid scarlet sparks erupted from her, and miraculously caught on the waterlogged wood. She added a crackling torrent of liquid Fire, for good measure, the two of us staring into the flames until the bones turned black and there was nothing left but ash.

Fergus gasped. "I... see her."

"You do?" I whirled around, searching the surrounding area for any sign of a ghost. But his love's spirit was for his eyes only. As a breath of wind sighed over the graveyard, Fergus dissolved into dust and drifted away in peace. And I prayed, with everything I had, that he'd be reunited with his long-lost love. That was the reward for a love that defied everything, wasn't it? It had to defy death, too.

Like my grandparents... I'd never met them, thanks to the evil of Katherine Shipton, but my mom had made sure to keep their memory alive in all of us. They'd been reunited in the afterlife, and it gave me hope for Fergus and Lorelei. Hadn't they waited long enough?

"I think we ought to retreat to a safe distance," Nathan urged suddenly, snapping me out of my reverie. "It looks as if there's about to be fireworks."

As a trio, with the pixies still sitting on my shoulders, we backed away from the Door to Nowhere. A deafening roar exploded from the gateway, the frame juddering violently. Charlotte dropped the shield and instructed everyone to run to safety, with Genie, Nathan, and me bringing up the rear. I looked back as I ran, watching the door beginning to break apart into shards of light that swirled in the center, spinning faster and faster as though the realm itself was imploding.

"Take cover!" I yelled, and not a moment too soon. Everyone dove to the ground as the gateway crumpled in on itself, before unleashing a shockwave so volatile that it took the tops off several headstones. When I glanced back, the Door to Nowhere had vanished, hopefully never to be seen again.

Lying flat on the ground, squelching around in the mud, I realized that it was finally over. The Door wouldn't take any more victims, and the Wisps had paid for what they'd done—not only to Lorelei, but to everyone they'd dragged into that realm, and everyone before that, whom they'd led to certain death. And my friend had returned to me in one glorious piece.

A voice cut through the ensuing silence. "Are those... pixies?" I didn't recognize the man who'd spoken, and instinctively lifted a hand to protect my monsters. It came as quite the surprise when Charlotte got to her feet and folded her arms across her chest.

"Yes, they're pixies, and if anyone even thinks about hurling Chaos at one, they'll have me to deal with," she said sternly. "None of you would be here if it weren't for them, so show some respect. The same goes for Persie."

I struggled not to cry as Genie helped me up and put her arm around my shoulder. "She saved us." She glared at the Institute folk. "And so did the pixies."

"Those monsters... helped?" Xanthippe looked dumbstruck. "Monsters don't help."

Charlotte nodded. "Well, these ones did, and a lot of them died to rescue you all. And if we'd kept on thinking they were the bad guys... Well, I don't need to keep repeating myself."

"Thank you, Persie, and... uh... thanks, monsters." Xanthippe took a step forward, looking at Genie sheepishly. "And I guess I owe you both an apology, for things that... I might've said. I had a bit of time to think, in that world. I guess people get things wrong sometimes. So, I'm... sorry."

Genie smiled and gave me a side-squeeze. "Apology accepted."

"Nathan also helped." I felt bad leaving him out, when his choice of book had been the catalyst in this rescue mission.

A rumble of gratitude spread across the graveyard, sounding like the murmurs of the dead. But it was a start—a sign of better days to come. Victoria would have to see that my pixies had been instrumental to our success in freeing everyone, and I hoped she'd appreciate their sacrifice. I allowed myself a sad smile, knowing that this victory had come at a price. But I'd succeeded, and I'd proven the innocence of the pixies. Maybe, just maybe, that meant everyone would start to realize that not every Purge beast was a bloodthirsty, mindless monster after all.

THIRTY-FOUR

Genie

Three days passed like three seconds, while life at the Institute gradually returned to normal. Well, sort of. Lessons hadn't restarted yet. Victoria had put out a blanket order for all of the returnees to spend a week in quarantine, in case of Fergus-world side effects. I'd chosen to quarantine in Persie's room, or I'd have died of boredom. Plus, Nathan snuck Boudicca out of her orb most mornings so she could keep us entertained. And man, did pixies know how to be the life and soul of the party. She taught us how to jig, pixie-style; she'd snazzed up some flowery headbands for us; and she'd started a tournament of what I liked to call "toothpaste archery." She'd also given us a few lessons in pixie-speak. Of all the monsters Persie had Purged, she was my fave.

As for my memories of Fergus's messed-up paradise, they'd grown fuzzy. I knew I'd yammered on about my dad and arranged marriages, but I couldn't recall the exact words I'd said. Still, it was therapeutic in a way. I felt like I'd hashed out my issues without intending to. That could happen when you were stuck on a loop for... however long I was in there. I knew, more than ever, that I wouldn't settle for an arranged marriage. The gut-wrenching Fergus-and-Lorelei story had further cemented my thoughts on love. I wanted what they'd had, minus the sacrifice and Wisp-trapping and anguishing death. I wanted a love that made people cry in a good way. If I couldn't have that, then I didn't want any of it. End of story.

"Relax, Mom, it's honestly fine." Persie's desperate gaze pulled me from my thoughts and back into reality. She'd called her mom on video chat to relay everything that had happened, and it wasn't being well received.

I dove into frame. "It really is fine, and you know I wouldn't fib where Persie's concerned. Victoria cleared her of all charges, and everyone's okay. No harm done."

Nathan had also been cleared and had somehow wrangled the benefit of not being stuck in his room all day. But I was secretly glad about that. I'd started to look forward to his morning Boudicca deliveries. He usually stayed to chat and watch the pixie's antics, and I sort of liked having him around. He suited a casual atmosphere. It warmed him up and loosened his natural stiff-upper-lip-ness. And, as it turned out, he had some funny bones of his own. Naturally, Persie had told me how livid he'd been when he'd heard me babbling about arranged marriages. I wouldn't say it had made me swoon, but I liked that he'd jumped to love's defense.

"I just don't understand why you didn't call me," Harley replied, her tone momified. "I could have helped."

Persie groaned under her breath. "I told you, the signal went down due to a storm." She hadn't told her mom about Victoria's Institute-wide comms block in case it made her more nervous. "We handled it, Mom. If things had gotten worse, you know I'd have tried to get in touch once the signal came back, but they didn't. And you're kind of missing the point—I managed to control monsters *and* rescue everyone, by myself. Well, with help, but mostly by myself."

I patted my friend on the back. "She even swam in a grave filled with water. I don't think I'll ever get the stink out of my nostrils." I winked at Persie. "You don't need to worry. Persie totally owned the show, and now everyone at the Institute is in awe of her. Myself included."

Harley reeled back in horror. "You. Swam. In. A. Grave?!"

"To reunite the bones. I told you that already." Persie shot me a did-you-have-to-say-that? look. "Everything really is fine, and people are being a lot nicer to us now." She paused, realizing she'd messed up. "Not that they weren't before! I just mean, we've found our footing a bit more. And people aren't as scared of what I can do, which is great news."

I even got an apology from that uppity cow. I grinned at the memory of a sheepish Xanthippe saying she was sorry. If I could've taken a picture, I'd have framed it. But the fact remained—we weren't pariahs anymore. Who knew that all it would take was my best friend saving a bunch of hunters and trainees from a lovesick spirit and a horde of evil Wisps? We'd have done that from the start, if someone had given us a heads-up.

"Ooh, and Persie's allowed to carry puzzle boxes at all times, so you don't need to have any more sleepless nights about her Purging something she can't catch," I chimed in, giving Persie a nudge. "Unless she spews up an army of, like, dragons. Even then, she'd probably just befriend them, so it's all cool."

Harley shook her head in despair. "I'm not sure I'll ever sleep well again."

"Mom, you have to trust me." Persie leaned closer to the camera. "I fixed everything. Don't I get some credit for that?"

Harley sank back in her chair and sighed the kind of sigh only a mother can expel. "I'm... insanely proud of you, Persie. What you did is incredible, by anyone's standards. And I know I'm being hypo-critical, worrying about you being in danger when I was doing similar things at your age. But it's my job to worry." She managed a half-smile. "Nothing you can say will change that. You could be in a cotton-candy bubble, and I'd still worry. But I *am* so very proud of what you've achieved."

Persie relaxed. "That's nice to hear."

"Will I be able to see these pixies in the Bestiary?" Harley asked. "I'm always curious to see what you've created. It used to be artwork, but I suppose Purge beasts are sort of like living art."

I snorted. "And the gargoyles are the really ugly portraits that make people giggle."

"Gargoyles have their merits," Harley said, laughing. "You've just got to make sure they don't get too fond of you, or you'll never get the slime out of your clothes. Murray has always been partial to licking."

Persie's eyes brightened. "Victoria let me keep the pixies here, in the Repository. She's not sending them on to the Bestiary, so you'll have to see them when you visit. I think you'd get along well with one of them." She grinned, and a flutter in the corner of the room signaled an eavesdropper.

"Victoria thought it would be important to Persie's develop-ment," I added sagely. "This way, she gets to visit the pixies and spend time with them, so she can relate to what she's created. They're genuinely amazing. I never knew monsters could have these huge personalities. Everyone in this place has a lot to learn from her."

Harley's smile widened. "I'm just glad you're both safe. I knew there was a reason you two were best friends. Just don't make this a habit, okay? Less saving the world, more learning." She leaned forward conspiratorially. "Kes is driving your uncle up the wall. He's so jealous of the pair of you. But now that Tobe has banned him from the Bestiary, he's diverted his efforts into monster-study so he can get into the Institute when he's old enough."

"Tell him there's a spell I can give him if he wants to sneak into the Bestiary without old Tobes knowing." I flashed a mischievous smirk, channeling my pixie friend.

"Don't even joke." Harley rolled her eyes. "He'd snap up the offer in a heartbeat."

I chuckled. "Who said I was joking?"

"From here on in, it's all about studying and training," Persie interjected before her mom had a heart attack. "And I swear I'll call you—"

Her sentence was cut short by a knock on the door. The hunter behind it didn't wait for permission to come in.

"Victoria wants to see you in her office," he said gruffly.

Persie immediately stiffened. "I'll have to call you back, Mom. And, seriously, you don't have anything to worry about. We're fine, everyone's fine." She pressed her lips to her fingertips and put them to the camera. "Bye. Speak soon."

She swiped the end-call button before her mom could reply. "What does she want now?"

"I'm betting it's good news," I encouraged. "She's already raked you across the coals for sneaking out and stuff, and you got away with a reluctant 'thank you' and a slap on the wrist. Now that things are getting back to normal, I bet it'll be about developing your control. She wants you to be here, Pers. Everyone does."

She sighed and stood. "Let's hope you're right."

With that, she left the room, leaving me and Boudicca to get started on another round of toothpaste archery.

THIRTY-FIVE

Persie

_____

I followed the hunter through the hallways, but he didn't lead me where I'd been expecting to go. Most chidings took place in Victoria's snazzy office, but he seemed to be taking me to the Repository.

My heart plummeted. Maybe she'd found out about Boudicca's trips out of her orb and planned to give me a warning about it. Although Nathan would technically get the rap for that, since he was the one who kept dropping Boudicca off like my room was some kind of pixie daycare. Not that I minded having her. In fact, I loved it, which was part of my concern. I didn't want Boudicca to have to go back into her orb full-time, not after what she'd done for me and the abductees.

"She's in there." The hunter ushered me through the Repository doors before turning on his heel and striding back the way we'd come.

Drawing in a deep breath, I stepped into the bubble jungle. Victoria stood by the window on the far side, staring out at the verdant scenery—the clash of greens and gray-toned blues, where the clifftop met the sea. Forcing my legs forward, I walked toward her.

"You sent for me?" I said to her imposing back.

She glanced over her shoulder at me. "Yes. I thought you might appreciate the change of scenery." She beckoned me to stand beside her, so the two of us were looking out at the landscape together. Her arms were slotted into their usual position behind her back, her torso straight like a soldier's. And I felt as though I was about to be put through my paces.

"Thanks," I replied dumbly.

She kept her gaze on the horizon, and the lack of eye contact unnerved me. "We haven't had a chance to properly discuss what happened. As you know, I have been busy arranging quarantines and having teams scour the new wing for any more unknown entities. Now, however, I think it's time we spoke frankly with one another."

I fidgeted awkwardly. "I… don't know what else you want me to say."

"Then allow me to begin." She sighed quietly. "First, I must thank you, once more, for the part you played in rescuing our missing people. I do not wish to minimize what you did for them. That being said, matters might have concluded more smoothly had you been truthful about the pixies being Purged from the outset, and had you come to me as soon as you discovered the existence of the Door."

I lifted my chin, just as my mom did when she was going into an argument. "Not to be rude, Ms. Jules, but you laughed it off when I told you about the Door to Nowhere. If I'd come to you, you wouldn't have believed me."

Victoria surprised me by laughing. "It's not rude at all. You're quite right. I should have trusted you, but you have to understand it from my perspective. You omitted the truth about the pixies being created, and that led me to believe that you might be lying again when you told me of their innocence. It sounded an awful lot like you just wanted to protect them."

"I did, because they were *innocent*," I muttered. And one omission of truth didn't make someone a chronic liar. "And you said you understood why I didn't tell you about the pixies being Purged, initially. You can't double-jeopardy me."

She nodded. "I concede that I was mistaken, and yes... I did say I understood, but that doesn't negate the consequences, even after forgiveness has been given. What I am trying to say is, we need to be able to trust each other from now on. That means I want you to feel like you can come to me with anything. I will not judge you for a Purge, or I wouldn't have invited you to join the Institute. You must never be afraid to ask me for help, or fear for your position here. If we are honest with one another, then you do not have to worry. I'm concerned because you seem to be expecting an axe to fall, and it clouds your judgment."

I bowed my head. "I guess I am expecting an axe to fall."

"Then it will be all the more important that we have an open line of communication, especially since some bad news has revealed itself." A muscle twitched in her jaw, her eyes turning steely. "It is to do with something you mentioned to me, about your mother."

"My mom?" I peered up at her, confused. "What do you mean?"

"One of the people who disappeared has not come back, a scientist called Charles Burniston. He went missing around the same time as Xanthippe, though he'd told one of his colleagues that he needed to go into town. That is why I did not, initially, add him to the list of missing parties. However, when he did not return to the Institute, I thought he might not have made it to town at all—I thought that he was taken from his quarters. Now, it is my belief that he was not taken by the Wisps as the others were, and that he *did* venture into town, but did not return."

I understood what she was getting at, though it sent a spike of terror through me. I'd assumed everyone who was missing had returned. Evidently, Victoria wanted to keep this within a very small circle of people, or the Institute would descend into panic mode once again.

"Are you going to speak to my mom about it?" At the beginning of the Wisp mess, I'd thought the missing Institute people were linked to the missing magicals in the wider world. Now, to hear that one person might be embroiled in that mess... It made my blood run cold.

Victoria finally turned to look at me. "I have instructed a team to liaise with her in due course. I apologize for not heeding your advice regarding the disappearances; I have grown so used to the Institute being insular that I forget there is help to be found beyond these walls." She smiled. "I imagine this experience has been educational for both of us."

"You can say that again." I lowered my gaze shyly, her black eyes too intense for comfort. Still, it felt good to be acknowledged. Fresh troubles might've been brewing on the horizon, but at least Victoria was reaching out to the right people. Maybe, with everyone putting their heads together, the issue of the missing magicals might get solved sooner rather than later. Although it set a dangerous precedent if this Charles guy *had* been snatched so close to home.

"Then we should part on good terms and move forward with honesty and trust." Victoria put out her hand, and I tentatively shook it. "You have my heartfelt thanks for what you've done, and the thanks of this Institute. However, I would urge you, as the head huntswoman, to be careful as you walk your path here—for your safety and the safety of those around you. Take risks only when they are necessary, and when someone is too stubborn to listen." She flashed me a knowing smirk and released my hand.

With that, she dismissed me. I'd gone in anxious, and I was

coming out feeling anxious in a different way. The notion that someone from the Institute had been taken had thrown me, even if the theory suggested they'd been snatched from a nearby town instead of from within this magical fortress. It was way too close for comfort, and I knew my mom would freak out when she heard.

Slipping through the Repository doors, I almost ran headlong into Nathan and Genie.

"What are you doing out here?" I asked, grabbing Genie's hand and pulling her behind a statue of a Nimean lion. Nathan hurried to join us, all three of us crouching low in the shadows in case Victoria came out.

"I wanted to make sure you were okay, and I found this one on the way." She thumbed at Nathan. "How did it go? Are you in trouble? Did she find out about Boudicca?"

I shook my head. "No, nothing like that." I peered through the lion's legs to make sure we were alone. "She told me that one of the magicals didn't come back, and we think it might be related to what my mom is working on."

"What?!" Genie gasped, her eyes bugging. "How come no one's mentioned it?"

"She'll want to keep it quiet until she knows more." Nathan frowned, evidently miffed that he'd been left out of the loop.

My gaze flitted between the two of them. "The thing is… I had this feeling that I was being watched when I left the Institute with Charlotte that night. I put it down to paranoia, and to being in a graveyard at night, and to all the crazy stuff going on with the spirits and the Wisps. But now I'm not so sure." I glanced up and down the hallway. "I don't think I was imagining things. I think someone really was watching me, and I don't think it's over." Our troubles with the Wisps had ended, but new troubles were stirring.

"We should be vigilant," Nathan said. "If there is someone watching the Institute, then we should do our best to act as lookouts. It could be nothing, but it could be something, and if Victoria is keeping things hushed up, then we will have to be her eyes and ears wherever we can."

"Which may mean giving the pixies a bit more freedom, if you can manage it?" I looked at Nathan hopefully. "After all, they're good at finding things that the rest of us can't see."

My fresh start hadn't gone exactly according to plan, but one incredible thing had come of it: I'd learned to tame the pixies and discovered that they had more heart than their size suggested. I'd stood on my own two feet and had rescued trapped magicals from a secret world. A few weeks ago, if someone had told me we were in danger, I'd have run to Genie, or my parents, and asked them for the solution. Now I knew I was capable of getting myself out of a scrape, and I intended to use this newfound courage and confidence as best I could to save more magicals from meeting a similar fate.

Whoever you are... We'll find you.

It was only a matter of time.

HARLEY MERLIN 20: Persie Merlin and the Witch Hunters

Dear Reader,

Thank you for reading Persie Merlin and the Door to Nowhere. I hope you enjoyed the ride!

Continue the journey in Harley Merlin 20: **Persie Merlin and the Witch Hunters** — releasing **July 17th, 2020**.

Visit www.bellaforrest.net for details.

HARLEY MERLIN BOOK 20

PERSIE MERLIN

AND THE WITCH HUNTERS

FROM MILLION-BESTSELLING AUTHOR

BELLA FORREST

See you there!

Love,

Bella x

P.S. Sign up to my VIP email list and you'll be the first to know when my books release: **www.morebellaforrest.com**

(Your email will be kept private and you can unsubscribe at any time.)

P.P.S. You can also follow me on **Twitter** @ashadeofvampire;

Facebook BellaForrestAuthor;

or **Instagram** @ashadeofvampire

Read more by Bella Forrest

DARKLIGHT

(Fantasy/romance)

Darklight (Book 1)

Darkthirst (Book 2)

Darkworld (Book 3)

Darkblood (Book 4)

Darktide (Book 5)

Darkbirth (Book 6)

Darkfall (Book 7)

Darkwilds (Book 8)

HARLEY MERLIN

Harley Merlin and the Secret Coven (Book 1)

Harley Merlin and the Mystery Twins (Book 2)

Harley Merlin and the Stolen Magicals (Book 3)

Harley Merlin and the First Ritual (Book 4)

Harley Merlin and the Broken Spell (Book 5)

Harley Merlin and the Cult of Eris (Book 6)

Harley Merlin and the Detector Fix (Book 7)

Harley Merlin and the Challenge of Chaos (Book 8)

Harley Merlin and the Mortal Pact (Book 9)

Finch Merlin and the Fount of Youth (Book 10)

Finch Merlin and the Lost Map (Book 11)

Finch Merlin and the Djinn's Curse (Book 12)

Finch Merlin and the Locked Gateway (Book 13)

Finch Merlin and the Forgotten Kingdom (Book 14)

Finch Merlin and the Everlasting Vow (Book 15)

Finch Merlin and the Blood Tie (Book 16)

Finch Merlin and the Legend of the Luminary (Book 17)

Persie Merlin and Leviathan's Gift (Book 18)

Persie Merlin and the Door to Nowhere (Book 19)

Persie Merlin and the Witch Hunters (Book 20)

THE GENDER GAME

(Action-adventure/romance. Completed series.)

The Gender Game (Book 1)

The Gender Secret (Book 2)

The Gender Lie (Book 3)

The Gender War (Book 4)

The Gender Fall (Book 5)

The Gender Plan (Book 6)

The Gender End (Book 7)

THE GIRL WHO DARED TO THINK

(Action-adventure/romance. Completed series.)

The Girl Who Dared to Think (Book 1)

The Girl Who Dared to Stand (Book 2)

The Girl Who Dared to Descend (Book 3)

The Girl Who Dared to Rise (Book 4)

The Girl Who Dared to Lead (Book 5)

The Girl Who Dared to Endure (Book 6)

The Girl Who Dared to Fight (Book 7)

THE CHILD THIEF

(Action-adventure/romance. Completed series.)

The Child Thief (Book 1)

Deep Shadows (Book 2)

Thin Lines (Book 3)

Little Lies (Book 4)

Ghost Towns (Book 5)

Zero Hour (Book 6)

HOTBLOODS

(Supernatural adventure/romance. Completed series.)

Hotbloods (Book 1)

Coldbloods (Book 2)

Renegades (Book 3)

Venturers (Book 4)

Traitors (Book 5)

Allies (Book 6)

Invaders (Book 7)

Stargazers (Book 8)

A SHADE OF VAMPIRE SERIES

(Supernatural romance/adventure)

Series 1: Derek & Sofia's story

A Shade of Vampire (Book 1)

A Shade of Blood (Book 2)

A Castle of Sand (Book 3)

A Shadow of Light (Book 4)

A Blaze of Sun (Book 5)

A Gate of Night (Book 6)

A Break of Day (Book 7)

Series 2: Rose & Caleb's story

A Shade of Novak (Book 8)

A Bond of Blood (Book 9)

A Spell of Time (Book 10)

A Chase of Prey (Book 11)

A Shade of Doubt (Book 12)

A Turn of Tides (Book 13)

A Dawn of Strength (Book 14)

A Fall of Secrets (Book 15)

An End of Night (Book 16)

Series 3: The Shade continues with a new hero...

A Wind of Change (Book 17)

A Trail of Echoes (Book 18)

A Soldier of Shadows (Book 19)

A Hero of Realms (Book 20)

A Vial of Life (Book 21)

A Fork of Paths (Book 22)

A Flight of Souls (Book 23)

A Bridge of Stars (Book 24)

Series 4: A Clan of Novaks

A Clan of Novaks (Book 25)

A World of New (Book 26)

A Web of Lies (Book 27)

A Touch of Truth (Book 28)

An Hour of Need (Book 29)

A Game of Risk (Book 30)

A Twist of Fates (Book 31)

A Day of Glory (Book 32)

Series 5: A Dawn of Guardians

A Dawn of Guardians (Book 33)

A Sword of Chance (Book 34)

A Race of Trials (Book 35)

A King of Shadow (Book 36)

An Empire of Stones (Book 37)

A Power of Old (Book 38)

A Rip of Realms (Book 39)

A Throne of Fire (Book 40)

A Tide of War (Book 41)

Series 6: A Gift of Three

A Gift of Three (Book 42)

A House of Mysteries (Book 43)

A Tangle of Hearts (Book 44)

A Meet of Tribes (Book 45)

A Ride of Peril (Book 46)

A Passage of Threats (Book 47)

A Tip of Balance (Book 48)

A Shield of Glass (Book 49)

A Clash of Storms (Book 50)

Series 7: A Call of Vampires

A Call of Vampires (Book 51)

A Valley of Darkness (Book 52)

A Hunt of Fiends (Book 53)

A Den of Tricks (Book 54)

A City of Lies (Book 55)

A League of Exiles (Book 56)

A Charge of Allies (Book 57)

A Snare of Vengeance (Book 58)

A Battle of Souls (Book 59)

Series 8: A Voyage of Founders

A Voyage of Founders (Book 60)

A Land of Perfects (Book 61)

A Citadel of Captives (Book 62)

A Jungle of Rogues (Book 63)

A Camp of Savages (Book 64)

A Plague of Deceit (Book 65)

An Edge of Malice (Book 66)

A Dome of Blood (Book 67)

A Purge of Nature (Book 68)

Season 9: A Birth of Fire

A Birth of Fire (Book 69)

A Breed of Elements (Book 70)

A Sacrifice of Flames (Book 71)

A Conspiracy of Realms (Book 72)

A Search for Death (Book 73)

A Piece of Scythe (Book 74)

A Blade of Thieron (Book 75)

A Phantom of Truth (Book 76)

A Fate of Time (Book 77)

Season 10: An Origin of Vampires

An Origin of Vampires (Book 78)

A Game of Death (Book 79)

A Veil of Dark (Book 80)

A Bringer of Night (Book 81)

A Circle of Nine (Book 82)

A Bender of Spirit (Book 83)

A Memory of Time (Book 84)

A Shard of Soul (Book 85)

A Break of Seals (Book 86)

Season 11: A Shade of Mystery

A Shade of Mystery (Book 87)

An Isle of Mirrors (Book 88)

A Sanctuary of Foes (Book 89)

A Ruler of Clones (Book 90)

A SHADE OF DRAGON TRILOGY

A Shade of Dragon 1

A Shade of Dragon 2

A Shade of Dragon 3

A SHADE OF KIEV TRILOGY

A Shade of Kiev 1

A Shade of Kiev 2

A Shade of Kiev 3

A LOVE THAT ENDURES TRILOGY

(Contemporary romance)

A Love that Endures

A Love that Endures 2

A Love that Endures 3

THE SECRET OF SPELLSHADOW MANOR

(Supernatural/Magic YA. Completed series)

The Secret of Spellshadow Manor (Book 1)

The Breaker (Book 2)

The Chain (Book 3)

The Keep (Book 4)

The Test (Book 5)

The Spell (Book 6)

BEAUTIFUL MONSTER DUOLOGY

(Supernatural romance)

Beautiful Monster 1

Beautiful Monster 2

DETECTIVE ERIN BOND

(Adult thriller/mystery)

Lights, Camera, GONE

Write, Edit, KILL

For an updated list of Bella's books, please visit her website:

www.bellaforrest.net

Join Bella's VIP email list and you'll be the first to know when new books
release: www.morebellaforrest.com